BUY ME, SIR

JADE WEST

Cover design by Letitia Hasser of RBA Designs

www.designs.romanticbookaffairs.com

Book design by Inkstain Designs

www.inkstainformatting.com

Editing by John Hudspith

www.johnhudspith.co.uk

All enquiries to jadewestauthor@gmail.com

First published in 2017.

Text set in Dante MT Std.

*This one is dedicated to a flash of inspiration on a cold
January afternoon whilst bingeing on Season One of Travelers.
And – even more importantly – bingeing on Eric McCormack.*

PROLOGUE
MELISSA

I guess it was desperation that compelled me to stalk a man as powerful as Alexander Henley.

That's what losing your parents in a late-night hit and run when you're barely eighteen does for you. It makes you desperate.

Not for the college life that trickles down the drain in the aftermath. And not for the stars you were reaching for in your dreams of becoming a criminal lawyer one day. Not even for a let-up in the despair that losing your whole world plunges you into – that soul-crushing pain at knowing you'll never ever see them again.

It makes you desperate to get your shit together for the baby you're now responsible for. The little boy that is now your everything.

That's why I took the cleaning position at Henley Grosvenor Legal in the first place, to provide for my baby brother.

And that's why I'm here now, in a suite at Delaney's Spa Resort, with twenty-five grand stuffed in my handbag, and Alexander Henley's beautiful cock in my ass…

I guess I'd better start from the beginning.

ONE

THREE MONTHS LATER

I'm late. I'm late. I'm fucking late.

Tube strike. Fucking typical on day one of my new job.

My reflection looks horrible as I race through the mirrored glass entrance. I'd hoped that cleaning for a firm as prestigious as Henley Grosvenor would have meant something a little more stylish than the scratchy baseball cap and hairnet they mailed out to me. More stylish than the green and white striped sack of crap apron I have to wear over a blouse and starchy polyester skirt, too. But beggars can't be choosers.

"Cleaning induction," I tell the pristine receptionist. I pull the crumpled instructions from my pocket as I catch my breath, and she glares at the dishevelled state of me. She thinks I'm shit. It's written all over her face.

"Fifth floor," she tells me. "You're late."

Like my burning cheeks don't make it clear I'm aware of that.

It feels like a walk of shame, pacing through marble pillars in such a shitty uniform. A badge of *minimum wage nobody* amongst the tailored suits.

I pick up pace as I see the elevator is already open, rushing through the plush seating area as my heart pounds in my chest. It's packed already, rammed full of legal staff with their morning papers and Starbucks, and so many of them are staring at me, so many of them see me coming and make no move whatsoever to hold the doors.

Until him.

My heart stutters in recognition, breath hitching as he puts out a hand and stops the doors for me.

I clatter in and ease myself tight into the corner, and I want to say thanks so bad, but I don't. I can't.

He doesn't meet my eyes, or even really glance in my direction. The doors close and he stares straight ahead as the woman at his side talks him through his morning schedule. Her voice is nasal and whiny, and she over pronounces her words. *Misterrr Cal-der, ten-aaay-emmm. Drunk dri-ving.* I press the button for floor five, one of the only levels not illuminated. Figures. And then I look at him, trying not to make it obvious.

Alexander James Henley. Jnr.

The man I've been dreaming about for four years straight.

It must be hard having Jnr. after your name your whole life, but I guess that's what happens when you take over an empire from your larger-than-life, legal legend of a father.

He looks just like I remember, and he smells like it too. Woody, like embers. Spicy, like oriental incense.

Black suit, white shirt, black tie. His hair is the same, as dark as his suit. His eyes, too, only now he's got the tiniest lines around the corners. They suit him.

He isn't smiling, not even a bit. His perfect jaw looks so stern and serious, his skin flawless apart from the tiny birthmark he has on his right cheek.

My fantasies of a sizzling moment of recognition shrivel and die. He doesn't remember me, and why would he? I was just a dumb kid when he bummed me a cigarette outside my school gates. He saw hundreds of kids that day, a sea of us packed into the school hall to witness his motivational speech about the legal profession. *Corporations in the Community*, they called it. Some government scheme or other.

I'd been late that morning, just as I'm late today. Too late to catch morning registration, so I'd stopped outside to roll myself a sneaky cigarette before facing the music. My tin was empty apart from the dregs. Dust and a couple of meagre tobacco flakes, barely enough to make even the skinniest roll-up, and there he'd been, propped against the wall in his tailored suit, lighting up a cigarette of his own before he went inside.

He'd watched me struggle with my excuse for a roll-up, and then he'd held out his cigarette packet.

Insignia. Scrawly font on a beautiful black box. So much more beautiful than the cheap cigarettes the kids at school smoked.

"Thanks," I'd said.

He'd sparked up his lighter for me and cupped his hand around the end of the cigarette, and I'd leaned in, trying my best not to look like an idiot as my stomach churned and my heart raced.

I'd never smelled success before, but he reeked of it.

"You could get arrested for this, you know." I'd grinned after taking a drag. "Supplying cigarettes to a minor."

He laughed the kind of confident laugh that made my heart race even more. "They could try."

I didn't know he was one of the country's top criminal lawyers back then.

Didn't know his name was Alexander James Henley Jnr. and he employed over five hundred legal staff at his swanky London law firm.

I had no idea at all that the papers called him the puppet master, or that I'd come to know he has a penchant for asphyxiation games and brutal fucking.

He'd just been a posh guy in a suit, until he'd smiled at me.

And that smile was enough for me to gift my heart to a man I'd probably never see again.

The elevator pings on the fifth floor, and I have to squeeze through the throng of suited bodies to step out. My elbow brushes Alexander's arm, and for the tiniest moment he smiles.

And then he's gone.

The doors close and take him away, and even though I'm late, I watch the floors creep up on the display. Six, seven, eight, right up the way to... eighteen.

It thrills me to know he's in the same building, just like I knew it would.

After all, that's why I took the job here, at the opposite end of the city. They'd asked at the interview, *why us, so far away from your home address,* and I'd given them my polished spiel about how much respect I have for Mr Henley's work, and that seemed to clinch it.

Phase one complete.

I'm in, and I've seen him. Actually *seen* him already.

I head off to find my induction with a smile on my face.

❧

I'm one of ten cleaners starting today. We all match. A roomful of green and white striped minions that they assume need educating on how to use a mop properly. I imagine that's what we are to them, nothing but cheap grunts, incapable of doing anything more with our lives.

"We pride ourselves on our professional standards," our new line manager tells us. "Everything *must* be perfect. *Always* perfect."

My fantasy of being assigned to Mr Henley Jnr's office gets a reality check as they divide us into pairs. Canteen kitchen, that's where I'm assigned. Scrubbing grease and cooking oil, taking out the food waste and disinfecting the main employee toilets along the corridor. Toilets that I doubt Alexander Henley ever uses.

I'm paired up with a girl called Sonya, and we head up towards floor seven.

I can see she's pretty, even under her shitty uniform. Her skin is rich and dark, and her eyes are burnt umber – the exact same shade as one of the wax crayons I had as a kid. She's blessed with the thickest lashes I've ever seen, and her hair is glossy even through her hairnet. Her braids are twisted into a bun, resting on her collar like a ball of coiled rope.

"What do you think, hon?" she asks. "Quite a ball breaker, our new manager, ain't she?"

I shrug. "Seems ok."

She rolls her eyes. "She gave me a load of abuse for using the escalator earlier. Seemingly it's forbidden for us lowly cleaning staff to use them."

"Forbidden?"

"An *eyesore* apparently. They don't want the likes of *us* on display, I s'pose."

I'm tempted to tell her that Alexander Henley himself held the door for me this morning, but decide against it. "So, we have to walk up seven flights of stairs every day?"

"Sure do. Just be glad we're not on the top floor, hey? Although I doubt we'd ever get up that far if we wanted to. That's where Mr Henley works."

The thought gives me shivers.

We step aside as another pair of cleaners come racing down with an industrial floor polisher, but Sonya keeps on talking. "Apparently not even his swanky clients go up there, he meets them lower down. That's what I heard, anyway." She sighs. "I think I saw him this morning, heading up from underground parking. Just for a second though."

"You did?"

"I mean, you can't miss him, right? He's gorgeous on an epic scale."

I smile. "Yeah. Yeah, he is."

She nudges me with her elbow. "Saving grace of working in this place. What I wouldn't give to be Mr Henley's personal scrubber, eh?"

I push open the doors at the rear of the canteen. "Maybe we could do it, get ourselves promoted up there."

She laughs. "Up to floor eighteen? Yeah, right."

"I'm serious," I tell her. "Why not?"

She locates the supplies cupboard we've been directed to and examines our stash. "Because... well... I dunno." She shrugs. "Because I guess everyone in this place wants to work on the eighteenth floor. I'd probably sniff his seat if I got a shot in there, then rub one off on his posh-boy desk. *Oh, oh... Alexander! Yes! Your mahogany feels divine!*"

She looks at me and her eyes twinkle. And then she gives a sniff to demonstrate, and it's funny, it's really funny, and it makes me laugh.

I think I'm going to like Sonya a lot.

"Everyone calls me Lissa," I tell her and hold out a hand.

"Everyone calls me Sonnie," she says and shakes it. She hands me a bottle of de-greaser and a fresh scrubbing sponge from the pack, and arms herself with an industrial-sized vat of cream cleaner. "Just my fucking luck to get the shitty floor," she groans. "They fired the last two. Thankless fucking task, the canteen, so they say."

A rush of horror sweeps through my gut. "Fired? How do you know that?"

She taps her nose. "I love knowing what's what. Made friends with one of the girls who cleans the IT suite. She told me. Said she used to work this floor, too, until she got promoted. Said she had to work her fucking sweet ass off to get out of this crappy gig. Rather sell a kidney than come back here, she said."

"Great…"

"Yep. Life's fucking rosy. Hope we last the month out at least, I got rent to pay."

Me too, I tell her. I've got a little brother to take care of, I tell her, then take a moment to pull out my phone from my apron and show her my screensaver.

"His name's Joseph."

"Aww, he's a cutie, hon. Got your eyes."

"From our dad." I take the handset and stare at my little brother. We really do share the same eyes. Big and blue, and cheeky. He has the same pasty skin as me, and the same wisp of mousy hair. Not the dimples, though, he got those from our mum.

I try not to think about it, not now.

She's weighing up whether to ask, I know it. I save her the anguish, giving her the clipped spiel about how my parents died in a hit and run last Spring.

"Shit, I'm so sorry," she says, and she is, her eyes are kind. "You having to pay for childcare? That crap gets expensive."

I shake my head. "I have a friend, Dean. He's cool. He helps out. I'm lucky."

Lucky. That's a joke.

"A friend friend?" she asks, and her eyes twinkle.

I smile. "No. Just a friend. Definitely platonic."

He is as well. I've never seen him that way. Never seen anyone that way, apart from Alexander Henley.

Suited me just fine holding onto my V-status anyway. Getting enough A-grades to one day be his peer was the only thing I was focused on.

I shove my phone back out of view, and Sonnie's staring at me strangely, as though she's wondering whether she's going to divulge some more insider info or not. I hope she does.

"Keep a secret, right?"

I nod, and she hands me her own handset. Two beautiful little girls stare back at me, their smiles the sweetest thing. "I got two little ones," she says. "But don't say nothin'. Didn't mention it at the interview, was worried they wouldn't take me, single mum and all that, iffy childcare arrangements."

"They took *me*."

She smiles. "Guess you're braver than me for risking it."

Braver or too desperate to care.

I shrug. "Having responsibilities doesn't stop either of us scrubbing their ovens just as well as the next candidate, does it?"

"Better," she says. "We'll be better. Coz we need to be. Mouths to feed."

She isn't wrong there.

She tips her head at me, and her smile is conspiratorial. "What say we give it a shot?" she asks. "Show 'em that us little minions from floor seven got what it takes to get out of this gig. We could do it, have this place cleaner than they've ever seen it. Clean enough to eat your lunch from their swanky toilet bowls. That'll show 'em."

"You mean go for promotion? Off this floor?"

She nods. "Yeah, off this floor. All the way up to floor eighteen, that's where I'm thinking. Hell, I ain't been one of life's winners, not up to now, but ain't much I don't know about cleaning."

I grin. "Floor eighteen? For seat sniffing and rubbing one off on Alexander Henley's desk?"

She laughs. "Hell to the yes."

"You've got yourself a deal, partner," I say.

13

My feet ache like a bastard when I kick off my shoes in the apartment doorway. That's what you get for buying budget footwear. Blisters and anguish.

Dean's voice is only just audible over the cartoon theme song sounding from the living room. *"Lissa's home, yes she is. Let's go see your poor tired sis."*

My heart swells to bursting as Dean steps into the hallway and passes the smiling little guy into my arms. Ignorance is bliss.

It's the best feeling, being home. Even better than smelling Alexander Henley.

"Hey, little man!"

Joseph smiles, but is clearly still far more interested in the cartoons than me. Tears prick at the relief that he hasn't been crying all day, but it doesn't stop the resurfacing of the guilt I feel. The first day away from him was always going to be tough ride.

I don't really want to be doing this – palming him off on Dean every time I have a shift to work. I don't want to palm him off at *all*, in fact, but the flip side is so much worse. A lifetime of benefit handouts and few prospects. That isn't the life I want to introduce Joe to. It isn't the life our parents would have wanted for either of us.

I drop him back on his beanbag and he stares at the cartoon dogs on screen.

"So?" Dean prompts. "How was day one?"

I head on through to the kitchen, and he follows me, grabbing two mugs from the side while I switch on the kettle. "Hard. Long. Tiring." I pause. "Shit."

"Shit? Really?"

I shake my head. "Nah, it's not all that bad. I met someone. Sonnie. She seems nice."

"A friend already?"

I nod, and then I smile. "And I saw *him*."

"And did seeing his criminal-aiding ass in the flesh again cure the infatuation?"

I shake my head. "Not exactly…"

I want to tell him so much. I want to tell him that Alexander Henley smells just as good as I remember. I want to tell him the birthmark on Alexander Henley's cheek is a perfect little circle, and his eyes have the faintest little lines in the corners, and that's new. Newer than four years, new.

I want to tell him that I broke the rules and took the main elevator, and even though that's strictly forbidden, he still held the door for me.

Dean stares, waiting for more, and I realise I'm grinning. Mute.

"He didn't recognise me," I admit. "But he wasn't ever going to, was he?"

"Nobody would recognise you in that shitty uniform, Lissa. It's God fucking awful."

"Even so, it was years ago. He bummed me one cigarette, I'm sure he barely even remembers the school, let alone me."

"Just don't get arrested for stalking," Dean says. "It's not as if they don't know how to prosecute."

He's joking, but not really.

He knows all about my stalker tendencies. He's been an accomplice to most of them.

But not this time. This time he's got to look after Joe while I go scrubbing toilets for money.

"So, what's the plan?" he asks. "Don't tell me you haven't got one. You *always* have a plan."

"I'm going to get to the eighteenth floor," I say. "That's where *he* is."

"And then what? Hope he likes stripy caps and polyester?"

I shake my head, and it seems funny again. It all seems funny again.

15

I throw my crappy cap at Dean's head. "And then I'm going to sniff his seat."

He catches it easily. "I'm not even sure you're joking," he says.

I shrug. Smile. Make our tea, but say nothing.

Because, truth be told, I'm not even sure I'm joking myself.

TWO

ALEXANDER

Brenda, my assistant, has a voice that makes my ears bleed. I've pondered it a great deal during idle minutes, and the closest comparison I've so far drawn is that of a poorly tuned trumpet, played through the nose.

It would be comedy, if she weren't so thoroughly fucking prissy with it.

It would kill me to hear her squeal my name in the bedroom, and since my personal assistant is the very *last* person I want in my bedroom, that is fortunate. And quite possibly one of the main reasons I decided to hire her in the first place.

That and the fact she's really fucking good at what she does.

Mr Austin is here to see you.

I'm sure her voice sounds even worse through the internal telephone system, as though some of the depth of tone is lost in transmission.

Believe me, she finds me as unbearable as I find her. But we tolerate each other. A courteous professional disdain that gets us both through the working day. I think it suits us both that way.

"I'll be down. Get him a coffee."

Yes, Mr Henley, sir.

Mr Austin is an arrogant, weasel-faced prick, and I've already seen more than enough of him this week. Another weekend late-night call, another visit to his local police station to bail him out when I should be busy spending money, not earning it.

Mr Austin is CEO at Lux Air, the pompous private jet firm, and believes owning an airline gives him special privileges.

Mr Austin believes he can drive his sports car while under the influence of alcohol at over double the speed limit through residential areas, without giving a shit for any lesser mortals who may share the same road space as him.

Mr Austin also believes I can get him off the hook every time, just so long as he pays me enough money.

He's right.

Like I said, he's an arrogant prick, but so am I.

And so we go again. The firm handshake, the pat of his hand on my arm, the warm, fake, professional smile. The same old routine as he bleats about how *thankful* he is that I came to his rescue last night, how it *wasn't his fault. They've set him up, again. Jealous assholes. Barely even a double shot of whisky.*

I take the same old notes and nod in the same old places. And then I do what I always do.

"I'll deal with it," I say.

"Good man," he replies, just like always.

And just like always, I deal with it.

This business is as much about connections as it is about the law. It's about saying the right things to the right people, with the right air of confidence. That and knowing all those tiny little loopholes that infuriate the prosecution every fucking time.

They hate me more than Brenda does, just as much as they hated my father before me. But that's okay.

You know what they say. You're no one unless somebody hates you. And judging by those rules, I really am *someone*. Just ask my ex-wife.

Today is like any other day at the office. An endless carousel of the same old faces making the same old fuckups.

Mr Austin, and then Mr Rand, the oil tycoon with a penchant for picking up women on street corners. Mr Kingsley, the dot com boomer who does far too many drugs and gets into scrapes with the law far too often for sanity. Some court paperwork, and a crappy board meeting that sees me staring numbly at my officially retired father for an hour across the boardroom table, and I'm done.

Once upon a time, before life – *divorce* – turned me into the cynical, jaded asshole I am today, getting people off the hook was all the exhilaration I needed. The rush of a serious court case, the heated negotiations behind the scenes, the high-end networking, and the money, always so much money. I loved it. All of it.

But these days it's not enough.

I'm barely out of the office foyer when I pull my second phone from my inside pocket. It's identical to my work handset in virtually every way, except this is an unregistered pay-as-you-go, topped up using cash only, and never in the same location twice.

My fingers feel clammy as I unlock the screen.

I scroll through my previous messages, the ones that I should have deleted minutes after bidding is closed, as per the rules. I used to follow them. I used to be careful, guarded. Sensible.

This week's offer is still in my inbox.

Britney Jane. 26. Brunette. 5'10. Athletic. D-cup tits.

The pretty girl stares out from the handset, lips pouted like a cheap porn star, legs spread to show the pretty pink slit of her pussy. She's had surgery, that cunt is far too perfect to be natural.

I hate perfect, but that isn't why I haven't placed a bid on Britney Jane. The list of ticked boxes beneath her photo show her as far too vanilla to warrant any kind of investment.

Far too vanilla for *me*.

I scroll back through the listings.

Candice. 21. Natural blonde. 5'2. Curvy. C-cup tits.

She'd been worth every penny and then some. The girl had very few hard limits listed under her photograph, and she'd been telling the truth. Believe me, I know. I pushed her on all of them.

I arrive at my car, and my mouth is dry and my jaw feels tight, waiting for the thrill that zips up my spine whenever a fresh listing appears, like an addict craving a hit. It's about time I went cold turkey for a few months, logged out of the network and weaned myself back to a state of mind closer to equilibrium.

But the thought is unwelcome, the prospect one of nausea.

I need this.

Need.

That's the downward spiral before me. The cycle of dependence and escapism that leads me down the rabbit hole. The same cycle I see every day in my office, rich men taking ever greater risks to get their rocks off, chasing the elusive thrill that comes from the shadier side of wealth.

Gambling. Drugs. Fast cars.

I've seen billionaires shoplift costume jewellery just for the rush of it. I've seen calm, responsible fathers snort a gram of coke from a hooker's tits and take them out for a joyride through leafy London suburbs. I've seen men with beautiful wives at home, hovering outside public urinals for the chance to shove their dick in some seedy guy's asshole before teatime.

I've seen it all, and I've excused it all, and somehow, somewhere along the line I became caught in the same rancid headlights.

I don't do drugs. I don't drive my cars at excessive speed. I don't visit bars and drink myself into oblivion. I don't even smoke expensive cigars.

I do sex.

Dirty, filthy, brutal sex.

I should sign up for some anonymous self-help group. Go along to some grotty community centre in the dregs of London for a Styrofoam mug of cheap coffee, and the pleasure of perching myself on one of their grimy plastic chairs as I psyche myself up to say it.

My name is Alexander, and I am a sex addict.

I'd get a round of applause, and then I'd have to tear up, eat a biscuit, and tell them all how good it felt to face down my own demons.

I have no intention of doing any of those things.

I remember the glorious pained grunts as *Candice* took my cock dry. I remember the soft flesh of her hips yielding to my grip as I held tight and pushed in all the fucking way.

I remember the way her pretty tits bounced, her big nipples so fucking ripe for my mouth.

I remember the way she wriggled and squirmed with my hands around her throat.

Paying *Candice* was a delight. Money well spent.

But I think I'll go with *Elena* this evening. I haven't seen *Elena* in a while.

I slip into my Mercedes and fire off a text message before I start up the engine.

Elena. Tonight. Nine thirty.

Sent.

I wait.

The handset vibrates in my hand as the message icon flashes.

Room sixteen. Harley's tavern. Your name is Ted Brown.

I'm smiling the first genuine smile of the day as I pull out of the car park.

MELISSA

It takes us three weeks of back-breaking effort to get a compliment, let alone a promotion. Another two weeks on top of that to get a regular smile from our line manager at the start of shift.

Week seven of scrubbing steel and grouting and toilet bowls until our hands are blotchy, and both Sonnie and I are questioning just how sound our ambitious little scheme is turning out to be.

She drops her sponge in the canteen sink and shoots me a look of pure apathy. "Whose idea was this?"

"Yours." I smile as I wipe down the air conditioning vent. "And mine. Alexander Henley's seat, remember?"

She takes a deep breath. "Mmm, I hope it smells half as good as I imagine."

"Oh, it will," I say. "He smells *incredible*."

"And there she goes… never quits with the bragging…" Sonnie's laugh makes me laugh too. "Tell me about it again, hon. I need the motivation."

I clear my throat. "It was a day like any other day… rushing my way through the back alleys to school, knowing I'm late for registration *again*…"

"Yeah, yeah," she prompts. "I got this bit. Late, sneaky cigarette, dregs of tobacco in your crappy tin, yada yada. I want the bit about *him*."

"You have no patience." I laugh. "He smells musky, deep… rich, like the orient… his eyes are dark… like…"

"Midnight…"

"Midnight in *winter*…"

She's already laughing. "Boy, we got it bad."

"Yes. Yes, we do."

"Imagine it," she says, and her eyes glint with that goofy sparkle that takes over every time she floats away into fantasy. "Being with a man like him. A man who has everything. Imagine waking up in the morning and being Mrs Alexander Henley. He has it all, right? The real deal, the full package. Mr perfect, living the dream…"

"Living the dream," I repeat.

She picks up her sponge. "I guess we'll just have to make do with sniffing his seat."

I wipe the damp from my forehead. "Yeah, well, you'd better get scrubbing. We're quite some way from the eighteenth floor."

"Amen to that," she says, and gets to work.

We're about to check out for the day when we're accosted in the cleaning corridor on floor five.

"A word, girls, please," our line manager says, and beckons us inside her office. Sonnie looks at me, and I look back, and I'm not sure whether I should be worried or excited.

Worried definitely wins out.

We step on through and I close the door behind us, hoping that's the right etiquette.

Janet. Our line manager's name is Janet, but should I call her Miss Yorkley? Janet or Yorkley?

"Sit," she says, and I hope I don't have to choose.

We sit. My hands are in my lap. My heel tapping.

I really want this job. *Need* this job. For Joseph, and for me. For my shot at smelling Alexander Henley's seat. For my shot at smelling Alexander Henley *himself.* Please God.

"What's your secret?" Janet Yorkley asks.

Sonnie looks at me, and I guess I have to answer for us both. "Sorry?"

"Your secret." She raises an eyebrow. "You must have one. Canteen's never looked so good, so they tell me, and our staff survey showed the floor-seven toilets as ten out of ten for cleanliness. We *never* have ten out of ten, for anything. These people just *cannot* be pleased." She leans forward. "But *you've* managed it, two newbies in the crappiest floor of this building, and you're the ones who got us a perfect score. So, what's your secret?"

"We, um… we work hard…" I begin.

"No shit," she says, and there's a smile on her face I haven't seen before.

I dare to smile back, but I don't think she sees, because Sonnie is leaning forward in her seat, and rolling back the cuffs on her crappy blouse.

"This," she says. "This here, this is what gets those toilets clean."

Sonnie's hands are rough. Her skin blotchy and tired.

Janet stares at her, and I wonder if she's made the wrong move. "You should use the standard issue gloves," she says. "Health and safety. It's in your induction booklet."

"Health and safety don't get them cubicles shining, Janet. Ain't nobody got time for that."

I nod. Because I think I should. "We do what it takes. Everything *must* be perfect, just like you said in our induction."

"I know what I *said*." She sighs. "But this is a cleaning job. I can't say there's many of your ilk in this building that give much, if any, consideration to perfect. They just do what needs doing and watch the clock until they can leave."

The thought is in my head. Just like that. *I guess they just don't want to smell Mr Henley bad enough.*

Sonnie nudges my foot with hers and I know she's thinking it too.

"Thanks," I say to Janet. "For the recognition. It means a lot."

She laughs, just a little. "I didn't get you in here for the *recognition*, Miss Martin. I got you in here to give you a promotion."

Promotion.

I can't stop the grin. "You mean we're off floor seven?"

"You're too good for floor seven," she says. "None of the senior executives use the canteen anyway. It's for the juniors and the admin staff."

Sonnie's eyes are nearly as wide as her smile. "So, where are we…"

Floor eighteen, floor eighteen, floor eighteen. I daren't hope.

"Floor sixteen," Janet says. "Senior conference suites. Where the top executives really will see your magnificent handiwork, so make sure you get it right."

I nod. Sonnie nods. I try my best not to feel disappointed.

"Thank you," I say. "We won't let you down."

"You'd best not." She stands and gestures that we're free to leave. "Because Mr Henley conducts his meetings there, and if there's one thing you need to know about Mr Henley, it's that he *demands* perfection. And you'd better deliver."

There's a bloom in my chest. A hope. The faintest, most beautiful little flicker of hope.

If it's perfection Alexander Henley demands, then I'll deliver.

I'll deliver anything he wants.

THREE

MELISSA

Dean jokes that we need champagne, not the chipped mugs of coffee we clink in my tiny cramped kitchen. He tells me he's happy for me, that it's a *job well done*, says that maybe they'll give me a pay rise big enough to make up for the extra bazillion stairs I'll be climbing up every day to get to floor sixteen.

He looks good today, his cropped hair a dark shadow, his brows heavy over bright blue eyes. A tight white tee under a loose checked shirt. Torn jeans and bare feet. Bare feet always look good on a man.

It's when Dean says he's happy for me for the tenth time that I know something's up.

It's in his smile.

Tense.

More like a grimace as he raises his mug. Again.

I put mine down on the draining board. "What is it?"

He shrugs and the smile doesn't even flinch. "What's what?"

I poke my head through to the living room to check Joe's still playing with his picture book, and then I fold my arms. "Don't give me that. You look like you're trying to hold in the shits or something."

The smile eases up. "It's nothing, I'm just…"

"Just *what?*"

He passes his mug from hand to hand, back and forth. "I just thought the novelty would have worn off by now. Plenty of places closer, Lissa. Plenty of places more flexible. Better pay, too." His eyebrows pit as he stares at my filthy apron. "Without a crappy uniform."

"There aren't…" I begin, but he shakes his head.

"Don't give me that. How long do you spend on the Tube every morning? Half hour? Three quarters?"

"I don't notice… it's not so bad…"

His eyes are so big and so genuine. "What you gonna do, Lissa? Floor sixteen this week, then what? What happens when you *do* make it to his office?"

When. Not *if.* I resist the urge to smile.

"Then I sniff his seat." I try to make light of it, but he doesn't laugh.

"Don't pretend this *thing* is a joke to you."

A horrible tickle in my belly. More like a scratch. *Desperation.*

"It *is* a joke." I laugh. "Me and Sonnie, we both say…"

"Like *she's* serious. Like she's *you.*"

I hate the way he says it.

I choke back the fake giggle and ease the door closed until I can only just see Joe through the gap. "I know this is hard on you, I know it asks a lot, you being here, all the time. You shouldn't have to, I know that… and if it's too much…"

"If it's too much then what?" His eyes are right on mine. I don't have an answer and he knows it. He sighs, and I feel like shit. "This isn't about Joe. I love having Joe.

I love helping out. I can start up college again next year, like we said."

I clutch at straws. "I could pay you, maybe... if they do give me that extra money... or a babysitter... so you can go back..."

He looks stung. "Like it's about money."

"But it could be..."

"Stop." He holds up a hand. "Just stop doing this."

"Doing what?" I flick the kettle back on.

"Deflecting." He has to tip the jar to scoop the last of the coffee granules into our mugs. Dregs. Story of my life – credit card debt from funeral expenses don't leave much of a budget for anything else. "This thing with Alexander Henley," he continues. "It's not... healthy..."

Like anything about my life is *healthy*. I don't say it.

"I know what I'm doing," I tell him. "It's just fun. Something to dream about. And I'm planning on working my way up, maybe be a team leader one day... maybe even an admin junior... and then who knows..."

"Right?"

"Right," I lie.

"And you aren't gonna do anything? Not when you get there? Not when you're close enough that his seat really is there for the sniffing?"

I take my coffee black, saving the milk for Joe's cereal in the morning. "Anything like what?"

Dean takes his black too. "Like stalking him. Like following the guy around until he catches on to you, and fires you, or sues you, or worse."

"Worse?" The thought makes me smile. "What on earth could be worse than being fired or sued?"

"I'm being serious, Lissa!"

His raised voice takes me aback, and I check the door for Joe. He's still flipping those picture book pages, smiling to himself, lost in his own little world like I used to be.

When I turn back, Dean's pulled his phone from his pocket and he's flipping across the screen, flipping through images I recognise from my own Google searches.

He turns the handset in my direction, and my stomach flips but I don't look away. I don't need to.

I've already seen it.

Already read everything there is to read on Alexander Henley Jnr.

"I did some digging," he tells me, "while Joe had his nap this afternoon."

My cheeks burn as I check out the headline on screen.

The legal Puppet Master pulling the strings of the dirty elite. Just who is Alexander James Henley Jnr?

I can't see the rest of the text, he pulls his phone away too quickly.

Like hell it was just this afternoon. I didn't find that crap, and I searched hard. Really hard.

Dean's eyes are fierce. "There's a woman here, or there *was* before she retracted her comments. Said he paid her. Said he's dangerous. That she was afraid for her life."

I roll my eyes. "Tabloid gossip, I'm sure. Sour grapes, maybe."

"And if it's not? There's plenty of stories, Lissa, if you dig hard enough. All retracted. All hushed up soon after. What if he *is* dangerous? Who knows what a guy like that's into? He's not like us. He's not from our world."

"So, you thought you'd better fill me in now I'm up nine floors?" I shrug, sip my coffee. "I'll probably never even get vaguely close enough to find out what he's really into. As if a man like him is ever going to be *into* a little scrubber like *me*. Christ, Dean, are you blind?"

I wonder how long he's been looking up Alexander Henley. I wonder whether he sees the beauty that I see.

I wonder if he's saved a picture. Maybe several.

I wonder if he knows quite which way he swings yet, and if he's still masturbating over gay porn when he thinks I'm asleep through the wall. I wonder if he's masturbated over Alexander Henley.

The idea of a stash of photos makes me jealous. My phone has a cracked screen and barely any storage.

"That's the thing," he says. "I think you *are* gonna find out what he's into. And I don't think you'll stop *'til* you find out."

I groan. "That polyester stripes don't really turn him on, Dean, that's what I'm gonna find out. That guys like Alexander Henley don't date girls like me. That I'm not good enough, not smart enough, not pretty enough for a man like him. *That's* what I'll find out."

He holds up his hands. "I don't think that, not *any* of that. And you shouldn't either."

"Yeah, well *he* will. Probably." That *scratch scratch* in my belly. The *scratch scratch* that seeing the job advertised in the paper managed to take away.

A *Saaaaa*, and then a *Dee deee* from the living room, and I push the door open. Joe is up on his feet, a big smile on his face as he claps his hands, picture book finished.

Dean sighs, and then he smiles, and I know it'll be alright. I know he'll never make me give up on my dreams, not while this little guy is depending on me to get us through this mess.

He grabs my elbow before I go to scoop up my Joe, and his voice is just a whisper, right in my ear.

"Henley won't think that, I promise you. Not about *you*, Lissa."

I could kiss him. Kiss him for the way he's looking at me, as though I'm still the girl with straight-As and a big future ahead of her.

"Thanks," I say.

"It's the truth," he whispers. "And that's what worries me shitless. That it's gonna be *you* who ends up hurt, and broken and retracting *your* comments when you make it a whole lot further than floor eighteen. Because you will. You *will* make it."

Hope.

It's a beautiful feeling.

I shouldn't smile, not when he's so worried, so I pretend it's all for Joe, and choo-choo trains, and the cruddy second-hand trainset I picked up with my first month's wages.

He deserves so much more than this. And I'm going to get it for him.

If Dean really pushed me, I'd tell him I really don't have a plan beyond floor eighteen, and I wouldn't be lying, not technically. The plan *post* being up close to the area Alexander Henley spends most of his working life is hazy. More a feeling. A feeling that I'll know what to do when the time comes. Doors opening into darkened corridors, and more doors, deeper and deeper. Like the detective novels I used to pick up from the charity shop as a kid, there were always so many breadcrumbs, a trail unfolding as you flipped the pages, and then BAM, at the end it would all come together, a sense of satisfaction as the whole picture came into view.

That's how I feel right now. Like I'm at the beginning of something, armed with nothing but that sense of *knowing.*

Maybe it'll be a late night. Mr Henley working late as I stumble into his office, and there'll be a meeting of eyes, a simmering recognition in the darkened room, just him and me, and maybe I'll tell him, tell him I'm the girl he bummed the cigarette to, the girl who was late.

Maybe he'll remember.

Maybe he'll invite me to sit down and ask me all about my life, and I'll pull the crappy cap from my head and shake my hair loose from my hairnet, and he'll see something in me.

Something.

Something he wants.

I'm such a fool. Even the thought makes me laugh as I whizz Joe's crappy train around the track and make the noises.

I'm pretty sure that's not how a run-in with Alexander James Henley, the *puppet master,* is going to go down. Maybe sniffing his seat and laughing about it with Sonnie will be the end of it, nothing but a crazy fixation until I find a way up and off this crappy rung on the life ladder.

Before some asshole going thirty over the speed limit ploughed into my parents I was a girl on a mission. Determined to qualify as a criminal lawyer and run into the man who'd stolen my heart over an *Insignia* cigarette. It was supposed to be one hell of a different story to the way this one's panning out.

See, we're from here, Joe and me. From this shitty rundown part of town. My parents too, and their parents before them. Mum and Dad worked shitty jobs they hated, struggling to make ends meet for me and Joseph. They never moaned, not once, not ever. But I was going to be different. I told them so, and they believed me.

Lissa's going to be a swanky lawyer, they'd say. *Not like us.*

But I *am* like them. They kept on going, day after day, working hard, just like *I'll* keep going, just like *I'll* keep on working hard.

They wanted so much better for me. For both of us.

Our Lissa would run through a wall if there was something she wanted on the other side. She'll never give up. She's that kind of kid.

I heard Mum say that once, to Mrs Manning who lived across the hallway.

She was right.

I wanted to step up after the accident. Wanted to hold the pieces together for Joseph, quitting my own A-Levels and taking on my parents' rent. I wanted to do all of this, and I did.

I want Alexander Henley, and I'll have *him*, too.

I just don't know exactly how.

Yet.

FOUR

ALEXANDER

It's days like these I wish I still smoked more than one a day.

Another last-minute fucking plea bargain as my client wrung his shaky hands in the corridor outside, and Cyril Westerton, prosecution lawyer, flapped his saggy jaw and told me my proposal was *preposterous*. An *outrage*.

Nothing's fucking *preposterous* as far as I'm concerned.

The guy's a joke, heading for nothing but retirement and a shitty gold watch, looking for one last case to put his name in lights. Well, it won't be this one. Not today.

It'll never be one of mine.

It's all but signed and sealed. A tap on the wrist for my client, some damages for the *victim* – some cheap hooker from Soho who took his cash then filmed him getting rough with her on hidden camera. He swore she begged him for it, told him it got her off.

As it turns out, I believed him. Not that that matters.

My digging proved me right, at least. Bill Catterson isn't the first guy the bitch tried to stitch up, but he will be the last.

I've ruined her. Dug up the dregs on her seedy life, on the money she blackmailed from rich guys who can't keep their dicks in their pants, on the games she plays, on her secret coke habit. On the fact she collects more STDs than I collect gemstones, and I collect a *lot* of fucking gemstones. Childhood habit – an increasingly expensive one.

My client, Bill Catterson, is a sad loser whose wife now hates his guts worse than she did before.

Once upon a time I'd have had some sympathy for the guy, but now I feel nothing but disgust. Maybe a sliver of pity.

He knows he's worthless today. The same as he knows he's riddled with genital nasties, and I suspect the guy will most likely never regain enough testosterone to get his tiny little dick up ever again.

It *is* tiny. I saw the fucking video. Hazard of the fucking job.

Anyway, the guy's broken. But he's not in prison. Not even close.

Jacqueline Catterson flashes me a smile, but her eyes are like spitting coals as we leave court. An air kiss and a *thank you, Alexander*, despite the fact we've never once been on first name terms, and she's off in a plume of *Dior*, with her wimp of a husband trailing behind her.

His farewell handshake is as weak as the rest of him. His hand is clammy, and I hate that. I fucking hate sweaty palms.

I wait until he's out of sight before I tug a handkerchief from my inside pocket. Be fucking damned if I'm wiping that guy's grimy body fluids on my suit.

I'm waiting for my driver when I catch sight of an even bigger loser, and now I really am craving a fucking cigarette.

They say nicotine cravings peak three to five days after quitting. Bull-fucking-shit.

Two years and counting, and I still think about lighting up at least twenty times a day.

The tabloid journalist piece of shit, known only to himself as Ronald *the digger* Robertson – a legend in his own tiny mind – closes the distance, trailing his goofy photographer behind him as he sidles up the street, deliberately lighting up and offering me one when I'm close enough to get a waft. Wanker.

His cigarettes are cheap, like him. *Cheaper* than him, and that's saying something.

I tap my watch. "Tardiness, *Ronald*, it's not very becoming of those in the fast lane of investigative journalism to be late."

"Been out the back with *Miss Whiplash*. Poor form, Henley. She's got little kids, you know, currently in care of Social Services now they've been tipped off about her *unfortunate* addiction. How the fuck do you sleep at night?"

I *don't* sleep at night, but I smile a triumphant smile nonetheless and offer him a wave of the hand. "No fucking comment, Robertson. Why don't you move along to someone who has a modicum of respect for your opinion? I'm sure you've got reality TV wannabes tripping over themselves to flash their tits in exchange for a centre spread."

His beady eyes flash with hate, and it fills me with fucking joy. That's how the loser started, interviewing nobodies about their five minutes of fame, only now he's turned *serious*. Criminal investigative journalism, but Christ he stinks.

"Think she's gonna divorce him now?" he asks. "I heard she's leaving town for her sister's place."

That's bullshit speculation. Jacqueline Catterson loves her husband's money much more than she hates *him*, but I'll never tell Robertson that. I'll never tell Robertson anything. Not purely down to client confidentiality, which I *am* thoroughly bound by, but because I can't stand the fucking cunt.

"That's the most sophisticated question in your repertoire?"

"Just getting started, one off the cuff." He flips out a grubby little notepad, but I'm done.

My driver pulls up at the kerb, and I turn away as the camera flashes, obscuring my face as I clamber into the backseat of the shiny black hulk of Mercedes.

I see her as we pull away, *Miss Whiplash*, real name Wendy Brown, her eyes puffy from the bad news as she teeters down the court steps in a pair of cherry-red hooker heels which really don't match the cream cardigan she's dug out for the occasion.

He's right about her kids. Packed off to Social Services. If my conscience hadn't long been hammered into oblivion, maybe I'd care. Maybe I'd even feel sorry.

But I've done worse. A lot worse.

I know how it feels to lose your fucking kids, but life goes on. Same shit, different day. Only Wendy Brown has a chance of getting *hers* back, a couple of months clean and some supervised visits, and they'll be back home, watching daytime TV while their mother fucks men for money in the room next door.

Poor fucking sods.

But that's the world we live in.

The world all around us, around every shadowy corner.

The world that speared me and left me for dead under the heel of Ronald *journalist scum* Robertson himself, but we don't talk about that. Not since my father paid him almost seven figures to keep my face out of his shitty paper.

The city passes by the window and I'm glad of the tinted glass. Glad that nobody can see me scrub my hands with antibacterial gel, as though that stands a chance of getting Bill Catterson's grime off me. But it won't.

Bill Catterson's grime is *in* me, along with all the others – all the other slimy cunts I've been paid obscenely well to divert justice for.

I'm full of them. Every backhanded deal, every character assassination I've undertaken in their name, every loophole in the law I've exploited to keep their records clean.

I pull out the phone from my inside pocket.

If I'm going to feel dirty it'll be on my own fucking terms.

I think it'll be a *Candice* evening tonight.

MELISSA

Floor sixteen is beautiful. Glass and chrome and thick carpet that your shoes sink into.

My entire apartment could fit inside one of the executive toilet blocks up here, and it makes my heart pang a little, the contrast – my life and theirs.

I wonder if they realise how lucky they are, in their smart suits and their trendy hair, kicking back during meetings, unaware that I'm waiting, watching, hovering to swoop in like a thief in the night and clean up their mess when they're done.

Discreet. That's what Janet Yorkley told us. *You have to be discreet.*

We really are an embarrassment, that's obvious. We aren't allowed to walk along the main corridors in office hours, rushing along the service passages behind the scenes, hiding out in alcoves in fear of being spotted by those so much more important than us.

Floor sixteen has greater advantages than those obvious ones. The staffroom behind meeting suite seven is the hub of the higher floors, and it's in there that we first met Cindy Harris, Mr Henley's personal cleaner. She does his office – right at the back of the eighteenth floor – and more than that, so much more that it gives me shivers, she cleans his home. His actual *home*.

She loads his dishwasher, and stocks his fridge, and collects his suits from the dry cleaners on the way.

And she changes his sheets.

His bedsheets.

Takes his dirty laundry from the hamper, washes and presses it and folds it neatly back in his dressing room.

Sonnie's face was a picture when she told us. She mouthed me a *sweet Jesus* and wiped her brow, and I knew then that the goalposts were moving.

Floor eighteen is no longer our final destination.

We're heading for Alexander Henley's bedroom, and it won't be his seat we'll be sniffing.

Call it fate, or another breadcrumb in the tatty novel that is my life, but we got a flash of good fortune at the end of our third post-promotion week.

Cindy likes us, and that's lucky as hell, because we're the first to hear her news, before it's official, before she's even told Janet Yorkley.

Her husband's taken a new job posting, in Canada, and with it will come her two-month notice period, tops. Two months for Janet Yorkley to select a replacement for Mr Henley's personal scrubber, two months to prove that we're the team for the job.

Providing there is a *team* for the job, of course. The thought of going head to head with Sonnie for the new position makes my heart race, and not in a good way.

Hell, we'll toss a coin for it if it comes to it, that's what Sonnie says, but we both know it won't come down to that. It'll be Janet Yorkley's call as to who washes Alexander Henley's boxers, and that knowledge drives us on that bit harder, like women possessed, scrubbing our assigned areas like competition athletes and hoping we've got the edge. Even over each other, although we'd never say it.

Cindy figures we'll get it, one of us if not both, she tells us so. She runs us through the opposition when we catch her on a break, and points out all the reasons they'll never get promoted over us.

Takes cigarette breaks, and nobody will ever be allowed a cigarette break around Mr

Henley's property.

Broke a company branded paperweight in meeting suite five last summer.

Four individual sick days this last quarter.

That leaves us, she says. It's bound to be one of us. *Both* of us. Who knows?

That's when she decides to run us through the ropes. Just in case.

I listen in awe at the end of our Friday shift, soaking in every single word as she tells us all about the inside of Alexander Henley's home, the inside of Alexander Henley's *world*.

Alexander Henley collects gemstones. Rare ones that she has to polish with a special cloth. He keeps them in a dedicated room on the top floor of his Kensington town house, in special cabinets with combination locks. She knows the codes by heart, even though he changes them every month like clockwork.

Alexander Henley has more suits than she's managed to count, but they're all black, and so are his ties. Every. Single. One.

Alexander Henley finishes every evening with a single shot of whisky from an expensive crystal tumbler. He smokes one cigarette, by an open window in his entrance hallway and leaves the ash in an antique inkwell she has to polish to gleaming every afternoon.

Alexander Henley only ever uses the same one set of cutlery, and would rather take it from the dishwasher than choose a fresh set from the cutlery drawer.

He listens to dreary melancholic blues to wake up in the morning. Sometimes it's still playing when she gets there. She hates it, but I know I'll just love it, like I love everything else about him.

My heart tickled when she told us about the framed photographs of his children, and how they have to be facing just so on his mantelpiece. She told us that they're gone, to Hampshire with his ex-wife and her new boyfriend, some football coach named Terry.

Maybe the biggest surprise of all came when she told us he has a dog. *Brutus.*

I can't imagine Alexander having a dog, and I don't know why, it just seems so… human. Not much seems human about Alexander Henley.

She shook her head when she gave us the warning, beckoned us in close, as though she was spilling state secrets.

"Brutus is a beast," she said. "You'll have to win his trust or he'll take your hand off, and you don't want that. The last thing you want to be doing is bleeding over Mr Henley's cream carpets."

We'd oohed and aahed as she told us about his favourite treats, these weird dried fish sticks she has to pick up from the vets in the middle of Kensington.

"Never run short," she told us. "Friendship is unsteady with that dog, and you'll never get him out for his afternoon walk if you don't have those to bribe him with."

It turns out that's another of Cindy's duties. The afternoon walk, and apparently she's gone through three different aprons after Brutus has tried to tug them off her halfway around the block.

"Why is he so mean?" I asked, and she'd sighed and shrugged.

"Rescue, I think, after his wife left. Guess he was lonely."

I can't imagine that, either. He always seems so… composed.

"Just remember," she told us, "Mr Henley notices *everything.* Every. Thing. Make sure you get it right, or you'll be out of there before your feet hit the floor."

We nodded. Nodded some more. Made little notes for later. Made notes to give us the edge.

And so we make a pact, Sonnie and me, at the end of another long week as we hobble down the bazillion steps to the ground floor.

No hard feelings, that's what we promise.

"May the best scrubber win," she says, and holds out her hand before we part ways on the street.

41

And I shake it, I shake it and smile, and wish her good luck, even though I know it won't be going her way.

Because there's no way on earth I'm going to let her win this one.

Alexander Henley's dirty boxers will be all mine.

FIVE

ALEXANDER

Most addicts won't accept they're addicted. That's a fact. Not a fact I read in some shitty self-help book, either. It's something I see every day, every time I have to pluck the same old assholes from the jaws of a custodial sentence.

That's the other thing about money – it grants the privilege of eternal self-delusion.

My clients aren't *addicts*, they're *professionals* with *hobbies*. No client has ever looked me dead in the eye and admitted they've got a problem, not even in the cold light of day with their back against the wall and their freedom well and truly in my hands.

There's always a million excuses. A *set-up*, *burning the candle at both ends*, *living life to the max*, and, of course, the best one – they went a little *overboard*.

That's what they call snorting drugs all weekend and setting fire to your five-star hotel suite – going a little *overboard*.

Addicts. I'm surrounded by them.

I *am* one.

Porn, webcam girls, escorts… a constant itch I can't scratch. A tick behind my eyes. A nausea… a *need*.

But there's no self-delusion where I'm concerned. I know exactly what I am. I know exactly where I've come from, too.

It was neither selflessness nor an amiable disposition that saw me agreeing with every single one of Claire's custody demands when she loaded up our boys and a couple of token houseplants and took off to Hampshire in her – *my* – new plate Range Rover.

I could have fought her, and I could have won. Hired myself a nanny, or checked the boys into full-boarding at their private school and fought her every step of the way until she was too tired to fight me anymore.

She'd run out of both money and stamina long before I ever would.

But I didn't fight her. Not because I didn't give a shit about losing my boys – believe me, I gave plenty of fucking shits – but because of the final seething line Claire delivered as she slammed the door on our life and me along with it.

You're just like your father, Alex. Just like your filthy fucking father!

I'd poured myself a whisky as the Range's tyres screeched down our driveway. Thought about it as I smoked a cigarette, and thought about it some more as I smoked my way through another, and another after that, until the whisky bottle was all but empty and my tie was loose around my neck, and no matter how hard I thought about it there was only one verdict.

Every piece of evidence stacked up against me.

Guilty as charged.

My sentence was the realisation that I love my boys even more than I despise my father. And that's exactly the reason I only see them once a week on a Sunday.

It's better that way.

For them, not me. Definitely not for me.

It's a shitty day today, the kind of light drizzle that makes the world look miserable as sin. I head away from London, with the headlights on low-beam in the dull afternoon, listening to nothing but the rhythmic thump of the wipers and Brutus panting in the passenger seat.

Claire hates it when I bring the dog. She trusts him less than she trusts me.

Under normal circumstances, I'd say she was right. The animal has a foul temper and his social skills skirt closer to nil even than mine. But Brutus loves our boys, just as I love them. Maybe *because* I love them. And they love him back, in spite of his mean eyes, and his truly monstrous overbite and the fact that his breath stinks worse than Bill Catterson's diseased little prick. They see right through all of it, and love him all the same.

I hope that's how they feel about me, too.

Adults rarely give kids credit for all that much. My parents certainly didn't when I was growing up. They thought I'd buy into the paper-thin smiles, and the hushed voices, and the bristling niceties they put on for appearance's sake, as though I was too young, too naive, too fucking ignorant to pick up on the hatred simmering under the surface in our household. As though I couldn't possibly see through their bullshit veneer enough to know they couldn't stand the sight of one another.

I've never wanted to patronise my own boys like that, so I don't.

When Thomas and Matthew asked me why their mother didn't love me anymore I told them the truth.

Because I'm an asshole.

Because I'm incapable of plastering a fake smile on my face for the sake of keeping the peace.

Because I can't leave my work at the office.

Because I don't love her and she knows it, she's always known it.

And they'd listened, and shrugged and nodded, and Matthew – being a couple of years younger than his brother – had shed a a few quiet tears, and that was that. They'd settled in Hampshire, with Claire's parents up the road, and every Sunday afternoon they'd be waiting for our allotted time together.

Despite the crappy weather I'm excited today. Rugby tickets, England vs Wales, the best seats in the house for the game next month.

I can't wait to see their faces. They love rugby, Thomas especially. His games tutor tells me he's good for ten years old. Broad and strong and resilient, fast too.

He doesn't quit, that's what I'm told, no matter how tough it gets, Thomas will always dive headfirst into the scrum and come up trumps.

He's a winner. Just like me.

Matthew, well, he's much more like his mother.

I pull onto the driveway, parking up right in front of the door to make an entrance, and the curtain in the main living room twitches just like always. Claire never comes outside to greet me.

I'll occasionally catch a flash of tight blonde curls, or a hint of a scowl as she shoots me daggers from behind the window, but she never graces me with the courtesy of a sneer to my face.

Today, it appears, is different.

I see her as the door opens, easing aside for the boys as they come charging out. I register the difference in a heartbeat, the change in her willowy curves, the Empire line dress. The way she's standing, one hand idly on her belly, rocking back on her heels as though she's a few months further along than she really is.

I'd say three months tops.

I get out of the car just in time for the boys to slam right into me, warm arms squeezing me tight as Brutus barks his greeting at them from the passenger seat.

Dad! Dad! I came top in the History test, Dad! Terry took us bowling, Dad, and I won a trophy, Dad! We both did!

Their happy voices are one of my most favourite sounds on earth.

My other favourite sounds aren't suitable for polite conversation.

Terry wraps an arm around my ex-wife's shoulders, making a right old fucking show of it. It all seems a bit primitive to me – his male-ego need to paw at something in order to demonstrate ownership.

I don't need to drape myself over a woman to show she belongs to me. It's all in the eyes. In hers, in mine. If a woman truly belongs to you it's written all over her. She smells of it. It's in her smile. In the flutter of her lashes. In the way her body pulls towards yours, like a magnet. A charge.

Claire was like that with me once upon a time.

Now she's gripped awkwardly under Terry's arm while he shows off like a cockerel in a coop.

The boys stay attached to me as I head towards the woman who used to wear my ring on her finger. My hand is already extended, and Terry takes it, squeezes overly hard, and I wonder again just what he's lacking down below to require such a macho shake.

Claire doesn't take my hand.

"We need to talk," she tells me. "Later."

I don't hide the glance at her belly. "News, I gather. I don't need it spelling out."

She shifts her weight onto her hip. "Not *that*, Alexander. About the boys. It's *important*."

I ruffle their hair and resist the urge to flip her the finger. Her prickly tone infuriates me, trying to stab little holes in the few measly hours I get with them every weekend.

"Fine," I tell her. "Later." I smile my fake professional smile. "Terry."

He nods. "Alexander."

I step away before they take up any more of my precious fucking time.

I take the boys for dinner at a tasteless burger joint just off the A3 they've insisted on frequenting every Sunday these past few months. The coffee is bitter and thoroughly disgusting, and the burgers taste too cheap to be edible, but the boys love it here.

Terry takes them, apparently.

Good for fucking Terry.

I wrap my godawful excuse for a meal in a napkin when they aren't looking. Brutus will get considerably more enjoyment from it than I will.

I wait until the boys have wolfed down their fries and shakes before I pull the tickets from my jacket pocket.

I've been waiting all week for this, for the sweet wash of happiness I'll feel when their eyes light up in recognition. I have the seats marked out on a map of the stadium on my phone, a 360 degree view of the ground so they'll know exactly what we're heading for.

I slap the tickets down in front of them with a flourish, and my heart is thumping.

Joy.

It feels quite alien these days.

"I've booked us the very best seats," I tell them. "Right at the front. We'll see everything, and after the game I've got us backstage passes. We'll meet the players, get you some photos." I'm smiling, and they're staring, and I'm waiting for the moment, the moment when their faces light up.

But it doesn't come.

Their smiles are weak and fucking awkward, and it stabs at me, right in the fucking gut.

"What?" I ask, and there's a brutality to my tone that I didn't intend. I take a breath.

It's Thomas who spits it out. "It's the twenty-second..."

"Yes. Four weeks today."

"But we're..." He looks down at the table. "We're going to the football... with Terry... we were going to tell you today... Terry said to wait, until he definitely had tickets, said maybe you could come on Saturday instead, or–"

"Or *what*?"

He doesn't want to say it, and I feel like an asshole for pushing when I know what's coming.

"Or *what*, Thomas? What did *Terry* say?"

It's Matthew that answers, his eyes so big and innocent. "He said maybe you could miss a week, for the football. He said maybe you wouldn't mind."

Cunt.

Terry is a fucking cunt.

"I didn't realise you boys liked football. Rugby's your game, no?"

Thomas doesn't answer, but Matthew shakes his head. "We like football now, Dad. Thomas says football's better. *Cooler*, isn't it, Thomas?"

Thomas looks fucking mortified.

"Well?" I prompt. "*Is* football *cool* now? Cooler than rugby?"

Thomas shrugs. "They're both good. But we support Portsmouth now, like Terry. It's his team. He got us shirts."

I feel the tick at my temples. The sour taste of rejection.

"I see," I say, and pull the tickets back to my side of the table.

"Sorry, Dad," Thomas says, and he is sorry. I wish he wasn't. I wish he'd look me straight in the eye and admit he thinks rugby fucking stinks now and he'd much rather eat shitty burgers with Terry than me.

"Sorry, Dad," Matthew says.

I choke down my disappointment. "Some other time, then. When the games don't clash."

They nod. Matthew slurps the remnants of his shake. Thomas folds his napkin into little triangles.

It's really fucking awkward, all of it. This shitty place. This shitty weekend arrangement. This shitty situation with their *cool new dad*.

"Are you angry?" Thomas asks, and it makes me smile. Direct. I like that.

"Disappointed," I tell him. "Not angry."

I have no intention of forcing their priorities into an order I approve of, that's not in my make-up.

The boys gather up their burger boxes and put their coats back on, and I guess we're done here. Allotted time counting down to zero.

"Let's go and give Brutus his burger," I say.

⚜

Once the new football thing is out in the open, the boys can't get enough of it. I hear all about it on the drive back – the Portsmouth team, their cruddy uniform, their goal-scoring history.

I try to care, but all I feel is the unholy rage in my stomach. The desire to tell Terry exactly what I think of his ill-considered loyalty test.

And I do tell him, just as soon as I've stepped over their twee little threshold and Claire's sent the boys to their rooms.

"Classy move," I comment, "booking up a football match on my day with the boys."

He acts the innocent, all flustered as he tells me he didn't know I had plans,

50

thought one weekend wouldn't matter.

"*Every* weekend *matters*," I assure him.

"I'll give you the money," he blusters, "for the tickets."

Like I want his fucking money.

He's living in the house I pay for, driving the fucking car I pay for, standing on the fucking carpet my money paid to have fitted, and he has the fucking audacity to offer me a refund on the day he's stolen from me.

Cunt!

Claire clears her throat and puts a hand on his arm. She's nervous and it's not about the fucking game.

"We need to talk," she tells me. "Terry and I, we, um, have plans…"

"I can see that." I raise an eyebrow. "I imagine the new addition was *planned* too."

"The boys wanted a younger brother or sister. Tyler, too."

Tyler. Terry's drop-out teenage son has the perfect name for his flunky personality.

"I'm glad they're getting what they want."

"They want us to be a proper family," Claire says, and it pangs. *A proper family.* One without me in it. "They're close to Tyler now, and Thomas, well, he wants to be like his cool older stepbrother, wants to go to a regular school like he does, so we thought… next term… we thought we'd move the boys into Grange High. It's close, and the results are good…"

I'm shaking my head before she's even finished, my brows heavy and my jaw gritted.

"The answer's fucking no. The boys stay in Oxton, end of discussion."

Her cheeks flush pink, her veneer slipping away in a heartbeat. "It's not *end of discussion*, Alexander. They live with me. It's *my* call."

"No," I tell her. "It isn't."

She sighs. "They want to be normal kids, Alex. They want to hang out with regular people, not with the stuck-up little toffs at private school."

"Fantastic. They can cast aside their future employability for the sake of fitting in with the *regular* kids. I'm sure they'll be very happy to end up working in that shitty burger joint they insist on dragging me to."

Her eyes are on fire. *"Alexander."*

I haven't missed that condescending fucking tone. As though she's some permanently aggrieved little fishwife, and I'm the big bad cunt of an ex-husband.

Although maybe that bit's true.

"They're not going to state school," I tell her, "and that's the fucking end of it. If *you* wish to send *your* offspring through a second-rate education system, you be my guest, but *my* boys are *not* going to a shitty fucking state school."

Terry shakes his head, and I shoot him a glare that tells him to keep his fucking mouth shut. "I've already booked them into Grange High," she tells me. "They've been on an official induction visit. I've already cancelled their places at Oxton."

"Then you'll have to *un*-fucking-cancel them, won't you?"

"No," she says. "I won't."

I smile a horrible smile. "I could take you to court. Enforce my terms. I could move you into a grotty little terrace somewhere, see how you really enjoy slumming it with the regular folk."

She laughs. "As if you would."

"Don't try me."

"Don't try *me!*" she hisses. "Your filthy fucking father can't keep bailing you out forever, Alexander, one day one of those women are going to talk. Maybe they'll talk to me, hey? Maybe I'll be able to get them to testify how much of a dirty fucking pervert you are? Maybe I should give that asshole journalist a call and let him know I've got a story for him. I've still got screenshots you know, still got logs of your seedy fucking browsing history."

"Which will mean fuck all in a custody battle," I sneer.

"Not to your father it won't. Not when he realises his company name is being dragged through the tabloids."

I take a step forward, and Terry's arm is around her shoulders again, his face white as a pissing sheet.

"Don't push me, Claire."

She knows I'm serious, my eyes digging into hers, my breath shallow and angry, right on the edge of composure.

She says nothing, just stares with a holier-than-thou expression on her face, and I'm done here, I'm done with their shit.

I'm through the front door and halfway back to the Merc by the time she speaks again, and her voice is a shrill little wail, an attempt at intimidation that falls pathetically short of the mark.

"They're going to Grange High, Alexander! Whether you like it or not!"

My tyres churn up her pretty pink gravel on my way out.

SIX
MELISSA

Sonnie's bought herself some *non-standard* cleaning cloths. I've seen them advertised on TV, *extra strong for extra shine*. She doesn't mention it, but I see them when I look in on her wiping down the glass table in suite four.

I'm hurt for a moment that Sonnie would be so out to win, but it's for the best. Definitely. It means I can whoop her ass without any guilt.

Being here, among the corporate glamour of floor sixteen, has only fanned the flames. Yesterday afternoon I was stuck in an alcove between suites seven and eight, and I managed to stare at him through the glass for ten minutes straight.

He doesn't smile much, not that I've seen. Not with colleagues, nor with clients. He doesn't smile when he's on the phone, or even when an assistant drops a Starbucks in between meetings. His face always has this constant sternness about it – his eyes steely, his mouth so perfectly impassive. *Perfectly perfect.*

Being this close to him is doing nothing whatsoever to ease my obsession. My heart thumps every time I step foot into the executive suites, knowing he might be there, just around the corner, near enough to study, far enough removed that he has no idea I even exist.

I think about him in bed at night, when Joe is asleep in the room next door. I think about him every morning on the underground, wondering if today's the day I'll run into him late at the office.

I think about him all the time.

And it's not just me and Sonnie that are suffering the Henley effect.

I checked Dean's phone when he was in the shower last night. I wasn't even snooping, it was right there, flashing on the coffee table. I only picked it up to stop it bleeping.

I didn't expect to find his gallery app open, and didn't expect to find five saved pictures of the gorgeous Alexander Henley staring back at me.

Dean says he's dangerous, just like the internet claims, and maybe he's right. Maybe the man they call Puppet Master *is* dangerous. Maybe he's involved with things I could never imagine, but that doesn't stop me playing with myself when I think of all the dark, dirty secrets those steely eyes might be hiding. In fact, it's the opposite. Juicy gossip about the skeletons in his closet turns me on all the more. Fucked up, but true.

I just want… more…

everything…

I just want… *him.*

And I'm pretty sure Dean's jerking off over him too.

Hot older guy syndrome – I guess it's an affliction we both suffer from.

That's why Dean ended up on my sofa in the first place – a not-so-secret crush on our History teacher at school, Mr Patterson. Dean was just a kid, and he didn't like to talk about it, especially not after his dad cottoned on and beat the shit out of him at regular intervals from that day forward. Street fighting, that's what everyone blamed it on, even Dean himself, no matter how many times I asked. But I knew, even if nobody else would believe me. I've always known his dad's a homophobic piece of shit.

So, when Dean arrived on my doorstep earlier this summer with a case full of clothes and the declaration he was going to stay awhile so I could get myself back on my feet I welcomed him in with open arms. He stepped on in and said nothing about his cut lip, or his swollen cheek, or the fact he was walking with a limp, and hasn't said a word about it since.

He doesn't talk about his family, or the way they call him a *filthy little queer*.

He doesn't talk about the men I know he wants, or the gay porn he jerks off to and thinks I don't know about.

I do wish he'd talk about Alexander Henley, for him as much as me.

Maybe one day.

But today is all about scoring my way into Alexander Henley's bedroom, even if it's only to wash his sheets. Sonnie might have her super-duper cleaning cloths, but I've got something she doesn't have. Absolute determination, with a side helping of crazy.

I'm definitely on the side of crazy today, fizzing with the prospect of stepping foot inside that Kensington house and seeing it all for myself – all his little habits, all his ways, in his most private surroundings. I want to walk barefoot across his plush carpets, strip naked and wrap myself in his bedsheets and breathe him in, so near but so far. I want to be the one to hang his suits up and load his dishwasher and walk his lovely dog. I want to be able to pretend...

I'm already pretending. Pretending I'm already close as I sneak through the service passage to meeting suite ten. I've seen the roster. I know he was in there just over an hour ago. I'll be wiping his fingerprints from the glass table top, polishing up the chair he's been sitting in. A ghost behind him, following him, *adoring him*.

Stalking him, Dean would say. He's not so far wrong, I guess.

The room is supposed to be long empty, that's what the roster says. I'm loaded up with cleaning products and committed to my entry as I shoulder open the door and step inside. The lights are dim, the London skyline bright through the floor to ceiling windows. I don't see his silhouette until my feet are already on the carpet, the door swooshing shut behind me.

Oh fuck.

Alexander Henley has his ear pressed to his mobile phone, his voice angry and curt as he barks out orders to the person on the other end.

I back into the door, heart pounding, mouth paper dry at the thought of the disciplinary I'm bound to be getting for this.

Discreet. You must be discreet.

I've really fucked up. My dream of promotion shrivels and dies in the air between us as Mr Henley himself turns to face me.

He steps forward, and the glow of a spotlight catches his forehead, his brows so pitted as he squints to make me out in the shadows. I lower my head, and for once I'm grateful for my stupid cap. I don't want him to see me like this. I don't want him to see *me*.

So much for the late-night office fantasy.

"Hold," he says to the handset, and he's heading my way. I'm doomed, a rabbit in headlights, unable to bolt and run because that would be too rude, unable to stay because Janet Yorkley will throw a fit at me when she hears about this.

The panic thrums, my mind spinning through my options.

Maybe I should beg him to forgive my error. Beg him to turn a blind eye and not let Janet know what a fuckup I made.

Maybe I should beg full stop.

I'd beg for anything from him.

I shrink into the door, my cap low and shoulders hunched, as though being small is going to save me. But weirdly, as my breath comes out ragged and my knees feel all weird and wobbly, it does.

He stops.

Stares.

I feel his eyes burning as mine stare at the handset lolling in his hand, the call still active. His hands are big. Long fingers. I can't raise my eyes.

"I'm so sorry, Mr Henley, sir," I whisper, clutching my armful of products like a shield. "I thought… it said the room would be…"

"Empty," he finishes. "Yes. I'll be out of your way shortly."

The handset rises to his ear and my eyes follow, and he gestures me forward, gestures I can carry on about my business. His laptop is still open on the table, but he indicates I can clear it to the side. His coffee cup, too.

My skin prickles. My eyes meeting his for just a moment as I dither and dawdle, and I must look petrified because he smiles.

He smiles.

Just for a heartbeat.

And then he's barking at the person on the other end again, pacing back to the windows.

My fingers are shaky as I unload my supplies onto one of the chairs. The polish makes a hiss as I spray, too loud for the room, and I see him turn again, staring as he paces. I can't look at him, I daren't. I give it my best as I scrub and buff, stretching over the expanse of glass, my arms tense with effort. I lift his laptop so gently, taking care not to look at his inbox on screen. I lift his coffee cup and buff underneath, wipe down the seat he's been sitting in, then rebuff the table until my reflection is crisp and clear and I can even see my terrified eyes.

I see him, too.

I see him watching me in the glass.

Shivers. It gives me shivers.

I don't stop working. I daren't stop working. I'm like a whirling dervish as I polish and wipe down the side cabinets, the corporate pictures on the wall, the leaves of the ornamental plants in the corners. I empty the wastepaper bin and make sure the new liner is perfectly even. I run a cloth along the skirting to catch any dust.

I'm wiping down the radiator cover as he hangs up the phone, and there's a lump in my throat, filled with apologies, a hundred words to stop him telling Janet Yorkley to fire my sorry ass.

I don't say a single one of them.

He clears away his laptop. I watch him from the corner of my eye, and I see that he's careful, picking up his things without touching the table, being so careful with his fingers.

I don't know why it surprises me so much, but it does.

He reaches under the table for his briefcase, and he pushes his chair in all the way when he's done.

And then he heads for the door. The thought of him leaving makes my chest pang, and I turn my head, bold for just a single moment.

He's looking at me, his elbow already through the open door.

"Goodnight," he says.

My voice is squeaky. Pathetic.

"Goodnight, Mr Henley, sir."

He smiles. Again.

He smiles at *me*.

And then he's gone.

ALEXANDER

There are myriad corporate species in this building, and almost all of them exist outside of my awareness. The pools of secretaries, the receptionists, the kitchen staff, the trainees.

The cleaners.

It occurs to me that I've existed in this space for more years than I care to remember, and yet not once have I ever seen a cleaner going about their business.

Not until last night.

Corporate efficiency – that's what my father would call it. The great divide between the lowly minions who clean up our shit, and ourselves, the untouchable lords at the top.

Like I said, my father is a prick.

So what that I saw a cleaner? Some girl in a shitty uniform going about her working life, just happening to collide with my space at the same time I'm inhabiting it – who cares?

What makes it so memorable, I decide as I examine it this morning, is the fact that I spend my recreational time paying an obscene amount of money to women who'll do my bidding. Women who are there purely to give me what I want. *Whatever* I want.

And yet not one of them has ever made me feel as powerful as that scared little creature made me feel last night.

I'm so sorry, Mr Henley, sir.

I wish I could recall her voice more accurately. The hunch of her shoulders as she recoiled from my stare. The dip of her head, the jitters almost unperceivable, like a ghost of a scent on the air.

Mr Henley, sir.

The women I pay never use my real name. I'm Ted, or Bill, or Vladimir, or whichever poxy name I fancy for the evening. I could be Henry VIII for all they give a shit.

Mr Henley, sir.

It's been a long time since someone called me that and really meant it.

My assistant Brenda never means it. She says it with as much of a sneer as she dares without landing herself out of a job.

The cleaner was just a ghost in the machine, I didn't even see her face, not under the stupid hat I assume we make them wear. Her face doesn't matter. Shouldn't matter.

And it doesn't.

Aside from the fact that her meek little apology gave me a hard on, the girl cleaned with more dedication than I've ever put into anything.

I wasn't just hard, I was fucking impressed.

I call up my corporate extension list, wade through the reams of names I've never had any reason to take notice of.

Janet Yorkley – Cleaning Services Manager.

I buzz Brenda and tell her I want to see this *Janet*, and not ten minutes later the woman is outside my door with red cheeks and an expression nothing short of terrified.

I beckon her in and point to an empty chair on the opposite side of the boardroom table. The same boardroom table.

I hold up a hand as she makes to pull herself in.

"Don't. Touch," I say, pointing at the glass. It's still perfect, pristine, untouched. I don't want Janet Yorkley's grubby prints on it. I tell her so. I tell her that's exactly what she's here to observe. "I want you to look," I tell her. "At the glass. Tell me what you can see."

The woman has no idea what I'm talking about, her breath still ragged from the ascent. Lord fucking knows why she didn't take the elevator.

"Look at what, Mr Henley, sir? I don't understand."

Her voice is nervous, but it does nothing for my dick. It's gravelly, hoarse. Too confident.

"The glass," I say. "It's perfectly clear. Perfectly. Not a single smear. Not a print. Not one."

She puffs up her chest like a proud little peacock. "Thank you, sir, our cleaning staff are dedicated to the very highest levels of…"

I shush her with a shake of my head. "Yes, yes, Janet. I don't need the brochure spiel, and this isn't an award ceremony."

Her mouth slaps shut, a little bit like a toad's.

"There was a girl here last night. A cleaner," I continue.

Her eyebrows go so fucking high. "You saw one of our cleaners?"

"Yes, Janet, I saw one of your cleaners. In here. Last night. I was talking, and she was…"

Janet Yorkley looks mortified. She holds out her hands, dithering in the air so as not to spoil the cleanliness of the table I just pointed out to her, and she's waffling apologies, assurances that it won't happen again, that the cleaner in question will be demoted. Fired. Dismissed *immediately.*

I tell her the table is perfectly fucking clean and she wants to fire the girl.

Imbecile.

I can't fucking stand imbeciles.

The woman isn't listening to a fucking word I'm saying, and I hate that. I think it's probably my biggest hate – people who won't shut their trappy fucking pie hole long enough to just fucking *listen.*

"I don't want her *fired*," I tell her, and my voice is irritated as sin. "I want her *promoted.*"

"Promoted?" Her eyes are like golf balls. "You wish to have her *promoted*?! The girl you saw? But she's in breach of–"

"Yes, *Janet*, I wish to have her *promoted*. To my *house*. To my office. To anywhere I'll get the best personal use of her talent."

Janet Yorkley bores me.

I can practically hear her brain clunking around her skull.

"To my *house*, Janet. Do you understand? I have an extensive collection of gemstones. My tumblers are Dalton Crystal. My dining table is antique walnut. I want that girl to clean it. All of it."

She nods. Her brain chugs around some more.

"She moved my laptop and she didn't even look at the screen. Not even a glance. Do you have any idea how difficult it is to find someone who cares so little for corporate snooping?"

It's a rhetorical question, but she goes to answer it anyway.

"We value discretion, in our induction we vet our candidates for–"

I wave her quiet. "My old cleaner is leaving us, yes? I got a memo, did I not?"

"Your assistant… I sent it to…"

"I see all my assistant's correspondence, Janet."

"At the end of the month… Cindy's moving away…"

Like I give two fucks who Cindy is or what she's doing.

"That girl will be my new cleaner," I tell her. "Make it so."

SEVEN

MELISSA

When we're summoned into Janet's office at the end of our next shift I hope it's only me who's going down for my fuck-up, and not poor Sonnie too.

The apology is already on my tongue since I've been rehearsing it all afternoon. I wonder if she'll let me off with just a slap on the wrist. Show mercy over one stupid moment of carelessness.

I don't get the impression they give many second chances in this place, and I'm petrified, now more than ever, because I was so close to him, just him and me, and he spoke to me, smiled at me... just for one moment... but it's a start... it's–

"Sit," Janet snaps, and I sit. So does Sonnie. "You girls know why you're in here, I'm sure."

Sonnie looks blank, shaking her head a little, and I feel so guilty. I should've said something earlier, at least she could've prepared for the shit storm.

I blurt it out, just to get it over with. "I'm really, really sorry. It was a mistake. It was dark, the roster said the room was empty..."

Sonnie's eyes are so wide. I wish the ground would swallow me up.

"I'm sorry," I say again. "I should've looked, should've checked, I was carrying things and I didn't think…"

Janet looks seriously unimpressed, her mouth so tight and mean. "I'd dismiss you for this," she tells me. "Discretion is one of our highest priorities, Miss Martin, especially where Mr Henley is concerned."

I'm nodding, and Sonnie is staring right at me as the realisation dawns. "You walked in on Mr Henley?! This ain't got nothing to do with me, Janet. Uh uh. No."

"It's got nothing to do with Sonnie," I reiterate. "She doesn't even know about it."

Janet nods. "As I said, *I'd* dismiss you for this. Luckily for you, Mr Henley has other plans."

She shuffles a load of papers and taps them on the desk as I gawp. She pulls out what looks like a pass on a lanyard from her top drawer, and a set of keys from a box she has to unlock with a special code.

"Other plans?" Sonnie prompts, and my heart is pounding.

Janet shrugs at Sonnie. "I was going to promote *you*, Miss Webber, but the decision was made for me. Miss Martin is going to be taking over from Cindy Harris as Mr Henley's personal cleaner."

"Me?!" I gasp. "But I—"

"*You*," Janet says. "Just as well you're an exceptionally thorough polisher, Miss Martin, otherwise you'd be out on your ear."

"I don't understand…" I start, and Janet rolls her eyes at me.

"You *impressed* him. Lord knows why after you bulldozed in on him like an incompetent ass."

Sonnie hides her disappointment well. "Congratulations, honey," she says.

I hate myself for Sonnie, but I adore Alexander Henley right now, even more than I did before.

"Thanks," I say. "You should really have the position, you're miles better than me," I offer, and Sonnie nods. So does Janet.

"Guess it was your lucky day." Sonnie smiles and shrugs, and I feel even worse, because she's so nice, and *competent*, unlike me.

"You'll be taking floor eighteen, Miss Webber," Janet says.

Thank God for small mercies. At least she'll still get to sniff his seat. But I don't think I'll win any favours by pointing that out to her.

Janet hands over the paperwork, the lanyard and the keys. I take them so gently. The Holy Grail. His *actual* house keys, the real thing.

"Cindy will need to show you the ropes," she says. "You'll be shadowing her for the next few days, and then she'll be moving on."

I thought we had weeks before Cindy left, but apparently Janet has other plans. *Or maybe Mr Henley does.*

I stop right there. Mr Henley liked my polishing. That's all. A lucky day, just like Sonnie said.

We're dismissed before I can say anything else, and I'm burning up, feeling quite sick as Sonnie and I make our way downstairs.

"I'm sorry," I tell her. "I thought she'd fire me. I had no idea."

"Ah well." She shrugs. "Guess the best scrubber won in the end."

But they didn't. She smiles anyway.

"I expect a full report, by the way. I want to know everything, like what his sheets smell like, if his toilet has skids in it, if he uses a sock to jerk off. *Everything.*"

I laugh. "Everything," I repeat. "You know it."

She slaps my arm as we reach the exit. "I'm actually glad you won," she tells me. "I'm pretty hot on the guy, but you… well… you're a whole load more batshit than I am."

I laugh again. "You got that right."

"We did it together," she says. "Remember that. We put our minds to it and we did it. You just keep on doing it."

In my mind's eye, I see myself scrubbing his toilet. See myself sorting his dirty laundry. See myself using his toothbrush. See myself rolling naked on his bed. See myself...

Sonnie grabs hold of my hands. "Girl, I have something for you."

She leans in really close, her mouth right to my ear. "Ask Cindy about Harley's Tavern. You want your man, you gotta get in there. Whatever it takes. You got it? You ask Cindy, she'll tell you, but don't say it came from me, alright? Janet told her I was likely getting the job, she filled me in on a few things..." She winks. "Private things. Private *Henley*-related things."

She's already on her way before I can ask any questions, so I blurt out the obvious one. "What's Harley's Tavern?!"

She freezes, spins back to face me and flaps her arms around like I'm being a clumsy idiot all over again.

"Jeez, girl, you gonna have to learn to button it if you want to keep this gig!"

"Okay," I say quietly, "tell me more. What private things?"

She taps her nose, gives me a wink, "You'll see."

Harley's Tavern is an old style pub north of the city. Dean looks it up on his phone for me while I make us a hot drink.

"What's so special about the place?" he asks. "Looks pretty regular to me."

"I have literally no idea, Sonnie said to ask Cindy."

"Henley's old cleaner?"

I nod.

"Maybe he takes his chicks there before he offs them." He laughs, but I don't. He holds my new keys up to the light. "Looks like he's got some helluva lot of security going on."

I stir my coffee, bouncing Joe on my hip as he sings *wheels on the bus*. "You'd hope so. I'm sure he's got plenty worth stealing."

"And plenty of secrets worth hiding." He smiles. "Well done, Lissa. You did it. I knew you would."

"I got *lucky*."

He shrugs. "Wasn't luck that polished that table up. Wasn't luck that got you promoted up there in the first place."

"*Was* luck that he cared enough not to fire my idiot ass."

The paperwork is still sitting on the worktop, detailing both my pay rise and the insanely intimidating non-disclosure agreement.

Dean sifts through it. "This is pretty hardcore."

"*He's* pretty hardcore."

"Dangerous, like I said. This stuff is like a military secrets act."

"He's a lawyer."

"With a lot to hide from the sounds of it, I'm not talking client confidentiality either."

I pull a funny face at Joe and he laughs, and then he wants down to watch some clowns singing songs on the TV in the living room.

"Maybe it's all the dead bodies." I smile. "Bodies, or snuff porn, or maybe a black magic temple in the cellar."

"I'm being serious."

So am I. I hope I'm going to find kinky sex toys and cock selfies rather than a couple of corpses, but Dean's got me pretty psyched up about those online stories. Maybe I'm his next victim… hopefully not to bury me under his patio, but maybe he wants me in his house to humiliate me and turn me into his dirty little sex slave.

The thought makes me grin and prickle at the same time, and Dean scowls at me.

"You're gonna get yourself into a whole world of trouble with him, Lissa, you know that, right?"

I'm counting on it.

ALEXANDER

Harley's Tavern is a dingy little pub out past the M25 towards Harlow. A nothing place, that's how it looks. That's why Claude uses it more often than not as his venue of choice.

I take the Mercedes down into the underground car park, and pull in next to his sparkling BMW. Harley's Tavern looks like a dive to the casual observer, just another spit and sawdust local showing football on the big screen at the weekends.

I wouldn't be seen dead here under normal circumstances, but venture upstairs and it's a whole different story.

I've called this meeting. I haven't seen Claude in months, not since he schmoozed it up at the same charity ball I was at last summer and shot me a few too many overfamiliar glances across the crowd. I generally prefer distance in our business communications, but my requirements are… changing.

He meets me by the entrance to the rear hall, the same slick grin on his face he always wears for business. His handshake is firm and not at all clammy.

"Alexander, it's been a while. I've booked us the bridal suite." He laughs and slaps my back.

This kind of boys' club camaraderie normally gets my hackles up, but I need Claude, so I let it lie. Every fucking time.

Need. It's a fucking disgusting word.

He leads us upstairs and slides his card into the lock. Memories of Candice hammer my senses. Her pretty ass spread wide for me last week, her groans as I opened her up all the way. She stretched so willingly that girl.

But she gave me nothing.

Tense calves. A grimace. Moans that were borderline over-acting.

She gave me fuck all.

They're always there for the money, and why wouldn't they be? I'm no fucking idiot, but cash-hungry girls going through the motions are no longer enough.

I want more than a couple of ticked boxes showing their hard limits. I want more than a little slut on her knees pretending she's loving everything I'm loving.

I want *real.*

And that's what I tell Claude in no uncertain terms.

He offers me a whisky and I wave it aside as usual. He pours himself a healthy measure and takes a seat on the leather chaise longue. I pace, back and forth by the four poster, sifting through memories of all the times I've been in this room, all the women I've paid to tie to its posts and fuck until I'm sated and they're considerably better off financially.

"The girls like it," he tells me. "Candice, well, she asks for you, often. I think she's got a real thing for you."

"Because I tip," I snap. "You know it and I know it."

He shakes his head. "She's a dirty girl, believe me. She was a star in the test run. She wants it one hundred percent. She wants *you* one hundred percent."

"I've no doubt she gets her thrills, Claude, but she's not really *exposed.* She doesn't let go. She isn't…"

His eyes glint like the black obsidian in my collection at home. "Isn't what, Henley? Isn't scared? Is that what you want? A girl who's scared of you? Some little slip of a thing who'll make you feel like your balls are made of fucking steel?" He takes a sip of whisky. "Is that what you're after? Power? Real power? I'm sure I can deliver, just tell me how far you want to go."

I shoot him a glare. "I'm not a *total* fucking psychopath."

I hate that he knows me. I hate that he knows what I like. Most of all, I hate the way he judges me without even realising he's fucking judging me.

He shrugs. "None of my business what gets you off, Henley. You just tell me what you want, I'll find it." He sighs. "Why the sudden dissatisfaction? You liked Candice last week, Elena, too. And Kimberly. You told me you liked Kimberly. You gave her two grand in tips last month, she told me."

I did like Kimberly. *Did.*

"I'm tired of Kimberly," I tell him. "Kimberly uses the first chance she gets to take it doggy style and get the kinky shit over with. Kimberly gets off that way, that's her priority. I gave her two grand in tips last month because she pushed her limits. That's all. She bolted like a smacked fucking horse afterwards."

He laughs. "Sure. She's not hardcore enough. So you want fresh meat. I got it." He grabs some papers from his briefcase. "For your perusal, off the books. First choice."

"Like every single thing you do isn't off the books." I take them from him, sit myself on the bed to have a look.

Girls. Five of them. Early twenties, pretty, spread pussies, perfectly filthy smiles. Keen.

Perfect.

All of them perfect.

An array of checked boxes under their pictures. Limits, so many limits.

I drop the pile at my side. "None of them."

"That little Lulabelle is a real treat. She'll be right up your alley, I promise. I can do you a deal. I'll call her in this weekend, on the house, try before you buy."

But I don't want Lulabelle, with her pouty lips and her perfectly perky tits. She looks like she'd be a squealer. She'd probably break glass.

"What's wrong with Lulabelle?" Claude asks again. "She's perfect."

Exactly. I don't say that. I don't want to share any more of my kinks with Claude than absolutely necessary. The slimy cunt already knows enough to turn my stomach.

"I said none of them."

Claude looks nonplussed. "Sure, well, your father showed interest. I guess I'll pass her on to him."

My finger jabs through the air before I can stop it. "Don't mention my fucking father, Claude. You know the fucking rules."

He holds his hands up. "Just saying. I'll pass them on, if you're sure."

"And you also *just said* this selection was just for me, *off the books.*"

He shrugs. "Me and your old man go back a long way, as you well know."

It makes me cringe, the whole fucking lot of it. Pandering to this seedy little back-alley business for *safety*, because my own tried and tested methods of scoring hook-ups landed me in the jaws of Ronald fucking Robertson and his fucking shit stain of a newspaper.

I grit my jaw. Breathe slowly. Calmly.

"Find me what I'm looking for, Claude. Send the others to whoever you want, I have no interest."

"You get first refusal, you know that…"

I laugh, because it's like a black comedy, this whole sordid affair. I'm watching my own train wreck unfold, tumbling down my own perverted rabbit hole. "First refusal in an open auction. Sure I do."

"You know what I mean, Henley. First refusal over some of my other clients…"

Clients.

He means my disgusting excuse of a father and his vile little network of associates. The man who bailed me out with company cash and insisted I use his more *secure* outlets for my *needs*.

The one condition: we never cross *purchases*.

Quite frankly I have no fucking interest in touching any woman my father has been within a five-mile radius of. I'd rather hack my dick off with a rusty knife.

I'd rather not be in a five-mile radius of *him* either for that matter, but I have no such joy keeping the old cunt out of my boardroom.

I wish I didn't know what the grim old bastard gets up to at all, but the memory is emblazoned in my psyche for all time. The wonders of teenage curiosity. I wish I could bleach the knowledge from my brain. Believe me, I've tried. My therapists made these pricey little sexcapades look like small change.

"Get me what I'm looking for, Claude. Something real. Someone with no ticks in the boxes. Someone who'll fucking fit."

He laughs. "Sounds to me like you want a girlfriend, Henley, not a hooker. That isn't my game."

The idea of a girlfriend is laughable. My heart shrivelled up and died a long time ago.

He stands and holds out his hand. "Leave it with me."

I shake it without smiling, then offer him back his paperwork. He doesn't take it.

"Think on them, I have other copies."

I'm sure he fucking does. "I don't need to think on them."

"Humour me, then." His grin is bright and professional, as though he's trying to sell me a fucking timeshare.

I fold the papers and slip them into my inside pocket, to *humour* the sonofabitch.

"I'll be in touch," he says.

I don't say goodbye on my way out.

EIGHT

ALEXANDER

Life wasn't always like this for me.

A sugar-coated veneer of normality once held the power to keep my darker impulses at bay.

Once.

Getting married was easy, I just had to pretend to be everything I wasn't.

Getting divorced was easier, I just had to stop pretending.

I never wanted Claire. I wanted her sister.

We met at a fundraiser for the Para-Olympics. Claire's sister is a double-amputee swimmer, and one of the most vivacious people I've ever met.

She was in an accident. One of those wrong place at the wrong time affairs that dealt her a shitty hand.

She lost both her legs below the knee, chewed up under a Transit van travelling far too fast on a blind bend. People grimace when she tells the story. Give it all the oohs and aahs and *you poor, poor soul*. But she didn't want any of that. Didn't need their sympathy. Just as the pressure in the earth forms mere rock into the most glorious crystals, her accident transformed her into something incredible, someone who came back stronger and all the more beautiful for her adversity.

I love people like that. Unfortunately, I see very few of them.

Which is why I wanted to propose to Emily Caldwell on the spot. Just like that. In front of a crowd of people at some snooty fundraiser. In front of my grotesque father and my vile excuse for a mother.

Just as well I was introduced to Emily Caldwell's fiancé before I could do anything ridiculous.

I was introduced to Emily Caldwell's sister shortly afterwards.

I think it was the tux that first snared Claire. Then it was the cool million my company donated to some Sports Relief gig as the champagne flowed.

Charity.

I despise the way it brings out the self-righteous in people. Far more effective than the confession box at church, because it involves no self-searching, no confrontation of the terrible things people do to further themselves. Give a million to some poor unfortunates and let the world know about it. Go out and fuck over those same unfortunates for some cold hard profit on your next dividend statement and nobody bats an eyelid. Smile for the media as you hold the cheque and the world tells you how generous you are. How wonderful you are. What a great example you are.

When *I* give personally to charity – and believe me, I give a lot – I give anonymously. Totally anonymously.

I don't want credit. I don't want salvation. I don't want my pearly whites all over some fundraiser on prime time TV. I don't want to impress some smiling Miss Perfect like Claire on the back of my generosity.

I don't want to impress anyone. I rarely impress myself.

Brutus, at least, is pleased to see me when I get home this evening. He's not a particularly expressive beast, just a meeting of the eyes and a wag of the tail, and we both know he's glad I'm back.

That does me just fine.

I get him his dinner, then pull Claude's shitty offerings from my pocket and dump the paperwork on the side. I grab myself some sushi to get food out of the way, and hit the treadmill downstairs for thirty to raise my serotonin levels.

I take out my case notes, prepare for another crappy day in court, getting my clients a retrospective free pass to do whatever they feel like.

I'm doing just fine when my phone rings.

My *other* phone.

I don't answer, just stare numbly at the incoming call. It stops flashing, and the ping of a message comes through. I open it.

Lulabelle. I'm taking her.

I reply instantly. *I don't fucking want her.*

Another ping. *Claude says you're turning your nose up at his merchandise. That's bad form, boy. Very bad form.*

I don't reply to that one, and another comes through.

We use Claude. No alternatives acceptable.

As if I'm interested in another fucking supplier. I go back to my case notes.

The phone flashes.

He's starting up the auctions again, for brand new merchandise.

I reply. *And?*

No more first refusal. We bid fair and square. I want my old meat in some fresh young meat.

My reply is instant.

You disgust me.

His comes straight back.

You disgust yourself, boy. I'm just the scapegoat.

Boy. I turned forty-four last spring, and the old prick still insists on calling me boy. I can hear his voice say it. A hiss and a jab of the finger.

You disgust *yourself.*

He's right about that.

Not for what I do with women. Not for buying sex as a service because I can't bear the thought of anyone coming close to me ever again. Not for liking to choke off some pretty girl's breath as she squirms around, spluttering as I drive my cock into her tight little asshole.

Not for treating them like I own them.

I *do* own them.

I've paid generously for the privilege and they know exactly that they're signing up for. *Exactly.*

I disgust myself because of the things I've *done.*

The people I've destroyed. The money I've taken. The cunts I've protected from justice.

The people I've destroyed. *I've* destroyed.

Not Henley Grosvenor in our ivory tower with our poncey graphite and mauve letterheads. *Me.* Face to face, eye to eye, destroying innocents in the courtroom. Taking away their justice behind the scenes. Taking away their rights, their validation, their fight.

Their soul.

Claire once asked me, a long time ago, why I don't just quit.

Claire's a fucking imbecile.

You don't just *quit* when you're in as deep as I'm in. When you know the things that I know. When you're in tight with the people I associate with, that my father

11

associated with before me.

My father's client list makes mine look like a fucking children's party.

That's the closest I've come to getting out.

I'm a long fucking way from getting out.

There is only this.

This.

More. Of. This.

My case notes blur into nothing. The curtains parting and showing me the bleakness beyond. The pointlessness. The complete and utter pointlessness of my existence.

My heart stutters, my gut twisting as my mind closes down.

Pointlessness.

Everything is meaningless.

Empty.

My life is empty.

Brutus stares at me as I get to my feet.

My steps are light on the stairs, my tie still perfectly knotted as I stare at my haunted face in the bathroom mirror.

I clear my throat as I ease open the cabinet door. A row of bottles, perfectly lined up. Prescription painkillers, easily enough to end it all, all lined up, just waiting for me.

My heart beats quickly. My mouth is dry as a bone.

I draw myself a tumbler of water. Pick up one of those pill bottles and shake its contents.

Empty.

My life is empty.

I picture my boys' faces as they told me they were going to the game with Terry.

Claire's twisted expression as she screamed *You're just like your filthy fucking father.*

I picture my filthy fucking father.

I can feel Bill Catterson's clammy handshake.

Ronald Robertson's tabloid sleazy grin as he stares at me.

I picture Vivian Rachel Farr. The hate in her parents' eyes as they screamed at me outside the courtroom on Lionshall Lane over a decade ago.

I shake that pill bottle.

It's not that I want to commit suicide. It's really not that dramatic. There isn't any wailing, or panic, or crushing sense of misery.

It's not any of those things that ensure I have a stock of medication on hand to end it all at any time of my choosing.

It's the nothingness. The pointlessness. The exertion it requires to get through day after pointless day, knowing tomorrow is going to be more of today, and the next day is going to be more of that. On and on and fucking on.

For nothing.

For no one.

Although that's not strictly true.

I hear Brutus on the tiles. His panting breath. He has such rancid breath.

The thought makes me smile.

I take a breath of my own.

Brutus was the most hopeless, desperate animal they had at the shelter. That's what I wanted, and that's why I took him.

Vicious. Untrainable. Unlovable. Haunted. Scarred. Ugly. Miserable.

Hopeless.

And less than twenty-four hours from euthanasia when I loaded him into the Merc and brought him home with me.

We're a good pair.

Vicious. Haunted. Hopeless.

He grunts at me as if he knows it.

I put those pills back in the cabinet and take a shower.

I jerk myself off to brutal pornography in my dressing gown.

I think about burying my dick in another man's asshole as I finally come, ignoring the sickness in my stomach, ignoring the memory of that public urinal all those years ago.

I let Brutus out for his late night shit. Give him a fish stick as a reward for basic bodily functioning.

And then I go to fucking bed.

NINE

MELISSA

I'm rattling with nerves as Cindy and I take the tube across the city. I've officially signed my life away to whatever non-disclosure criteria Henley Grosvenor insisted upon. I didn't even read it, not completely, just signed my name in the box and landed it back on Janet's desk first thing this morning, much to Dean's despair.

Cindy is quiet on the crowded carriage, and I bite my tongue, holding back the stream of questions zipping through my mind. We get off at Kensington and Cindy hands me the company expenses credit card outside the vets. She shows me the exact treats for Brutus inside, some gross dried-up fish things that barely look edible, even for a dog.

"Always these," she tells me. "Never walk through that door without them. Seriously, that nasty little shit will take a bite out of you."

"I guess he's a guard dog," I comment, handing the card to the woman behind the counter. Cindy hands me a little black book and flips to a page partway in. The company credit card pin is written amongst a load of random numbers.

"Guard dog my ass. The thing's a menace."

I hold back judgement until I meet him for myself.

Mr Henley's house is an impressive white building on a leafy corner. The garden is neat but plain, ornamental hedgerows and wood-chipped flower beds. The front door is thick and black, standing at the top of some fancy white-tiled steps. I'm full of butterflies as Cindy talks me through the set of keys, turning one at the bottom before adding a second key to the top.

She pauses before opening the door. "You don't have long to disable the alarm," she tells me. "The number's in the book."

I flip through the pages. "Seven seven six, three four five nine."

"That's it. Keypad's under the stairs, to the right. Brutus is always in the conservatory, you've got time to sort out the alarm without him causing problems."

"Got it," I say, and she opens the door.

The countdown bleep of the alarm sounds right through the house, and I make a dash for it, heading to the little white door under the stairs and searching inside. There are coats in here. They smell of him. *Him*. Butterflies. So many butterflies in my belly. *Seven seven six, three four five nine*. I sigh in relief as the alarm goes silent, and turn to find Cindy smiling at me.

"It'll become second nature after a while. *Everything* about Mr Henley becomes second nature after a while."

I can't believe I'm really here, standing inside his house. His actual house, where he eats and sleeps and showers. I spin on the spot, trying to memorise it all, every little detail – the red-tiled floor, the leafy plant at the bottom of the stairs, the wrought iron balustrade climbing to the upstairs landing. There's a table by a low window, on it sits his bottle of whisky, and next to that is a single glass tumbler, and the antique inkwell Cindy told me about. I feel heady at the sight of the *Insignia* cigarette packet.

And then there is Brutus.

His growl is absolutely terrifying, a horrible low snarl behind me. The hairs on my arms stand on end, and I take a breath before I face him, turning slowly towards what looks to be the kitchen doorway.

"Don't walk away from him," Cindy hisses. "Hold your ground."

Easier said than done.

Brutus really is a brute. He's big and black, some kind of Rottweiler cross from the looks. But shaggier. Meaner. If that's possible.

He's got a big scar under his right eye, and his lips are curled back, showing some monster teeth.

"Hey, boy," I say, and he growls all the louder.

I'm relieved when Cindy comes to my side, and she talks to him like a baby, as though she's not scared, even though she's as white as I must be. "Fish sticks," she whispers. "Give him a fish stick."

I fish in my handbag for the packet, and his ears twitch at the rustle. I pull out the treats, tear into them with shaky fingers.

"Throw one," she says, but it's not my game plan.

I'm in. Totally. All or nothing.

Come on, boy. Let's be friends, right? Please let's be friends.

I step forward and drop to my knees and Cindy grabs my shoulder, curses that I've got a fucking death wish, but I shake her off. Edge closer. A stinky dried up fish treat in my outstretched fingers.

"Hey, Brutus. Do you want this?"

He's still growling, and I'm totally shitting it, but I force that down and take a breath.

"Hey, Brutus. Good boy. Come on."

"You're fucking batshit," Cindy tells me.

Yes. Yes, I am.

A flash of panic as Brutus comes toward me, and it takes every bit of steel not to get to my feet and bail a retreat. He sniffs the treat in my fingers, his face so close to mine. And his breath stinks. It really stinks. Enough to make me splutter.

"Geez, boy, you're quite a honker." I dare to laugh, smiling with my face in his, that gross bit of fish wedged between us like a peace offering.

It feels like that dog is staring right into my soul, his big dark eyes so cold and mean. I feel like he can see everything, and that's good, because there's no way he'll be able to look inside me and not see how much I want to be his friend.

I really want to be his friend.

Because I love his owner. I love his owner so much it takes my breath.

And I've worked so hard to get here, given everything to get here.

"It's for you," I whisper. "Come on, Brutus, take the yummy treat."

Cindy gasps as he actually does take it. He takes it gently, right from my fingertips, then sits back on his haunches and crunches it with a big slobbery gnashing of teeth.

I get to my feet slowly, very slowly, but he doesn't seem that interested, just finishes up his treat and drops to lay on the floor with his head on his paws.

"Fuck me," Cindy says. "Do you moonlight as Cesar fucking Millan or something?"

I shake my head. "I just want him to like me."

"No shit. You could've got your face bitten off."

But I didn't. The relief feels amazing.

"So," I say, before my confidence burst fades. "Tell me everything about Mr Henley."

She smiles. "Everything?"

I nod. "Everything."

"I'll talk as we work," she says, gesturing to the kitchen.

❧

I wipe down Mr Henley's gorgeous granite worktops as Cindy cleans out the inkwell. One solitary cigarette butt. That's all there is.

"He really is magnificent," she says. "If you get to see the corporate suite reception on floor ten, you'll see all his legal awards lining the main corridor, Mr Henley senior's, too."

"He's the best," I say, "I mean, I know that. I wanted to be a criminal lawyer myself."

She raises her eyebrows. "Shit. What happened?"

I shrug it off. "Life."

She shrugs back. "Cool beans. Anyway, he's incredible. He's smart, *observant*, totally demanding of perfection. For real make sure you do a good job in here, because if there's so much as a fingerprint on a candlestick he'll notice it. Well, he *would* have done."

"Would have?" I slow down my scrubbing to look at her, and she's dithering, weighing me up. "Please," I say. "I need to know this stuff."

Her eyes are so pointed. "Everything?"

"Yeah, everything. I want to know everything."

She stops cleaning and I do too. "I've been doing this nearly four years, and it was a whole different gig when I started, believe me. The kids were here then, and Claire, his wife. She was nice, the kids were cool, it wasn't this stealth operation we have now, I'd knock on the door and she'd let me in, and we'd have a coffee sometimes while I was working."

"And then the divorce?"

"Yeah, she took the kids."

"Why?"

She grins. "You're hot on him. I know. Sonnie told me, like it needed pointing out. It's written all over you."

I'm so embarrassed I feel sick, so far from professional that I wish the ground would open up. "Sorry, I just…"

She shrugs. "He's beautiful. Talented. Smart. Driven. I get it."

"You do?" Of course she does.

"Yeah, I get it, but if you've got any sense in that pretty head of yours you'll steer well clear of him. The guy's damaged. Broken."

"Broken?" The thought seems ridiculous. Alexander Henley seems anything but broken. He's the most together person I've ever laid eyes on.

"He used to be careful," she says. "He still is. His passwords and security codes change monthly, like I said. He's got a shredder in his study, and that gets plenty of action, but he's not…"

"Not what?"

She pauses. "Not like he used to be. It's like he's careless on purpose, leaving loose ends hanging, like he wants to be caught somehow."

My heart is thumping. "Caught doing what?"

She laughs. "Jeez, girl. Sonnie really did keep her mouth shut, kudos to that one."

I just gawp. Mute.

She sighs. "Mr Henley has some *issues*. Not just the weird little habits he has like only using one set of cutlery, and smoking one cigarette before bed, none of that crap. The guy likes… pornography."

I smile.

"A *lot*," she adds. "He used to lock everything down. You'd never even get into his TV without a twenty digit passcode. Now he doesn't care, let's it all hang out, his browsing history sometimes still glaring on screen when I come in in the morning."

"So he likes porn." I shrug it off. "Show me a guy who doesn't."

"Not like this. You'll see, that's all I'm saying."

I want to ask her more, but she goes back to cleaning.

I squirt some cream cleaner into his Belfast sink. "Ok, so he likes pornography. Anything else I should know?"

"He has cases full of sex toys in his dressing room, all lined up ready to go."

"Ready to go where?"

"It's none of our business. I'm just telling you so they don't shock you too much. Some of them are… yeah, you'll see."

I decide to chance my luck. "Harley's Tavern," I say. "What is it?"

She smirks. "Maybe not so much kudos for Sonnie's big mouth after all."

"She told me to ask you."

"Seriously, you don't want to be getting any ideas."

But I'm getting plenty. Ideas of dashing into the TV room and scrolling through that browsing history, rushing upstairs and looking through all those toys. Rolling naked in his bedsheets and waiting for him to come home, and then begging him, begging him to–

"Harley's Tavern is a venue for upmarket room hire. The kind of room hire you rent by the hour, no questions asked. He buys women and takes them there," she says. "Fuck knows why, the guy could pick up whoever he wanted."

It really wasn't what I was expecting. The idea seems absurd. "He pays? For sex?!"

"Pays a lot of money for a *lot* of sex from what I can make of it. This isn't any vanilla shit, either. You'll see soon enough, just like *I've* seen. Pictures on his laptop, when it hasn't shut down properly. His bedside drawer has… paperwork… pictures of some of these women… what they'll do…"

"What will they do?" My eyes feel like saucers.

She sighs, then digs in the front pocket of her apron. "I gathered these up when we walked in, right before you saw them. See, this kind of shit, this careless shit, this is new. Six months max."

She hands over some folded paperwork. I hold my breath while I open it.

Five girls. Pretty girls. *Really* pretty girls.

My poor heart pangs.

There's a load of checked boxes underneath. Hard limits, the text says.

Anal. BDSM. Pain. Watersports. DP. Fisting. Multiple partners.

Jeez.

There really are skeletons in the closet. I'm tingling all over, and I shouldn't be. I really shouldn't be, but I can't stop.

"He keeps the ones with fewer ticks in the boxes, just so you know." Cindy holds out her hand. I give her the paperwork and she shoves it back into her apron.

I still absolutely can't imagine it, Mr Henley paying for sex. I mean he's... gorgeous. *Perfect.*

I tell Cindy so and she laughs, shakes her head. "He's gorgeous, alright. Gorgeous and talented and sharp as fuck. But he's broken, just like I said. The guy has some serious issues. His wife told me."

"His *wife* told you?!"

Cindy looks really pleased with herself. "Bits and pieces. I'm only telling you so you know what you're walking into. You signed some pretty hardcore non-disclosure shit, don't even think about blabbing this around."

"I wouldn't," I tell her, and I'm not lying.

"I've said enough. The rest you'll pick up for yourself."

She heads for the utility room and drags out a vacuum, and I feel bereft, desperate to crawl inside her mind and soak up every single thing she knows about Alexander Henley.

"You don't seem put off any," she comments, and I realise I'm still gawping at her.

"The guy has kinks… that's ok."

"The guy has more than kinks. The guy's seriously messed up."

Skeletons in the closet. The adrenaline is pumping, excitement fizzing, and I shouldn't be like this. I really, really shouldn't be. Because I'm just a silly cleaner who managed to bag a promotion, not one of these girls, I don't know anything, I've never *done* anything.

But I *want* to.

I want *him,* if I'm being paid for it or not.

"Seriously," Cindy says. "Stay away from him. He's bad news. I mean it's pretty tragic, losing his kids and all that, but he's… dark…"

"Damaged…" I repeat.

"Yeah, all fucked up." She sighs. "Such a shame, the guy is fucking gorgeous *and* fucking loaded. Guess he had to have some pretty major flaws to balance all that out, right?"

I'm not interested in loaded. I'm not even interested in gorgeous right now.

I'm interested in all fucked up. Damaged and dark.

Broken.

Like me.

But I don't pay for kinky sex in some weird pub on the outskirts of London. I don't have a closet full of sex toys and a browsing history bad enough to come with a warning.

And those girls on the pictures are so pretty… so perfect…

And I'm so… not.

Cindy groans. "Sonnie said you wouldn't give a shit about my warning. I guess she was right."

I stare blankly. "What do you mean?"

She eyeballs Brutus as he comes into the room, edges around the island to keep him at safe distance. "I *mean* that you're already thinking about it, how to get to Harley's Tavern. How to be one of those girls."

Even the thought jabs me in the ribs, because I'm not one of *them*. I couldn't be one of *them* if I tried.

I laugh it off, but my voice sounds pained. I tell her I could never be one of *them*. They're beautiful, with great hair, and perfect makeup, and manicured nails and... other bits. I feel a billion miles away from that in my crappy uniform, without so much a drop of foundation on my face.

She closes the distance and pulls the cap from my head before I can blink. She yanks my hairnet loose and tousles my hair, then tips her head and pulls a face.

"You could be one of *them*, if you tried."

I shake my head, cheeks burning, and gather my hair back up. "You're being kind."

"I'm being *honest*. You *could* be one of them, but you'd need your head examined if you went in for that crazy shit."

The thought pricks.

Hope.

It's both beautiful and dangerous.

Like Alexander Henley himself.

"So what? I just rock on up at that tavern and put myself up for sale?" She laughs and I fold my arms. "What?"

I flinch as Brutus grumbles in the doorway, but he settles just fine.

"You think you just roll on up with your pussy on show and hope Alexander Henley turns up for a good time? That really isn't how it works, honey."

"So how *does* it work? Do you know?"

She grins at me, and then she tuts. "You really are batshit. Sonnie told me you would be."

"Sonnie knows me pretty well."

"Yeah, and *I* know Mr Henley pretty well for someone who's never officially met the guy. And you will too." She vacuums before she says anything else, being careful not to venture too near the resting Brutus. I finish up the sink, wondering, thinking. *Hoping.*

One day in his place and I'm already going insane. *More* insane.

Christ help me. Sex toys, and prostitutes and hardcore pornography. I haven't even seen his bedroom yet and I'm tumbling in deep.

Cindy finishes up and I squeeze out my sponge.

"Sonnie says you'll find a way to get to Harley's Tavern whether I help you or not. She says it's only a matter of time. That once you set foot in this place you'd be on some crazy mission. I may as well set you straight, she said."

"Sonnie's probably right," I admit, holding her stare.

"Is that why you're here? To get close to Alexander?"

Alexander.

I can't imagine being as close to him as she has for four years, and never even exchanging a simple hello.

The thought is unbearable. The torture of being so near and still so far.

I decide to be honest, and why not? She's leaving in a few days, and she can help me, save me a bit of time that I'd otherwise spend finding all this crap out for myself. "I'm here because I *always* wanted to get close to him. This cleaning job was my best shot. My *only* shot. I met him when I was at school, he did a presentation. I wanted to be a lawyer."

She nods. "That's some kinda crush. You have real balls spelling that out for me. I admire that."

91

"So tell me," I push. "Tell me how I'd get to Harley's Tavern. Tell me how I'd get a shot, presuming I could be... good enough..."

"You really want to know how to line yourself up as Alexander Henley's next hooker? For fucking real?"

"Please."

She smiles. "I'll point you in the right direction on one condition."

"What's that?"

She unplugs the vacuum. "On the condition you look through his browsing history first."

I nod. "And if that doesn't put me off?"

"If that doesn't put you off, you're even crazier than Sonnie says you are."

I picture Sonnie saying it and it makes me grin. "I might well be crazier than Sonnie said I am. A whole load crazier..."

"We'll find out," she says. "The TV room is through here."

TEN
ALEXANDER

I didn't cheat on my wife. Not once in the entire decade we were married. That may well surprise some, including her, but it's true.

I took my marriage vows seriously, for better or worse, and with that came… sacrifices. Sacrifices I was prepared to make for the sake of having a family. A *real* family – not the pathetic excuse for one I'd known growing up.

Just how many sacrifices I'd have to make didn't become entirely apparent until after the rings were exchanged, when Claire dropped the bombshell I imagine so many newlyweds are unexpectedly burnt by. *But I thought you'd change… I thought things would be different, now we're… married.*

My *wife* Claire was a lot less keen on a rough anal pounding once that band of gold was on her finger. She no longer felt the urge to sidle up to me at social events and let me know how keen she was for *later*. My *wife* Claire turned her nose up at my dirtier sexual advances.

Can't we just do it like normal people, Alex? I'm too tired for all that tonight, Alex.

Can you be quick, Alex?

I've got a headache, Alex.

And then we had our two beautiful boys.

Not now, Alex.

Not that, Alex.

Why do you have to be such a fucking pervert, Alex?

I had some choice answers for that question, but I digress.

My point is, I understand restraint. I'm capable of restraint. Or I *was*.

I'm determined I shall be again, which is why I walk into my office on Monday morning with a steely determination to plough myself into my caseload, and why my *other* phone is still at home on my bedside cabinet.

I'm done with Claude.

I'm done with paying for dirty sex.

I'm certainly done with this grotesque bargaining-waltz I'm obliged to perform for the sake of sharing the same *escort* agency as my grubby shit-stain of a father.

Cold turkey. It's the only fucking way.

And so it begins.

I tell Brenda she has free rein of my diary and focus back on my client list like a rookie with a point to prove all over again. I organise catch-ups with my key networking associates, reinforcing once again why the industry not-so-affectionately labelled me the Puppet Master, and I give my clients my absolute undivided attention. I manage to get three driving offences thrown out of court in the first three days, and convince the local authorities that prosecuting Mr Rand for cannabis possession is a waste of both their resources and mine.

I scope out upcoming matches for Portsmouth football club, swallowing down both my pride and my own preference for rugby to ensure I give my boys a good time on our Sundays, and then order them a couple of shirts to be delivered to

Claire before I'll see them next.

I manage three days without jerking off to porn. Three nights of lying in bed at night, wide awake with a raging hard on I refuse to fucking finish.

Day four since shooting my load and I'm irritable and foul-tempered, desperate to empty myself inside some dirty little bitch's asshole and find some fucking relief.

That's why I finally switch on the *other* phone. Not to go crawling back to Claude and his seedy *new meat* auctions. I don't go in for the new meat – virgins don't hold any special interest for me. Not only do they not have a fucking clue what they're doing, they also have no fucking clue what *I'm* doing. I'm not in the market for fucking up some naïve little plaything, staring at me doe-eyed, in blissful ignorance as to what exactly she's signed up for.

No. I switch on my *other* phone to re-engage with my other pastime. The only thing that's ever been a semi-effective balm to soothe my self-loathing.

It's a band-aid on a bullet wound, but hell, I need *something*.

Something more than *this*.

I call the number as soon as I'm safely back through my front door. My cock is so fucking hard it actually hurts, my balls tight and aching, my temples pounding for relief. It's Annabel who answers on the third ring, and the warmth in her tone takes me aback.

"Ted! I was only talking about you yesterday! We've missed you."

I utter a load of bullshit apologies, tell her how I've been so busy, travelling across the country selling stationery, a lie I made up on the spot eighteen months ago and have upheld ever since. A conference, I tell her. No rest for the wicked, trying to plug my wares to hit targets. Boss is a ball-breaking wanker, blah, blah.

She tells me she understands. Tells me they hope I can come back soon.

I clear my throat and check my diary, and then I commit to coming back *real* soon.

"Tomorrow?!" she asks. "Wow, that's great! We could really do with the help.

Stacie's son is sick, we've barely had enough hands to get the food prepped. You know what Fridays are like, Ted, always a nightmare."

I tell her I'll be there. Right on time.

And I will be.

I hang up and then feel a flash of concern.

It's been months since I last put on my incognito jeans and baseball cap, and I haven't seen them since, which wouldn't be any reason for alarm should I not have a new cleaner, and should new members of staff not inevitably feel the need to deviate from just about everything their predecessors did. I head upstairs to search through my dressing room, and the crisis is averted as I find the clothes I'm looking for in the *odds and sods* clothes drawer.

I'd say I'd almost forgotten I have a new cleaner, but that would be a lie. There's no way I *could* forget about the new cleaner, because the place looks impressively immaculate when I step through the door every evening. The old cleaner was good, but the new cleaner is something else, just as I'd hoped she would be.

The new cleaner turns the corner of my bed sheets back. An odd little touch that makes the bed all the more inviting, even if I still can't get to sleep at night.

The new cleaner must have noticed the empty vases in the living room – the ones Claire used to fill – and has taken it upon herself to fill them with fresh white orchids to match the decor. It's surprising both how much I appreciate them, and how much difference they make to the room.

The new cleaner is getting my eggs from a different supplier, and I've had two double-yolkers for breakfast this week.

It turns out that the new cleaner is also the reason I jerk myself off in bed on night four without using pornography. She's the reason I shoot my load without any thought for some seedy guy's asshole, and the reason I don't feel the need to scrub my hands clean afterwards.

The new cleaner is the reason I abstain from looking at Claude's string of messages, although that makes no rational sense whatsoever.

I've never even properly seen her face, but she's there. A hazy figure at the edge of my consciousness, almost ethereal as I picture the meek little picture she cut as she shrunk away from me, the tenderness of her apology just a whisper in my memory.

I'm certain my sex-starved mind is distorting things – shrinking her stature and making her voice all the more reverent. The desperate fantasies of a man battling his demons, turning some poor little slip of a girl into a glowing figure of hope in my unconsciousness.

I smile at my own ridiculousness, my fingers still sticky with cum.

ELEVEN

MELISSA

I had three days shadowing Cindy to drag every little scrap of information out of her. She'd tut and shake her head, giving me a look that made me feel even crazier than I felt already, but then she'd spill the beans anyway.

I guess she owed it to me after I sat and happily watched her scroll through the last four weeks of Alexander Henley's porn browsing history.

She wasn't lying, the stuff was... brutal. Not handcuffs and riding whips type brutal like I was expecting. The stuff Alexander Henley watches is not nearly so... I dunno... *theatrical*.

His porn tastes are dark and animalistic – grunts and pounding flesh and sweat, sometimes one on one, sometimes several men on one woman as she's pushed and pulled and thrown around, fucked raw by big dicks in every hole. *Many* dicks in every hole. So many positions, so many settings – some gross and grimy, and some crazily plush, some with tiny little women and some with much bigger women. Sometimes they spit on her, and sometimes they slap her about, and sometimes they even… pee on her… but not all the time…

I wanted the ground to swallow me up as Cindy stared at me staring at a woman getting peed on on Alexander Henley's giant TV screen, but it didn't. I had to sit through it, all twenty minutes of that particular video.

When she asked me what I thought, I told her I still wanted to know how to get to Harley's Tavern.

She told me I was definitely batshit if I could be even slightly interested in that crap.

I'm interested in all of it, because I'm interested in all of *him*. I watched it as though it was one of those prize-winning memory games they show on TV, where you have to memorise every single item for recall, because to really stand a chance with Alexander Henley I need to stand a chance of knowing exactly who Alexander Henley *is*.

And exactly what Alexander Henley *likes*.

Those videos showed me three constants:

The first being that these women get fucked until they are utterly exhausted. Until they're nothing but a broken, sweaty, whimpering, cum-splattered mess at the end.

The second being that these women are always like puppets, doing exactly as they're told without hesitation. There's this obedience to them that I can't really put into words, I just *felt* it. I felt it *everywhere*.

And lastly, on every single video without fail, these women get… strangled. Hands-around-the-throat until they choke. Like properly choke. Sometimes they fight, sometimes they don't. Sometimes they have these glassy eyes without any fight in them at all, and sometimes they cry. Sometimes they even smile. Sometimes they cry as they smile.

It made me hurt inside. A weird, tender kind of hurt.

The kind of hurt I've tried to close away since the night my life was taken away from me. But this time it was different, this time it was... beautiful...

Peaceful.

I can't even begin to explain how fucked up I must be to feel like this. You can't understand until you're in these shoes. Not unless you've lost everything. Not unless every day is a fight you're not sure you want to be fighting.

Not unless there is one single dream in life you're grasping onto with every tiny part of your broken soul, not unless laying yourself before him and offering up your everything is the only destination at the end of a really painful road.

Cindy told me she's pretty sure Mr Henley is into it in real life, *asphyxiation*. She told me this shit is dangerous and fucked up, and if there was any truth in the things his wife told her that I'd be crazy to risk finding out.

I'm crazy, alright.

I didn't tell Cindy that Mr Henley's browsing history made me burn up. Made me flush hot and cold and shiver all over. I didn't tell her that I had to clench my thighs all the way through, unsure whether I wanted to faint or play with myself right then and there.

I didn't tell her *he* is my final destination.

The thing that keeps my soul alive enough to care for Joseph and keep on breathing.

My breaths are borrowed. Loving him gives them to me. Loving him keeps me hoping.

He can take them away.

Literally if he wants.

I guess I passed her craziness test anyway, because Cindy put the TV back to standby and carried on with the rest of her tour. A tour which ended in Mr Henley's actual bedroom, and Mr Henley's cases full of sex toys.

She wasn't lying about those either. Some of those toys could never be used, at least I don't think so, you'd have to be... loose... to take some of them. Like real loose.

Maybe I'm not the best judge since I've never done *any* of it before, but I know enough to know what might fit and what might not.

I told Cindy that and she laughed and said I should scroll further back through his browser history and I might change my mind on that.

We'd cleaned the whole house before she finally beckoned me over to Mr Henley's bedside table. I held my breath as she eased open the top drawer, peeking inside as she so carefully flipped through some paperwork and pulled out a business card.

"This is your gateway to Harley's Tavern," she told me.

The card looked innocent enough. I turned it over in shaky fingers, looking for more, but if there was any meaning it was lost on me.

Claude Finch, senior auctioneer. Finch Hamilton.

The address listed one of those posh auction houses in Chelsea.

"That's who hooks him up," she said.

"How do you know that?"

"He has a private email address, some random account under the name Ted Brown. It was open on his screen one day, there were loads of emails there from CF. Emails showing women with all the usual tick-boxes underneath."

"So you don't know it's definitely this Claude guy?"

She rolled her eyes. "CF. In the bedside drawer with all the dodgy paperwork. He's an auctioneer."

"Yeah, but…"

"No buts," she said. "It's him."

"And if it's not?"

She shrugs. "Pretend you dialled the wrong number."

The idea of actually calling this guy launched my heart into my throat. I wrote his number in my little notepad and slipped that business card straight back into the drawer, exactly as it had been.

"I'm glad I'm not going to be around to see what a whirlwind of shit you get yourself into," she said.

And so am I.

For all the insight and tips I got from Cindy during our handover, I've never been as excited as the moment she hands me her work mobile, loaded up with Mr Henley's real-time schedule, and finally says her goodbyes.

I feel the craziest rush of freedom, this weird naughtiness at the thought that it's just me in his space now, me on my own, free to rummage and root through his life as much as I like.

It takes me two days without her to pluck up the courage to strip naked in his bedroom and slip between his bedsheets. My heart is thumping, right between my legs, my thighs all clammy and jittery as the cotton brushes my skin. I press my nose into his pillow and breathe him in, and I can smell him there, that same deep scent, gorgeous enough that I never want to breathe normal air ever again.

I play with myself in his bed on my third day alone. And again on my fourth.

I drink out of his whisky tumbler and put my lips around the cigarette butt in the inkwell.

I run my fingers around his toilet seat, knowing his bare ass has been right there.

I put on his worn shirt from the laundry hamper, wrap his tie around my neck and imagine him choking me with it as he takes my virginity.

I smell his boxers. I smell his bedsheets where his cock must've been.

I put his toothbrush in my mouth, and my reflection in his bathroom cabinet makes me feel so sick, so out of control that it takes my breath.

So I stop. Stop doing this crazy shit and focus on something more practical – on finding out everything I need to know to be close to him for real.

I clean and snoop in tandem, working so hard I get blisters on my fingers. I buy some big white orchids for the empty vases in his living room just because it looks so cold and bare, and just hope my streak of initiative doesn't get me fired. I gain the confidence of Brutus as best I can, and by the end of the week I'm sure I see him wag his tail when I open the door, just one sweep, but it's enough to give me hope that we really can be friends.

Friday evening comes around so ridiculously quickly. I turn down his bed, just so, and take a lingering look at the room before I leave.

I say goodbye to Brutus on my way out and check the orchids have enough water to survive until Monday.

And then I wait.

I linger just down the street, pressed in the shadow of an ornamental hedgerow with a decent view of his front door, the work handset in my hand as his schedule switches from *court* to *clear* and the sky turns dark overhead.

I wait for almost an hour until he shows, and it's worth every second to see his car pull onto the driveway. I'd have waited an hour all over again just to watch him climb his front steps and unlock the door I cleaned so thoroughly this afternoon.

I watch the lights come on, imagine him walking from room to room. Imagine the pad of paws as Brutus follows his master around the place.

Imagine the scent of orchids in the air.

Imagine the scent of Alexander Henley with my nose nuzzled into his neck.

I'm about to leave for home, really I am. I'm tired and sated and ready for real life. Ready to cuddle with Joseph on the sofa and get him bathed for bed. Ready to drink coffee with Dean and tell him all about my latest adventures at Henley's palace.

I've turned on my heel and taken a step in the direction of the underground when I hear the familiar thud of that heavy front door closing.

I hold my breath as he locks up behind him, and my eyes are wide, because I can't believe it. It can't be.

But it is.

Alexander Henley, whose dressing room consists almost entirely of tailored black suits and ties, is wearing a baseball cap, jeans and a scuffed old coat that's seen better days. I dip behind a parked car, crouching in the darkness as he passes.

My skin prickles.

All of me prickles.

And I follow him.

Because wherever he's going, I'm now on a mission to get there too.

TWELVE

ALEXANDER

I hate taking the underground. It reminds me exactly why I have a driver.

It's a strange phenomenon that when I'm dressed to be *incognito* I feel more noticeable than ever. The discomfort is palpable this evening. I feel *observed*. As though every pair of eyes on this carriage are boring into me. Staring.

They aren't, of course.

A simple three-sixty makes it obvious I'm just a guy amongst a regular crowd going about their business. Just good old Ted Brown heading across town to do his bit for the community.

Maybe I can add paranoia to my list of sexual-abstinence side effects.

I didn't pick some random homeless charity to absolve me of my self-loathing. The decision to volunteer at *New Start*, at the Brickwood branch, was an accidental choice, made for me one Friday evening after too much whisky.

The tube station is the same grimy shithole it was a few months back. I head up to the street amongst the stream of people disembarking, being careful not to dirty my hands on the filthy handrail.

Vivian Rachel Farr, the girl who haunts my dreams, died on the streets here. A heroin overdose. They found her body in an alleyway I'll have to walk past this evening, a note for her parents written on a greasy old fish and chip paper in her pocket.

That's before I managed to get her rapist an acquittal six months later, and before her parents screamed in my face on the court steps, their haunted faces burned into my memory for all time.

Annabel Pilcher found my drunken ass in the very same alleyway Vivian took her last breath. She smiled down on me as though I was one of life's unfortunates – just as Vivian had been – and offered me a mug of hot soup. Enough to sober up my sorry ass.

Sober me up it did.

Permanently.

If Annabel Pilcher had been on hand with a mug of hot soup when Vivian was facing her final dark night, then maybe she'd have made it through. Taken a sip of watery tomato goodness and lived to see another day. Just as I did.

Unfortunately *New Start* was just a fledgling community effort back then, struggling for both the funding and manpower to make a difference.

In me they found both an anonymous donor – generous enough to finance the opening of three branches across the East End – and good old Ted Brown, on hand every Friday evening to help cook up meals in their community kitchen and offer them out on the cold London streets.

I was worried they'd have put two and two together by now. Ideas for expansion tossed around over cook-up time invariably led to yet another anonymous donation. As if by magic. By miracle.

Our angel has answered our prayers again, Ted! We've got to secure another kitchen, Ted! Our donor came through again!

It doesn't mean I can sleep at night. There isn't any donation great enough to secure that pleasure. But it enables me to face my reflection in the bathroom mirror every morning, and as far as I'm concerned that privilege is priceless.

People always pull a sympathetic face then they talk about the homeless. *Poor souls. So awful.* They'll throw a pitiful glance along with their loose change at a beggar on the street, then head on into a boutique coffee shop for a huge latte with their conscience squeaky clean.

I've pondered this a lot, the disconnect between surface level social-driven empathy and the kind of genuine desire to help the world that people like Annabel Pilcher are consumed by.

I'm not a good man and I know it. I'm fully aware of my distinct lack of moral fibre. I don't pretend to myself that I'm anything other than a self-serving, ethically-corrupt sonofabitch.

It's the people in the middle that add most to the social apathy in our world. The people who share the horror stories with a simple click of a social media button, thank their lucky stars they're one of the *ok* ones, and move along.

They wouldn't be homeless, because *they* don't make bad life choices. *They* wouldn't be a drug addict because *they* have the will power to just say *No.*

Poor unfortunates. So sad. But it couldn't be them. Oh no.

Except it could. It could be any of us.

Born under different circumstances, tried by life pressures greater than we could comprehend. A few badly dealt cards from life, and that could be any one of us, huddling in an alleyway at night, injecting poor quality drugs just for a break from the mental torment.

I get that.

I *feel* that.

Most of the time these days I'm just relieved I feel *something.*

Annabel has a big genuine smile for Ted Brown this evening.

She wraps me in warm arms and her hair smells of cheap soap. The press of her body to mine always feels alien and leaves me feeling strangely emotional. I experience the simultaneous urge to push her away but hold her for longer.

"Ted!" Her voice is muffled by my coat. She squeezes me and then lets go. "So nice to see you!"

"Nice to be back," I tell her, and I'm not even lying.

Frank and Mary are already chopping vegetables. They smile and wave as I hang my coat up, and I say hello as I pass them on my way to the sink. I scrub my hands with their *basic essentials* anti-bacterial soap and take up position at the hob.

Annabel unpacks the Styrofoam cups and we get to work.

I'm not much of a chef. I choose my own meals based on simple acquired tastes and nutritional value, not from any desire for culinary expression.

Nobody on the street cares whether I have a five star rating on *food genius* though.

"How have you been, Ted?" Frank calls. His eyes are kind and well-meaning, but I hate small talk at the best of times, not least when I'm lying through my teeth – which is a lot of the time.

"Same old, Frank."

He shakes his head. "You wanna tell that boss of yours to get stuffed. Works you too hard."

"Bosses, eh? All the bloody same."

He nods. "Profit, profit, profit."

Frank starts up his trademark rant on how it should be *people not profit*, and my cover is safe for another week. He's a union type, campaigning for justice and fair treatment for all. He doesn't just do Friday night soup kitchen, he does all three branches and he works like a trooper.

Works and talks.

He talks a lot.

That's the thing about people. Most prefer talking to listening. Set someone off on their own little monologue and nod in the right places, and you'll have a friend for life.

These people think they know me. They'd call me a friend, and yet they don't know anything much about Ted Brown. They don't know where he lives, or which company he works for. They know he's in his forties, has a couple of kids but no significant other.

They know he makes an average soup at best, but they don't seem to care about that.

The thought makes me smile, and Annabel smiles back.

"It's gonna be a cold one tonight," she says.

I nod. Agree.

Freezing.

The irony is that the street is the only place I ever truly feel warm.

MELISSA

Cindy didn't know everything of note about Alexander Henley.

She didn't tell me about his Friday night moonlighting at a soup kitchen for the homeless.

She didn't tell me that Alexander Henley wanders around the streets with a cap down low to cover his eyes, handing out hot drinks to people with nothing when he could be drinking champagne in some posh cocktail bar somewhere.

This blatant oversight is what renews my vigour to find out *everything* about

Alexander Henley.

Everything.

Every. Little. Thing.

Dean doesn't think an evening volunteering for charity makes any difference. He maintains I'm in too deep, that the man whose house has become my own fantasy playground is just as dangerous as the internet rumours make him sound.

He doesn't know about the escorts. I didn't tell him that bit. Not yet.

He hasn't admitted to me that he's got photos on his phone, so I feel ok about withholding the truth, just for a while. Just until I'm certain of my next move.

Brutus barely even growls this morning. He pads through to the entrance hallway as I disable the alarm, stares at me with mean eyes, but doesn't make any move to see me off his property.

Progress.

It usually takes at least twenty minutes for him to stop growling at me, fish treats or no, even if I do get a little happy swish from his tail.

I've got fresh orchids as well as fish treats, and some outdoor-reared bacon that I charged to the expenses credit card.

My last impromptu food change seemed to be a win. Mr Henley now has two eggs every morning rather than just the one he had before.

Maybe Mr Henley likes smoked outdoor-reared bacon too. We'll see.

I can't stop beaming as I realise he's topped up the water in the vases. He likes the orchids.

I change them for fresh, even though they're barely wilting, and I wrap up the old ones. I'll take them home until they're long dead, a piece of this place in mine.

Yes, I like that.

I clean fast but thoroughly, taking just a moment to smell the scent on his clothes before I do his laundry. His Friday night clothes are right in the middle of the hamper, clearly stashed amongst the pile of shirts, as though that will camouflage them. I have a sniff of those, too. The worn denim shirt smells of vegetables, but I can still smell him, that spicy smell. It's enough to make my tummy flutter.

And thinking of spice, I clean out his kitchen cupboard today, making a note of the opened spice jars amongst the sealed ones. He likes paprika. Paprika and… chilli. Turmeric too.

And then I head upstairs, to the storage room at the far end of the landing.

Cindy said we don't clean in there. She shrugged when I asked her what was inside and told me *nothing of note.*

Boring paperwork, she said, and yawned at me.

I no longer trust Cindy's idea of nothing of note, so I step on inside and survey the boxes.

Paperwork. Lots of paperwork. She's right about that. But there's more.

A floral crockery set that I can't ever imagine him using.

An old games console with about a billion boxed up cartridges. I can't imagine him using those either.

The next box takes my breath.

Boys' toys. An old stuffed rabbit. Some scribbles on coloured art paper. An old punctured rugby ball from a few years back.

His kids.

It feels so sad to see their things in here, all boxed up.

The boys staring out from the mantelpiece look happy and confident, full of life as they smile for the camera. I wonder how much he sees them. Cindy said not much. She said they're over in Hampshire with his ex-wife and her new boyfriend. I seal the box back up and move along to the next.

His wedding album.

It makes my heart pound, and I can barely look. I turn the page just once, to see them smiling on a lawn somewhere, his hand in hers as she smiles up at him. Blonde hair with a natural curl. Blue eyes. Pretty.

The people to the side of him must be his parents. His mum looks... stern. Her hat is this crazy big thing with feathers and roses on, and her smile is so obviously false.

Alexander Henley looks like his dad, but I knew that before I saw this photo. I knew a lot about his dad from browsing the internet. His dad is one of the greatest legal legends of all time. They quote him in text books. I know, I had them. Before...

Anyway.

I seal that box right back up again and move along.

The next looks older, much older.

And I hit the jackpot.

At least it feels that way. Like peeping into someone's soul.

Alexander Henley's old school books. Several old reports writing home to tell them how *exceptional* a student he is. How serious. How dedicated. How talented.

There's an old clipping of him in a rowing team, his hair longer, with a hint of curls.

Some postcards with no writing on the back. Egypt. New York. Sydney.

And then, in the bottom, an old packet of condoms with one left in there. A dirty magazine that looks *thumbed*.

And...

Pictures of a blonde woman in a zebra print dress. Debbie Harry, I think. Her blonde bob blowing in the wind as she poses. There are loads of these, pictures of her, clippings from magazines, and a couple of old CDs.

It makes me smile to think of a young Mr Henley, cutting out pictures of his crush.

One is particularly tattered, with the sticky tape still on the corners from being on a wall. She looks so innocent in this one, eyes wide for the camera, in a pale pink dress with lipstick to match, her hair messy and at odds with her outfit.

He liked this one.

He liked her.

He likes blondes.

My hair is mousy. A nothing colour that's never really bothered me one way or another.

I could be blonde.

I forget about that for now and move along to the last box.

More paperwork, but this one has been packaged more carefully. I have to lift the lid slowly so as not to damage the tape on the sides.

Divorce paperwork.

It gives me flutters.

The decree absolute is right on the top. Eighteen months old.

And underneath is a file of... correspondence... settlement figures that take my breath.

Emails back and forth. C.Henley to A.Henley. Unreasonable conduct.

I shouldn't look, but I do. Of course I do.

It leaves me under no illusion that the divorce was in any way amicable. Her emails are vicious and persistent, accusing him of sleeping with other women, so many other women, having *perverted* interests... and...

My eyes widen.

...fucking men.

...wanting men.

Disturbed by childhood abuse, the text says, and a reply from him denying that. Strongly. But he doesn't deny the other.

He doesn't deny fucking men, just denies that he *fucked any other asshole* in all the time they were married.

She tells him that's bullshit. That she found the emails from other men. The videos they sent him. The chat logs from the *bareback* forum he'd been logging into from their office computer.

Shit.

I close the box up tight and put it right back on the shelf where it belongs. And I'm thrumming, tingling, filled with… nerves… and excitement.

Because I'm close. So much closer than I ever dreamed.

And my head is spinning, full of ideas I'm not yet aware of, just the beginnings of something… crazy…

Something *really* crazy.

Something…

Big.

THIRTEEN

MELISSA

And so it begins.

The goalposts move from playing with myself in Alexander Henley's dirty sheets, to playing with him in them.

After the accident I couldn't imagine myself ever making plans again, ever using my brain again, not properly.

I was living for Joseph and that was fine. I didn't want anything else.

I couldn't *do* anything else.

My dreams of being a lawyer were crushed into oblivion. But not my dreams of Alexander Henley. The fantasy of a life in the arms of the man I've been fascinated by for all those years held strong.

And now here I am. So close. So very close.

I'll be a whole lot closer if I manage to pull off my crazy scheme.

It *is* crazy. It's so crazy I should probably never speak it out loud, not to Dean and not even to myself.

But I'll have to, because I'll need his help.

I drop into an internet cafe on my way home, and the soup kitchen location I followed Mr Henley to is easy to pinpoint. *New Start*. A charity-funded initiative with three branches across the city.

Newtown Lane on a Monday.

A place called Eastspring on a Wednesday.

And Brickwood, where he went, on a Friday.

I call Eastspring in my finest telephone voice and tell them my name is… *Amy*… and I'm… looking to volunteer… on a Wednesday… *this* Wednesday…

The guy's name is Frank and he seems really nice. He tells me they'd love to have me, *Amy*, and I should head on down for seven o'clock sharp, with some warm clothes and a smile and that's all I'd need.

But it isn't all I need.

I pick up some hair dye and bleach at the local chemist when I get off the underground, and dig out my makeup bag once Joseph is bathed and in bed.

Dean watches me sorting through my old lipsticks until I find a light pink, and the expression on his face lets me know he's expecting an explanation.

"It's nothing to worry about…" I begin as he hands me a coffee.

"If it's to do with Henley it's plenty to worry about."

I ask him for his help with the hair dye, just so I won't have to see his face when I explain myself.

He gloves up with an expression of impending doom, and the silence is heavy as I sit in the chair, an old towel slung around my shoulders.

When he's safely out of my eyeline, I confess in one long monologue that I've discovered Alexander Henley uses escorts, about the paperwork in his drawer, about the porn I've seen on his browsing history, but I don't stop there, rattling off all the things I've seen and all the things I've learned. Big things, small things.

Any things.

I tell him I'm going to volunteer at Eastspring, and then, when the time is right, I'll transfer to Brickwood, I'll run into Mr Henley and I'll introduce myself as someone other than his cleaner, and it'll be great... it'll be just fine...

I take a breath. A long breath.

"What do you mean, *it'll be fine*? Are you ..."

I twist in my chair and I don't need to say anything as my eyes meet his. His widen, the bottle of dye paused in mid-air as he realises what I'm really planning.

"No," he says. "No fucking way, Lissa. Just no."

"For Joseph," I tell him. "I have to get him out of here, Dean. He's only got me, and this place, and it's not enough. Being a cleaner's not enough. He needs more."

"He has *me*, too," Dean snaps. "And he'd rather you were poor than dead."

Dead.

The word hits hard.

I take a another breath. Compose myself.

"I saw the guy's card. Some swanky auctioneer from Chelsea. They don't *kill* people, Dean, that's crazy. They just pay them... for sex..."

"And you've never *had* sex. You've never *been* an escort. You've no fucking idea what these people are into, Lissa, *swanky* or not."

"I *want* Alexander Henley. Being paid for it is..."

"Insane, Lissa. It's fucking insane!"

"My only shot..." I close my eyes. "I'll put the money in a trust fund, for Joe, if they'll even have me on their books, that is. All of it, every penny, and I'll keep working... keep cleaning... I won't get carried away... I won't..."

His hands land on my shoulders, and he squeezes so hard, as though he's trying to squeeze some sense into me.

He can't.

I'm a lost cause.

I know that much.

"For fuck's sake, Lissa. What if it's not even him? You even thought about that? What if it's not Henley who rocks up in some seedy hotel room somewhere, but some slimy random. Some creepy old guy who's paid to be your fucking first?"

The thought chills me, but it's nothing I haven't considered myself.

I gesture to the bottle of hair dye, and he resumes the application with a sigh. "I'm doing everything I can to make sure it is him who rocks up. He likes blondes. He had a crush on Debbie Harry when he was young, I've seen the pictures in a box of his old things and…"

"Oh, well that's just brilliant, then. Dress up a bit like Debbie Harry and I'm sure it'll be him who shows. Have you lost your fucking mind? Do you have any idea how fucking crazy you sound?"

I shrug, because it does sound crazy, and I lost my fucking mind a long time ago, before I ever got close to Henley's bedroom. But there's hope. Just a bit.

And that's enough.

Money for Joe and hope for me. It's as good as it gets right now.

He takes off the plastic gloves and moves away from me, staring out the window at the shitty street below with an expression like death.

I slip on the gloves without a word and apply the rest of the dye.

"I need to do this…" I tell him.

"You really fucking don't," he snaps. "You could do back to college, study like before."

I shake my head. "I can't and you know it. Not with Joe, and my head is… fried… I just can't…"

"Your head is full of that fucking asshole of a man."

"Better that than the alternative. If I stop, Dean, even for just one second. If I stop… hoping… if I stop dreaming… then I won't get up, I won't be able to breathe."

He sighs, and his eyes are softer when they land back on mine. "Don't say that, Lissa. You've got Joe, you've got me."

"And I love both of you, but I have to do this. Please don't stop me doing this…"

He groans. "Like I could if I wanted to."

And I've got him. I know I've got him.

The victory doesn't feel great.

I apply the last squirt of dye and wrap my hair in the plastic cap. "I'm sure they pay well, I mean it's Chelsea, right? I'll earn enough to make sure Joe's ok. And us, we'll be ok, too. I can get a babysitter and you can go back to college… you can have a life, too."

"Please don't pretend this is for me."

So I don't. I don't pretend anything. I stop speaking, sitting quietly as the dye matures.

"Is there anything I could say to change your mind?" his voice is quiet. Heavy.

"No."

He exhales a long breath. Shakes his head.

"Fine," he says. "In that case, how can I help?"

ALEXANDER

I'm in relatively good spirits for an average Tuesday morning.

I put that down to the smell of fresh orchids. That and a hearty breakfast. Bacon and eggs on a nice thick slice of wholemeal. The breakfast of champions – as long as those champions aren't overly concerned about their waistline.

Nothing a good session on the treadmill can't remedy.

I tell myself there are a variety of factors contributing to my good morning, but there's no illusion. That's why I left a simple note this morning.

Thank you.

And then the afterthought. A radical impulse.

Please help yourself to breakfast.

It pleases me to think that maybe she'll take me up on my offer. Maybe she's sitting at my kitchen island right this minute, listening to the radio as she eats, enjoying the space considerably more than I have these past few years.

It's not her cleaning standards that inspired the note, nor is it any one individual change she's made to my space and routine. It's her thoughtfulness.

Her thoughtfulness creates the illusion my house is a home again. That illusion is priceless.

I'm thinking about her mysterious presence all the way through my early client meetings. Wondering if the note made her smile. If she'll leave one in return.

I wonder what her handwriting is like. What her smile is like. Whether she licks her fingers clean after she's eaten.

I wonder what her name is.

I force myself not to look it up.

"Christ, man. And I *really* have to go on this ridiculous fucking *speed awareness* course?!" Mr Calder's voice disturbs my equilibrium. "As if I haven't got better things to do with my fucking time."

His face is piggy and infuriating, his bluster doing its best to ruin my happy vibe.

Ungrateful prick.

I've got better things to do with *my* time than bail him out of his stupid fucking mistakes, but *I'm* not sitting in *his* office moaning about a perfectly commendable outcome.

"Unless you want to take your chances in court. We could call your mistress in as a witness, I'm sure she'd be able to tell them you weren't *all* that drunk while she sucked you off at twenty miles an hour over the speed limit." I smile sarcastically. "Take the fucking speed awareness course. You're fucking welcome, Andrew."

His mouth flaps open, and then he thinks better of a smart comeback.

He rises to his feet as I do, shakes my hand with a nod.

"Thanks, Henley. Much appreciated. I'll get my secretary to book it in."

"You do that." *And stop drinking and driving like a fucking imbecile.*

I don't smile.

He doesn't linger.

The door swings on its hinges as he leaves, and his silhouette is replaced by an even bigger cunt. Just what I fucking need.

"Let's talk." My father closes the meeting room door behind him. He's wearing a red tie today. I fucking hate the colour.

"Let's not."

I don't even attempt to hide my disdain as he takes a seat opposite me. "People are talking about you."

"Which fucking people?"

He laughs. "Ok, so *I'm* talking."

"Talk all you want, I have no intention of listening."

His eyes turn dark. "What in the name of holy fuck is wrong with you? Turning your nose up at Claude, ignoring your messages."

"Ignoring *your* messages."

"This *silliness* ends now. Claude's offered you a free sample. You will take it."

"I'm not interested in Claude's free fucking sample. I'm done."

"Like hell you're done," he sneers. "You don't know *how* to be done."

"Speak for yourself, old man. I'm doing just fine." I bristle with false confidence, my arms folded tight.

He pulls an envelope from his inside pocket and slides it across the table. "A gift. Take it. Enjoy it. I hate to worry about you, Alexander. You know how it makes me uncomfortable to worry. I may have to keep a closer eye on things..."

His threats mean nothing to me. "Are you quite fucking done? I have work to do."

His eyes are steely but so are mine. "For now."

"Good." I get to my feet. Again. "Next time you want to *talk*, book a fucking appointment."

"This is *my* office," he snaps. "Don't you forget it."

"*Retired*. Don't *you* forget it."

We stare each other down for long seconds.

"Your mother misses you."

"That's a shame."

"She misses the boys."

"I'll pass on her regards."

He shakes his head. "You're such a belligerent prick, Alexander."

"We both know where I learned it from."

"We both know where you learned a *lot* of things, boy. Call Claude. I don't expect to have to come here again."

"That would be nice." I gesture to the door. "Close it on your way out."

It slams with a thump that shakes the glass surround. His frustration makes me smile.

I put his envelope straight through the shedder unopened.

MELISSA

I hardly recognised myself in the mirror this morning. The bleach worked its magic, and the dye took well on top, and there I was, a new blonde version of me. I've never been blonde before. It looks strange, alien. Not that you'd ever know the difference under a hairnet and stupid cap.

Dean helped me cut my hair shorter, armed with nothing but a pair of general purpose scissors my mum used to use to open stubborn food packets. My new long bob looks pretty good for a home-done effort. A few random snips to vary the length and the look is definitely a little *Debbie-Harryesque*. Even Dean agreed.

I slapped on some pink lipstick and ruffled my freshly dried hair, and he called up a couple of old pictures of her on the internet and said he thinks I'll pass.

Charging up and down a billion stairs every day these past few months has helped my physique. My legs are more toned than they've ever been, and although I'm far from the perfect women pictured in the bedroom drawer, I think I look alright.

If it's not enough, it's not enough, but I don't want to dwell on that.

I'm lucky that I have a similar jawline to Debbie. High cheekbones and big eyes. My nose is a little bit pointier than hers, but I can compensate for that with similar makeup.

There's a lot more to my plan than a makeover though, which is why I've borrowed Dean's phone today. He has a much better camera, and I'll need to take a fair number of shots.

The codes for the gemstone cabinet are in the little black book Cindy gave me.

I have the special buffing cloth in my apron pocket, inputting the numbers so carefully to make sure the cabinet doesn't autolock me out of there.

It opens with a click, and I get to work, snapping pictures as I go. I make sure all the names are in focus, a clear enough picture of the gemstones that I'll be able to look them back up at home and memorise them.

Alexandrite. Poudretteite. Topaz. Red diamond. Benitoite. Musgravite. Bismuth.

I'll never be able to afford anything like these, so I hope he's interested in more mundane specimens as well as these weird little rocks. It just has to be a common interest. A convincing one.

I close up the cabinet when I'm done, and then I photograph his music collection. He doesn't have many CDs on the shelf, and most of them are by the same band. A blues outfit called Kings and Castles. I check out the listing on the back, and I'm pretty sure the one song – *Casual Observer* – is his dreary morning wake-up soundtrack.

I like it, just like I thought I would.

I venture down to the kitchen last thing today, my heart calming now I've got my illicit practicalities out of the way.

His plate is on the island, the dirty cutlery arranged so nearly on top. The sight of the pan on the hob makes me smile. Bacon fat. He had the bacon.

I've loaded it into the dishwasher by the time I notice the piece of paper propped against the fruit bowl.

My stomach flips, because it can't be. It really can't be.

But it is.

A perfect scrawl, so beautifully penned on fine grain paper.

Thank you.

Please help yourself to breakfast.

To me?!

My fingers are shaky as I run them over the text.

He wrote it for me. For *me*. For the bacon. He liked the bacon.

I smile so hard my cheeks hurt, and I'm not hungry, not in the slightest, but his offer is too generous to ignore. I don't want to ignore him. I couldn't ever do that.

I take the pan back from the dishwasher and fry myself up some bacon, cut myself a thin slice of bread and add a single egg to the pan.

It gets the attention of a grumbling Brutus, who flops down at my feet as I try to manoeuvre. I guess he wants some bacon too.

It's the strangest feeling, eating breakfast at Alexander Henley's kitchen island. My feet tap against the base of the bar stool, nervous even though I'm the only one here.

The bacon tastes better than any bacon I've ever had before.

Brutus seems to agree with me. He takes the rind in one greedy swallow.

I clear down the sides thoroughly, then stand with a cheap biro in my hand, wondering what on earth I should write in reply.

I tear a page from my notebook, because I want to take his home with me, and I try for my very best handwriting, even though my hand is trembling.

Thank you very much, Mr Henley, sir.

I don't sign my name. Because why would I? I'm just a nobody.

I prop it up against the fruit bowl, right where his had been, and then I do it. I just do it.

I input Claude's number into Dean's handset, and take a swig of water before I press to call.

Three rings and all I can feel is my own thumping heart.

I'm ready for it to go to voicemail, half *hoping* it goes to voicemail.

But it doesn't.

"Claude Finch."

I clear my throat. "Mr Finch? I'm sorry to call so randomly, it's just I'm... I'm looking to sell something... and I was hoping you could... help..."

I hear him rustling through paperwork. "If you could call the main sales line,

I'm sure they'll be able to take your details."

My throat is so dry. "I was hoping maybe you'd be… the right person…"

"That depends. What kind of item are you looking to sell?"

My voice is so weak. Such a whisper. "Well, I'm… I'm looking to sell… *me*…"

A pause. Such a long pause.

I feel the panic rising.

"Where did you get this number?"

"I, um… a friend…"

"What kind of a friend?"

"A female friend… she said I should…"

"This isn't for discussion on the telephone," he snaps. "Please forward a photo of the item to this email address." He rattles off a series of letters and numbers that I scrabble to write down.

I read it back and he grunts, and then he hangs up.

I feel so wired I can't keep still. Pacing up and down Mr Henley's kitchen as I open the random email account Dean set up for me and attach the photo in my best underwear he took last night.

The nerves take over as soon as it's been sent, and the pressure builds to breaking, my whole plan resting on a random guy and his reaction to one semi-slutty photo.

I feel like I've bared my whole soul for nothing, like he'll laugh at me, tell me of course I'm not good enough, I'm not of the calibre they're looking for.

I'm getting ready to take Brutus for his walk when the handset vibrates in my apron pocket.

1 new email.

The sender is *CF*.

I can hardly bring myself to open it.

Bring the item along to the saleroom with a copy of your ID.

There's a date and time listed underneath.

I'm so excited I nearly pee myself on Alexander Henley's freshly mopped floor.

FOURTEEN

MELISSA

Brutus and pornography are usually my only two incentives for stepping foot through my front door every evening. Tonight I have a third. A most ridiculous third.

I drop my keys on my smoking table and deactivate the alarm, and then I head straight through to the kitchen, which of course is immaculate, without so much of a clue as to whether someone sat and ate bacon in my absence this morning. I open the fridge, and a glance at the packet of bacon thrills me.

Two slices missing.

An egg, too.

It makes me smile, which is unusual. My muscles feel tight and out of practice.

My note is missing, and in its stead, propped so neatly against the fruit bowl, is a torn scrap of notebook paper.

Thank you very much, Mr Henley, sir.

Shit.

My cock aches, hardening at the memory of her nervous apology at the office.

Her script is flowery, a tiny circle over the *i* in sir. The letters are evenly spaced, the curves drawn with effort.

She cared how it looked.

I imagine her gripping her pen, the precise flow of her fingers.

I should stop this silliness before it starts, accept my interest as nothing more than the idle fantasy of a desperate mind, but of course, I can't do that.

My cupboards are embarrassingly barren, and for the first time in months I take a detour from my usual dog-walking route, looping Brutus' lead over a post outside the late-night store while I nip inside and grab a handbasket.

I run through the things I like. Some organic muesli and some fresh peaches. A pot of luxury Greek yoghurt that I think Claire bought me once when we were on some weird health kick. Dark chocolate with orange segments, the most expensive on the shelf.

I'm losing my fucking mind and I know it as I check out. Selling out my sanity for some grandiose illusion that a moment with a terrified cleaner in a dark office meant something. That the note in my pocket is anything other than a kind young girl being polite to her employer.

Brutus sniffs the shopping bag as I retrieve his lead, and it amuses me to think the grumpy old beast knows so much more about the mystery woman than I do. What's surprising in itself is that the teething period with a new member of staff in the house has been surprisingly dog-issue free. I was expecting at least one emergency call out as she'd found herself trapped in a room with a growling Brutus on the other side of the door. But no. Nothing.

Maybe he likes her.

I trust his judgement as much as I trust my own. We're two peas in a very cynical pod, him and I, and yet he's accepted an intruder without spilling any of their blood over the carpet.

"What do you think, boy?" I ask him as we walk. "Is she nice?"

His ears prick at the sound of my voice, his tongue lolling as we pace the final stretch back to home turf.

"Let's see if she likes a bit of muesli in the morning, shall we?"

Brutus pads through to the kitchen as we head inside, as though he knows. He parks his stinky arse on the tiles and stares up at me as I unpack the shopping. I take one of Claire's flouncy old serving trays from the bottom cupboard and arrange a display on the kitchen island. Muesli and a fresh peach, one of my finest china cereal bowls and a silver spoon from the cutlery drawer. And the chocolate. Of course the chocolate.

I take a fresh piece of paper from my writing pad and pen her another note.

Your bacon was a superb suggestion. Here's one of mine.

Muesli with chopped peach. A generous spoon of Greek yoghurt (fridge) covered with a fine grating of dark chocolate.

Let me know your thoughts.

Regards, AH.

I fold the note on the tray and head up to bed before I can think better of it.

MELISSA

Dean and I shopped on the internet last night, looking for cheap second-hand designer bargains to carry off the illusion that I'm a high-class woman worthy of high-class clients.

I've spent the final scraps of my wages on this crazy quest, but I've got a few outfits on their way which look as though they'll do the job for me. A slinky pink gown with a killer split, some sparkly heels, a faded pair of designer jeans and a trendy cami-top. A fitted jacket was the most extravagant of my purchases, but the weather is shitty at this time of year, and I'll need it unless I want to freeze my tits off on the way to meet *CF* at his swanky sale room.

My appointment is on Friday at eight p.m.

In the interim I have my new gig at the soup kitchen this evening, and I have to pull that off, too. My trial run in my new identity.

Dean helped me concoct the perfect cover story. A girl named Amy Randall, aged twenty-one, older sister of Dean's friend Sammy that we used to go to school with. It's *her* details that Dean messaged over to a dodgy contact lower down on the estate last night. He says they owe him a favour, so last night he disappeared with one of my passport photos and came back with the promise they'll deliver a convincing fake ID in time for my Friday meet up.

I hope he's right.

It feels weird to steal someone else's identity, especially someone I vaguely know. But I need any background checks to hold true. My fake address is Amy Randall's real address, my fake date of birth is her real one, stolen from Facebook along with every other scrap of info we could find on there.

Her social media is locked down pretty tight, just a photo of her cat as a profile picture to anything other than friends.

I hope it'll be enough to hold my cover.

Leaving Dean in charge of Joe for so much of the working week makes me feel guilty, but I try not to dwell too hard on that, just focus on the time we do have and keep on pushing for the better future I have planned for him. For *us*.

He doesn't seem to care, just as long as he has someone to play choo-choo trains and make his dinner just so. Dean's doing a sterling job on both fronts.

Dean's also doing a sterling job of hiding his attraction to Alexander Henley. There's still no mention of the pictures on his phone, still nothing more than fear that the guy is some kind of crazy psychopath out to spill virgin blood.

Maybe if I pull this off… maybe if he sees that I lived through a night with Alexander Henley and managed to walk back through the door as right as rain.

If I walk back through the door as right as rain.

If I get a night with Alexander Henley at all.

Brutus doesn't growl at me this morning. I swear he could be smiling, his tongue flopping out the side, eyes bright, and my heart blooms at the triumph. I give him a fish treat without even thinking about his scary teeth, and he settles down nicely on his big cushion once he's chomped it into nothing.

I'm getting used to the routine here. Polishing the table and washing out the whisky tumbler. Cleaning out the inkwell and shining it up to perfection.

The dusting and the vacuuming, and the gorgeous scent of Mr Henley on his dirty laundry.

The sad music of his alarm clock still playing more mornings than not.

There's no pan on the hob this morning, and I'm a little disappointed until I notice the tray on the island. At first I think it's his dirty breakfast bowl, but his is in the sink, already soaking.

Muesli and peach, and some fancy looking dark chocolate, and a note.

A NOTE!

My throat is so dry I can barely swallow.

Your bacon was a superb suggestion. Here's one of mine.

Muesli with chopped peach. A generous spoon of Greek yoghurt (fridge) covered with a fine grating of dark chocolate.

Let me know your thoughts.

Regards, AH.

132

I have to read it through at least five times before it really sinks in.

He wants me to eat breakfast. *His* breakfast.

I have no idea why, and my mind spins, trying to work out if this is some kind of weird test to try my professionalism. To eat the muesli or not to eat the muesli?

Of course I have to eat the muesli. I *want* to eat the muesli.

I want to eat the whole damn lot and lick the bowl clean.

I follow his instructions exactly, chopping up the peach into neat chunks and adding it to the bowl along with the cereal. A dollop of yoghurt from the fridge, and I find the grater, unwrap the chocolate so carefully to use just a little.

My heart is a fluttery mess as I spoon up the first mouthful, my eyes still fixed on that note, looking for hidden meaning.

AH.

His note says he wants my thoughts. Like my opinion matters.

Why does my opinion matter to him?

Why does he even care?

I'd have lied about the breakfast even if it tasted like crap, but it doesn't. It tastes delicious. The perfect mix of tart and creamy, a mix of tastes that blend into this yummy goodness.

I feel young again, excited like when Mum let me have the lump of cream from the top of the milk bottle on my cereals in the morning. A real treat.

I haven't really eaten breakfast… not since they…

Not since we used to eat together in the morning, all of us crammed in the kitchen with our cereal bowls in our hands, bickering and laughing before we went our separate ways.

A normal family. A *happy* family.

And now it's all gone.

No. That's not true. Joe's not all gone, and I'm not all gone, and while there are still two of us we're still family. Just a much smaller one now.

But not as small as Alexander Henley's, just him and Brutus in this huge place, eating alone.

I have no idea what to reply to him. No idea how to sound like a gushing food critic, so I don't try.

Peach, muesli, yoghurt and chocolate are a delicious combination. Thank you so much, Mr Henley, sir.

Warmest regards,

Your cleaner.

I look at the note. Read it back to myself. *Your cleaner* sounds so dull. So cold.

I add an *MM* to the bottom, and hope that's not too unprofessional.

AH and MM.

MH.

In my dreams.

I smile to myself, wrap the rest of the chocolate up neatly and put it in the fridge. I clear the muesli away into one of the cupboards and get rid of my peach stone, wiping the side down as though I've never been here.

And then I take Brutus out.

Today's the first time I don't have to tug him over the threshold.

I think he may actually like me.

⚜

It's a rush to get home and change before heading out to my *New Start* meeting.

My heart is in my mouth as I plaster a smile on my face and push my way between the swing doors.

Amy Randall, Amy Randall, Amy Randall.

"Hi, I'm Amy," I tell the gathered volunteers, and one of them steps forward with his hand outstretched. His smile is big and bright.

"Frank Peterson," he says. "We spoke on the phone. Really pleased to have you here, we can always use another pair of hands."

I tell him I'm really pleased to be here, too. That I hope I can be of use.

I'm lucky, because this place is so busy and understaffed that they barely have time to ask me any questions about my fake life. I smile and muck in as best I can, chopping up vegetables for soup and stirring the big steel pans.

It's hard work, but good work. The people here are full of smiles and effort. There's a genuine sense of community that I haven't felt for a long time, not since I was part of an estate clean-up team back at school in the summer holidays. It feels a lifetime away.

It doesn't take much time before I've forgotten all about being here on a mission, and instead believe I really am part of the team, just doing my bit, the same as they are.

It becomes a lot more real when we load up the trays with soup mugs and venture out onto the street.

It's bitter cold out, even with my mum's old fluffy scarf up around my ears. My fingers feel numb as I hand out food to the people who need it, and I get it, I get why Alexander Henley goes so far out of his way to do this.

These people, the ones with nothing to their name and every reason to be bitter, are some of the nicest people I've ever met in my life. They take everything with thanks, and ask me about my day with genuine interest, like they haven't got better things to worry about than my cruddy life away from here.

Frank knows everyone, literally every single person that comes up to us. I follow him as he makes conversation. He asks one guy about his bad leg, and some poor old woman about her grandkid's birthday last weekend. She tears up as she tells him she got to spend time with him at the foster shelter, and I tear up too, because there is something so real and so raw about this place and these people, something so sad and so warm all at once.

I'm so homesick for my old life that I have to fight the urge to curl into a ball and never get back up. I twist my cold fingers in the tassels of mum's scarf and push the pain back inside, dishing out those hot soups to those less fortunate than I am and counting my limited blessings.

At least Joe and I have a roof over our heads. It may take every penny I earn to run the place and keep it that way, but Joe always has food in his belly and warm cuddles at night.

Maybe that's why Mr Henley comes here, to feel gratitude for his lot in life.

Who knows.

I guess Frank does, because on the way back to the kitchen he tells me how he works at all three branches, how once he started this work he couldn't just walk away at the end of the evening.

Looking after people on the street is everything to Frank. His volunteers are like a second family to him, he says, and so are the people out there in the cold.

I wonder if Mr Henley is like second family to him. The thought feels weird.

I help him pack away, even after everyone else has gone, and he's turning off the lights for the evening when he asks if I'll be back next week.

I tell him I'll definitely be back next week, and every week after that if he'll have me.

He calls me Amy and I smile like it's the most normal thing in the world.

The weirdest thing about all this?

On my way back to the underground I realise I'd be back next week regardless, Mr Henley or no.

FIFTEEN

ALEXANDER

MM.

Maybe she's a Margaret or a Millicent or Mollie. A Mary, or a Maddie, or something trendy like a Miley.

Mary Moore.

Miley Montgomery.

Margaret Mackenzie.

I could just look her up on my employee database, of course. A few keystrokes and I'd have every *M* name on our books at my fingertips.

But I don't.

There is something so ethereal about this girl's presence in my home. One wrong move could blow that sweet illusion away.

At the other extreme, knowing her actual name might give me dangerous options, so I force myself to remain ignorant.

I name her Molly May instead.

I like that. Sweet Molly May.

Molly May enjoyed her breakfast, her note told me so.

This morning I didn't leave another, just made sure there was an empty bowl and spoon on the tray on the island, trusting she'll know what it's there for.

I'm disappointed to find nothing in its stead when I return. No sure way of knowing if Molly May ate her fill or simply put the empty bowl back in the cupboard.

I tell myself it's done, our ridiculous little note exchange nothing more than a passing fancy. She's most likely relieved, free to carry out her daily tasks without having to concern herself with looping her letters just so for her fool of an employer.

Despite my rational mind telling me it doesn't matter shit whether my cleaner left me a stupid little thank you note or not, there's definitely a pang of frustration in my gut.

It's annoying.

Distinctly annoying.

I console myself with the pornography I've committed to avoid, then finish myself off to the fantasy of little Molly May with my hands around her throat, retching streams of saliva all over her stripy uniform.

It's the best orgasm I've had in months, and that's distinctly annoying too.

MELISSA

The notes stop.

I try to shrug it off and pretend it doesn't matter.

I'm sure it doesn't matter, not to him. He was just a powerful man taking a moment to make his lowly cleaner feel comfortable.

The disappointment only makes my plan all the more important, because now I've had a taste, just the tiniest little taste of how good it feels to be known by Alexander Henley, I can't bear to let that go.

So here I am, trying to hide my bellyful of nerves behind a calm smile as I teeter on my new-old heels through the centre of Chelsea en route to meet CF.

It's dark, and I'm glad. It already feels like everyone is staring at me, like they know I'm an outsider, that I don't belong around these parts, with my second-hand gown and the jacket that needed stitches on the inside seam.

I have to take a minute to calm my breathing when the posh signage for Finch Hamilton auctioneers comes into view.

The main entrance claims it's closed for the day, but there's a little light shining above the posh oak reception desk I spy through the window. The door is locked when I try it, so I press the intercom.

"Side entrance," a voice barks, and it's him, CF, I recognise him from my first phone call.

The side entrance is dark, and I'm slow on my heels. The door is already open when I reach it, and Claude Finch is a huge shadow beyond, big and broad and dressed in a pinstripe suit. He beckons me in, then locks it.

He slips the keys into his inside pocket, and the hairs on the back of my neck prickle. He's older than I expect, a silver fox with a slick moustache. He looks as though he should be wearing a monocle.

"I'm Amy," I lie, keeping my smile confident and hoping he doesn't realise my legs are wobbly.

"Alright, Amy," he says, "come on through." He points to a door at the back of the corridor, and I walk on ahead of him. I feel his eyes on me, know he's hanging back to check out my ass in this slinky dress.

Judging me. He's definitely judging me.

It feels grimy, but I don't care. I just want to be good enough.

His office smells of old leather, his desk covered in guides to antiques and reams of paperwork. The seat he offers me squeaks as I lower myself into it. He stares at me from across the desk, opening his hands to offer me the floor.

I feel so small. So pathetic.

"I want to... I'm hoping to..."

"Sell yourself," he says. "Yes. I have buyers."

Buyers.

My nerves jangle. I can't speak. I don't know what to say.

Claude sighs and I feel like I've already failed. "So, tell me, Amy, have you ever offered your services for sale before? My clients have... particular tastes. We are a niche agency."

I shake my head. "No. I'm, um..." I can't find the words, and I wonder if I should say them at all, because he might not want me if I'm inexperienced. He might tell me to come back when I've sucked a few dicks and know what the fuck I'm doing.

Maybe he'll offer me his, and I don't want it. I really don't want it.

"You're what?" he prompts, and he's impatient. The kind of guy that wants it straight or he'll chuck you out on your ass.

"I'm a virgin," I tell him. "But I can learn... I'm a fast learner..."

His eyes widen, and I'm petrified he's going to tell me to fuck off out of here. "A virgin? A genuine, honest-to-God, un-fucking-touched virgin?"

I nod. "Yeah. But I..."

"A medical will have to confirm."

I nod again. "Sure."

The biggest smile creeps across Claude Finch's face, and it's scarier than the scowl he was wearing before. "You want me to put your sweet little cherry on the market? First time goes to the highest bidder? I hope you're not playing games with me, sweetheart."

No. I want my sweet little cherry to go to Alexander Henley.

I can't say that, so I smile instead. "Yes. That's what I want. Please."

He laughs. "Alright then, Miss…"

"Randall," I lie. "Amy Randall."

"And you brought ID with you, Miss Amy Randall?"

I dig my fake passport from my clutch bag, hoping beyond hope Dean's dodgy friend delivered a decent forgery.

Claude nods as he looks it over, and then he slams it onto the photocopier at his side. "For my records," he says. He taps away on his keyboard, and I wish I could see his screen. He pulls a face. "Good, good. I see you have a good credit rating, Miss Randall. We like that. We don't take… *desperates.*"

I keep smiling, my foot tapping in mid-air as he leans down to a desk drawer. I hear the rattle of keys, and my breath hitches as he presents me with a questionnaire. I lean to take it but I can't stop staring at the camera in his hand, some high end digital thing. It lights up as he angles it towards me.

"Are you, um… is that for pictures of me?"

"Video. Call it a brochure. Just fill in the questionnaire first so I know how to catalogue you."

Catalogue me.

I recognise the tick boxes on the form. I've seen them listed under the girls' photographs in Mr Henley's beside drawer.

I remember Cindy's words. *He keeps the ones with fewer ticks, just so you know.*

I hand the form back untouched. He looks at me like I'm a total idiot.

"No, sweetheart, you have to fill those *in*. Check the ones you definitely won't do. Err on the side of caution."

"I have," I tell him.

He laughs. "Amy, sweetheart, if there's any terms you don't understand you have to ask. Believe me, you'll want to know what you're signing up for."

I shake my head. "I understand them all, and I'm done. I don't want to tick any boxes, thank you."

His expression is strange, a weird mixture of bemused and excited, his eyes glinting in the glow of his banker's lamp.

"Miss Randall, I'm going to be frank here, my clients have extreme tastes, some of these men will be looking for these services, and they'll expect you to deliver."

I tip my head. "Will any of your clients kill me, Mr Finch? That's all I really need to know."

He scoffs at me. "Good God, no. What kind of agency do you take this for? If you've got some kind of fucked up suicide wish, this really isn't the place."

I laugh, because this is crazy. This whole thing is insane. "No," I tell him. "I mean if I'm walking out of there alive, then I'm good. I don't care what else they want to... pay me for..."

He raises an eyebrow. "You're willing to say that in your introduction video? That you're hard-limit free?"

I nod. "Sure, if that's what you... want me to do."

He's really excited now, and I know it, trying to hide his grin under a steely nonchalance, but it's too obvious. He's practically slavering.

"Well then, Miss Randall." He points to a chaise longue at the back of the office. "You'd better make yourself comfortable."

✜

Claude flicks on a table lamp at the side of me and I sit in the glow, perched awkwardly on the edge of his chaise longue while he fumbles around with the settings on his camera. I'm still not really sure what he wants from me, and it's all I can do to breathe, in and out, holding onto the single little thread of composure keeping me from freaking out.

"Take your jacket off, please."

I shrug it from my shoulders and he takes it from me. He hangs it on a coat stand.

"And your dress." My eyes must look like saucers, because he shakes his head. "No need for shyness, Amy, believe me, the real experience will be considerably more intimate."

I have to stand to shimmy my dress up and over my head, and I'm glad I chose my very best underwear. I'm in pink lace, a cheap but pretty set I bought from the discount store on our estate. The bra is slightly too small, but I guess that's ok, because Claude's staring at the spill of flesh over the top of the cups, and he looks pleased as Punch.

"I need you to be yourself," he tells me, and I nearly laugh out loud. Like anyone could be themselves in this place, bared in skimpy underwear while some random old guy pulls out a video camera. "Just relax, we have time to do a few takes if necessary."

He pulls up a stool real close, his camera in his hand as he angles it for a decent view.

"We really need to do this?" I ask, although I'm sure it's a pointless question.

"It's imperative we offer video for our auctions. It makes our buyers more *invested*."

I wonder if he jerks himself off to them afterwards, then force the idea away.

"Lay back," he tells me, "make yourself comfortable."

I do as he asks, leaning back on my elbows. I flinch as he lands a hand on my knee, taking a breath as he eases my legs open.

"That's good," he says. "I'll be doing this as an interview, so answer honestly, and do exactly what I ask."

I nod, and he clears his throat.

"Our auction lot four of the evening is *Amy*, a rare specimen indeed. Amy, tell our bidders of your sexual history."

My voice is so quiet. "I'm a… I'm a um… a virgin…"

I stare up at the camera, and the light is on me, it obscures Claude's face, and I'm glad. I close my eyes, and in that moment I forget I'm here, in this place with a man who plans to sell me like it's the most normal thing in the world. I pretend I'm in front of Mr Henley, imagine him watching this video later, imagine him bidding on me.

I take a breath.

"And you're twenty-one?"

I nod. "Yes."

"Tell me, Amy, what are your hard limits?"

This is my moment, and I know it. I imagine Mr Henley's stern expression, the way he'll be watching this video, the way he'll be wondering if I'm worth bidding on.

"None," I tell the camera, and I make sure I'm looking right at it. "I have no hard limits. I'll do… anything…"

"No hard limits, you're sure about this?"

I force a smile and nod and in my head I'm looking at Mr Henley as he stares down on me like he did when I barged into his meeting room. "I'm sure."

Claude's voice grows softer, and my skin prickles, my breath evening out.

"One of our fine bidders is going to win you, Amy, is that what you want? You want one of our fine gentleman purveyors to take your virginity?"

144

"Yes."

"And you want to fulfil their every fantasy, yes?"

I picture Alexander Henley's hands around my throat. How it will feel. *"Yes."*

"Are you a dirty girl, Amy? Show our buyers what a dirty girl you are. Show them what feels good."

Panic. I feel it snaking around my belly. But there's something else, something that makes me feel so... hot.

Him.

Claude's voice sounds so far away. "Let our buyers see you, Amy. Take off that pretty little bra."

My fingers just do it. They fumble with the catch at the back and let the bra fall loose. My tits aren't really that impressive, so I push them together to make them look bigger, and my nipples are hard as I thumb them.

"Has a man ever touched those sweet tits, Amy?"

I shake my head. "No."

"How about your tight little pussy? Have you ever had a man touch you there?"

I shake my head again. "No."

I know what he's going to say before he says it, so I take a breath and spread my legs for the camera, knowing full well he's going to be focusing in on my little lace knickers.

I shaved. Everywhere.

I'm so glad I did.

"That's good," Claude tells me and I wonder if he's hard. "Show me how you touch yourself."

Me. Show *me.*

It's not him I think about as I slip my hand between my legs, rubbing my clit through the lace of my knickers. I shift my hips and my thighs fall open, my heart pounding as I focus on how much I want this. How much I want Alexander Henley to see me like this.

I imagine myself in his bed, the scent of him on his sheets, the way I came over and over as I thought of his body against mine.

I can do this.

I close my eyes, and I'm with him. His dark eyes so stern and his jaw so tense as he tells me what he wants from me. What he *needs* from me.

I tip my head back and my fingers move faster, circling my clit in quick little motions, my back arching as I bring my knees up.

"Take them off," Claude tells me, and his voice is croaky.

I hook my fingers into my knickers and wriggle them down, letting them slide from my feet. They catch on my sparkly heels for just a second before they drop to the floor.

"Very nice," Claude says. "Show me."

My fingers spread my pussy lips, and I hope I've got it right. He moves the camera closer, and I guess I'm doing ok.

"Wider please," he says, and in my mind it's Alexander Henley doing the ordering.

I hitch my thighs wider still and I pull my lips apart so hard it hurts.

The camera moves so close between my legs, "Nice," he says, "clench for me, Amy."

My pussy pulses with heat at his words and I clench for him.

I hear him swallow. Hear him licking his lips. My God.

"Beautiful," he says, pulling the camera away and focusing on my face.

My legs are shaky and my breaths come out shallow, but I keep Mr Henley's image close in my mind.

"The man who will take your virginity, Amy, tell me what else you would like him to do to you. Tell me what turns you on, Amy."

I know exactly what I need to do. "This," I say and let go of my tingling pussy, trailing my hands up my stomach and over my tits, and then I wrap my fingers around my throat and squeeze just a little, pretending its him, pretending it's him watching me right now, and it works, my clit is fluttery and the muscles in my belly are tight.

I stare at the camera, the glaring light. I can hear him breathing. Heavy breathing.

"Come for me," he says.

My own breaths are ragged. So hot. So scared as my trembling hands leave my throat and I'm hitching my legs, my heels scrabbling against the fabric of the chaise longue, but I don't care as I touch my aching clit.

Don't care as I rub like crazy.

Don't care as I hiss and my eyes burn at the camera.

Don't care as I feel myself losing control.

When I come it's a rush and a shudder, my thighs clenching around the fingers on my clit. A little murmur that I stifle with my hand, and my head lolls back, waves of white rolling through me.

And then it stops.

It all stops.

A shivery rush as I realise I'm naked, naked and exposed, and that my stupid heels are digging into Claude's posh furniture.

"I'm so sorry," I whimper as I scrabble to change position. "My heels! I should've been more careful... I'm so sorry..."

But Claude doesn't seem to care. He doesn't say a word as I look up at him with wide eyes, and then I hear the click as he turns the camera off.

He adjusts his trousers, and suddenly I feel sick.

"Can I get dressed now?" I'm already yanking up my knickers as I ask him.

He hands me my bra, and tosses me my dress from behind him.

I get dressed as quickly as I can, and then I sit, my knees tight together as I wait for his verdict.

He stares at the camera screen as I stare at him, nodding his head with a smirk.

"Very good," he says.

My hands are twitchy, I have to clasp them in my lap. "What happens now?"

"We work out the fine print," he says.

ALEXANDER

Once I've shot my load over my faceless cleaner I can't fucking stop.

A day of shitty client meetings with a constant fucking semi, and not even my stint in the soup kitchen can ease the fucking cravings.

I watch porn until I my eyes are bleary, trying to come over any fucking thing other than the thought of choking her in her uniform, but it doesn't work. Nothing fucking works. My cock is sore and aching from my constant jerking, and yet nothing will tip me over the fucking edge.

In desperation I try a different search, one that makes my gut lurch.

Gay bareback rough.

Christ, what have I fucking become?

I'm minutes away from accepting defeat and checking out Claude's listings just to regain some fucking sanity when the guy on screen takes a big fat cock in dry, his face a grimace as it ploughs all the way to the balls.

And I come.

Thank fuck, I fucking come.

I'm a wreck. My thighs tense and straining, my temples pounding as I gather my breath.

This has to stop.

I've got to stop.

I take as hot a shower as I can stand, scrubbing myself down as though body wash has any chance of cleaning away my own disgust.

I browse my regular dealers for current listings of rare gemstones, and spend twenty-five grand without even thinking about it.

I take Brutus out after midnight and barely notice the rain.

I smoke three cigarettes this evening instead of one.

And then, when I finally slip between my perfectly folded back sheets, I find I'm fucking hard again.

I tell myself it's just one more time. Just once more that I'll allow myself to jerk off over that poor little oblivious cleaner. But I've come twice more already by the time I finally get some fucking sleep.

MELISSA

I try to remember everything as I prepare to tell Dean what happened with Claude.

It's late by the time we have a coffee and I've checked in on Joe. He's fast asleep, none the wiser of my crazy mission, thank God.

Sweet dreams, little one.

I kiss his head before I head out to face the music.

Dean looks terrible, pacing around the living room with his hands behind his head.

"I'm fine," I tell him. "Seriously, Dean, I'm fine."

149

"For now," he says.

I feel better for meeting Claude, as weird as that sounds. He didn't seem to think I'd be walking into a snuff movie, and if that's really what he has planned for me then he's a damn good liar.

Before I left he presented me with a ream of paperwork that made the NDA I signed before cleaning Mr Henley's house look like a love note. Why would he bother if I wasn't going to make it out of there?

I glanced over it at best, then signed Amy's name at the bottom. What does it really matter what it said? It'll either be Mr Henley that wins me or it won't. An epic win or an epic lose.

At least the twenty grand in Joe's trust fund will go some way to softening the blow.

That's how much I'm getting. Twenty grand for one night.

Claude asked me what my expectations were, said he could offer me a figure right there and then if I didn't want to risk losing out at auction.

I accepted his first suggestion, before he changed his mind. I've never seen anything like twenty grand, I've no idea what that kind of cash would even look like.

But I'll find out.

He says the client will pay me in the hotel room, assures me they will be good for it.

There are rules, of course.

I'm not to count it until I've left. I'm not to talk about money. I'm not to swap any personal details with the client whatsoever.

When the successful bid has been accepted I'll be notified of the appointment. I'll be sent the venue details, and I'll be booked into a hotel room for the evening.

My buyer will decide how they want me dressed and an outfit will be waiting for me in the hotel room wardrobe.

I'm to be shaved as per the client's preference. I'm to wear makeup in line with the client's preference.

I'm to do *everything* in line with the client's preference.

In the interim I'll have to undergo a medical at a private Harley Street clinic, and although it usually takes a few months for a satisfactory screening, Claude says mine will be cleared in days, what with me being a virgin and all. My bloods should be whistle clean, he said.

Dean listens as I tell him all this, shaking his head all the while.

The only details I leave out are the buyer options Claude wanted me to agree to.

A boob job and a labiaplasty should the client require it, at their expense. Apparently there will be a bonus expenses payment for that. A bonus payment should I leave the appointment with any marks which last longer than a fortnight, too.

I said I'll have to get back to him on the whole boob-labia stuff. I'm really not sure I want to undergo surgery for this craziness. I mean there's Joe to consider... and work... my actual work...

What if it isn't Mr Henley who wins the auction, and I have to leave my job for the sake of surgery that some other man thinks I need. I mean there's the money... but... I can't bear the thought of walking away from Mr Henley's house...

I daren't even think about that, so I don't, just assure Dean again that this is all going to be fine and I'm cool with everything, really cool with everything.

"You're fucking crazy," he snaps. "This is all fucking crazy."

I can't really argue with that, so I don't.

My auction will happen in just under a week, all being well. A Friday evening to leave the weekend clear. That's standard practice, Claude says.

Until then I'll wait.

Wait and dream.

SIXTEEN
ALEXANDER

It's great to see my boys on Sunday afternoon. They're wearing the new shirts I sent them, full of smiles at the prospect we can share this new football craze of theirs.

I play along, pretending to the best of my abilities that I'm as excited as they are by the upcoming fixtures, and it leaves me with no uncertainty that they're changing. Rugby is old news, and no matter how much I try to fight it, it's only a matter of time before I become old news too.

Football, and Hampshire, their *cool* older step-brother and new younger sibling on the way.

And Terry. *Cool* dad Terry.

This is their life now, and I'm… well, I'm still the same old workaholic they knew in London.

I'm pained as I make the drive back to the city, as though the final shreds of my soul are bleeding out through the cracks. It's been a long time coming.

My fingers feel dirty as they grip the steering wheel. The kind of grime no antibacterial gel can scrub away.

I've spent my entire adult life pulling the strings of those around me, as my father did. Still does.

Clients, judges, juries, boys' club fraternity members. The women I pay to serve me. The women I don't.

The people whose fate rests in these filthy hands and what I choose to do with them.

People may despise me for the outcomes I manipulate in order to fulfil my legal duty, but they respect my ability to deliver.

People do what I tell them because the alternative is unfavourable.

Plenty fear me, but not a single person who has truly known me has ever come out the other side loving me. Sad but true.

My boys still have that obligatory affection for their father that all young children have before they learn better. My boys will learn better as they get older, just as I did.

I'm feeling it already. My word is no longer God. My idea of *fun* is no longer their absolute benchmark for a good time.

Brutus stares out of the passenger window for the entire journey, giving occasional grumbles as though he's sorry to leave them behind too. I'm probably reading too much into it. Seeing things that aren't really there.

I've got into a habit of that lately.

It's another sad truth that having the house feel like more of a home is beginning to highlight the fact it really isn't one.

There's a sadness around the scent of fresh orchids tonight as I walk in through the door. Their delicate floral radiance unable to counteract the knowledge that someone was paid to put them here.

Paid to turn my bedsheets down and stock up my kitchen with necessities – as nice as they may be.

And yet there is still a fragile spark of hope in me.

It's dangerous.

Dangerous to feel touched by someone's consideration.

Dangerous to want more of it.

"What's she like, boy?" I ask Brutus as I eat yoghurt straight from the tub.

He stares at me, angling for whatever I'm having.

"Is she nice? Pretty?"

His lolling tongue tells me nothing other than he wants yoghurt too, and it's grotesquely adorable enough to let him lick the remnants from the pot.

I guess I'll have to find out for myself what she's like.

MELISSA

I've been poked and prodded and jabbed with needles at some expensive clinic in Harley Street, all paid for, no questions asked.

They said nothing about my general state of health, making no comment whatsoever as they weighed me, and took my height, and checked in my eyes and ears, and… *everywhere else…*

They asked me about my menstrual cycle and informed me I'd been listed to receive a contraceptive injection. I let them jab me in the ass with it without argument.

I'm just glad it's over as I race across town to finish up at Mr Henley's house after lunch.

I'm rarely out at this time of day, normally up to my elbows in scrubbing and polishing. That or playing with myself in his bed, although I'm trying to do less of that now. *Trying.*

My work handset shows me he's in court all day today, and my internet search this weekend told me he's got some big case going on. They showed a picture of him leaving the courtroom, steely and immaculate as his client – some rich oil tycoon – trailed behind.

I wish I still had the dream of being a lawyer ahead of me. I wish it was me in an expensive suit representing clients in court, the excitement of the trial, the hushed negotiations behind the scenes.

Maybe one day I'll be able to live the excitement through him, maybe he'll confide in me as we lie in bed at night, asking my opinion as he whispers client secrets in my ear.

Or maybe I'll end up trapped in a hotel room with some random guy who wants to fuck me up in exchange for twenty grand.

There's a sweet little street market open in Kensington as I head back to the house. I feel ok about glancing at the stalls today, feeling more presentable with my crappy uniform stuffed out of sight in my shoulder bag.

The clothes and jewellery are so out of my price range it's not even worth a thought, but there's a boutique cupcake stand at the far end, and I can't resist a quick look.

That's when I see it. A dark chocolate and orange swirled muffin with a vanilla yoghurt fondant.

I think of him.

Of course I think of him.

I don't care that it's unprofessional as I root in my handbag for my purse.

I leave it on the island as I finish up for the day, looking so pretty with its deep purple cupcake case. I make sure it looks inviting, placing it just so on a cute little stand I found in the cupboard, and cover it up with a clear glass bowl that I guess someone used to use for baking.

I hope I'm not totally overstepping my boundaries, hoping he'll forgive me rooting around his kitchen to leave him a gift.

My throat is dry as I tear out a piece of paper from my notebook, my fingers shaking as I find the right words.

Dear Mr Henley,

I saw this and thought of you. I hope it's even half as nice as your breakfast recipe.

Thank you for being so generous with your muesli.

MM.

I'm convinced I've made a professional faux pas as soon as I am back on the underground, but my calendar tells me it's too late to undo my mistake even if I wanted to.

ALEXANDER

I don't bother heading back to the office after court today. My driver picks me up as soon as I'm done, which is just as well since I narrowly avoid a pointlessly antagonistic run-in with Ronald bastard Robertson on the steps outside. I've got no time for his crap.

Nor have I any time for the congratulatory calls my father attempted several times today after the quarterly board report showed we're twelve percent up on last year's turnover.

It would have meant something once.

All of this meant something once.

Winning meant everything to me.

My head's fried with the whole sorry lot of it as I step through the front door, dropping the keys on the smoking table and giving Brutus a pat on the head as I make my way through to the kitchen for a glass of water.

I'm not expecting it. Not in the slightest.

The bacon was a thoughtful professional gesture, but the cupcake waiting for me on the cake stand is something entirely different.

I stare at it as though it's some kind of optical illusion, as though it may disappear in a puff of smoke and leave me gawping like a fool.

I read the note before I dare touch it.

Dear Mr Henley,

I saw this and thought of you. I hope it's even half as nice as your breakfast recipe.

Thank you for being so generous with your muesli.

MM.

She saw this and thought of me.

The strangest stabbing feeling in my ribs. A beautiful revulsion. A beautiful pain.

Thought of me.

I can't remember the last time someone thought of me.

I can't remember the last time I received a gift that wasn't a branded fountain pen.

I lift the bowl so carefully to uncover the cake.

Dark chocolate and orange.

I smile.

Of course.

Brutus grumbles as I tease down the cake paper, but he can grumble on.

"You're allergic," I tell him, and he cocks his head. "And you can go fuck yourself, boy, this is all for me."

Sinking my teeth into that muffin is the greatest culinary pleasure I've ever experienced. Not because I have a particularly sweet tooth, and not because I'm even particularly hungry, but because it's such a thoughtful gift.

A vanilla filling. Thick, like creamy yoghurt.

My smile grows wider.

She thought of me.

MELISSA

An email from Claude tells me my medical was satisfactory. I'll be up for auction on Friday evening.

I wonder how it works, trying to shake off the horrible little fear that Alexander Henley won't even be there to bid. He'll be out on the streets, dishing out hot meals, nowhere near the Chelsea saleroom.

But Claude would know that, there must be… early bids, remote bids… I'm not sure how it even works, but I'm sure it does.

I breathe.

I'm definitely sure it does.

There's a breakthrough today as I step through the door. Brutus comes padding up before I've even deactivated the alarm, and his tail is wagging. It's actually wagging.

I dare to ruffle his ears as I grab him a fish stick and he doesn't even flinch.

He likes me. For real, he likes me.

And so does someone else.

The sob chokes as soon as I see it, a crazy sense of excitement zipping through me at the sight of a plate on the kitchen island.

It's a cookie. Chocolate chip and topped with pink icing.

Thank you it says in iced yellow letters.

There's a note, but it takes me a few moments to calm down enough to read it.

MM,

Touched, genuinely.

I saw this and thought of you.

With my thanks,

AH.

It's the greatest cookie I've ever eaten in my life.

SEVENTEEN

ALEXANDER

Every evening I receive a gift.

A cake, a fresh pineapple, a bottle of freshly squeezed orange juice from the health-food deli two streets down.

Every morning I leave one in its stead.

A Belgian truffle, a tub of candyfloss, a selection of vintage cheese.

Finally, on Friday morning, I leave her a bottle of wine.

It's an expensive one, thoroughly extravagant. Ridiculously extravagant.

I write her a note along with it telling her to enjoy her weekend.

It's the craziest phenomenon, how this little gift exchange brightens my disposition.

I've been excited when I walk in through the door at night, smiling as I set out her daily surprise on the kitchen island before leaving for work.

So it's no surprise that I'm feeling the disappointment now the weekend looms, knowing the house is about to turn cold again.

that proves to be a fucking pain in the ass to boot.

Board meeting. My disgusting father nodding at me across the meeting room table.

He accosts me as everyone leaves, insisting I stay behind as I stare pointedly at the clock on the far wall. I'm supposed to be meeting Mr Rand at his office in forty minutes for a Friday night celebratory social. I hate those at the best of times, but right now it feels pretty damn inviting.

"What?" I snap. "I've got places to be."

His smile is sickening. "Yes, so do I. Auction, yes?"

I stare blankly. "Auction?" And then it dawns. Claude's seedy fucking new meat offering.

My cock twitches instinctively at the thought of getting some fucking snatch, but I don't care today. I don't care at all.

"Have you seen the lots?" my father asks, and his eyes sparkle with delight.

It sickens me. I tell him so.

"Get off your fucking high-horse, boy. We both know you'll only last so long."

"We'll see about that."

He laughs. "Yes, we will. It's at eight. Don't be late."

I hate the way he has such little respect for my resolve.

I hate the way he has such little respect for *me*.

"A bit old for little girls aren't you, old man?"

"I do just fine, thanks for your concern." He leans in close and it makes my skin crawl. "Nothing a few little blue pills can't remedy. I can hook you up, if you like?"

I shunt past him without the grace of a response, and my heart is thumping, hands so clammy I repulse myself.

I wipe them down as I head to the car, and my breath is shallow, raspy.

Panic.

I'm on the edge of a fucking panic attack.

It amuses me so much I stop to laugh.

A fucking panic attack.

I haven't had a panic attack since Geoffrey Rogers smashed a cricket ball into my temple and I thought he'd smashed my skull in. I was twelve.

It won't ease off as I get into the car, not even after a minute of staring blankly through the windscreen and breathing in to seven out to eleven.

I call Brenda, she answers in two rings.

"Mr Henley?"

I tell her I've changed my plans. Tell her to inform Mr Rand that we'll have to reschedule.

I give her no time to drill down into detail, just hang up and scroll through my weekly schedule.

I'm marked out as busy for at least another ninety minutes, time enough to get home before rush hour.

Which means…

And I get it. I get the panic attack. I get the urgency of having to cancel Mr Rand's silly fucking social.

I'm officially losing my fucking mind as I put the car into reverse and get the fuck out of there.

MELISSA

I'm absolutely crapping myself knowing that tonight's the night my fate will be decided.

I've made preparations, spending a chunk of my latest wages on setting up life insurance and writing out one of those stupid standard legal templates to set up a will naming Dean as Joseph's legal guardian should I…

Well, just should I…

I don't want to think about that.

Mr Henley has left me a bottle of wine, I choose to think about that instead.

I wish it didn't have to be this way. I wish I could leave him a note telling him that my name is Melissa Martin and I've loved him since I was fourteen.

I wish I could tell him that it was my dream to be like him, and I'm sorry we had to meet this way, but to give me a chance, just one little chance to introduce myself.

I wish I could tell him that being in his house is the greatest honour, and I'd give anything just to share breakfast with him, just once in person.

But I don't.

I can't.

Because tonight Mr Henley will be seeing my face on some seedy auction screen. Tonight Mr Henley will be seeing my spread pussy and my sparkly heels, and listening to all the things I said to Claude last week.

I'm just Mr Henley's cleaner, and Mr Henley is a kind employer.

I don't want Mr Henley to be a kind employer, I want him to be the man who takes my virginity.

And that's why I can't take the bottle of wine from him. It's vintage. Expensive.

It's too much for a lowly little cleaner like me, and I don't want to drink it without him.

My note is simple this evening.

Dear Mr Henley,

You are too generous.

Thank you, but please enjoy the bottle yourself.

MM.

I hug Brutus without even thinking about it as I prepare to leave and he stiffens but doesn't growl at me. I slip him an extra fish treat and ask him to wish me luck.

My Henley's calendar shows some work social thing, but I want to get across the city in time to avoid rush hour.

I want to cuddle my baby brother and forget my body is about to be bid on by a roomful of strangers.

And then I shall wait for the verdict.

Terrified.

I close the door behind me and step into the cool twilight, bracing myself against the chill. The street is quiet and I smile as I realise I really have missed the rush hour.

In half an hour I'll be snuggling up with Joe on the sofa playing choo-choo trains as Dean puts the kettle on.

The glow of headlights behind me makes a long shadow of my silhouette, and then they swing away onto a driveway. And I know. I just know.

I stop.

Wait.

I dare to glance back over my shoulder in time to see Mr Henley step out of his Mercedes.

I'm too far away to see him clearly, but I want so desperately to watch him make his way inside.

I take a couple of small steps back towards his house, close enough that I see he swings the door open quickly, with an urgency that hitches my breath.

This is risky. Too risky.

I've resumed walking when I hear the thump of his front door for a second time.

The hairs on my arms stand up, my throat tight and scratchy as I pick up my pace.

Please don't see me like this, please don't.

I stop dead as I hear him call after me.

ALEXANDER

She's not here, but the alarm is still running through its activation cycle, so she's close. Really fucking close.

I just want to see her.

I want to look her in the eye and thank her for her gifts.

I want to tell her she's doing a great job.

I want to ask what her name is.

I want to ask her her life story.

I want to *know* her.

The door slams behind me as I dash back into the street, and I know I'm acting like a crazy. I know I'm out of my fucking mind.

And there she is, a tiny figure in stripy green walking away towards the underground.

"Hey!" I shout, and I feel like such a fool. "Miss Moll..." *Fuck*. That's not her fucking name.

Fuck.

What the fuck do I fucking shout?

She stops.

And I'm scrabbling for words, pacing towards her without a fucking care for how deranged I look.

What the fuck do I say?

Hey, Miss fucking cleaner? Hey, MM. Come and say hi to your idiot fucking boss.

I'm trying to find the right fucking words, trying to get this crazy fucking impulse under control and not appear like an absolute fucking crazy when she keeps on walking.

She hears me and she keeps on walking.

It fucking floors me.

I stare in horror as some poor freaked-out little employee makes a dash for it, and I know I'm way out of line.

So out of line I can't do anything other than stumble back to my front door.

Jesus Christ.

My head spins.

I'm a head case, a fucking lunatic.

My fingers fumble with the door handle and I barge back through to safety on the other side.

I head straight through to the kitchen to splash myself with cold water, and that's when I see the bottle of wine still on the island.

I tear into the note.

Dear Mr Henley,

You are too generous.

Thank you, but please enjoy the bottle yourself.

MM.

I laugh a bitter laugh.

Of course.

She doesn't want the wine.

She doesn't want to fucking know me.

She's just a woman doing her job, and I'm a fucking imbecile.

An imbecile who's too much of a fucking addict to think straight. This cold turkey is sending me fucking nuts.

It has to stop. Right fucking now.

I fire off an email to the New Start volunteers, telling them poor Ted can't be there tonight.

And then I call up Claude's messages.

It's time to put a stop to this craziness.

EIGHTEEN

MELISSA

Walking away from him breaks my heart.

I feel it shatter into pieces, my belly churning as I rush down to the underground and away from there.

I want nothing more than to change my mind, turn on my heel and batter his front door down, apologise for my rudeness and beg his forgiveness.

But I can't.

Because in a couple of hours' time he'll be seeing my naked body on a screen somewhere, if he hasn't seen it already.

I'm all in, committed to staying the course, committed to whoever wins this auction tonight.

Please God, let it be him who buys me.

Please God, let him show mercy on his rude cleaner and let her keep her job.

My cuddles with Joseph soothe my heart enough to breathe through the panic.

Dean makes me a coffee and joins us on the living room floor, resting his head on my shoulder without words, knowing just as well as I do that my fate is about to be decided somewhere across the city.

I'm glad he's my best friend, my constant in this craziness.

We put Joseph to bed together after dinner, and I slump down exhausted on the sofa, beyond hope that my mastermind plan is going to work out well. I snuggle up to Dean and he puts his arm around my shoulders. There's a difference in him, an acceptance. I guess he's as exhausted as I am.

And that's when he says it, just a whisper in the darkness.

"I get it," he says. "I get why you're doing it. You've been through so much, lost so much."

"I'm scared," I admit, and he sighs.

"If it's not him, you get out of there, fuck the money."

I nod, but I know it's not going to be that simple. There's no way it will be that simple. You don't just walk away from crap like this, not from people like this.

"Would *you* do it," I ask, "for twenty grand?"

His breath is on my hair. "Henley?"

I nod, and feel him smile.

"Hell, Lissa, I'd probably do Henley for free."

ALEXANDER

I'm contemplating Candice or maybe Elena. Maybe even that perfect little slut Britney Jane if she's available.

It doesn't really matter, I just need to pound my cock into some tight little pussy and wrap my fingers around her throat.

I've got a backlog of messages from Claude, some new girls, some older offerings whose exclusivity agreements have expired. None of them interest me in the slightest.

I sigh and check out the auction listings. Five pieces of hot new pussy ready to go to the highest bidder.

A pretty dark-haired girl with blue eyes, nice, but literally every single fucking box has a tick in it.

A chubby little redhead with a cute smile, she's a definite maybe, but the app tells me there have been ten pre-interest bids on her already, and she won't do anal. Fuck that.

A natural blonde with ridiculously unnatural tits. No. Definitely not.

A girl who's going for the sexy librarian look but failing miserably. She's no fucking librarian. No fucking way.

And the final listing. The hot piece of the evening. A certified virgin with hundred grand reserve, Jesus Christ.

I click on the link and up comes her image.

It stops my fucking heart.

She's young, maybe early twenties, big pretty eyes staring up at the camera. She's in pink underwear that doesn't fit very well, a soft innocence on her face that belies her surroundings.

Her light blonde hair is cut in a jagged style, her body petite and pale.

Like Debbie Harry.

She looks like a young Debbie Harry.

My cock twitches and I'm smiling.

I'm a teenager again, jerking myself crazy over the tatty posters on my bedroom wall. Fuck knows how many times I've come thinking about fucking that woman. I've still got the posters somewhere, folded up in a storage box for prosperity.

And here she is, a good enough replica that my cock's already pulsing.

I need this. I really fucking need this, virgin or not.

I call Claude and he answers after a single ring.

"I was wondering when you'd grace me with your voice," he laughs.

I'm not in the mood for jokes.

"I want the virgin," I tell him. "How much? I'll get it transferred."

He ums and ahhs, acting like he's in a real fucking corner. "No can do, I've got pre-interest. A *lot* of pre-interest."

"Fuck the pre-interest," I snap. "Just give me a fucking price, don't be a prick."

"Bidding starts at eight," he says. "I'll see you there."

I haven't got time to argue before the cunt hangs up. I curse the fuck out of him and then I check my watch.

Twenty fucking minutes to get to fucking Chelsea.

I grab my fucking coat.

I pull into Claude's bastard saleroom car park, piling out of the car with a haste that revolts me.

A doorman lets me in when I rap on the front entrance, then locks up behind me.

"Mr Henley, sir."

I wave him away and pace on through to the back.

Everyone is already assembled, at least fifteen men from my social circle with their crappy bidding cards in the air for the librarian girl. Fifty grand she's going for.

They are welcome to her.

I ease myself into the back of the room, hoping that nobody gives me a second glance, but old man Kennedy, one of the senior players at the House of Lords, clocks me in the corner of his vision. A nudge to his associate and a smile in my direction, and the whole room is alive with whispers.

My father turns his head, and the grin on his face makes me sick to the stomach.

He heads in my direction and I bristle when he clamps a hand on my shoulder.

"Good call, boy, I knew you'd make it. You here for the librarian, nice piece of pussy, isn't she?"

"I'm not here for the librarian," I sneer, and his eyes light up.

"Of course, Blondie, yes." He tips his head. "You'll be going up against your old man, Alexander. I've got my eye on that one."

The idea makes me seethe. "Back off," I hiss. "I get first choice, remember?"

He shakes his head. "Not this time, boy. Not when there's a pretty pink hymen on offer." He laughs and slaps my back. "May the best man win."

There's no best about it. I try to shrug off the disgust as he heads back through the crowd.

I'm about to walk away on principle, fuck this whole fucking spectacle, but the hammer comes down at sixty-five grand on the brunette, and the next lot flashes up on screen.

Amy.

Twenty-one.

Virgin.

No limits.

I have to look twice at the screen to make sure, but it's right, Claude confirms it in his summary.

No limits, not a single one.

My throat is bone dry as they play her intro video, and I know the girl shouldn't be here, she's too innocent, much too innocent. The nervous sparkle in her eyes, her shy smile.

I can barely look, but I can't turn away.

She's absolutely fucking beautiful.

She tells the camera she has no limits, none at all. She tells the camera she's a virgin. She tells the camera she wants this.

Claude zooms right in on her untouched pussy like the seedy cunt that he is, and she's perfectly imperfect, her pussy lips puffy and uneven. Her tits aren't perfect either, natural and fleshy with tight little pink nipples.

There's an intimacy about her that makes me uncomfortable as I watch her play with herself on screen, as though she's staring right into me, right through me.

I have to swallow a weird lump in my throat as she wraps her fingers around her throat and tells Claude that's what she likes, and I nearly come in my fucking pants, right then and there in this disgusting fucking place with these disgusting fucking people.

The bidding starts before I've even regained my fucking clarity.

One hundred grand.

One twenty.

One two five.

My father comes in at one fifty.

I head him off at two hundred grand, my eyes meeting his and hoping my stare burns him to fucking death.

He nods. Two twenty.

Two fucking fifty, I say.

Another bidder, some idiot who can't see what's going down here. Two sixty.

Three hundred grand, my father says. *And let that be a fucking end to it.*

But no, no fucking way.

"Three twenty," I say to Claude.

My father tips his head. "This girl, she'll have a tit job, yes? And get those dangling fucking pussy flaps trimmed off?"

I could kill the sonofabitch with my bare hands as Claude responds in the affirmative. "Buyer's expense, of course."

My father nods. "Three fifty."

"Four hundred," I counter.

Claude's eyes widen, a greedy smile on his face as the room murmurs. It's safe to say everyone else is out of the running.

"Four-fucking-twenty!" my father shouts. "Don't be a fucking fool, boy!"

But I am a fucking fool, a fucking fool with a raging hard on in my fucking trousers and an unstoppable desire to block his chances of ever laying a finger on that poor girl.

"Five hundred grand!" I snap.

The room goes silent. Dead silent.

Claude's gavel hangs paused in the air.

My father shrugs, laughs to the crowd. "He used to have a crush on Debbie Harry, silly little teenage thing."

The rooms laughs with him, but I don't care. I'm past fucking caring.

"Five hundred grand," Claude says. "Any further bids?"

Once, twice, three fucking times, and the gavel comes down with a bang that makes my heart soar.

NINETEEN

ALEXANDER

I've paid a cool half a million for one night with some little blonde slip of a girl who doesn't know what the fuck she's signed up for.

I think my fixation with the cleaner was less insane than the craziness I'm involved with now, but that doesn't matter. My heart soars, and it's a welcome rush.

It would have been worth it just to win the standoff with my cunting father, but there's more to it than that.

Amy.

She excites me.

The prospect of pushing her limits excites me. It's base, and thoroughly immoral, the intent to corrupt something so innocent, but this is not a charity endeavour. I'm going to take my money's worth.

The only saving grace is that she'll spend her first time with me and not my father. She's dodged a bullet there, one she'll never be aware of.

I fill in the specification form as soon as I'm home, listing my preferences for tomorrow evening. My criteria is easy. Simple.

Wear whatever she likes.

No preferences on makeup, or waxing, or what kind of scent she has on.

I want her, as her, exactly as she is.

Claude's message tells me he'll confirm ASAP, within the hour.

Good.

I'll be waiting.

MELISSA

Both Dean and I jump to attention as the email alert sounds on his phone.

I can't look. I really can't look.

I ask him to read it for me, perched on the edge of the sofa with my heart in my hands.

His fingers are shaking as he calls it up, his voice croaky.

"Tomorrow night."

I can feel my heartbeat in my temples. *Tomorrow*. I really didn't think it would be so soon.

"Does it say anything else?"

"An instruction box with client preferences."

"And?" My eyes feel like dinner plates.

"And it says none."

"None?"

He turns the screen and I scour the text. He's right, it says none.

"So I wear what I like?"

"I guess so."

Guess. I can't believe we're guessing over something like this.

"What do you want me to do?" he asks. "Reply or... it's not too late to change your mind..."

I take the handset from him. Click the button to confirm my availability.

"I guess I'll hear more before then."

"Before you rock up to fuck some random in a hotel room somewhere? You'd fucking hope so, Lissa."

I nod.

He's right.

The confirmation goes through, and I wait.

It's all I can do.

ALEXANDER

She's available.

I scan Claude's suggestion. *Harley's Tavern. 8pm.*

But no. Not this time. I've used Harley's so many times over the past couple of years, but this is *different.* I don't want to take her first time in a place I've been so many others' *every* time.

No, I reply. *Book Delaney's spa.*

Reckless. Close to home. But I'm feeling it, dancing on the edge.

I'm not sure I care about falling off.

A ping straight back.

That'll be extra.

Cunt. Like I haven't paid enough already.

Fine. Let me know it's confirmed.

Another message. *This purchase also comes with compulsory five percent cash tip on the night. It's in the small print.*

Sure it is.

My fingers jab the handset as I type out my response.

Just fucking book it.

I toss my handset to the side.

MELISSA

Another email. I feel heady as I stare at the screen, weirded out by how surreal this is.

I'm expecting Harley's Tavern, of course. I've already looked it up again on Dean's phone.

I've scoped out the route on the underground, know just how to get there.

But no.

Delaney's Spa Resort. Kensington Gardens.

I'm shaking so bad.

"It's not Harley's," I tell Dean, and his eyes widen.

"Is that good or bad?"

"I don't know. But it's Kensington…"

He looks as stressed as I do. "That's gotta be good, right? Close to his house…"

I shrug. "I really don't know."

I scroll further down.

You're booked into room 216. Your client will be waiting in suite 12 at 8 sharp.

Dress to impress.

Ok. I breathe. Room 216. I guess I check in as Amy Randall. Cool. I've got that.

A couple more lines of text reinforcing the earlier rules about money, not talking about it, not counting it.

And then finally, one final little line.

Your client is Ted.

I remember Cindy's voice, so clearly. *He has a private email address, some random account under the name Ted Brown. It was open on his screen one day…*

A breath. A gasp.

Surely… surely it has to be…

A moment of staring at Dean in crazy, mute shock.

And then I dance around my living room.

I barely sleep a wink, but I feel ok for it, running on adrenaline and more than a bit of excitement.

Dean holds up a picture on his phone as I feed Joe his breakfast cereals.

I stare at the metallic crystal and take a breath.

"Native bismuth is known to be found in Australia, Bolivia, and China."

Dean nods. "Good." He holds up another.

"Moldavite, found in the Czech Republic. Known as the Holy Grail stone."

"You got it."

I've only got one final job on my list today.

We take Joe to the park to feed the pigeons on the way, and I soak up the sunshine, realising all over again that tomorrow I will be twenty grand better off, and not a virgin anymore.

Ted.

I pray to God it's really him. Really, really him.

I wish I had a bigger budget as I step inside the New Age shop on the corner of Barrow Street.

I pick out a couple of nice looking stones. A sparkling amethyst and a tiny little lump of garnet. A green banded malachite.

And an angel hair quartz, its sides so smooth. I roll it in my palm.

This one. This is the main event.

Dean takes it from me and holds it up to the light. "Nice."

I smile. "Angel hair, for good luck."

"You'll want it." He nudges me, then hoists Joe up on his hip.

I pay for my crystals and a little velvet pouch to put them in.

ALEXANDER

I count twenty-five grand from my safe in used bank notes.

I put the envelope in the case with my sex toys.

And then I choose my suit for the evening.

It's an easy choice.

Black, white, black.

I polish my shoes to a mirror shine.

I shower and shave.

I get dressed. I choose my finest cufflinks.

I let Brutus out for his final crap of the evening.

And then I go.

MELISSA

My choice of dress was easy. I only have one that's anything like suitable.

My sparkly heels clack loudly on the marble floor of Delaney's Spa Resort. I'm early, a good hour ahead of schedule.

I paste on my brightest smile as I head up to the reception desk, and I must look ok, because the woman behind the counter smiles right back.

"Amy Randall," I tell her. "Room 216."

She taps on her keyboard, then scans a keycard. "Welcome, Miss Randall. Your room is on the second floor. Do you need a porter for your bags?"

I don't have any bags. I feel myself burning up.

"No, no need," I bluster. "They're not arriving until later."

She hands my card over. "Enjoy your stay."

I can't hide my shaking fingers as I take it from her.

My room is incredible, huge and cream and modern. The lighting is low and sensual, the bed the biggest I've ever seen.

But I'm nervous. Too nervous to enjoy it.

I pace back and forth in my stupid heels, sipping water from the complimentary bottle in the minibar.

Forty minutes. Thirty-five.

Twenty.

Fifteen.

I check my makeup. Reapply my pale pink lipstick and fluff up my hair.

I check Dean's phone is on silent and screen-locked. I check I have my crystals and fake ID in my clutch bag.

I adjust my tits in the stupid lacy bra I wore for my video.

Five minutes.

Fuck.

Fuck, fuck, fuck.

I turn off the lights on the way out.

And I head up to the top floor.

The corridor is empty, the thick burgundy carpet soft under my heels as I head to the mahogany door at the far end.

Suite twelve. Its gold lettering looks so regal.

My belly is a twisted knot of butterflies.

Moment of truth.

I tap gently. Once, twice.

And then I breathe.

Please, God. Please, please.

The door opens so slowly and I see the cream carpet first. I don't even know I'm looking at the floor until I clock the freshly shined shoes, the tailored trousers.

The shirt I pressed yesterday before I left. The tie I hung on the inside of the closet.

He's immaculate.

Perfect.

I look up at the face I've been dreaming of, and I have to check myself, squeezing the clutch bag in my hands as though this whole thing is going to vanish into a cloud of dust.

His eyes are dark, his jaw tense as he steps aside to let me in.

"Amy," he says, and I can't stop staring, not as I brush past him and step into the room, my eyes wide open and fixed on his.

The door clicks shut.

"Hi," I say, and it sounds so lame.

I drag my eyes away to take in the room, and it's amazing. Everything is amazing. The lighting is low and warm, and there's champagne in ice on the dresser. I don't know what to do, so I do nothing, just balance on my stupid heels, shying away as he steps by so close.

I'm gripped by this terrible impulse, this crazy urge to gabble it all out, the whole thing, tell him who I really am, and how much I wanted this. I want to... I really want to...

"Champagne?" he asks, and I nod.

"Please."

He pours me a glass and my fingers touch his for just a moment, just like they did when he offered me his cigarette packet all those years ago.

There's a weird lump in my throat I can't swallow down, not even with a mouthful of champagne.

He doesn't take a glass for himself. He stands still and easy, his gaze piercing. *Judging.*

I realise in that one shuddery moment that he doesn't know me, and I know it's crazy that somewhere deep down I felt like he would.

His stare is cold and unfamiliar, his face stern and guarded.

Dangerous.

"I don't enjoy small talk," he tells me.

I nod. "Sure."

"You specified you had no hard limits. Is that true?"

My belly lurches. "Yes..."

I sip my champagne and try to ignore the disappointment inside. The horrible little spark of disillusionment.

I'm not the woman he left a *thank you* cookie for. I'm not the woman who ate muesli in his kitchen. I'm not the woman he chased down the street last night.

I'm not even the schoolgirl he shared a cigarette with outside the school gates.

I'm a prostitute.

I'm a hooker who's staring at the man she wants more than any other dream she's ever had, staring him right in his cold eyes and wishing hers weren't welling up.

"Are you ok, Amy?" His question is demanding, his tone is brusque.

"I'm fine, thanks."

I don't sound fine and I know it, my voice is thick with stupid tears that threaten to spill, and my legs are all shaky and pathetic.

"Do you want a moment?" He gestures to an armchair by the dresser.

I perch myself in the seat with my knees together, cursing myself for how ridiculously wrong this is going.

He looks unimpressed, reaching down into the minibar and pulling out a bottle of mineral water. He fills a tumbler and swaps it for the champagne in my hand.

"Amy, I'm going to ask you a question, and I need you to answer me honestly." He rests on the arm of the chair opposite and his tone is so curt.

Oh shit.

I nod, gulp down some water.

"Do you want to call this off? The door is right there, one chance only." He tips his head to the exit, and I feel myself pale.

"No!" I insist. "No, that's not what I want. Please. I'm just…"

"A virgin who's sold her first time to a stranger, yes."

His words hurt, a wash of indignation at the thought he assumes I'm so cheap. But why wouldn't he?

"That isn't… it…" I say. "I, um… I want this."

He smiles for just a second. "Amy, darling, you don't know what *this* is, I can assure you."

I'm losing him. I can feel my dreams unravelling and slipping away. And I can't let them. I can't let that happen.

I get to my feet, relieved to find my legs toughen up enough to hold me steady. I pace straight up to him, close enough that the gorgeous scent I know so well hits me in the temples, and I keep my eyes dead on his as I pluck the champagne flute from his fingers and raise it to my mouth.

He nods, ever so slightly.

I'm close enough to see the fine lines around his eyes. The faint shadow of stubble on his jaw. The tiny birthmark on his right cheek.

"I have no hard limits," I say. "I didn't lie."

He stares right through me. "Is that so?"

"Yes. I'll do anything you want."

"Anything I want?" His eyes are cold, and it hurts, but I'm excited. A flicker between my thighs that wants to throw myself on the floor at his feet and beg him to take me. Beg him to do it all, every dirty thing he's ever dreamed of.

"Anything," I whisper.

"Fine," he says. "Then let's do *anything* I want."

He takes the glass from my fingers and the clutch bag from my shoulder. He places them both on the dresser and takes me by the hand.

My fingers clasp his as he pulls me through to the bathroom and flicks on the light.

It's a harsh contrast to the softness of the bedroom, my eyes blink as I adjust.

His hand pulls from mine and lands on my shoulder, firm as he demands I drop to my knees.

He points to a spot at the side of the toilet, and I shuffle along until he positions himself before me, his hand on my head.

"Anything, Amy, are you sure?"

"Positive," I tell him.

He unbuckles his belt and steps closer, and my heart jumps. He takes out his cock, and it's bigger than I expected, much bigger than I pictured. He's already hard, the head of him swollen dark.

He takes a handful of hair and tips my head back, but my eyes are still on his cock, watching his hand move back and forth.

Transfixed.

I'm transfixed.

I want to touch him so bad but I'm scared. Scared I'll do it wrong.

"Look at me," he says, and I do. I do look at him, staring up into eyes that show no emotion whatsoever, even though my heart is spilling out through mine. "I'm going to piss in your mouth and you're going to swallow every drop, do you understand me?"

My poor heart hammers. "Yes."

I clench my thighs, and even though this isn't what I planned, isn't for a second what I dreamed of, I still want this. I still want *him*. Still want *everything*.

"I understand," I say.

"Open your mouth. Nice and wide."

I open my mouth nice and wide. Position myself right under his cock, my tongue out and waiting, my eyes on his, even though I'm so scared I could be sick, even though my nerves are jangling and my clit is going crazy between my legs.

I whimper as he presses the head of his cock to my bottom lip, but I don't pull away, not even for a heartbeat.

I take a breath, and grip his thighs to keep me steady.

"If you spill a single drop I'm going to make you lick it from the floor."

I stick my tongue out further ready to catch the flow.

"Are you ready?"

I nod, just a tiny tip of the head.

"Drink it all down like a good girl."

I keep my eyes on his.

I'm ready. I'm really ready. My fingers squeeze his thighs, my eyes wide open. *Do it. Just do it.*

"Very good," he says.

He turns away from me and aims the stream for the toilet.

I gawk in shock, watching that stream of piss as it lands innocently in the bowl.

"Did I do something wrong?" My voice is so pathetic.

"Not at all," he says, and shakes himself off. He fastens his trousers and flushes the chain, then lathers his hands in the sink and dries them off. "It infuriates me when people bluff."

"But I wasn't bluffing…" I tell him.

"Yes," he says. "I know."

"Then what?" I begin, but he cuts me off, taking hold of my elbow to lift me to my feet.

"It was a test," he tells me. "You passed."

"I passed?!"

He smiles and it's beautiful. "Yes, Amy. You passed."

I really don't think I should say thanks, so I don't. "Don't you want to… do that?"

He smirks. "Lord, no. What the hell do you take me for?" He steps back into the bedroom. "You haven't even finished your champagne yet." He gestures to the bottle still chilling. "Anyway, piss play isn't really my thing."

"It's not?" I think of all the porn I've seen at his house. All the times I've watched men pee all over women on screen.

"No. It's not."

I follow him out. "So, um… what now?" I ask, and I realise my breath is steadier. My nerves evening out.

"We start over," he tells me. "You can call me Ted."

TWENTY

ALEXANDER

It was a cunty move and I know it, but the girl was a wreck when she walked in through that door, barely able to string a sentence together.

Nerves and fear. An unpleasant combination at the best of times, not least when you're about to give your cherry to some random in a hotel room, I imagine.

As it turns out, *Amy* has steel behind those big doe eyes.

She's more beautiful in the flesh than she was on Claude's seedy video. She's unsteady on her heels, which indicates she doesn't walk on them often, and she keeps fidgeting with the fabric of her dress, as though she's not sure it fits properly.

It fits perfectly.

The light pink of the fabric highlights every slope and curve of her body. The pale flesh of her cleavage showing nicely, without being slutty.

I take a seat on the edge of the bed and pat the spot at my side for her to join me.

She sits down close, much closer than I expected, and I'm pleased my asshole f an initiation hasn't sent her running. She's far from running.

She looks strangely euphoric, shy but transfixed as she looks at me. Stares at me. The girl has been staring at me since she came in through the door.

"This is quite a way to spend your first time," I comment.

"I want this…" she begins, but I wave my hand.

"We're past that," I say. "I apologise if I scared you." I make sure my eyes are on hers when I deliver the next statement. "But I'm likely to do it again, and next time won't be a test. My interests are… extreme."

Her eyes are incredible, thick eyelashes that I want to feel flutter against my skin, even though I rarely go in for contact that personal.

"Will they kill me… these interests?" she asks, and the question is serious, delivered so matter of factly that it takes my breath.

"No," I tell her. "Of course not."

She smiles. Her smile is beautiful.

"Then I don't care," she says. "I don't care what you do to me."

She can't be serious, *shouldn't* be serious, but she is. There's a simple honesty in the way she angles her body towards mine. A calmness in her breath that I feel against my cheek.

I've paid a lot of money for this girl, but honestly, I'd have paid double for the experience I'm having right now.

I've needed this, *craved* this, someone like her. Someone *real*.

She feels so real to me.

I can barely believe this is happening.

"Is there anything you want to tell me?" I ask. "Anything you want me to know? About you, about what you like?"

She shakes her head. "No. Just please don't… hold back… I want it to be good… for you…"

Her words go straight to my cock. The soft tone of her voice brings out the demons, and it's been too long. Too long to keep control.

I should tell her to leave. Send this sweet girl away to a far more fulfilling experience with someone who isn't a filthy cunt.

"Please…" she whispers, as though she can read my mind. "I really want this…"

And I believe her.

I believe her when she leans in so slowly, her eyes open as she dares to guide her lips towards mine.

"I'm going to be rough," I warn her.

"I don't care…" she says.

And neither do I.

I kiss her, her soft lips so sweet as they press to mine. She opens her mouth without hesitation, her tongue yielding as she murmurs. I take a handful of hair and hold her tight, and her hand comes to my wrist, her fingers so light against my skin.

She kisses me back, her tongue circling mine as though she really wants me, her breath quickening as she edges closer.

I break the contact long enough to tug her dress up around her waist. She picks up where I've left off, hitching it up and over her tits, then tossing it free over her head.

She's wearing the same bra and knickers from the video, the underwire digging into the flesh at the side of her tits. Much too small.

I press a hand to her ribs and guide her backwards, and she falls so easily, reclining back onto the bed and bringing up her knees. I unfasten the buckles of her sparkly heels, and pull them free.

She has perfect ankles.

Perfect little toes.

I shunt her further up until she reaches for a pillow and places it under her head. I watch the rise and fall of her chest as she breathes.

I watch the damp patch on her knickers as she spreads her legs for me.

She wants me.

Fuck knows why, but she does.

MELISSA

He drapes his jacket over the armchair and tugs the tie loose from his neck.

I've pulled that same tie taut around my own neck and pretended it was him.

My pussy flutters.

I'm not scared. Not anymore.

I love the way he kisses. I love the taste of him. I love his breath on my face.

I love the way his fingers feel in my hair.

I love the way he looks so dangerous right now.

He does look dangerous. His eyes dark and wild and his jaw so tight.

He unbuttons his shirt and takes out his cufflinks. I lift myself on my elbows for a clear sight of him, and he's everything I dreamed. His chest is toned without being bulging muscle, a smattering of dark hair leading down to his bellybutton.

He takes off his belt and his eyes don't leave mine.

"Let me see you," he says.

I slip my fingers around my back, unclasping my bra without hesitation and tossing it away to the side.

He drops his trousers, and his cock looks even bigger than it did in the bathroom, jutting up towards his belly as he leans forward and takes hold of my knickers.

I squirm to help him, and he yanks them down and off, then spreads my legs to stare at my pussy.

I feel so exposed. Crazy exposed.

I can't believe this is happening as he climbs onto the bed alongside me. I reach out to touch him and his skin burns my fingers; I can't stop grinning.

His thumbs brush my nipples and it makes me moan.

His lips land on mine and I wrap my arms around his neck and pull him closer.

I'm a wriggling mess underneath him, his chest pressed to mine as my legs hook around his. His tongue is fierce and deep, the ridge of his cock grinds against my belly.

I want him inside me.

I want him to do it.

I try to position myself, spreading my legs nice and wide. But he won't. He won't do it.

He breaks the kiss.

"No," he says. "Not like this. Not yet."

Not yet.

My breathing is heavy, my senses reeling as he frees himself from my grip and lowers his mouth.

His tongue flicks around my nipple, and then he sucks. He sucks me.

Oh fuck, he sucks me so hard.

His hand trails down my belly and slips between my thighs, and I'm wet. I can hear how wet I am as he strokes his fingers around my clit.

He presses hard. It aches and tingles. His thumb rubs me as he sucks on my tit, and I'm delirious, my fingers in his hair, begging for more.

Begging.

Oh fuck, I'm begging.

I look down at him sucking my nipple, and his eyes are staring right back at me.

Oh fuck.

Oh please.

His tongue flicks, his thumb circles, and I can't stand it.

I can't.

I really can't.

It takes me by surprise when I come under his fingers. A rush of breath and a squeak, and I worry I'm going to pee myself as I shudder and jerk and thrash my feet around the bed.

My nipple plops from his mouth and he sucks his fingers instead, and then he slips them into my mouth.

"Taste," he says, so I do. I suck and suck until he tells me to stop, and then he brushes a thumb across my puffy lips. "Hold your knees," he orders, and I hitch them up to my chest. I bite my lip as his fingers spread my pussy, groaning as his tongue digs its way inside.

"Virgin pussy," he says. "You are a fucking delight."

"Take me," I hiss. "Please. Please... Mr, *Sir*... Take me..."

His eyes darken, and I know he likes it. I know he likes me to beg.

I beckon him up with my arms outstretched, but he doesn't come. Instead he yanks me sideways and flips me, pinning me on my front with my eyes fixed on his in the mirrored wardrobe.

"I want you to see this," he says, and I nod. "This is going to be rough."

I nod again.

His knees part mine. His fist in my hair tugs my head back. He lowers himself behind me and I feel his cock pressing against my pussy.

I didn't think I'd lose my virginity this way, not on my front, with Mr Henley at my rear about to fuck me like a bitch in heat.

It's supposed to be deeper this way... much deeper...

"Look at me," he says, and I do. "This will hurt," he says.

And it does.

It does hurt.

I cry out as he pushes in. A burn and a tear, and it feels hot, and deep. It hurts so bad it takes my breath, and my eyes well up.

He grunts as he pushes deeper.

So deep. I feel so full. Full of *him*.

I stare at him in the mirror. His big hands gripping my hips. His skin pressed tight against mine.

His dark eyes staring back at me, the slightest hint of a smile on his beautiful lips. "That's it," he whispers. "That's all the way."

Even though it hurts, I clench to feel him.

He grunts.

I clench again and it makes me moan.

"Fuck," he growls, and I want it. I want him to fuck me.

I want it to hurt.

I want to know I'm his.

"Do it," I hiss. "Please, sir, fuck me…"

TWENTY–ONE

ALEXANDER

The girl's pussy is a fucking dream.

I stay still as a fucking statue, catching my breath with my dick buried to the hilt inside that beautiful little slit.

She clenches and my balls tighten, ready to fucking blow.

"Do it," she hisses. "Please, sir, fuck me…"

Her eyes are hooded and hazy, fixed on mine in our reflection. Her pretty little tits move with her breath, her hair soft in my grip.

If she thinks I'm going to fuck her hard and fast to get this over with, she's mistaken. Very fucking mistaken. But I don't think that's what she's angling for.

The want in her eyes is all real.

She whimpers as I slowly pull out, sucks in breath as I ease myself inside her a second time, and I tug her hair, arching her back until her pale throat is exposed in the mirror. Her eyelashes flutter, and she turns her head as far as I'll allow, angling and her lips press to my skin, a gentle kiss that makes my stomach lurch. Like a rollercoaster. A fucking rollercoaster.

I let go of her hair and wrap my fingers around her pretty throat. She doesn't flinch, doesn't shy away as I squeeze just enough that she'll feel the pressure.

"Please…"

Her breath is a whisper, her open lips brushing my cheek.

I kiss her. A crash of my mouth against hers, deep and hard as her tongue comes forward to meet mine.

She shivers. Moans for me.

And it's strange.

Insane how my heart aches in my chest.

Insane how real this feels.

Insane how much affection I feel in this stranger's kiss, in the way her body yields to mine, the way she grinds her hips to meet my thrusts, even though it must hurt like hell.

I hitch up on my knees for more momentum, and she yelps but she's smiling. I kiss her temple and breathe into her hair, and my fingers squeeze tighter around her throat, holding firm as I pick up speed, opening that tight little pussy to take me.

And then I stop. Stop before it's too late. I pull out, my dick throbbing as her pussy fights my exit.

I flip her. She rolls so easily onto her back, her arms snaking around my neck as I lower myself on top. Her feet glide up my calves and hook around my thighs, her eyes staring right into mine, her smile so gentle.

As though she loves me.

And I'm lost, taken beyond my control, beyond any scrap of reason in my jaded fucking mind.

I've barely composed myself before my cock demands back in. One push and

I'm all the way inside her, propped on my elbows with this beautiful girl's eyes sinking deep into mine, and I can't stop kissing her. Can't stop myself slowing down to savour every crazy fucking second of this madness.

Her hands slide down my back, her fingertips gripping, teasing, feeling me. Her legs wrap around my waist and squeeze, urging me deeper, and there's no whimpering, no murmur of pain as I take her harder. Take her faster. Take every fucking thing from that gorgeous little pussy.

I'm getting close, my breath frantic as my heart pounds, and I can't fight the urges. I don't want to fight them.

"Trust me." My voice is a rasp. A desperate rasp.

And she nods. She fucking nods.

"Don't fight," I insist.

"I won't," she whispers.

And she doesn't. Not when I pin my weight on one elbow, not when my hand slides around her throat and grips tight.

Her eyes are just inches from mine, my breath on her face as hers stops.

"Trust me," I repeat.

Her chest strains, her mouth open as she struggles to take a breath, but she doesn't stop me, not even as she gasps for breath, over and over, she makes no move to stop me whatsoever.

And fuck, how I fucking fuck her.

I fuck her like a man fucking possessed, her body shunting under me as I keep my grip tight around her pretty neck.

She splutters, her eyes flashing involuntary panic, squirming just a little as she strains for breath that won't come.

I kiss her. Plunging my tongue inside her breathless mouth as she chokes for me.

She should fight, but she doesn't. Her hands grip my shoulders, her fingers digging in so tight, and I know she's struggling against the panic, struggling to let this be.

Her eyes are scared and raw, welling up with tears as she battles the urge to wrestle her way free.

And it's beautiful.

It's fucking beautiful.

I wait. Steady. So fucking steady.

I feel her going there, watch her so intently as she calms.

She smiles as she reaches the other side of panic, the quiet place I know so well.

"Trust me," I breathe, and she blinks. The tears flow.

I know she feels herself slipping, I know the pull of the void. Her fingers loosen their grip on my shoulders. Her eyes flutter, holding onto mine.

And then, in those final moments of consciousness, she strokes my face. Her thumb sweeps my cheekbone with a tenderness that defies reason, defies everything.

I count down from five, savouring the way she's slipping away from me.

And then I let her go.

She comes back in a heartbeat, gulping in a long rasp of air as her eyes come back to focus. I'm still inside her as she splutters, still inside her as she turns her head to the side and coughs and gasps and gulps until her breathing returns to normal.

I stroke the hair from her forehead, then tip her face to mine.

"Ok?" I ask.

The girl underneath me smiles, and then she giggles.

It's the most beautiful sound in the world.

"Do it again," she says.

MELISSA

I want to die in his arms. I want his eyes to be the last thing I see. His beautiful voice the last thing I ever hear.

But not tonight.

I'm euphoric, giddy as my breath returns to normal, and he smiles at me. He actually smiles.

I don't think he realises he's doing it, the lines at his eyes crinkling as he brushes the hair from my forehead.

"Ok?" he asks.

I smile back, because I am. I really am ok. Better than ok.

I giggle because this is crazy. This shouldn't be good, but it is. It's so good I can't stop grinning.

"Do it again," I say.

He's still inside me, and I love how it feels. I love how all of this feels.

"Soon," he tells me, and then he kisses me.

I love how he kisses me.

I love how he breathes into my mouth as he pushes in deep.

I love the way I've made him so horny. I've definitely made him horny.

It's different when he fucks me this time, frantic and desperate, his skin clammy under my fingers as I hold his face to mine.

"Please…" I ask, and I don't know what I'm asking for.

He does, because he gives it to me. Deep thrusts that make me cry out noises that don't sound like me.

I hold him so tight, my lips on his as he shudders and moans, and he's so close, his eyes right in mine, as I feel him lose control.

He tenses. Grunts. And I feel it. I feel him come.

I made him come.

It's only when he stops that I realise how sore I am. How tender my pussy feels.

It's only when he pulls away and pulls me up with him that I realise I've bled over the perfect white bedding.

Horror. I'm so horrified I try to wipe it away with my fingers, but the pink stain just smears worse.

"I'm so sorry…" I tell him. "I'm really, really sorry, sir."

My eyes are wide and scared as they meet his, because I don't want him to be angry. I don't want to disappoint him.

But he's not angry.

His eyes are dark, but they're not angry at all.

He stares so weirdly, and my heart races, because I think he knows. I think he knows who I really am.

"There's nothing to be sorry for," he tells me.

But he's still staring. Still thinking.

I'm burning up. My cheeks on fire as I bluster a smile.

"I'd better get, um, cleaned up a little…" I say, and head for the bathroom.

ALEXANDER

"I'm really, really sorry, sir."

I can't stop staring at her, can't tear my eyes away from the sweet panic in hers. The hunch of her shoulders as she frantically tries to wipe her blood from the sheets.

As if I give a fuck about the sheets.

She's beautiful. Too much of a delight to be real.

So it can't be real. *She* can't be real.

She tells me she'd better get cleaned up a little, and I watch her retreat to the bathroom. She smiles before she closes the door behind her, and it makes me smirk to myself to think of her dithery fingers wiping herself clean.

I plan to head in after her, but I need a moment. I've already clocked her bag on the dresser, and I'm straight over before she can catch me in the act.

I make sure the door is still closed before I undo the clasp and take a look inside. A purse, which I don't open. A phone with a locked screen, an older handset, nothing special. A lipstick, a hairbrush. A little velvet bag, some chewing gum, and finally, slipped into the hidden pocket, her passport.

I flip it open quickly.

Amy Leigh Randall.

Age twenty-one, just as she said on the video.

I note her address. East End, but not in too bad an area. Her photo looks older. Her hair is longer and light brown, her face glowing natural with barely any makeup.

I shove it back in her bag.

Amy Leigh Randall.

It's not a name I recognise. Not one that's ever crossed my path before – I'm good with names.

I smile to myself.

Her familiarity must be a welcome illusion, my mind playing tricks on me.

A lucky find. Fate some may say, although I don't go in for that shit.

I guess Claude just came through this time. I'll forgive him the extra charges after all.

This was the best half a million I've ever spent.

I turn the bathroom door handle.

MELISSA

Alexander Henley is in the room next door.

I can't believe this is happening to me. I can't believe this is real.

I'm still bleeding, but it's not so bad. It's pale now, and mixed with... *him*... his cum... and I didn't think it would be possible to want him any more than I did before tonight, but I do. I want him more than ever.

I never want this to end.

I touch my neck, run my fingers where his held me tight, and I smile.

I feel so alive. Never more alive than I did when I felt myself slipping away. Scary, and exciting, my heart pounding in my chest as he choked off my air, and then... peace.

Calm.

A blackness creeping in. My ears ringing.

And him.

I hope this isn't it. I hope we're not done already.

I'm wiping myself for the final time when the door opens. I clench my thighs when he walks in, and he sees me. He sees and he tips his head.

"Feeling ok?" he asks.

"Yes, thank you," I tell him. "I feel great."

I get to my wobbly feet and flush the toilet, so aware of how naked I am under the hard lighting.

He watches everything. The way I soap my hands in the sink. The way I shake them, then dry them on the hand towel. I watch him right back in the mirror, burning everything to memory. The broad strength of his shoulders. His dark nipples on his toned chest. The trail of hair over his belly, to his cock. His cock is still hard.

I'm pretty sure that means we're not done already.

I fluff up my hair before I turn to face him, trying to strike my most confident pose, even though I don't feel confident at all.

My skin prickles as he steps closer, tipping up my chin to examine my throat.

"No marks," he says. "Good."

I wouldn't care if there were. I wish I could find the words to say that without sounding like an idiot.

His hands rest on my shoulders, and I realise how big he is compared to me.

"You must be thirsty," he says.

I nod. "A little."

It makes him smile, and it's only fleeting but it's addictive. I love to see him smile.

"Come," he says, and takes his hands from me. "Champagne."

I follow him back through to the bedroom, hoping I'm not still dripping pink. He tops up my glass and hands it to me, and he toasts me with my glass of mineral water from earlier.

"To your first time, Amy."

"To my first time, sir."

He clinks my glass, and I drink down the bubbles. It's good. The champagne is really good. I tell him so.

He examines the bottle. "You like? I'm not much for champagne myself." He reads out the name on the bottle, some posh French word.

I shrug. "I'm not really much of a drinker... especially not the good stuff. I normally stick to juice. Less of a hangover."

He nods. "Indeed. I'm of the same mind myself."

Mr Henley takes a seat in one of the armchairs by the dresser, as though sitting naked in a hotel room is the most natural thing in the world. Maybe it is to him.

He gestures to the chair opposite him, and I sit, wondering what he's thinking. Wondering where this is going.

"What brings you here, to a stranger's bedroom, Amy?"

I smile. "I didn't think you enjoyed small talk."

He tips his head. "I don't, but I'll make an exception now we're... acquainted."

I shrug. "Not much to tell. I thought it was about time. I thought the money would be... useful." I meet his eyes. "I didn't want to be a virgin anymore. I thought this would be... memorable."

"And is it?"

"Memorable?" I feel the grin creep across my lips. "Oh, yes."

"And what now?"

"I hope we do it again," I tell him honestly. "The night is young, right?"

His dark eyes twinkle. "Yes. The night is young."

"And what about you, Ted?" I ask. "What brings you here?"

"A bad divorce and peculiar interests," he tells me. "That and a sixty-hour working week, plus the added bonus of finding almost every human being I come across thoroughly intolerable."

I nod. Smile. "Yep, I guess that'll bring you here. I hope I'm not too... intolerable..."

"Not at all," he tells me. "So far you've been thoroughly entertaining."

"So far so good." I laugh.

"So far so very good." He takes a sip of water. "Are you at college? Studying?"

I shake my head. "No. I wanted to be a lawyer, but I, um... it didn't work out. Maybe sometime soon, though."

"A lawyer?"

I practice my poker face. "Criminal, yeah. I'd love to be a criminal lawyer."

He smirks. "I'd rethink that if I were you. It's really not all that glamorous."

I let my eyes widen. "You're a lawyer?"

"I'm *Ted Brown*," he tells me, as though it's an inside joke. "I sell stationery."

"And what else does Mr Brown do besides sell stationery?"

He laughs a little. "Mr Brown strives towards world peace, and fucks pretty little virgin girls in expensive hotel rooms."

I laugh along with him. "Then I guess Mr Brown is very good at selling stationery." I gesture to our surroundings. "He must be."

"Mr Brown is very good at a lot of things." His eyes are dark again.

I take a breath. "I don't doubt it."

He opens the dresser drawer. My heart thumps as he pulls out a briefcase, one of the ones I know so well. He unclips the catches and I see the set of sex toys I've been thinking about non-stop since I found them in his bedroom. He hands me an envelope. A thick envelope.

"This gets the practicalities out of the way," he says, then lowers himself back in his seat.

I nod. "Thank you."

I realise this could be my moment. Maybe my only moment.

I take my handbag from the side and make a mountain of pulling my things out to fit the envelope snugly. I act like I'm clumsy, juggling my lipstick and purse in my splayed fingers as I slip it inside.

And then I let the little velvet bag tumble. I watch it fall, watch it bounce on the carpet between us, then scrabble for it as he does, making sure I'm a couple of seconds too late.

"Phew," I breathe as he hands it back. I jangle the bag. "Thank you. I really don't want to lose these."

He takes the bait. "These?"

I shove everything else away in my bag. "You'll think it's silly," I tell him.

"Silly?" He raises an eyebrow. "If that's a bag of white powder, then maybe so, yes."

I laugh. Then I tip the crystals out into my palm.

His poker face is good, but his jaw tightens.

"I keep them for luck," I tell him. "Stupid maybe, but I love them." I hold the little red stone up to the light. "This is garnet."

"From Rajasthan, I imagine," he says. He takes it from my fingers. "They mine most of the gemstone grade quality there."

My belly flutters. "You know about crystals?"

He holds out his hand and I offer him another, the green one.

"Malachite," he tells me. "They have the most incredible vase made out of malachite at the Hermitage Museum in St Petersburg. It's really very impressive."

"Have you been?"

"Yes," he says, and reaches for another. I give him the amethyst. "Very pretty. I have an extraordinary piece from Siberia. It's the very deepest purple. Stunning."

"You collect them? Really?"

"You could say that." His eyes meet mine. "What a coincidence."

I shrug it off. "Oh, I'm not a collector. I don't really have the funds. I just love them."

"Love them enough to carry them in your handbag." He smirks. "I may collect them, but I don't carry them around in my pockets, so I think you win."

I smirk right back at him. "I may carry them around in my bag, but I don't have an amethyst from Siberia. I think you win, Mr Brown, sir."

He tips his head, stares at the palm I've been so carefully rolling my quartz in. "And that one?"

"Oh this one?" I meet his eyes, determined to make him see what I want him to see. "This one's special. It's my favourite. I carry it with me, all the time." I laugh.

"Normally in my hand like an idiot. It's like my lucky charm."

He holds out his. "May I?" I hand it over gladly. My heart thumps as he holds it up to the light. "Rutilated quartz."

"Angel hair, yeah."

He squints as he stares inside, and he looks so serious. "This is a very nice specimen."

"Thanks." I will him to hold it in his palm like I did, will him to roll it in his fingers. Will him to like it.

He does roll it in his fingers. He really does. "I can see why it's your favourite."

"Nice, isn't it?"

"Very nice. I don't have one. I'll have to put it on my list."

I act surprised, even though I know his collection by heart. "You don't?"

"No. I've not yet had a specimen come up that I liked."

I shrug. "Guess I got lucky with mine." I hold out my palm, and he places the stone back in it, but my fingers grasp his before he pulls away and flip his hand over. I don't let go, not for a long moment. "Keep it," I tell him. "To remember me by."

He raises his eyebrows. "Oh no, I couldn't."

"Please," I insist. "I have more, at home. Maybe it'll bring you luck too."

I'm sure he's going to protest. His eyes burn mine, but my smile is easy. "Please, Mr Brown. I'd like you to have it. A memento."

Mr Henley smiles. A proper smile this time. It lights up his eyes. He grips the stone between his fingers and examines it some more. "Maybe I'll have to take to carrying one around in my pocket after all," he says. "For luck."

I raise my glass. "For luck."

When he holds it up to the light for a second time I feel it in my tummy.

Mission accomplished.

I down the rest of my champagne.

ALEXANDER

Extraordinary.

I run my thumb over the cold smoothness of the quartz, staring unapologetically at the delightful creature whose cherry I just popped.

I shouldn't take her lucky crystal. I should thank her for her generosity and hand it back, but I don't want to. It's so smooth in my palm, so pretty under the light. Not rare, or expensive, or even high grade. It's just a plain old tumbled-quartz gemstone from any old hippie shop in town, and yet I've not wanted a crystal as much as I've wanted this one for a long, long time.

I've not wanted a pussy as much as I've wanted this one for a long, long time either.

Her eyelashes flutter as she catches my gaze, her breath quickening as she registers my intent. She places her empty glass so gently on the dresser, then drops her other crystals back in her handbag.

My case is still open, my collection of toys in full view, and I feel like a cunt as she looks over them. I feel like a cunt for bringing them here to this girl's very first time.

She makes light of it. "That's an, um, interesting collection…"

I bluster it away, make to close it and take it out of view like it's nothing, but her hand lands on my wrist and squeezes.

She's close. Her eyes big and transfixed. Her breath shallow.

"Show me," she whispers. "Please."

"You've done enough," I assure her. "I paid for your virginity and I took it."

She shakes her head. "You paid for more than that."

"And I've already got my money's worth." I brush my thumb across her cheek.

"Really, Amy, you don't need to do this."

She shifts her weight onto her hip, and her eyes are hooded as she takes my hand and places it on her breast. "Please..." she whispers.

Her nipple is hard against my palm, she leans into me as I squeeze her, wrapping her arms around my shoulders as I pinch that beautiful pink little bud between my fingers.

"I want to see everything," she whispers.

"Everything?"

She nods. "You brought that stuff here for a reason, right?"

"Peculiar tastes, like I said. You've already sampled some of them."

"So show me the others." She murmurs as I palm her sweet little breast, pressing her hips to mine and pinning my cock to her soft belly.

"On the bed," I tell her, and she lets me go.

Her smile is beautiful as she climbs up and waits for me.

I slip the crystal safely into my jacket pocket before I join her.

TWENTY-TWO

MELISSA

I watch him as he slips the crystal into his jacket pocket, and my heart swells.

He likes it. He really likes it.

And my body really likes *him*.

My skin is shivery and sensitive, my belly a knot of butterflies as he heads over with the case in his hands. It pains me that he believes I'm here for money, but that doesn't seem to bother him, doesn't stop his eyes burning into mine as he climbs up onto the bed beside me.

I inch towards him, desperate for contact, and he runs his fingers down my ribs. They tickle my belly on their way between my thighs. I open wide for him.

"Are you sore?"

"Not too much." I flinch as he slides two fingers inside.

"I think that sweet little cunt's had enough this evening."

The disappointment pangs. "But I'm fine..." I insist.

He dangles a string of purple beads over my face. "No need to worry, Amy, I have many interests. Pussy is just one of them." He trails the beads down my body and the bumps tease my nipples. "I need you to hold your knees up for me, nice and high." I do as he asks without hesitation, and he lowers himself down the bed.

I'm nervous. My mouth dry as he taps the beads against my pussy. They're rubbery, heavier than they felt on the rest of me. His fingers splay my pussy and I suck in breath, hoping I'm not still bleeding. I gasp as his tongue flicks against my clit, moan as he sweeps all the way down. He digs inside, and then he sucks. He sucks my pussy and it feels so good my feet twitch.

And then he licks my ass, circling his tongue and it makes me squirm, makes me quiver as the tip pushes inside.

"Take a breath," he tells me, and I do.

I hear him spit on his fingers, craning my neck to see. His dark eyes are fixed between my legs, a look of concentration as he pushes one long finger inside.

It's uncomfortable but nice and I can't think straight, can't tear my eyes from the way he's staring at me.

"I think your sweet little virgin ass may be even tighter than your pussy." His voice is deep velvet, his words sound so dirty. "We'll find out."

He wriggles his finger and I moan and throw my head back. He slides it in and out and I'm his forever.

"That's so nice…" I whisper, and it is. It's really nice, even though it feels like I might need to go back to the bathroom.

I feel raw and open as he takes his finger away. I smile as I hear him spit again. It lands right on my asshole and my pussy tingles in response. I couldn't imagine a man like Alexander Henley spitting before tonight, but I love it. I really love how dirty he is.

The first bead is small, I feel the ridge sink in, and the next after. The third feels bigger, a bit of resistance before my ass lets it in. I hold my knees, grit my teeth as he pushes the next inside.

"Good girl," he says. "Relax."

I try. I try really hard.

"And easy does it," he says as he pushes hard on the next.

I grunt as it plops in. He follows it up with another and it makes me hiss.

"That's good," he tells me. "And again."

This one burns and fills me up. My toes curl.

"Last one," he whispers, and his thumb strokes over my clit. I clench my ass around the beads, and he likes that, I hear him moan as his tongue digs around the spot. It's still there when I feel the final bead against my ass. It's tight. So tight.

"Yes…" I hiss, and he pushes it in.

"You know what pleases me as much as filling up someone's ass?" he asks, and I'm sure he doesn't want an answer, but I meet his eyes anyway. "Emptying it again," he tells me, and then he yanks on the end.

The beads tug out in one long bumpy motion.

I arch my back, my knees dithering in mid-air as I groan. My breath is ragged, embarrassment burning at the sure belief I've just added worse stains to the ones I made earlier. I hitch myself onto my elbows to see, but if I really have made a mess he doesn't care. He lines the beads back up at my clenched ass, tells me to lie down as he does it again.

They go in easier this time.

They come out harder.

In and out. Burning. Filling me up.

I'm a grunting, wriggling mess, unable to control my spasming asshole.

I'm not prepared when he slides two fingers in, completely at his mercy when he circles them deep inside.

"Tight," he says. "Beautifully tight, but we'll remedy that."

"Please..."

He laughs so quietly. "I think we've found ourselves a dirty little girl."

He pulls something else from the case, but I don't see it. It's between my legs before I can tell what it is. I feel it, though. Feel the hard ridge of it pushing inside.

"Don't fight it," he tells me.

I won't. I won't fight it. I hold my knees high and spread wide, smiling down at him as his eyes scorch mine.

The cry from my mouth as he shunts it in surprises me, and that makes me giggle. He taps the base of whatever it is and it makes a funny slapping noise. I feel the vibrations right the way through me.

"A pretty little plug for a pretty little asshole," he says. "Now we just need to give it a while."

"A while?" I ask.

"A little while and that little hole of yours is going to be begging for cock." He smirks, and my tummy flutters. "Let's see what other delights we can discover."

I'm still holding my knees as he comes to my side. Still holding them high as he tilts my face to his and flicks his tongue across my lips. He pulls away as my mouth opens for him.

"You're a dirty little thing," he rasps. "Open wide." I open wide and he slides two fingers right to the back of my throat. I retch but he pushes them deeper. "Swallow," he says, but I can't. I retch again and he pulls them out, complete with a long string of spit. My ass tightens and whatever's in there makes me tingle.

"Sorry, sir," I splutter.

"No need for apologies," he says, and his fingers are ready again. I open my mouth without being asked, fight the urge to cough as his fingers push right back there. "Suck," he whispers. "Suck and swallow."

I suck. I suck as hard as I can, and he likes that, he presses his hard cock against my hip.

"Swallow," he insists, and I do. I swallow and his fingers are right there. It makes my eyes water. And then I retch again, harder this time. My mouth fills up with spit, so wet as he pulls his fingers free.

He kisses me before I've caught my breath, his tongue pushing deep as I splutter, and the kiss is wet, it's so wet.

"Now for my next trick," he whispers. "Time to fuck that pretty little virgin throat."

He shunts up the bed and rolls me towards him. His cock slaps against my cheek, and he takes my hair, angling me just right for his cock to press against my lips. I open right up, stick my tongue out as he pushes inside.

His cock tastes beautiful, so musky I just want to suck on it hard. The head strains my jaw as it pushes past my teeth. He moves, fast, and I'm like a ragdoll, gagging and choking as he fucks my face. My eyes are streaming, my hands gripping my knees so tight to my chest.

"That's right," he growls. "Don't fight it."

I won't fight it, not ever. I grunt around his dick as his fingers find my clit, and he rubs me so hard, so fast, making me gurgle wet noises.

I let myself go for him, giving him my throat like the dirty girl he wants me to be.

The dirty girl he needs.

I open my eyes wide, caring little for the tears rolling down my face. He looks divine from this angle, the shadow of stubble on his jaw, the crease of his throat as he stares down at me.

"Fuck," he growls. "Your tight little throat is going to empty me."

His fingers make me buck, make me squirm, make me clench around that hard toy in my asshole.

There's a warmth as he groans and thrusts deep, a saltiness at the back of my throat as he comes in my mouth. I fight the urge to retch with everything I've got, and that's good, because he's watching, he watches like a hawk as he pulls free.

"Swallow," he says, and I do.

I must look a mess underneath him, still squirming against his fingers as he pinches at my clit. My hair feels sticky, my skin clammy, my breath wild as I look up at the man who obsesses me.

He's the most beautiful thing I've ever seen.

He takes his time, staring down at me as his fingers work. He's steady, concentrated, his movements so skilled as my breathing quickens.

"That's good," he encourages. "Good girl."

I can smell him, his thigh pressed to my cheek, the scent of him so close. I can still taste him.

"I... I'm gonna..."

"I know," he says, and quickens his fingers.

And I do. I tip over the edge with my head lolling in his lap and my eyes open wide.

I come hard. So hard I thrash my legs, all thought of holding my knees forgotten as I ride the waves.

I'm still riding the waves as he pulls the thing from my ass and slips three fingers inside.

"Nice and ready," he whispers, and his body guides mine, rolls with me as he eases me onto my front and bears down on top of me. His thighs part mine, and I feel his cock stiffening as he presses it to my asshole.

"We're going to take this slow." His breath is on my ear. "Nice and slow."

I feel the head plop in, and he grunts.

He pushes forward and my ass takes him. I clench tight around his shaft just to hear him groan.

"Fuck me," I hiss. "Please, sir. Please fuck me."

And he does.

Slowly.

So fucking slowly.

My ass feels slack and hungry and so nice as his cock burns inside.

"Final act," he whispers, and it pains, the thought pains.

I twist my face to his and his mouth is waiting.

I kiss him like I love him because I do.

He kisses me back like he knows and it's so wonderful I could cry.

And then his hand clasps around my throat. I slide my arms behind me and lay my palms flat against his thighs. His grip on my throat takes my weight and my air with it.

I'm not scared, even if my body is. Even if my heart panics and races. Even if my lungs cry for breath.

I focus on the heat of his cock inside my ass. Focus on how deep he feels, how loose he's making me.

How much I want him.

I give Alexander Henley my breath. He takes it with his lips pressed to my cheek.

"Beautiful girl," he whispers, and I wish I could tell him how my heart feels.

My body knows what to do when he loosens his grip. He gives me air. One, two, three long gulps before he takes it away again. Over and over, breathing and choking, breathing and choking.

I could do this forever.

ALEXANDER

I keep her in the half light, coasting on just enough air to maintain consciousness.

I love the way her throat gurgles. I love the way she doesn't fight when it does.

I love the way her ass loosens up for me, and I love the way my cock slides all the way in.

This must be hurting. I know she's going to struggle to walk tomorrow.

I love the way she doesn't care.

One load left and I'll have taken my fill. Her sweet little asshole does its best to milk me dry, but I don't want this to end.

Her eyes are so blue as they stare into mine. They tell me she's all in.

It's more than I can resist. I'm going to come in her ass and I'm powerless to stop myself.

If I wasn't paying her I'd play with her sweet little body all night. I'd suck her clit until she couldn't take any more, and then I'd shower her, towel her dry and do it all over again.

But I *am* paying her. She's here because of the cash in her handbag, and her portion of the insanely generous half a million Claude will be depositing into her bank account.

I let her breathe. Press my cheek to hers as her breathing returns to normal, my cock still gliding in and out, my balls on the verge of blowing.

I shudder as they go. The ripples rush right through me, pumping my seed into her perfect asshole, my cock still twitching as I come down.

She groans as I pull out all the way. Groans again as I move away from her.

Her eyes follow me as I head to the bathroom.

I take a piss and freshen up, and she's still staring at the doorway when I return.

I smile as I pick up my shirt, and she shifts on the bed, winces as she moves to the edge.

My heart pangs with the urge to kiss her. It's so laughable it turns my stomach.

"So, um... what now?" she asks.

"You're free to go," I tell her.

"Okay," she says, and if I didn't know better I'd swear she sounded disappointed. The idea is ridiculous.

She's going to walk away from this experience with enough money to set her up for the next ten years and there's nothing I can do about the fact I'll most likely never see her again.

My sweet Amy will likely take the bonus twenty-five grand in her handbag and buy herself a stiff drink in the all-night bar downstairs. I only wish I could join her, but that's not what I've paid her for.

"Was I, um... okay?" she asks.

"You were more than okay. You were excellent."

Her smile is hollow. "Thanks."

"Thank *you*, Amy."

"You're welcome, sir. I, um... I really enjoyed it."

Polite. I like that.

I button up my shirt and she gets to her feet. She gathers up her knickers, bra and dress from the floor and retreats to the bathroom. I don't follow her.

I'm fully dressed when she returns, and so is she.

The tension is palpable, her fingers twisting in front of her as she struggles for the right words.

"Your room is booked all night," I say. "You could stay if you wanted." I put the toys back in the case and clasp it shut. "Or you can stay here, if you prefer. I believe this suite is better."

"I need to get home," she says.

"Yes," I tell her. "So do I."

I hate goodbyes. The emotional awkwardness disturbs me. I've normally made an exit by this point already, disappearing into the night with nothing but a curt thank you.

I take a step forward, and the sweet girl that she is closes the distance. She presses her tiny body flat to mine and wraps her arms around my neck.

I hate the way it makes me feel. Hate the way my heart quickens and that fucking lump comes up in my throat. I stiffen and she feels it. She pulls away.

"Thank you for everything," she says.

Money. Thank you for the money. That's what she means.

"Take your time, they do excellent room service here if you're hungry." I lift my case and head for the door, cursing myself that I didn't take one last taste of her pretty mouth before I was done. I stop before I turn the handle, take a moment to soak her in as she buckles up her sparkly heels. "Get yourself into a decent law school," I tell her. "There are plenty of firms who'd give you a shot with a decent degree under your belt."

I fight the urge to tell her that I own one of them.

She nods. "Maybe one day. I hope."

"Goodbye, Amy."

"Goodbye, Mr Brown, sir."

I close the door behind me.

MELISSA

My fingers are shaky as I call a taxi from Dean's phone.

I head through reception quickly, taking just a moment to leave my key card on the counter.

I don't say a word all the way home, just stare out of the window, unsure whether I want to laugh or cry.

He was everything I dreamed and more, and then he was gone.

My heart breaks at the thought I'll never see him again, yet it soars at the knowledge I had him.

I can still feel him, everywhere. My body is fucked raw, battered and bruised, but I feel amazing. I'd do it all over again right now.

Dean looks out through the window as I step out of the taxi. He's already in the doorway when I climb the communal stairs to the landing.

He lets me through the door before he speaks, but as soon as I'm inside he's one long stream of questions.

Am I okay? Did he hurt me? Did he pay me? What was he like?

I pour myself a glass of water and drink it down in one before I answer, and then I take the huge stuffed envelope from my handbag. His eyes are like dinner plates.

"No fucking way."

I nod. "Yes way."

"Have you counted it?"

I shake my head. "You can."

He takes it from me and I smile as he dashes through to the living room. He clears the coffee table and tips out the notes. Jesus Christ, no wonder my handbag was so heavy on my lap in the taxi.

He flicks through one bundle. "These are thousands." I watch as he stacks them up. "Twenty-five. Shit, Lissa, he's given you twenty-five fucking grand."

My heart pounds. "But that's too much."

"There's twenty-five here," he says. "Count for yourself. Fuck."

But I don't want to. I don't want this to be about the money, even though it is. I'm going to treat Joseph to a brand new trainset, and maybe a nice meal or two for the three of us, clear my credit card of the excess, and then I'm going to deposit the rest in Joe's trust fund.

"What is it?" Dean asks, and I shrug. "Did he hurt you?"

I wince as I take a seat beside him, but it's not that. I tell him I'm fine.

"Then what?" He holds up a bundle of notes. "Lissa, you just earned twenty-five fucking grand."

"I would've done it for free."

He squeezes my elbow. "But you didn't. You got so much money. You could quit the cleaning, go back to college…"

I smile. "I'm not going to give up the cleaning. This is all for Joe."

He nods. "Sure. So it's for Joe's trust fund, that's still good, right?"

It is good. It's really good. I force this silly mood away. I'm pining before the night's even over, and it's stupid, it's really stupid.

Dean clocks the change in me. He turns to face me and his eyes are wide and curious. "So what's he like?"

The grin comes from nowhere. "He's amazing."

"No danger of going off the guy then." He pauses. "Spill. What did he do?"

My cheeks burn at the memory. "Gory details?"

"Hell yeah." He grins. "Gory details."

I give him gory details. I give him every detail. Every single little squirmy one of them.

He hardly looks away as I recount the whole lot of it, and he's shifting in his seat, clearing his throat when I talk about how rough he was, how hard he fucked me.

How he took my asshole and made it feel so good.

"Shit," he says finally. "You really earned your fucking money."

"I'd do it for free." I smile. "And you would, too."

He shrugs. "Don't know about that," he says.

But I do.

I'm absolutely positive.

TWENTY—THREE

ALEXANDER

I keep that tumbled stone in my pocket right through my Sunday afternoon with the boys. I roll it in my fingers while they eat their shitty burgers. I grip it tight in my palm as I hug them goodbye. And I grip it tight all the way home.

I tell myself I'll put the stone in the cabinet with the rest of my collection, but it's on my nightstand when I slip into bed, and back in my pocket in time to leave for work in the morning.

Amy Leigh Randall. Brooklyn Road, EC1.

I have a good memory for detail.

I hold it up to the window in my office. Examine every little inclusion. *Angel hair.* Blonde strands, like hers.

I remember how she smelled. How her eyelashes fluttered. How her tight little pussy gripped me so perfectly and sucked me dry.

And then I talk some sense into myself.

I shove it away in my desk drawer amongst my gifted fountain pens, just another useless gift that means nothing whatsoever.

So she likes crystals? Big fucking deal. A lot of people like crystals.

She probably thinks they transmit some ethereal energy from Heaven above. She probably rests a piece of malachite on her forehead and chants some *zen* bullshit to ward of headaches, leaving her little bag of stones under the light of the full moon to charge up their *juju*.

I don't have time for mumbo fucking jumbo.

I take my meetings. I scan through reams of court paperwork. I threaten people with the full weight of the legal power invested in me, calling in shitty back-hand favours behind the scenes to ensure a favourable outcome for my asshole clients. Just another week of the same old grind with the same old people lying through their teeth about the same old things, as though I haven't heard every excuse for piss poor behaviour a thousand times before.

Sweet little Amy should sit in my seat for a week – that would be ample enough opportunity to rethink her career goals.

Maybe a week in my shoes would make the prospect of selling me her pussy on an ongoing basis a more preferable option.

I've been thinking about it, of course – contemplating the likelihood of a repeat performance.

I'm not one for holding my breath, having paid her enough money to set her up for the long haul, and I'm certainly not one to expose myself to the embarrassment of a *thanks but no thanks*.

No. If she wants to barter a deal then Claude will be in touch. That's his job – just a standard middle-man peddling pussy for sale.

But when he calls me from his *off the record* mobile on Friday evening, catching me on my way across town to cook up soup with that pissing gemstone of hers right back in my pocket, the rush in my chest is anything but fucking standard.

MELISSA

Almost a week, that's how long it took for me to hear a peep from Claude Finch.

I figured I'd been substandard, that maybe Mr Henley had reported back I really wasn't as good as the other women on offer.

I'd told myself that was okay, that at least I'd *had* him, even just once, but I'd been fooling myself.

Being back in his house Monday morning was nothing but beautiful torture, deep breaths against his pillow nothing but fuel to my despair.

The notes stopped. The gifts stopped.

Everything stopped.

I smiled thinly as I dished up meals for the homeless on Wednesday evening, and faked my laughter while I played with Joseph at dinner time.

I even tried my best to hide my despair from Dean, settling down for coffee and TV at night with a shrug of the shoulders in answer to every question he asked about my day.

And then it had come – a call from *number unknown* on Dean's phone on Thursday evening. Someone asking for *Amy*, and there he was, Claude Finch, his voice clipped and professional, asking whether I'd be interested in relisting my *item* for general sale.

My reply was instant enough that Dean raised his eyebrows across the room. *Yes, please. Yes!*

And so I'd trekked across the city on Friday lunchtime to renegotiate the small print. I used the main entrance this time, and there was no lamplight in his back office, no video cameras demanding a performance, just Claude in his pinstripe suit, asking me to sign more paperwork.

I didn't even think to ask about money. The only question out of my mouth was whether I'd be assigned to Mr Brown again.

Mr Brown will get first refusal, Claude told me. *Standard practice.*

I'd nodded. Smiled. Tried to keep my cool, even though my knees were knocking under the desk.

Three grand an evening, that's what Claude offered, and I'd stared mute, trying to gather my dropped jaw from the floor.

The money was insane – dwarfing my monthly cleaning salary in just one evening, so much for a poker face – the overwhelm was written all over me.

"Yes. Thank you!" My words tumbled out before Claude could rethink his offer.

"I'll be in touch with Mr Brown. Please keep your weekends clear, he prefers a Saturday evening."

And so I waited.

I scrubbed his kitchen until my fingers were sore. Pressed his clothes to perfection and hung them so neatly in his dressing room.

I took Brutus on an extra-long walk and gave him an extra fish treat.

I replenished the orchids before I left for the weekend.

And then I went home to Joe and Dean.

ALEXANDER

"I've had a lot of interest," Claude tells me with greedy eyes. The man is like a pig in shit, leaning back in his chair with a grin on his face as he tells me he's contemplating another auction for Amy's next *appearance*.

"Fuck the fucking auction," I snap. The very fact I'm in his fucking saleroom at close to midnight on a Friday evening – dressed in fucking denim in my haste to get this shit negotiated – tells him everything he needs to know.

The slimy cunt has me over a barrel, and we both know it.

He offers me a whisky from his desk drawer. I wave it away. "Exclusivity is going to cost."

My stare is ice-cold, practiced and pointed from years in court. "Don't dick me about, Claude. I'm open to negotiation."

"Twenty grand," he tells me. "Twenty grand a session, exclusivity assured for a six-month initial term."

I laugh out loud. "Twenty fucking grand a session? I could hire Elena ten times over."

"And Elena is average stock," he tells me. "We both know it."

"That's not quite what you said when you presented her."

He shrugs. "Elena is Elena, Candice is Candice. Amy is…"

"No longer a fucking virgin," I finish.

"*In demand,*" he tells me. "I've had five enquiries already this week."

I'd normally call the cunt's bluff, but not this time. This time I'm worried the prick is serious.

"Ten grand," I tell him, because I'd lose all self-respect by accepting his first offer.

"Fifteen," he says. "And that's generous. An extra twenty-percent cash tip on the night, compulsory."

If looks could kill he'd be dead already. "Twenty fucking percent? It was a five percent compulsory cash tip last time."

"It is what it is." His eyes are so fucking smug. "If you don't like it…"

I should walk. The number one rule of negotiation, never be afraid to walk away, never accept the weaker position.

But I don't. I don't fucking walk.

"And how much does she make from this? Amy?"

He laughs as though the question is absurd. "Seventy percent as standard. One hundred percent of her cash tip, of course."

"*Of course.*"

I contemplate the prospect of signing away the best part of twenty grand to sweet little Amy every weekend, contemplate how likely she is to stay a six-month course. But it's pointless. My heart is already pounding in my temples, frantic beneath the surface of my poker face.

"Fine," I tell him. "Delaney's. Weekly. Right through until breakfast, at my pleasure."

He holds out a hand. "I'll set it up."

It makes me cringe to shake it. "Six-month term, Claude. Don't fuck me about."

He nods. "It's done."

MELISSA

I can hardly breathe when the email pings.

Dean calls up the message and clears his throat.

"Well?" I quiz. I try to read his face, but he's still scanning the screen.

He smiles at me. "It's good. Really fucking good."

My heart thumps as I leap from my seat and join him on the sofa. I grab the handset from him, my eyes hungry for detail.

Six month exclusivity. Weekly schedule. Saturdays from eight at Delaney's Spa Resort.

Small print about referring to the original sale paperwork, more small print about accepting absolute exclusivity as a condition of sale.

And then finally, the piece of information I've been waiting for.

Your client is Ted Brown.

A click box to confirm the agreement.

I click without hesitation.

Dean stares at me. "You really want to sign up to this shit for six months?"

"You're kidding, right? I'd sign up for sixty years."

He shakes his head. "I'm being serious, Lissa. Who knows what crap can happen in six months?"

My belly flutters at the thought.

A lot.

A lot can happen in six months.

I'm counting on it.

TWENTY-FOUR

ALEXANDER

I spend my entire working life facing people down without so much as breaking a sweat. I never lose a stare-off, haven't done in all my years in the courtroom.

I don't *do* nervous. I've never done nervous.

But tonight, as I check the knot of my tie is positioned *just fucking so*, I'm definitely feeling a shiver of trepidation.

I don't know why this one night is even registering on my radar. It should be nothing more than a dirty little fuckfest, no different to any other time I've reached in my pocket and paid generously for the experience I want.

But her lucky stone is in my trouser pocket. Her pretty eyes are in my head.

The promise of a second round on her tight little cunt has my dick standing to attention before I've even fastened up my cufflinks.

I feel the ridiculous urge to buy her something. A beautiful bouquet of orchids like the ones downstairs. Belgian chocolates maybe.

But cliché gifts seem cheap and unoriginal, and a girl like Amy is anything but cheap and unoriginal. I have a half a million shaped dent in my bank account to prove it.

I take a bundle of notes from my safe and slip them into my jacket pocket, Claude's ridiculous *compulsory tip* sorted.

There's a niggle in my gut as I say goodbye to Brutus, and that niggle won't let me cross the threshold.

I already know what I'm going for as I head upstairs. I input the code to my cabinet and my eyes sweep immediately to the second shelf down. A polished fire opal, its colours so glorious in the light.

This stone transfixed me, captured my eye at an auction in Dubai almost a decade ago.

I had to have it, at any cost. I paid well over the fucking odds for it, but I didn't care. I felt nothing but relief as that gavel came down.

It's a fitting gift.

I wrap it in a burgundy silk handkerchief, slipping it into my pocket along with the cash.

The niggle in my gut is gone when I face my front door for the second time.

But not the nerves.

The nerves are still right fucking there.

MELISSA

I had to buy a dress today. I chose a pretty red number that fits tight at the bust and flares over my hips. Dean approved in the store this morning, and even Joe clapped. A definite win.

And so was the red lipstick to match.

I picked up the shoes and handbag at a discount store on the way back home, and they may have been bought on a budget, but I feel just fine as I head on through Delaney's reception with a smile on my face.

Round two.

I'm really going in for round two.

I've had a smile on my face all day, and I'm happy. Lighter than I've felt since… just *since*.

It feels so strange to feel this light inside.

I count down the minutes in my assigned room on the first floor, my eyes twinkling through my last second mirror check, and then I'm up and away, heart pumping as I make the ascent to the top floor.

Mr Brown in suite seven tonight – Claude's confirmation email told me so.

I count down the doors. Ten, nine, eight.

Seven.

Door number seven is in an alcove on its own.

It swings open as soon as I knock, and I'm not looking at the floor today. My eyes meet his in a heartbeat, my smile bright as he stands aside to let me in.

"Amy," he says.

Black suit, white shirt, black tie. A ghost of stubble.

"Hi," I say, and the flutters in my tummy are too much. I take a breath.

"You look considerably more at ease this evening," he says, and there's a smile there, just a hint. I can't stop staring as he crosses the room. "Champagne?"

He pulls the bottle from an ice bucket before I've answered, pouring me a glass even as I'm nodding.

"Please."

I notice the case on the bedside table. I notice how his scent lingers in the air between us. I notice the way he's looking at me, as though he's a cat about to pounce.

It's familiar here, the layout of this suite is similar to the one previous. Virtually identical.

I drop my handbag on the dresser.

He already has a tumbler of water. "Cheers," he says, and I raise my champagne.

"What are we toasting?"

"A long and mutually beneficial working relationship," he tells me.

Long.

"To us," I say simply, and his jaw tightens. He closes the distance to clink my glass, and stays there, his body so close to mine.

The scent of him makes me heady, and so do the bubbles on my tongue.

I want to kiss him, but I don't know how.

I want to slip my hands inside his jacket and hold him close.

I want to feel the hardness of him against my belly.

But I stand still. Waiting. Wanting.

"I'm assured you've accepted a six-month exclusivity term," he says. His voice is super professional. Guarded.

"Yes."

"I trust you read the small print?"

I attempt to recall the bits I noted, but my mind is fuzzy. Excitement and nerves aren't the greatest recipe for flawless recall. I tell him so with a smile, and hope that excuses my ignorance.

"Excitement?" He seems taken aback, even though his gaze is steady and his jaw is firm. It's just something in his eyes, something I can't put my finger on.

My cheeks are burning, and I don't know what to say. I don't have a smart quip to hand, or some sexy one-liner that makes me sound like a sex goddess. I don't have anything to offer him but the honest truth, which is such a joke in itself given the route I've taken to get into his bed in the first place.

My eyes are on his, my throat dry as I cough up my answer.

I hope he can't see my pink cheeks under my foundation. "I, um… I wanted to see you again."

No. That's not the truth. Not anywhere near.

I love you. I've always loved you. I can't stop thinking about you.

I'm Melissa Martin, the girl who bought you a cupcake. The girl who ironed the shirt you're wearing. The girl you bummed a cigarette to outside my school gates.

He reads people for a living, and I know it. I can feel how he's reading me right now.

His eyes are dark and fierce, the steel of his jaw just as intimidating as it was in the meeting room weeks ago.

My confidence deflates, my breath unsteady as I dip my head. I'm back to staring at his feet, the mirror shine of his brogues so stark against the cream carpet.

I feel the heat of him. I feel his breath on my hair.

And then his fingers are under my chin, tipping my face to his.

"Flattery is unnecessary."

My eyes widen. "But… it's not…"

His stare could cut me in half and leave me bleeding on the floor.

I want him to kiss me. I want him to wrap his fingers around my throat and take away my ability to speak any more stupid words.

But he doesn't.

He reaches inside his jacket and pulls out an envelope.

"I like to get the practicalities out of the way first," he says, and I feel weirdly sad as I take the money from him. Feel strangely deflated as I thank him and drop the bundle in my handbag. He finishes up his water as I clasp it shut. "I hope you weren't too inconvenienced in the aftermath," he says.

"Tender," I admit. "But it was no problem."

"Good to hear." He clears his throat. "In other practicalities, you'll be staying until morning. We'll meet at this time every weekend."

"Okay."

"If you've revised your hard limits after our last encounter, now is the time to air them."

I shake my head. "No revisions."

He doesn't understand me, and I know it. I can see his mind whirring behind those dark eyes, digging and reasoning and trying to fit my pieces together. I feel it. I feel *him*.

But he won't. He can't.

He's trying to solve a puzzle without all the pieces. Without *any* of them.

"You're quite extraordinary," he tells me, and I feel that, too.

"So are you, Mr Brown." I can hardly breathe. I can hardly think. I can hardly do anything but yield to the way my body feels when he's near.

I watch his throat as he swallows. I watch his mouth as he takes the breath I'm craving.

My body moves as his does, my tummy fluttering as we meet in the space between us, and my hands really do slip inside his jacket, my mouth already open for his as he lowers his face to mine.

I'd burn all the cash in my handbag for one single moment like this.

I'd give him everything I owned just for one breath of his breath.

And I think he knows, somewhere deep inside. I think he knows this isn't Amy Randall, some random girl being paid for sex with a stranger.

I think he knows he knows me, because he groans when his fingers twist in my hair, and I feel his heartbeat against my shoulder. It's fast, it's really fast.

Nearly as fast as mine.

He tugs my dress up and over my head, and unclips my bra and drops it loose.

His fingers hook inside my knickers and shimmy them down my hips, until there's only me, naked in discount shoes. He parts my thigh with his, and the fabric of his trousers is so soft against my pussy. He hitches my ass and holds me tight, and I rock against him, loving the swell of his crotch against my belly.

I wrap my arms around his shoulders for leverage, and he takes my weight, grinds against me until I'm panting into his mouth, my eyes hazy and unfocused as he urges me faster.

I'm going to come in his arms before he's even taken his jacket off, and he wants it, I know he wants it.

"Horny girl," he breathes, and I shudder.

My clit grinds against his thigh. My chest presses to his as I suck his tongue into my mouth.

I lose my mind as I tip over the edge, squirming against him without a scrap of reservation as I moan like the whore I technically am.

And when I stop, he doesn't. He doesn't let me go as I breathe ragged breaths into his mouth. He doesn't let up his grip on my ass as he walks me backwards to the bed and lowers himself on top.

His tie falls between my tits and tickles me. The lapels of his jacket are smooth under my fingers.

"You like the suit," he comments, and I nod.

"I love the suit," I tell him, and I guess that's why he stays in it. I guess that's why he unbuckles his belt and pulls his cock free with his clothed flesh against my nakedness.

I groan as he pushes inside, but my pussy is ready for him this time. I grunt with discomfort at the stretch, but he's hard and fast, shunting deep as my thighs part to take him.

"Fuck me," I hiss.

And he does.

He fucks me so hard I bite his shoulder to quell the grunts, his ear against mine as he takes me. I take his ass in my hands and urge him deeper, even though it fucking hurts, and I can hear the noises my pussy is making, the wet slaps as he pounds my flesh.

"This is insane," he growls, and it makes me smile.

He has no idea.

"I love it," I whisper, and he lifts his face to search my eyes.

I hold him, one hand in his hair as my thumb brushes his jaw, and there's nothing I can do to hide how much I want him. Nothing in the world I could do to play this cool.

So I don't.

I kiss him. Hard.

He shudders.

I stroke his face and he groans.

I wrap my legs around his waist and roll my hips to take him deeper, and I'm groaning too.

He comes with his forehead pressed to mine.

"Fuck!" he says with a grunt and his eyes closed tight.

He's tense as he explodes, his whole body taut as his heart races through his shirt.

And then he collapses. I love taking the weight of him, love the way he crushes me into the sheets.

I listen to him breathe, my fingertips teasing the back of his neck as he calms.

When he meets my eyes his are no longer cold.

"I have a gift for you," he says.

ALEXANDER

I feel completely fucking unhinged as I prise myself from her arms.

I feel like I've just been inside Amy's fucking soul, not just her pussy.

She's either the best hooker in the world, or the worst – either playing a straight up scam with world-class stealth, or falling in deep with the man who popped her cherry.

I'm not sure which I'm most afraid of, and I'm no longer nervous. I'm fucking petrified.

And yet I can't fucking stop.

Her smile is gentle. Her fingers brush my arm as she rolls to face me. "A gift?"

She's still breathless. Her lips are puffy from kissing so hard.

I prop myself on my elbow before I can think better of it, dipping straight into my inside pocket for the fire opal. Her eyes widen as she catches sight of the handkerchief and she gasps when I tumble the gemstone free. It lands on the bed between us, and her fingers dither halfway, her mouth open.

"But this isn't…" she starts. "This can't be…"

"A gift," I tell her, and press it into her open hand. "A lucky stone to replace yours."

"Fire opal," she whispers, and my heart starts pounding again. "It's too much…"

I hate those words.

I hate the way they make me feel.

Over-generous. In too deep.

Rebuked.

Like leaving vintage wine on a kitchen island and finding a *thanks but no thanks* note when you get home.

"Do you like it?" I ask, and my tone is harsher than I intended. I register the shock on her face.

"It's beautiful," she tells me. She runs her thumb over the smooth face, back and forth.

"Don't offend me. I want you to have it."

And I do fucking want her to have it.

I want her to carry a piece of me with her, in her handbag, everywhere she goes. I want her to carry that ridiculously priced gem around every day, checking just to make sure it's still with her.

The likelihood is that it will never stay in her handbag, and I know it. She'll probably shove it on a windowsill somewhere, maybe in a drawer for safekeeping.

Maybe she'll even sell it on to a raw stones specialist. Maybe I'll find it listed at my next specialist auction.

But none of that matters.

What matters is the way she's looking at me. The shock in her eyes as she realises I'm being serious, that this beautiful stone really is for her.

"One of your collection?"

"Yes."

"Is this your favourite?" she asks, and I know I'm definitely fucking insane when I answer her.

"One of them."

"Thank you. I'll treasure it," she says, and then she smiles.

My emotional discomfort eases the moment I see the pleasure in her eyes.

She loves it just as much as I do, maybe even more. She tips it to the light and the red inclusions sparkle.

She sighs a happy sigh. "It's lucky," she tells me.

Her contentment makes me smile. "How do you know?"

She stares me right in the eye as she answers, and I was right. Her fucking soul is swallowing mine whole.

"Because it's from you," she says.

TWENTY-FIVE

MELISSA

I can't stop staring at the opal.

I was expecting months of hard work, months of giving my best just to feel him kiss me and mean it. I was expecting the angel hair quartz to be nothing more than an ice-breaker, a token hint that we have something in common.

I wasn't expecting to be lying at his side with one of his prized collection gripped in my fingers a week later.

I've seen this stone.

Three across, two shelves down. I polished its little plinth last Tuesday.

I feel bold with this treasure in my hand. I feel like anything is possible. It really is lucky, I know it is.

And so am I.

"I love the suit," I tell him. "But I'd love you more out of it, please."

My voice is a whisper tinged with desperation as I reach for his tie. I pull it loose, and he kisses me as I push his jacket from his shoulders. My fingers fumble with his shirt buttons, the opal still gripped in my palm as I sweep my hand over his chest.

He is beautiful.

He is everything.

My breath is shallow as he pushes me onto my back and kicks his trousers off. Skin on skin feels divine, his cock hard against my thigh as he lowers his mouth to my nipple. I stare at his mouth as he flicks his tongue, and it takes me by surprise as his fingers find my clit.

"You're going to come for me until you're exhausted," he tells me, and I moan for him. His fingers sink inside, and I feel a pressure as he moves them. "Until you're exhausted," he repeats and I nod.

His fingers are fast and deep, the pressure inside grows intense, building higher and higher until I can't keep still. My legs wriggle and my ass bucks from the bed, my throat making stupid groans as I grab at the sheets.

His arm pistons. I can hear how wet I am.

"Nice and wide," he whispers, and I spread my legs for him as wide as they'll go, not caring that I look like a frog. Not caring that my hair is sticking to my clammy forehead, or that I'm probably wearing more red lipstick on my chin than my mouth.

He kisses my belly as he lowers himself down the bed, and his arms wrap around my thighs and pull my pussy to his mouth.

He sucks. He sucks right on my tender clit with his fingers inside me, and it's too much.

I grip his hair as I come, and he likes it, he growls at me and sucks harder. I wrap my legs around his shoulders and pin him tight, and he likes that too. He slides a finger into my ass as I buck for him, and I cry out over and over.

I worry as I catch my breath, worry that tonight should be about his pleasure, not mine. But his cock is so big as he gets up to retrieve his case, his eyes hungry as he unclasps it on the bed and takes out a massager.

He plugs it in behind the nightstand.

"Until you're exhausted," he says again, and turns it on.

The big purple head of it buzzes. He trails it across my tits and it vibrates all the way through me. It tickles my belly on the way down, and I'm already crazy when it reaches my clit, already hissing as I know what's coming.

He lies at my side, my thigh sandwiched between his, his cock at my hip as he presses the massager tight against me. He nuzzles my neck, and his mouth is at my ear, his breath warm and raspy.

"I want to know what turns you on," he tells me. "You're going to tell me."

"This..." I whisper, and he nips my ear.

"I want to know what you think about when you play with yourself."

"*You*," I tell him, and he nips me again.

"Don't lie to me, Amy," he growls, but I'm not. I tell him so.

He turns my face to his, and I tell him again.

"*You. I play with myself and I think about you.*"

"That's..."

"Crazy," I tell him, and I don't care. "I know. But it's true. And I can't stop. I don't want to stop."

He looks torn, and I hate that. I hate the way he's fighting what he already knows.

"Why me?" he asks, and flicks up the speed of the massager. It makes me squirm.

"Because..." I begin, and I don't know how to answer.

"Why?" he repeats.

But he's too late, because I'm already tumbling, already riding the wave, my body a clammy wreck against his.

He doesn't take the massager away, not even when I'm wriggling at the contact.

"You play with yourself and you think of me, why?"

"Because... because you're... everything..." I breathe, and it's such a stupid thing to say. He stares down so hard on me. "Last weekend... when you took me... it was everything... you took everything..."

He blinks, and I think I've got away with it.

"You... when you choked me... it felt so good..." I tell him. That gets a reaction. I feel his cock twitch against my hip. "And I want more... I want so much more... it's not just... about the money..."

"Why are you here?" he growls, and his lips press to the corner of mine.

"Because... of you..." I hiss. "Only you..."

"And what if it wasn't me who'd bought your exclusivity?"

"I wouldn't be here..."

I don't know if he believes me. I hope he does.

"You don't even know me," he says.

I meet his eyes. "I feel you," I whisper, and I'm going all in. My clit is sending me insane. "And I think... I hope... I hope you feel it, too... because it's crazy... but it's true... I *feel* you..."

The only sound above the massager is my own raspy breath. He's silent. And I can hardly look at him, can hardly face the rejection I know is coming.

Only it doesn't.

"I think about you," he tells me. "So I guess we're both fucking crazy." He breathes against my lips. "I'm dangerous," he rasps. "My tastes are dangerous. You shouldn't be here."

My eyes bore into his. "Do it," I tell him. "Please... do it."

He pauses for just a second, long enough to press his lips to mine.

And then he closes his fingers around my throat.

ALEXANDER

I'm always controlled. Steady.

But when I clasp my fingers around her pretty throat this time, I'm neither.

My left hand is clumsy. My weight is precarious on my elbow as I cut off her air.

I keep the bodywand to her swollen little bud, piling on the pressure as she squirms and splutters and shivers for me.

The girl is fucking crazy. And so am I.

I feel the strain of her throat and it makes my balls tighten. Her airless mouth makes my cock twitch, and I want to fuck it. I really want to fuck it.

But not yet.

Her eyes are watery pools as I rise to sitting, and I have a great vantage point from here, staring down on her as she grips her thighs to stop herself fighting.

I wait until the last moment, until I feel her slipping into unconsciousness, and then I let her take one long gulp before I hitch onto my knees and plough my dick straight into her open mouth. She retches. I feel her throat constrict, and I love it. I fucking love it.

She's wriggling under the massager as I shove my cock down her throat. I love the way it bulges for me. I run my fingers over her neck and I feel myself in there.

"You're everything... you took everything...." Her words have fucking addled me. I'm riding the crazy train all the fucking way.

I ride her fucking throat with fucking *everything*.

I wait until she's coming under the massager, her whole body fucking wired before I let myself shoot my load.

She coughs as I pull out, and my cum splatters down her chin, creamy white mixing with smeared lipstick.

She looks fucking beautiful.

I scoop it back into her mouth with my thumb. "Another gift," I tell her, and she swallows. She swallows every drop and then she smiles.

I turn off the massager and she sighs in relief.

She flinches as I brush my thumb over her swollen clit, but she doesn't stop me.

I'm getting the impression she'll never stop me, no matter what I do.

The prospect that I'm going to find out fills me with fear and awe in equal measure.

TWENTY–SIX

MELISSA

The sun is rising through the crack in the drapes as Alexander Henley comes in my ass for the final time this evening.

I'm exhausted, and he must be too. His chest heaves against my back as he recovers.

My ass is on fire. My clit is swollen and aching. My throat is raspy and raw.

He must be done. *We* must be done.

I'm disappointed, even though my body is absolutely spent. Beyond spent.

We don't move, either of us, just stay entangled with his cock pulsing against my sore asshole.

I wonder if he'll want me to leave now. If he'll get up and leave like last time with nothing but a parting goodbye, but when he lifts himself from my body he pulls me with him. I move so easily, his chest still hot against my back as he rests his chin on my head. His arms wrap around my waist, and he holds me.

"Fuck," he says, and I can tell he's smiling.

It takes me by surprise, and I giggle.

"That was… intense…" I hold up the opal to the morning light. "Lucky," like I said.

"Lucky?"

I nod.

"You're putting a good anal pounding down to a lucky crystal, are you? Tell me how lucky you think it is when you're limping through the foyer later."

Later.

He realises what he's said, I'm sure of it, because he reaches for the remote control on the nightstand and flicks on the TV clock.

It's gone six in the morning.

"You must be tired," I tell him.

"I don't sleep."

"You don't?"

"Not easily."

I turn over to face him. "Not even in a comfy bed at a swanky spa resort?"

"Not even in a comfy bed at a swanky spa resort." His eyes are so tired. "But *you* could."

My tummy flips. "Here?"

"If you would like."

I'm stupidly nervous given that he just spent the whole night in every single part of me. "And you? Will you stay too?"

He takes a breath. "I have to get home."

"Okay," I say, and I can't hide the disappointment. I don't want to.

He looks as though he's going to add something, so I wait quietly, giving the pause he needs.

It works. I can't believe it works, but it does.

"I've got a dog," he tells me, and my heart jumps at the fact Ted Brown told me something real about Alexander Henley. He stares right through me. "But I could stay awhile. Until you get to sleep."

I smile so bright. "I'd like that."

He shunts enough to pull back the bedcovers and I slip inside. He fluffs up the pillows and rolls to face me.

"I don't sleep," he says again, "but don't let that stop you."

But he does sleep. I know that because I'm still watching him through pretend-closed eyes as his close for real.

ALEXANDER

It's gone ten when I get home to poor Brutus. A cunty move that takes me completely by surprise.

I wasn't lying – I don't sleep. Only I *did* fucking sleep. I slept like a fucking log for four fucking hours straight, tangled in the limbs of a stranger with her pretty face against my shoulder, as though I was in the arms of a fucking angel.

Yes, it's that fucking ridiculous.

I feel grimy in yesterday's suit, my shirt crumpled to fuck and my hair fresh from fucking bed in my haste to get back for him.

My grumpy black beast pads nonchalantly through from the conservatory as though he's hardly noticed I've gone as I deactivate the alarm. I love how he plays it cool.

He's left me a couple of parcels by the back door, and looks surprisingly pleased with himself as I busy myself cleaning up.

"I'm a prick," I tell him. "I fell asleep. Who'd have fucking thought it, hey?" I ruffle his ears when I'm done. "A dick move, boy. It won't happen again."

He grunts as though he understands me, and I think all is forgiven as I dish up his breakfast.

I'll have to be more fucking careful next time.

Oversleeping. Racing through spa foyers like a dirty stop-out on my way home. Sharing a bed.

None of this is me. Not even close.

But I feel strangely sated. More relaxed than I can remember in years.

My balls are well and truly fucking empty, my cock sleeping the dead kind of sleep that fucking all night long gifts to you, and my mind is quiet.

Free.

I slump down in the armchair I haven't enjoyed for an age, breathing in the scent of orchids, and I feel fucking amazing.

I could sleep again, right here right now, with a smile on my face and the smell of Amy's gorgeous pussy still on my fingers, but Brutus has other plans.

He nudges my elbow, glaring up at me with his overbite in full gruesome splendour.

"You want out?" I ask, and he gruffs at me. Yes, he wants fucking out.

No rest for the wicked, but that's okay. I can live with that.

I grab his leash.

MELISSA

Joe calls *Saa* at me happily when I step in through the front door, bouncing along to his favourite TV show as Dean tries to give him lunch.

Dean doesn't look quite so impressed. He drops Joe's little train fork in the bowl.

"Jeez," he snaps. "Where the hell have you been?"

He's worried, of course he is, and he has every right to be. I tell him so.

And then I tell him how I slept in Alexander Henley's arms and he slept too. I tell him how he smiled at me as he left this morning, taking a moment to kiss my lips before he shot out through the door in a cloud of expletives.

"You could've phoned!" he tells me, but I couldn't have. How could I? How could I have possibly explained a call to a male friend at home taking care of my baby brother?

I explain my logic and Dean shrugs. "So what *are* you gonna tell him?"

I stare blankly. "What do you mean?"

"You *are* gonna have to tell him something, Lissa, You can't keep this act up forever."

"Just for six months…" I say, and I realise how stupid that sounds.

I don't need Dean to spell out the obvious, but he does it anyway. "Six months is a long time. One day you hardly know the guy, the next he's sleeping next to you, signing up to pay you crazy cash every weekend for half a year straight. This is crazy, Lissa. It can't work. You have to tell him."

"Tell him what?"

He shrugs. "The truth?"

I laugh out loud. *"That's* crazy."

"No," he says. *"This* is crazy. He's gonna find out, sooner or later. He's gonna find out and he's gonna be pissed. Fess up now, get it over with."

My stomach lurches. "He wouldn't want to know me… not if he knew…"

He shrugs again. "You don't know that. Guy seems pretty keen to me."

But I do know that. Of course I know it.

I feel Dean's glare. "Stop it now," he says. "Before you get in too deep to get out. I'm serious, Lissa, this ain't gonna end well, not unless you fess up and iron this crap out before it gets out of hand."

I'm already in too deep to get out, and my face says it all.

He shakes his head. "This is so messed up," he says, and I don't argue. I couldn't argue.

So I don't.

I get him to count my money instead.

ALEXANDER

I order Brenda to summon Janet Yorkley to my office first thing on Monday morning.

She's dithery as she presents herself at my door. I wave her in, and silence her as she starts gabbling on about how she hopes the new cleaner is doing a good job.

"The new cleaner is fine," I tell her. "She's excellent, in fact."

Her relief is palpable.

I don't give her chance to enjoy it. "Which is exactly why I want to increase her hours. I need her on a Sunday morning. Early. My dog needs walking."

"A Sunday morning?" she asks.

I hate having to repeat myself, so I don't. "I may be in, or I may not, but that's irrelevant. I need her to let herself in before seven regardless, feed him and take him out. She should be done before nine."

Janet nods. "I'll arrange it, Mr Henley. I'm sure Melissa will be pleased to assist."

Melissa.

Her name zips right up my spine.

"Advise *Melissa* to be careful of dog presents in the conservatory. He may well have had a long evening."

"I'll let her know," she says.

She plasters on a fake smile as I dismiss her, being so careful to close my door quietly on the way out.

Melissa.

Not a Molly May after all. Not even close.

It would have been handy to know this before I attempted to chase her down my fucking street a few weeks back, but none of that matters now.

I have other interests to keep me occupied.

MELISSA

I feel sick as I head for Janet Yorkley's office, freshly summoned via my work phone before I'd even finished clearing Mr Henley's breakfast things away.

She calls me inside as soon as I tap on her office door, and the sickness eases off just a little. She's smiling. That's got to be good, right?

She tells me to take a seat and I do.

"Excellent news," she says. "Mr Henley has expressed his approval of your cleaning standards. Very well done. His praise doesn't come easily."

I feel like such a fraud as I grin back at her, as though she'll see straight through me and realise I've been up to no good. As though she'll know I'm overstepping every boundary in my employee handbook and then some.

"Thanks, I've been working really hard."

"I don't doubt it," she says. "And you'll be working harder from this week onwards."

I stare blankly and she keeps on smiling.

"Mr Henley would like to increase your hours. You'll be taking his dog out on a Sunday morning before seven. You should be done by nine."

I feel the blood drain from my face. "Sunday morning?"

She nods. "He advised he may be in, or he may not be, but not to let that deter you. Of course, we prefer discreet, *always,*" she waffles on and on as I struggle to form words.

Finally, she stops. Waits for a response.

"But I, um... *Sunday?*"

She groans. "Yes, Miss Martin. Sunday. *Every* Sunday, seven a.m. at the latest."

I can't even begin to hide the horror. "But I can't! I really can't... not on a Sunday..."

Her eyes turn cold in a heartbeat. "What do you mean you *can't?* We don't do *can't,* Melissa, not where Mr Henley is concerned."

"But Joe..." I bleat. "My brother... he needs me... I said at interview..."

"Your responsibilities wouldn't be a problem. *That's* what you said at interview."

And she's right, I did.

"I really can't," I tell her, even though it pains. "There's no way I can do a Sunday, really there isn't. I'd love to, really I would, but I can't..."

She raises a hand. "You want me to tell that to Mr Henley, do you? That you just *can't?*"

My mind spins.

He wants a cleaner on Sunday morning because...

"I can't," I repeat. "I'm really sorry, Janet, but I can't."

The stand-off takes forever. My fingers fidget under the desk, contemplating the inevitable, contemplating having to walk away from this. But I can't do that either.

I really can't.

"This is worth losing your position over, is it?" she snaps. "Plenty of our staff would love to work in Mr Henley's house. It's a privilege."

"I'm lucky," I say. "I know it, but I just can't."

It doesn't matter how many times I say it, her eyes are still piercing. Still angry.

I lay it on the line, because I can't see any other option. "I'll resign," I say. "I'm sorry to let you down."

Her mouth opens. *"Resign?"*

I nod. "Please send my apologies to Mr Henley."

There's a tickle of relief under the disappointment once the words are out there. *Maybe I'll never have to tell him, maybe he'll never know who I really am.*

It's clutching at straws, but straws feel pretty good under the circumstances.

"Shall I leave my uniform?" I ask, ready to pull the cap from my head. It would be more than a tickle of relief to ditch this crappy outfit.

Now it's Janet struggling for words. "Let's not be hasty," she says, and then she tuts at me like I'm a naughty child. "I'm disappointed, Melissa, but under the circumstances maybe someone else can take the Sunday shift."

My heart pounds as she picks up her telephone extension. "I need Miss Webber down here, quickly please."

I wait in silence.

Janet does too.

When Sonnie enters the room she looks just as worried as I was. She takes a seat at my side nervously, clearly trying to work out what the hell she's done wrong.

"An opportunity has come up," Janet tells her. "We need you to clean Mr Henley's house on a Sunday morning. You'll be taking his dog out in particular. You're available, yes?"

Sonnie looks as horrified as I did. "But isn't that Lissa's job?"

I hope my eyes tell her how sorry I am. I know she has little kids at home. I know she didn't mention it at interview.

"Miss Martin is *unavailable*," Janet says, and I feel like an asshole. "Please don't tell me you are too."

I'm waiting for it, the stream of excuses as Sonnie tries to get out of it, but she doesn't. Although she looks stressed as hell she plasters a bright smile on her face.

"I'll do it," she says. "Hell, I'm always up for a promotion."

"Then it's done," Janet tells us. "I'll find a stand in for your duties this week, Miss Webber. You'll be shadowing Miss Martin in preparation for the weekend."

I smile.

Sonnie smiles.

Janet smiles too.

I'm a long way away from her office by the time I breathe easily again.

TWENTY–SIX

MELISSA

"Whoa,". Sonnie says. "This is some pad."

I swell with pride as I lead the way to Mr Henley's front door. Stupid, I know.

I hand her a piece of paper with the alarm code written down. "The keypad is under the stairs, you have to be quick."

"I'll be like lightning." She nudges me with her elbow as I sort through the keys. "Look at us little scrubbers from floor seven, making it all the way to Mr Henley's place. Did you really do it? Sniff his underpants?"

"Course I do. I wear them on my head while I'm scrubbing." I shoot her a goofy smile, and she laughs as I turn the key in the lock. "You have to be careful of Brutus," I tell her. "Never come here without fish treats. I'll give you a pack."

"Cindy warned me already. Said he's a monster."

I feel strangely protective. "He's not a monster. He's just… misunderstood."

"Like his master, eh? Up to no good sticking his dick in hooker pussy." She grins. "I know Cindy told you. Said you looked damn like you were gonna get yourself down there to Harley's tavern yourself."

"She told me a lot of things," I say, and my cheeks burn as we step inside. Sonnie really does make a dash for it, scooting through the hallway in her bid to deactivate the countdown timer. I'd forgotten how efficient she is.

The alarm stops beeping and she takes a look around the place, jaw open.

"Yep, just as I thought. Swanky as hell."

She hasn't seen anything yet.

And she hasn't seen Brutus yet, either.

He takes her by surprise, his growl crazily intimidating as he checks out the intruder in his house. It's a sound I haven't heard in a while, and I'm dithery as I rustle for the treats in my apron pocket. I toss them to her.

My heart is thumping as she catches them, and she's even more dithery than I was.

Shit.

"Hey boy, good boy," she flusters, but he isn't having any of it. He stalks her with his teeth bared, and she backs away before I can tell her not to. It's a mistake.

He launches himself in her direction, and she tears off with a shriek, heading right back out the front door as he throws himself against the other side.

"Brutus!" I call, but he isn't listening. "Shit, Brutus, no!" I shout, but he's still clawing at the woodwork as she grips the handle tight on the other side.

"Help!" she calls, and my actions are automatic. I just do it.

I put on my bravest voice, just like I heard on that dog whisperer show, and head over calmly to take hold of his collar.

"Stop!" I tell him. "No!"

He's still growling as he turns his head, teeth still bared as he clocks my expression.

"Brutus! No!"

I'm sure he's going to bite me, positive I really will be fired for spilling blood over cream carpets, but the fight in his eyes simmers down, and he grumbles, groans a bit before sitting his ass down on the floor.

"Christ, Lissa. Is it safe? Are you still alive in there?"

I tug Brutus away from the door. "Stay," I tell him, and hope he knows that word. I ease it open just a crack and Sonnie's terrified eyes greet me on the other side. "Sorry about him," I say. "He takes a while to get used to new people."

She's shaking as she eases herself back through the doorway. "Ain't you who's got to be sorry, hon. He ain't *your* monster."

A tiny pang in my stomach, and I realise why I've been feeling so off since we set off from the office earlier.

Reality. The burst bubble that comes with realising I really am just a cleaner and this isn't my house, or my dog, or my life.

Brutus isn't my monster, and neither is Alexander Henley. Not even if I wash his underwear and smell his sheets.

Or take his beautiful cock in my ass all night long.

Alexander Henley doesn't even know my name.

Sonnie flinches as Brutus drops to the floor, but he's not doing anything other than giving her the eye. "How'd you get him to like you so much?"

I shrug. "Persistence and fish treats." *And love.*

The addition shoots through my mind, and it gives me a shiver. That's the key, when it really comes down to it. It's all about love. All about putting your heart on the line for someone and trusting they'll see right through to your soul. Like Brutus did with me when I offered him the first fish treat from my fingers and stared him right in the eye.

"Persistence and fish treats," she repeats, and takes a breath. She pulls one from the packet and tosses it between his paws. "There you go, boy. Nice fishy snack. Nom nom."

Brutus nudges it with his muzzle, sniffs but doesn't bite.

He doesn't want it.

He doesn't want her.

I shrug. "Early days," I say. "He'll get used to you. Just give it some time."

But I hope he doesn't.

I hope they can never send another cleaner in here ever again.

Because I belong here now.

Only me.

❧

Sonnie is excited again once the Brutus commotion has died down. She snoops around the kitchen, just as I did first time in here, and she comments on the contents of his fridge, all the things I buy him.

She comments on everything, and as much as I love her, I really don't enjoy the feeling of sharing.

"Cindy told me about his porn habits," she says as we enter the living room. "You gonna show me what he's into?"

I tell her she's welcome to look, just as I was, and she flicks on the screen with twinkling eyes.

But there's barely anything there.

Gem auctions. He's been viewing a lot of gem auctions and very little else.

The revelation makes me tingle.

Sonnie groans. "I was expecting so much more. Cindy's such a bullshitter, she really egged this up." I don't say anything as she flicks the monitor back off again. "Anything else tasty?"

I shrug. "His laundry basket?"

She finishes polishing the mantelpiece and I have to rearrange the pictures of his kids just so.

"His bedroom." She grins. "I wanna see where he sleeps."

I show her where he sleeps, and she dips her head to his pillow and breathes him in. I try to ignore the pang of intrusion, because it's stupid.

"Yum," she says. "Midnight in winter, that's what he smells like."

It makes me smile. "He smells amazing."

She reaches inside the laundry hamper, and my face is on fire as she pulls out his crumpled shirt from Saturday night. And then his trousers.

My heart races as she lifts them to her nose and takes a decent whiff. And then she grimaces. Her eyes screw shut as her nose wrinkles.

She fake retches. Wipes her nose with the back of her hand.

"Hell almighty! Someone got laid this weekend. I can smell pussy all over them."

And she can.

Of course she can.

I came all over them with his thigh pressed right to my clit.

"Ain't gonna be sniffing none of that again," she says and throws them back in the hamper, and even though my face is burning up, I laugh. I can't stop laughing.

And when Sonnie laughs, I laugh harder. I laugh until my eyes are watering with the craziness of it all. With the crazy urge to tell her it was me. That *I'm* the one who came all over Mr Henley's thigh on Saturday night.

But I don't.

Of course I don't.

"I missed your laugh," she tells me with a giggle.

And I've missed hers, too.

ALEXANDER

I believed a six-month exclusivity arrangement would be more than enough. That a once-weekly session with Amy's tight little body would be enough to keep the cravings at bay.

But it's not enough.

I'd be happy to write this insanity off as pure addiction running wild, but if that were truly the case I'd be happy to stave away the beast with porn or webcam girls, or even a cheaper rut with Elena or Candice in the interim.

But I'm not happy with any of those options.

There is only her. Only her tight little cunt and those big blue eyes. Only the way she takes whatever I give her.

As I cruise through my workday with a distinctly sunnier disposition than the one I've come to know, I wonder whether I'm teetering on the edge of some kind of mental breakdown. Yet, I've been there before and it wasn't like this. I've stared into the abyss of meaningless compulsive paid-for sex and come out the other side unscathed, time after time, and *this* isn't *that*.

This feels different.

She feels different.

Different enough that I message Claude on Wednesday morning and order him to book both Delaney's and Amy for this very same evening.

Looming mental breakdown or no, I'll be having that girl's pussy tonight.

TWENTY—EIGHT

MELISSA

Even Dean can't hide how impressed he is when I tell him I'm on again for this evening. He makes me dinner as I search through my wardrobe, scouting for something vaguely suitable that Mr Henley hasn't seen me in already.

It's no good. I've got nothing super dressy other than the red and pink I bought especially, and so it's done. A choice taken out of my hands.

I'm going to have to go as myself this evening.

I hope that the floral patterned tunic dress is enough. It's not fitted or fancy, but it's pretty. At least I think so.

I give Joe his bath before I leave, playing with his floating boat toys amongst all the bubbles and lather. He laughs as one capsizes and it makes me laugh too.

I love how he smiles. I love how his eyes sparkle.

I love how happy he is.

I tell Dean so once I've settled Joe into bed. Tell him how grateful I am here's here to support me. How great he is with Joe.

He nods. "I love the little guy," he says, and I believe him. It's written all over his face.

I gulp down my pasta and finish up my makeup, and I have no time to take the underground across town this evening, so I take a cab. I have to call Frank at New Start on the way across town, apologising so hard that I won't be able to help out this evening. But as it turns out it's a major win of monster proportions, a stroke of lucky fortune much earlier than I'd intended it to happen.

"Not to worry," Frank tells me. "These things happen. It's a longshot, but we have a team running at Brickwood on Friday if you fancied stopping by." He's already backtracking as I answer. Already telling me that I shouldn't feel pressured.

"I'd love to," I say. "Friday works."

I take directions like I'll need them, confirm the times as though I don't have a clue what they are.

He tells me he's looking forward to it, that he can't wait to introduce me to the Brickwood team.

My heart races with it all.

I just hope it's not too soon. It could be way too soon.

I push that worry away as the cab pulls into Delaney's.

I'm early, but only by ten minutes tops. Barely enough time to check into my own room and head up to Mr Henley in time.

But it turns out that doesn't matter.

I'm paying the driver before I see him. Giving my thanks as I catch Mr Henley from the corner of my eye.

He's waiting. Watching. Making no secret of the fact that he's staring as he waits for the car to pull away.

I gesture to my outfit before I've even said hello.

"I'm sorry," I say. "I was in a rush. Little warning. I, um…"

He looks me up and down. "No apology necessary," he says, "I like it." The smile at the corner of his mouth makes it clear I've passed the wardrobe test.

I take a breath. "Hi," I say.

"Good evening, Amy," he says.

And screw etiquette, because damn if I know how a paid-for escort is supposed to act in public. I close the distance and wrap my arms around his neck, and he smells absolutely gorgeous as I press my lips to his cheek.

I pull away but he doesn't. His hand rests on my back as he opens the door for me, and stays on my back all the way to reception.

I watch his handwriting as he checks in, love the way he flourishes his fake signature with a flick of his wrist.

I'm not expecting the receptionist to recognise me, not dressed like this, but she does.

"Will you be checking in too, Miss Randall?" she asks with one of those super professional smiles which always make me nervous.

Mr Henley looks at me, and it must be obvious I don't know what to answer, because he does it for me.

"Miss Randall will be staying with me," he says, and she nods.

"Enjoy your stay."

His smile is all for me as he answers. "We will, thank you."

It's so strange stepping into the elevator with him. So strange to be staring up at him in just the same way I did at Grosvenor Henley in my stupid uniform on day one.

"I'm glad you could make it at such short notice," he tells me.

"I wouldn't miss it," I reply.

I take a breath as we step out onto the top floor corridor, and my hand brushes his as we head over to suite twelve at the far end. He takes it, his fingers possessive as they land on mine. His grip is firm. Demanding.

"I have an early start," he tells me as we get to the door. He slides the key card into the lock. "I must be out of here by six."

"Six," I say, and I can't stop smiling. It's later than I thought, longer than I thought.

He closes the door behind us, and he's still so close. His hands land on my waist as he walks me backwards into the room. His fingers trail up my spine as I raise my face to his.

"I'm not in the habit of mid-week appointments," he tells me. "I have to be focused. My job is demanding."

"Selling stationery," I whisper with a smile. "Yes."

His breath is warm against my lips. "I lied," he tells me. "I've never been a salesman in my life."

And it's right there, the urge to tell him I lied too.

But the urge leaves the moment his mouth lands on mine. Fades to nothing as his hands tangle in my hair and hold me firm.

"I've been thinking of you," I whisper between kisses. "I can't stop thinking about you."

His hands land under my ass, and he hitches me, lifts me up and onto the dresser where it's so easy for my legs to wrap around his waist. I tug his tie loose and drag it free, and my fingers are so much more certain this time as they work their way down his shirt buttons.

He breaks the kiss enough to reach inside his suit jacket, and I know he's going for the cash, *practicalities first*. But I don't want him to. I don't want to pull away and put that money in my bag. I don't want to cheapen this.

I push his shirt and jacket from his shoulders in one motion, and he doesn't fight me, just lets them slip to the floor.

His body is divine. His skin so firm under my fingers, the tickle of hair so perfect against my palm. I kiss his neck, and he tastes as good as he smells. I feel his groan as my lips press to his Adam's apple, and his stubble tickles my cheek as

I sweep to his ear.

"I'm crazy about this," I whisper, and he stiffens in my arms. "I'm crazy about you."

"You don't know me," he says, and reaches for my chin. He brushes his thumb over my mouth as he stares right through me. "You don't even know my name."

Touché.

"And *you* don't know *me*," I admit. "But what's in a name?"

His eyes are so dark. So serious.

"Amy Leigh Randall," he says. "Thirty-four Brooklyn Road, EC1. Twenty-one years old. Two younger sisters, Gemma and Belle. Your mother is a nurse, works at Saint Richmond General."

My mother is dead.

My stomach lurches. My shock is all genuine.

He brushes my cheek as he continues. "One credit card with zero balance. No driving offences. No criminal record."

"But how do you…"

"You studied business and management," he tells me. "But you dropped out last spring to take a position as a cattery assistant. I guess you like cats more than you like law, Miss Randall."

"But I…"

I have no words. I don't even like cats. I like dogs. *His* dog.

"I searched through your bag," he admits. "I wanted to know who you were."

"You searched through more than my bag," I whisper, and he nods.

"In my line of work I have to be… thorough…" He pauses. "I understand if you wish to leave, Amy."

But I don't. I've never been further from walking away from him in my life.

"You didn't have to tell me…" I breathe. "I wouldn't have…"

"Known?" He isn't smiling. He's stern and serious, and so beautiful he takes my breath. "No, you wouldn't have known. But you do now."

I unbuckle his belt. "Why did you want to know me?"

He grunts as I slip my hand around his cock. I work him fast, hoping I'm doing this right. Hoping he likes this.

He rocks his hips, shunts into my grip, and he's so hard. His cock throbs against my fingers.

"Why did you want to know me, Mr Brown?" I ask him. My voice is so soft, barely more than a hiss.

He tugs the neck of my tunic down enough to see my white lace bra. "Because I can't stop thinking about you," he admits, and it sounds pained. "Because this is sending me fucking insane."

Oh fuck, how I smile. I work his gorgeous dick in my fingers and the dresser bashes against the wall with a thud, thud, thud as he thrusts back at me, and I smile. I smile at him.

"My name's not Ted fucking Brown, either," he tells me. "It's Alexander."

"*Alexander.*"

It feels so good to say it.

He pinches my nipples through my bra, and the sparks are electric.

"Fuck me, Alexander," I hiss. "Please God, fuck me."

ALEXANDER

This girl. This fucking girl is sending me out of my mind.

I practically tear her dress over her head, shunting her against me as the fabric drags from under her ass. I have her bra off in a heartbeat, my mouth hungry for those sweet rosy nipples. I love the way her dainty fingers tangle in my hair. I love the way she moans for me and her legs grip me tight.

She wriggles as I tug at her knickers, and she's soaking wet when I slip my fingers between her thighs. Two straight in, my thumb rolling around her clit as she tilts her hips for me.

I drop to my knees and her thighs scissor my head as my tongue laps at her. Her pussy is heaven. The way she squirms is religion enough for me.

I grab her thighs and lift them, tip her back on the dresser with her legs spread wide. She spreads her pretty pink cunt for me without being asked, and it's so easy to suck that sweet little bud, so easy to make her beg for more, for harder. For everything.

Three fingers and she gasps.

A fourth, in her tight little asshole, and she cries out.

She wants cock. The hunger is in her eyes, her teeth gritted and feral as she hisses my name. My *real* name.

I haven't heard anyone scream my real name in far too long.

I haven't *known* anyone in far too long.

It's dangerous. Everything about this is dangerous. But I don't care.

She's ready as I get to my feet, her pussy taking my cock in one thrust. She arches her back and I palm her beautiful tits, and it's too inviting. She groans for me as I wrap my fingers around her throat.

"*Yes…*" she whispers, and I tighten my grip as I fuck her, her throat straining with every stroke.

Her whole body tenses as I angle my hips for the spot, her eyes screwing shut as I fuck her deep.

I let her breathe. Once, twice, three times, before I take her air all over again, and my balls are tight and desperate, my own breath ragged as she goes without.

I've only got a short window, but my own fuse is about to blow. I keep my eyes fixed on hers, soaking in the change in her pallor as her chest heaves.

I'm going to make her come without breath. I'm going to take her body to the edge without sound, without voice, in that hazy light of unconsciousness where there is only me.

Her hands grip my wrist but don't push me away. Her eyes wide as the pull of orgasm takes a grip of its own.

Her pussy clenches around my cock, her hips bucking for more even as she struggles for air.

She shudders. Squirms.

I feel everything.

Every tiny undulation as she comes for me. Every tremor as her body milks me dry.

I'm over the edge as I let her go, my cock pulsing deep inside her, my exhaled breath the first she takes into her lungs.

She coughs. Rasps. Her chest heaving under mine as I press my lips to her forehead.

I don't want to pull out of her.

I never want to pull out of her.

Her eyes come back into focus, her fingers a ghost against my cheek as she calms.

"*Alexander…*" she whispers, and my name is magic from her lips.

I hold her to me, cradling her head as I pull her up to sitting, and her legs squeeze me hard, her arms wrapping around my shoulders as though she never wants to let go.

She amazes me.

Her trust in me amazes me.

"Does it scare you?" I ask her, and my voice is more unsure than I'm unaccustomed to.

She shakes her head. "No."

I smooth her hair, my gaze not letting up as I search her face for more.

"No?"

Her eyes are so big. So vulnerable.

"You said you wouldn't kill me." She smiles so gently. "I trust you."

And *I* trust *her*.

I trust the way she looks at me. I trust the way she wants me.

I trust the way she trusts me.

Even if I don't quite trust myself.

MELISSA

My heart pangs with all the lies I've already told.

I feel them in my stomach, twisting around.

But I can't.

I can't risk it.

That seems crazy, even to me, given that I trust him to choke me until I see stars.

I trust him with my life, but not my name.

Yeah, that's crazy.

"I love the name Alexander," I tell him as he pours me champagne.

"Thank you," he says. "I'm glad you approve."

"You look like an Alexander."

"And you look like a sweet little peach." His eyes twinkle as he hands me the glass.

My hair must be a mess, my makeup all but destroyed as I cross my legs in the armchair, caring little for how on display I am.

I can still feel him inside me. I can still feel the throb of where he's been.

My throat is scratchy and it welcomes the champagne bubbles. My clit aches for more of his mouth.

He recovers his jacket and drapes it over his chair, reaching into his pocket for another envelope to add to my collection.

I tell myself it's all for Joe as I thank him, picture the figure rising in his savings account as I slip it into my handbag.

"Why cats?" he asks as he takes a seat opposite me. He looks more relaxed than usual, his cock hard but unassuming, still wet from me as it lays against his belly. His ankle rests on his knee, sprawling more contentedly than I've known him.

The hair is dark on his calves. I resist the urge to stroke them.

"I like animals," I tell him, careful to avoid lying any more than necessary. "Cats, dogs… hamsters…"

"Cats or law. I guess cats won."

"For now," I say. "Sometimes it's doing what you need to, in order to do what you want to, right?"

He looks so thoughtfully. "I'll let you know when I end up doing what I want to. Maybe someday."

"You don't like what you do?" It takes me aback enough that I drink more champagne to hide my surprise.

"No. I don't like what I do."

"But it buys you gemstones, right?"

He smiles. I love how he smiles. "And you, Amy. It buys me you."

I want to tell him I'd be here without the money, but the words won't come.

He pats his thigh and beckons me over. I finish up my champagne and place my glass on the dresser as I go to him.

It's so easy to lower myself onto his lap, so warm as he wraps his arms around my waist and lands a kiss on my shoulder. I relax against him, my head reclining so snug against his collarbone, and he hitches me, positions his cock just right as he lets me drop.

"You have a beautiful pussy," he whispers.

"You have a beautiful cock," I tell him, and he laughs.

"Mine's the only one you've known."

"The only one I want to know." I'm giggling but it's not funny. The way he breathes into my ear and holds me so tight isn't funny. It's bliss. Pure bliss.

"Show me what feels good," he says, and I do. I move slowly, carefully, up and down on his gorgeous dick as he stays still.

My breath quickens as I angle myself forward, the pressure too good to bear. His fingers dance up my spine and it's heaven. They tangle in my hair and I want to tell him I love him. I love *this*.

I surprise myself with what I want. I'm in shock as I lift myself enough to press his cock against my ass.

"Fuck," he rasps, and takes my hips. "Steady," he tells me, and I am steady. I'm really steady.

It burns an amazing burn as I ease down, and the stretch is incredible. I grit my teeth to take the whole length of him, and his thighs are tense as he sinks in all the way.

"Dirty girl," he grunts as I start moving, and I like that.

His cock in my ass drives me crazy, even through the burn. I rub my clit as I ride him, and I could come like this so easily, with my tits bouncing and my ass slapping against his lap.

"You're going to be the death of me," he growls, and it gives me shivers, like someone just walked over my grave.

The death of me.

It's raw. Everything about death makes life so raw.

I'm glad I'm grunting. Relieved I'm gasping and moaning through the urge to tell him he's been the *life* of me.

He thrusts back at me, flesh slapping flesh, and I fold forward, my hands balancing on his knees as he takes my weight.

"Give it to me," I hiss. "Please, Alexander, give it to me."

His arms wrap around my waist as he rises to his feet, his cock buried deep in my ass as he moves us to the bed.

I fall forward onto soft bedsheets, and his grip is on the back of my neck, pinning me down as he fucks me. Hard.

I cry out, my ass on beautiful fire as he thrusts.

"Don't come..." I moan. "Please don't come... not yet..."

"I won't," he grunts.

And he doesn't.

He fucks me until I'm a sweaty mess. Until my ass is slack and aching.

He fucks me until I don't know my own name anymore. I couldn't even tell him if I wanted to.

And finally, when he does fill me up with the perfect seed of him, my lips swollen from his kisses and my clit so tender it hurts, it's all I can do to get to my feet when he's done.

He reaches for his jacket and shrugs it on, and I have no idea what he's doing until he's eased my arms into his discarded shirt and buttoned me up.

He moves to the window and pulls back the drapes, swings it open wide on its hinges before he grabs a miniature whisky from the minibar.

He pours one for himself and opens another for me.

My nose wrinkles as I take a sniff.

"A routine of mine," he tells me. "A whisky before bed."

I smile. "I can do that."

My heart flutters as he pulls out his *Insignia* cigarette packet. My stomach tickles as he offers me one.

He flicks the lighter and holds the flame for me, and I hope I don't cough and splutter since it's been so long.

"Whisky and a cigarette," he says before lighting his own. "Two little vices before bedtime."

We stare at each other in silence, blowing smoke out through the open window as the first hint of dawn bleeds onto the horizon.

And then we go to bed.

TWENTY-NINE

MELISSA

I'm on borrowed time, playing this crazy game with an even crazier prize at the end of it.

Double or bust.

I'm dancing with disaster with every lie I tell, digging myself deeper with every step I take.

Turning up at his house to meet Sonnie without my uniform on Thursday morning, bed-headed and bleary-eyed as she grilled me on who I'd spent my night with.

She told me she wouldn't snitch to Janet Yorkley about my non-standard work attire, and I know she wouldn't.

It pained me to shrug off her questions about my *mystery man*, made me feel queasy when we reached Mr Henley's bedroom and found his bed still perfectly made from the day before.

How she'd grinned.

"Seems Mr Henley got himself lucky last night, too. I wonder who the lucky cow was."

I could've told her and I know it.

I could have confessed it all and trusted her to keep my secrets.

But I didn't.

Because as fucked up as it seems, I don't want to betray him any more than I already have by telling someone else before him.

And so here I am, heading across to Brickwood with another working week completed. Ready to serve up soup and sandwiches and looking forward to my Saturday with Joe and Dean.

Maybe he won't even be there. I don't know for sure Alexander turns up here every week, but my question is answered the moment I step in through the door and find him already at work at their industrial hob, a dark cap pulled down over his forehead.

I'd recognise him a mile off, even in crappy denim.

It takes every scrap of nerves not to bail and run, but I couldn't anyway. Frank is already heading in my direction, already calling out my name and telling me how pleased he is I could make it.

He wraps his arm around my shoulder as though we're old friends, and leads me through the kitchen introducing me to strangers.

Annabel, Mary, Christine. All nice. All smiling. All welcoming and happy to have me here.

And then, finally, he introduces me to Ted.

Ted turns to face me so slowly, as though being social is nothing but a headache.

He holds out a hand before he's even seen my face, and he tenses as I take it, his eyes shooting to mine in a heartbeat.

"Ted, this is Amy," Frank says. "Amy, this is Ted."

This was a mistake. I see it in his eyes.

They burn dark. His jaw fierce.

"Amy," he says and I burn up so hot I feel faint.

"Ted," I say and the word feels like glass in my throat.

Frank whisks me away to the vegetable station, and it's all I can do to stare back over my shoulder as Alexander's eyes eat me up.

"I'm sorry," I mouth, but he looks away.

ALEXANDER

My mind spins. Slurps around in a fucking mess as I stir the shit out of the soup pot.

I have no fucking idea why she's here, so far away from her fucking house.

I hand the stirrer to Annabel and stalk Frank right out into the storeroom, and I've grabbed his arm before I can stop myself. His eyes widen as he spins to face me.

"Amy," I say. "How do you know her? What's she doing here?"

He looks so fucking shocked, his mouth flapping like I'm a fucking lunatic.

And I am.

I am a fucking lunatic.

"Eastspring," he says. "She volunteers at Eastspring."

"Eastspring?"

He nods. "Yeah, Eastspring. But she couldn't make Wednesday night, said something came up. I suggested she come here instead." He pauses. "You know her?"

I'm out of control.

My paranoia tumbles down as I realise what a fucking fuckup I am.

"We've crossed paths."

He smiles. Poor sod has no fucking idea. "Ah yes, the volunteering circuit is a small place. She's been a godsend at Eastspring, works like a trooper."

278

It's innocent.

Frank's easy to read, an open book if ever there fucking was one.

A ridiculous coincidence, but one that has my heart racing.

"It's nice of her to change venues," I say.

"She's a good one," he tells me. "Sweet girl, very kind."

"Yes," I agree. "Very kind."

He slaps my arm. "Maybe she'll do both venues, we can hope, right?"

But she won't be doing both venues, even if our *anonymous donor* has to cough up the cash for a paid member of staff in her stead.

Her Wednesday nights belong to me now, even if she doesn't know it yet.

I feel like an asshole as I head back through to the kitchen. Amy looks terrified, staring over with scared eyes as I resume my station at the hob.

"I'm sorry," she mouths again and I feel like such a cunt.

I shrug, and then I smile.

She breathes in relief and pretends to wipe her brow, and she's beautiful. Absolutely beautiful in her dress-down clothes. A pair of jeans and a t-shirt under a fitted jacket.

"We'll talk later," I mouth and she nods.

I stir the fucking soup with a hard on until it's time to fucking go.

MELISSA

He's good on the streets.

He doesn't say much, but he's genuine.

There isn't a hint of snobbery as he hands out hot meals. There isn't any smug self-satisfaction in the way he works so hard.

I feel humbled.

I feel a fraud.

But I'm not a fraud, not entirely. I really do like it here.

I love the way the people are so kind. I love the way the people on the streets communicate from the heart, without any stupid sense of importance. I love the way it feels to help people and have them appreciate it, genuinely appreciate it.

It's late by the time we wipe down the counters back at the kitchen, stacking up all the trays ready for next week.

I get ready to leave with no assumptions, ready to make a sharp exit if Alexander seems uncomfortable.

He takes my arm as we get outside, angling me in a different direction to the others as we all say our goodbyes.

I wait until they're out of earshot before I speak, and I can't help myself, the apologies come tumbling out of my mouth before I've even properly said hello.

"I'm so sorry! I had no idea! Frank said come, because of Wednesday... and I wouldn't have thought..."

He shakes his head. "No," he says. "*I'm* sorry. My work makes me suspicious. It was unexpected, it's as simple as that."

"I won't come back," I say. "I'll tell Frank I can't make it..."

His eyes are piercing. "Why would you do that?"

I shrug, and I feel like shit for doing this. The whole thing feels like a bad idea going horribly wrong.

It probably is.

I can practically hear Dean's warning blaring in my head.

"Because of you... because I don't want to make you feel uncomfortable..."

"You think I'm uncomfortable?"

My eyes meet his, and I hate how they feel watery. "Aren't you?"

"No," he says. I'm sure I don't look convinced and he sighs. "Amy, it was a shock. I'm allowed to be shocked, aren't I? You must be shocked too. This is... unusual."

"London's a small place," I lie.

"So it appears." He takes his hands from his jacket pockets and sighs again. "Please let's just start over." He takes my hand and places something in my palm, and I know what it is straight away.

"You really carry it?" I say as I hold the stone up to the streetlight.

"It's lucky," he says.

I smile. "How do you know that?"

"Because you told me."

I wish his cap didn't hide so much of his face.

"I guess there must be something in all this *hocus pocus*," he adds, "because it brought you here."

"And that's lucky?"

His smile tickles my tummy. "I like to think so."

I hand him back the quartz and reach in my jeans pocket for the fire opal. I can't believe I'm doing this as I present it in my palm.

"It's lucky," I tell him. "It brought me here."

We stare at each other for an age. I don't move, and neither does he, trapped in no man's land on this grubby street corner with nobody else around.

"I should get going," I bluff, "I'll see you tomorrow."

"Yes," he says. "You will."

I've only taken two steps towards the underground before he calls me, and his voice gives me tingles all over.

"Do you have somewhere to be?" he asks as I turn around.

I shake my head. Another lie.

He looks as though he's struggling. Looks like a sailor lost at sea.

I wait.

Give him space.

It works, just as I know it will.

"My gemstone collection," he says. "I could show you, if you like."

"Now?" I ask, and my heart races. I feel it right through me.

"If you have time."

I smile, and I go to him. I link my arm through his, and rest my cheek against the scratchy denim of his shoulder and he doesn't pull away. I love how he doesn't pull away.

"All the time in the world," I say.

THIRTY

ALEXANDER

As I stand with Amy's arm through mine on that street corner, I'm not just waiting for the cab I just ordered, I'm waiting for my common sense to come piling back in to tell me this is a fucking stupid idea.

She doesn't even ask where we're headed as the taxi arrives, just piles herself into the backseat and shuffles along to make room for me. She doesn't even move fully to the other side – her body stays pressed to my side, her thigh tight against mine as she buckles herself in.

It's a comfortable silence. Strangely comfortable.

Resting my hand on her knee feels like the most natural thing in the world, even though it shouldn't be.

I've no idea why I feel like I've known her my whole fucking life, but I like it. I like it too fucking much to stop.

I pay the driver as we arrive outside mine, and if she's shocked by the grandeur

I take her hand as we head to the front door, and turn to face her as I slip my key into the lock.

"My dog is… difficult," I tell her. "He really doesn't like strangers."

"Don't worry," she says. "I'm good with dogs."

I want to apologise for him in advance and tell her the dismal story of his existence before I saved him from death row, just so she'll give him a chance, but she's already shivering from our evening in the cold.

"He'll be aggressive," I tell her. "But don't worry, I promise I won't let him hurt you."

"It's okay," she says. "I'm not scared."

But she will be. I know full well she will be.

I open the door and head on through to deactivate the alarm. She looks so dainty in my hallway as I get the lights. I can't stop staring as her eyes soak the place in.

I'm still staring as Brutus comes charging through, and he's so much fucking faster than usual. He's a dog who stalks from a distance, growls like a fucking demon before he attacks, but not tonight.

I lunge but I miss him, I yell his name and tell him to come fucking back, but he ignores me completely.

My blood runs cold as I charge down the hallway, and I'm shouting at her not to run, please don't fucking run.

But she doesn't.

She drops to her knees and the horror hits me in the gut.

She holds out her arms for him and I swear he's going to tear her pretty throat open.

But he doesn't. He fucking doesn't.

His tail is thumping as he skids to a halt, his tongue lolling out as she *coo coo*s in his face and scratches his ears. And I stare. Mute. Fucking astounded.

"What's his name?" she asks.

It takes me a moment to find my tongue. "Brutus."

"*Brutus!*" she says, and his tail thumps harder. "He's lovely."

"He's not usually," I tell her.

"Rescue?" she asks, and I nod. "He's lucky you found him."

"I'm the lucky one. He's great when you get to know him."

He's still staring up at her like a sappy poodle when she gets to her feet, and I can't believe it. I can't fucking believe it.

"You have a beautiful house," she says and I thank her. "And a beautiful dog," she adds, and I think she really believes it, even though he's hardly going to win a beauty pageant any time soon.

Maybe he doesn't need to. Maybe she sees through all that.

I shouldn't even be hoping, but I am. I shouldn't be this invested in some pretty girl who moonlights as a prostitute, but I am.

"Are you going to give me a tour?" she asks and I come to my senses enough to stop fucking gawping at her.

I lead her through to the kitchen and ask if she'd like a drink, and she sits herself at my island with her cute little feet tapping against the stool. Brutus plops himself down at her side, his head on his paws like she's part of the furniture.

Un-fucking-real.

"A coffee would be divine," she says, and I ditch my stupid incognito cap and get to work putting the beans in the machine, trying to work out if I've had a woman in this place since Claire. I haven't.

I'm still making the drinks when Brutus gets to his feet. He needs a piss, I know it as soon as he barks, but it's not me he's asking. He's barking at her, as though she'll know what the fuck he's asking for.

But she does.

She slips from the stool and heads for the back door like it's the most natural thing in the world.

"He wants to go out, right?" she asks, and I nod.

"Please."

She catches me watching and tips her head. "What? What is it?"

"Milk?"

She nods. "Please. Two sugars." She smiles. "You weren't wondering if I take milk, were you?"

I hand her a mug without saying a word, but she won't let it up.

"What?" she says, and giggles. "You're making me nervous."

I look about the room, look anywhere. "Just this," I tell her. "This is strange. Brutus is strange."

"Dogs can tell who their kind of people are," she says.

"So it seems."

"I'm glad he likes me." She smiles.

I have a niggle in my gut I can't place. It feels tender – as though the tiniest green shoot is poking its fragile form up through charred soil.

It's not entirely pleasant.

Brutus pads nonchalantly back inside and I wonder what the hell he's thinking as his eyes meet mine. His eyes say nothing other than he loves our new guest, and I trust him. I trust his judgement as much as my own.

I force that niggle aside. Force myself to go along with this insanity, because why not?

What else is there to do?

How could I possibly walk away from this?

Amy locks the back door without being asked. I watch her drink her coffee and enjoy the way the colour comes back to her cheeks.

"It was cold out there," she says. "But worth it. I love working with the homeless. It makes you so grateful for what you have, right? I'm just glad I can do something to help, even if it's just a little."

"I fell into it," I admit and her eyebrows lift.

"Fell into it?"

But I don't want to expand on that. Not today. Maybe not ever.

I finish up my drink and she follows my lead.

"I'll give you the tour," I say.

She holds out her hand and I take it.

MELISSA

This is so much harder than I thought.

My heart is pounding despite my easy smile, so worried I'm going to give the game away with some silly oversight. Like knowing the way his dog barks.

Knowing where his bathrooms are.

Knowing the names of his kids when he unavoidably points out their pictures on the mantelpiece. I ask about them as though I don't know.

"Thomas and Matthew," he says. "They live with their mother in Hampshire."

"That must be hard."

"Very," he admits, and I see a flash of pain in his eyes. "But it's for the best. They're thriving. Happy."

"They must love the dog," I say, and that makes him smile.

"They do, yes. And he loves them." He lifts one of the photos as though he's looking at it new. "My ex-wife isn't quite so fond of him."

I don't think it's my place to ask about his divorce, so I don't.

The pressure of acting ignorant is building up behind my eyes, but I don't show it. I keep my questions light and vague, oohing and ahhing over the place as though I'm seeing it all for the first time.

"I love the smell of orchids," I say, and a shiver zips up my spine as he angles one to my face for a sniff.

"My cleaner gets them," he admits. "She's excellent. They're a nice touch."

She's excellent.

My smile feels ridiculously bright on my face, but he doesn't seem to notice.

I don't know if I can really go through with this phase of my master plan, not now it feels so personal in here. Not now I feel so... overwhelmed.

As we step past the entertainment unit I'm forced to make my decision.

I make it in a heartbeat.

I spin so quickly towards his selection of CDs, my expression one of pure fake-shock as I pull out an album from the pile.

"Oh my God! You like Kings and Castles?!"

My fake-shock has nothing on the surprise on his face. "You know them?"

"Do I know them?! Hell yeah, they're my all-time favourite band!"

I hate this even as I'm doing it. Hate the shock in his eyes. Hate the fact I feel so obliged to perform like a circus monkey to make him fall in love me.

"That's extraordinary," he says. "Hardly anyone knows they exist."

"Crazy, right? I'm always saying it. I mean take Casual Observer, that song is my all-time favourite. How it doesn't get more radio airplay I have no idea. Criminal, don't you think?"

"Criminal, yes." He stares right through me. "That's my favourite too, actually."

I put a hand on my heart. "Wow. What are the odds?"

"Slim," he tells me, and he's not kidding.

I rattle off my imaginary history with the band, how my dad loved them, how I knew the singer dedicated a song to his dying grandmother, how I think their first album is seriously underrated, and how terrible the first mainstream music journalist who tore them to shreds in his column was for destroying their chances before they'd really started.

He listens. He nods.

I tell him how I love the lyrics in Casual Observer. How deep they are. How well they capture the loneliness of being surrounded by people and yet feeling so utterly misunderstood. So alone.

He's barely even nodding now. Just staring. His eyes piercing and raw.

"Sorry," I tell him. "I get a little carried away. I just love them so much."

"That's ok," he replies. "I do, too."

I slide the CD back in the collection and hold out my hand for the rest of the magical mystery tour.

He shows me his office, and the conservatory, and the dining room he barely uses. He tells me he has a bit of a gym set up downstairs, but doesn't take me down there.

I comment on the little things, the innocuous things, being so careful and considered. And fake.

I've never felt so fake in my entire life.

My heart is in my throat by the time the downstairs tour is finished, choked up with guilt and the crazy desire to tell him I've already been here. That I really do like Kings and Castles, but it's because of him. Because I heard them here.

To tell him that I already know him.

But he's no longer awkward or guarded, not like he was when I first pulled out that CD. He looks relaxed, even excited now the shock has left his beautiful face.

And I don't want to risk it. I can't risk it.

He takes my hand at the bottom of the stairs, and all thought of a confession zips out of my mind.

"Let me show you my collection," he says.

ALEXANDER

Kings and Castles. They have a hardcore following, but to say it's on the small side would be generous.

Barely anyone even knows they exist.

But Amy does.

I'm not sure this shit could get any more fucking weird if it tried.

I'm no bloody sap. I don't believe in happy ever afters, or soulmates, or twin flames or any of that other mumbo jumbo shit they use to sell dating site memberships and Valentine's Day cards.

I don't believe in anything other than two people deciding they can tolerate each other enough to make it through life in the same building, with maybe a bit of mutual affection along the way.

And sex. I believe in sex.

My heart is racing ten to the fucking dozen. My throat feels dry as I lead this girl upstairs, and there's a tickle in my gut driving me insane.

A tickle that daren't hope. That would be insane to even fucking hope this crazy connection between us could mean something.

Yet she feels so fucking real. The soul in her eyes is so fucking real. The way she wants me feels too insanely right to be wrong.

I'm terrified how much I fucking want this.

I lead her straight through to the crystal room and flick on the light.

Nobody has ever seen my collection, nobody that would give a shit about it anyway. Barely anyone finds these wonders of the natural world as beautiful as I find them.

But Amy does.

Her eyes widen as I input the cabinet code, she gasps as the light hits the gemstones and makes them sparkle in all their glory.

"My God," she whispers. "This is insanely awesome."

I stare at her as she surveys my collection open-mouthed, and I've misjudged her by thinking of her as a new-age hippy type. Of course I have.

Nothing about this girl any longer surprises me.

"You have poudretteite! I've wanted to see one in the flesh for years! I read about it when I was a kid, how they found it in Mont St. Hilaire!" Her fingers dither in the air. "And musgravite! From the Musgrave Ranges in Australia! This is crazy!"

Yes. Yes it is.

I listen to her in awe. Her knowledge of rare gemstones is incredible, better even than some of the hardcore collectors I go up against in auctions, those trigger happy types who take the listing details as gospel and care nothing for the actual stones themselves.

"You can touch them," I tell her, and she gasps.

"I couldn't!"

I take out the musgravite and place it in her hand, and her fingers are trembling.

I'm taken aback to find that mine are too.

"I had no idea you were so…" I begin, and I struggle to find the words without sounding like a condescending cunt.

She giggles. "Serious? It's alright. I have a couple of cheap stones in a little velvet bag. It hardly reeks of sophistication."

I feel like an asshole, but she looks at me like I'm the greatest man alive.

"You amaze me," I tell her, and she takes a breath.

"You amaze me, too," she whispers, and then she giggles some more. "I can't believe this. I can't believe any of this."

Neither can I.

I can hardly breathe. Hardly think. Hardly fucking speak as I watch that girl hold the musgravite up to the light.

She puts it back so gently on its display stand, and her fingers drift down to the empty space where the fire opal once rested.

"It was one of your favourites," she says as she runs a finger over the plinth.

"I have a new favourite," I tell her, and take the quartz from my pocket. I place it on the plinth and even though it looks so thoroughly out of place amongst the others, I love it more than any of them.

Her cheeks flush pink. "You need a new display card."

"You can write me one," I tell her, and dig around on the shelf for a piece of card. I present her with a fountain pen and wait for her to fill in the details, but she hovers. Dithers.

"My handwriting will be messy," she says. "You should really print one."

But I don't want a printed one. I want her to pen it by hand.

I tell her so.

"Your handwriting will be neater," she protests, but I shake my head.

"Please, Amy."

Her fingers are still shaking as she writes out the description. It's hardly what I was expecting. No weight, or mining location. No crazy new age properties.

Instead there is a simple description.

Angel Hair Quartz. From me to you, Alexander, with love.

With love.

She seems embarrassed as soon as she's written it, placing it front of the empty plinth with a shrug.

I can't stop myself as my hand reaches for hers, can't fight the urge as I pull her into my arms.

She comes so willingly, and I feel her heart beating through my shirt.

"Stay tonight," I whisper.

Her eyes are unsure. "But I, I didn't... I didn't come here for that... that isn't why I came here..."

Another asshole move. I feel like a dick as I squeeze her shoulders. "Fuck, Amy. I'm sorry, I didn't mean... That isn't why I invited you." I press my forehead to hers. "I'd pay, of course, I don't expect this to be..."

She shakes her head, her forehead brushing mine. "That's not what I mean. It's not the money... I just didn't want you to think I was... angling..."

And I don't want her to think I was angling either. I press my lips to hers.

"We're dancing a merry dance. Getting our wires all tangled up," I tell her.

She nods. "Let's start over?"

"Please."

She smiles a beautiful smile and breathes out a sigh. "I'd love to stay. Please. If you'll have me, and it's not about the money..."

"What is it about?" I ask her, and my voice sounds strangely uncertain.

"You know what it's about," she whispers, and her eyes stare right into my soul. "This is... crazy... I've never felt like this..."

I'd tell her I was feeling it too if she'd let me, but her mouth presses to mine and finds me desperate.

She tastes of everything I ever wanted.

THIRTY-ONE

MELISSA

wish the want I feel in his kisses was all for me and not for the crazy illusion I've spun, but I can't stop.

I can't stop this.

He smells of hard work and spicy tomato soup.

He tastes like every dream I ever had.

It's weird undressing him from tattered denim. It's weird to feel the ridges of his chest under a plain black t-shirt.

He tugs my top over my head and unbuttons my jeans, and I step out of them as we leave the crystal room. The thick carpet on his landing is so familiar under my toes.

He kisses me again as he opens his bedroom door, and I have to pull away to comment on how beautiful it is in here.

He shushes me with his mouth, and his hands are on my face, in my hair, all over me.

My bra falls away, and my knickers slip down my thighs as I fumble with his belt.

Skin on skin as he lifts me into his arms, and my legs wrap him tight as he kicks off his jeans and boxers on the way to his bed.

It's bliss as he lowers me onto the sheets I made up so nicely this morning. It's a dream to be here with him.

His mouth sends me crazy as he kisses my neck. The ridge of his cock rubs against my needy clit and makes me squirm.

I'm desperate as I grip his ass, already way past the point of no return as he thrusts his hips and spears me in one and I cry out, tell him how amazing he is, how amazing it feels.

I'm prepared for his fingers when they land on my throat. I'm prepared for the darkness in his eyes as they bore into mine.

But this time he doesn't take my air. His grip is firm but not restrictive, and I breathe freely, quick gasps of air against his lips.

"Do it..." I whisper.

But he doesn't.

I cry out as he changes position. He rolls me onto my side and presses himself to my back, his legs hooking mine as his cock slides in from behind and I cry out all over again. His breath is hot on my neck as he wraps an arm around to take me in a chokehold.

The pressure is divine. The heat gives me perfect shudders.

And here, wrapped up so tight in his grip, my chin pressed tight to the crook of his elbow, I find peace.

His free hand finds my clit and he starts fucking me. I'm panting like crazy as his thrusts match the rhythm of his fingers.

"You never did tell me what really turns you on," he whispers.

"This," I groan.

He asks me again as he rolls my clit between his fingers.

"*You*," I hiss. "Fuck, Alexander, It's you I want. You're the only thing I want."

I don't think I'd be getting away with such vague answers if he wasn't already close to the edge.

He holds back until my body trembles for him, controls his urges until I'm already crying his name, and then he joins me there, cursing through gritted teeth as he fills me up.

I'm still panting as he pulls away, my arms are reaching for him as he stalks across to his dressing room and grabs one of his sex toy cases.

"You're going to tell me what turns you on," he says as he plugs in the massager. "You're going to tell me everything."

Everything.

Sudden paranoia burns at my face. I look away, head down. The buzz against my throbbing clit makes me groan, but I'm rocking for him, easing my hips up to take more.

"What turns you on, Amy?" His tone is so dark, so dirty.

"You," I whisper, and he flicks up the speed on the massager.

"*Fuck*," I hiss. "I like... I like it when you're rough... I like it when you're in my ass..." I cry out as he sucks his finger and pushes it right in there.

"What else?"

"I love... I love it when you choke me... I love how it feels..."

"How does it feel?"

I can't stop the smile. "Like I can't take it... and then like I can... I float... and it's amazing... it's beautiful to see the stars... to see you..."

"And you're not scared?"

I shake my head. "No..."

I'm going to come so hard. I feel it from my clit to my toes.

"What else?"

I'm sweating. I can taste it on my lips.

"Amy, what else turns you on? What do you think about when you're alone?"

I don't want to do this. I don't want to say this. I'm already in way too deep.

I murmur that he's everything. That I want everything *he* wants. He pushes another finger in my ass and I'm on fire.

I can't hold back the words. Can't hold back the thoughts I've had in bed at night.

The thoughts about that divorce paperwork.

The thoughts about the filthy things he likes.

I can't hold back the thoughts about him and Dean.

"I want to see you…" I whisper. "Oh God…"

"See me what?"

He moves so quickly. Pinning himself on top with his cock poised against my open lips.

He's so hard. I can taste the wetness on his tip.

"See me do what, Amy?"

He pushes into my mouth until I gag, and then he pulls right out again.

My clit sparks like fucking crazy.

His balls are heavy on my forehead. He smells incredible.

His voice is raspy. "I have very few hard limits. You just have to fucking tell me."

And I do.

My confession is nothing but a whisper choked in the air.

"I want… I want to see you… with another man."

He comes in my mouth with the words still hanging in the air.

He comes with a grunt that sounds feral, spurting to the back of my throat without warning as I gag on my own orgasm.

I'm a mess. Wriggling and squirming and gurgling his name as my legs thrash the bed.

And when I'm done I can hear my heartbeat in my ears. My breath feels like fire in my chest.

He unplugs the massager without a word, and my endorphins shrivel away.

Fuck. I've fucked this up.

I tell him I shouldn't have said that. That it's no big deal, just a crazy fantasy.

I tell him it's stupid. That my stupid mouth was running away with me.

But when he talks, he talks right over me.

"How the hell did you know?"

ALEXANDER

My question leaves her open-mouthed. Her eyes wide and fluttery. "How did I know what?"

My heart is pounding hard, my breaths ragged from the spontaneous eruption of my fucking balls.

She rises to sitting. "What? What do I know?"

My gut is in fucking knots, as though I've been exposed raw. Guilty pleasures are so fucking guilty.

I spit it out. "How the hell did you know I want men?"

"You *do*?!" Her cheeks flush pink. "I, um… I didn't…" If she's a liar, she's a fucking good one. She looks mortified. "Shit, Alexander! You asked and I answered. It's just a stupid fantasy. I didn't think you'd… I wasn't even going to say anything…"

And she wouldn't have.

It took a fucking bodywand on high speed and two thick fingers in her asshole to unravel her enough to confess.

"I haven't done it for a long time," I tell her. "Since before I was married."

"It's really none of my business, you don't have to tell me..."

But I want to. Because if this is real... if she really...

I rub my temples. "I struggle with this. With this... *interest.*"

"You feel bad about wanting sex with other men?"

Her question is so innocuous, so unassuming, and it makes me feel like a fucking douche for my hang-ups.

"I have my fucking father to thank for that," I admit. "And my judgemental fucking bitch of an ex-wife."

"You don't have to talk about it..."

"It's not that I don't want to talk about it." I hate the way my voice snaps. "I'm just not used to talking. I'm not used to..." My arms gesture to nothing. "*This.* Any of this."

"It's just a silly fantasy." Her voice is so calm. "It's not a big deal. I don't want to make you feel uncomfortable."

But I can't deny the truth to myself.

I *love* how uncomfortable she makes me feel. I love how on edge this is making me, how fucking desperate I feel inside.

I love the glimmer of hope in the darkness. And I love that I hope this is something.

I feel like a fucking fool for it, but I do.

I relax onto the bed, my head propped on my elbow. "Tell me about your fantasy."

She mirrors my position, her eyes so hungry for mine. "I'm not sure I should..."

"Tell me," I insist, and she shrugs.

"I think about you fucking another guy. I think about watching. I think about your cock in another guy's ass, I think about you... being rough... I think about you, um... choking him... like you choke me." She pauses. "I think about watching you kiss another guy. I think about you with his cum in your mouth. I think about how it would make me feel..."

My mouth is bone fucking dry. "How would it make you feel?"

She gasps, and this is real. The truth of it prickles my fucking skin as she slips her fingers between her thighs. "It makes me come... when I think about it..."

My words are parched. "Show me..."

And she fucking does.

She circles that tender fucking clit with her little fingers until she squirms. *"Oh God,"* she whispers. *"Oh fuck, I want to see you fuck someone so hard..."*

"You want to see my cock in another guy's dirty fucking asshole?" My cock twitches. I can't hide how fucking hard I am.

She screws her eyes closed. *"Yes. Oh God, yes..."*

I can't stop myself wrapping my hand around my dick. "You want to see me pound some other guy's filthy fucking hole?"

She groans. *"Please, oh fuck... fuck..."*

"And what would *you* be doing?"

Her eyes are so hooded when they meet mine. *"Watch... I want to watch... I want to see everything..."*

"Just watch?"

Her voice is fragile. Timid. *"I don't know..."*

"I'm rough," I grunt. "When I fuck like that... it's rough..."

She moans, and her fingers are fucking frantic between her legs. "Fuck, Alexander, I want that... I really want to see that..."

I can't come again so soon, it's fucking insane, but my balls are aching all fucking over again, my cock jerking like a fucking fish in my palm.

She braces herself against me, her fingers tight on my shoulder. "I come every time I think about you with another man..."

And so do I.

It hurts when I shoot my load against her belly. My dick is raw and pulsing, my balls pained as they fucking blow.

I stare dumbly as she drags my cum down between her thighs and rubs my creamy fucking seed around her clit.

Her eyes have a filthiness in them I've never seen. I'm open-mouthed as she takes hold of my hair and urges me down between her legs.

"*Please*," she whispers. "*Oh God, Alexander... please...*"

She wants me to lick myself from her fucking pussy.

She wants to see me with my own fucking cum in my mouth.

My heart is fucking frantic. The girl is sending me fucking insane.

I know right now I'm doomed, snared by this beautiful fucking creature in my fucking bed.

So I do it.

I lick my lick every drop of cum from her fucking pussy, and I open wide to show her. My dirty fucking secrets are right there for her to see, my eyes fucking desperate as I let my own fucking cum dribble from my filthy fucking mouth.

She comes. Hard.

My fingers dance with hers around her sopping clit, and her mouth is open for mine as she rides the fucking wave. She drags me to her and she feels as desperate as I do.

I've never wanted anything as I want to please this fucking girl.

I'll do fucking anything to please this fucking girl.

She moans around my tongue, sucking the taste of me. She tips my head back and her eyes are hooded once again as she waits for me to swallow.

I swallow and she smiles.

Her smile is *everything*.

I wait until our calming breath is the only thing between us.

The words burn as they come out.

"I'll do it," I tell her.

THIRTY-TWO

MELISSA

I t feels grubby to take his money in the morning, but he insists.

He hands me the envelope when I'm finishing up my muesli and won't hear any of my protests.

"How is it?" he asks as I scoop up the final dregs of milk from the bowl, and I have to smile another stupidly-ignorant smile.

"Delicious. I love how the peaches taste with the chocolate. It's so unusual."

He seems to like that. "One of my silly little specialities. I'm not much of a chef."

I tell him I disagree, but he laughs it off.

His laugh is divine.

He asks my plans for the day and it catches me off guard.

My heart pangs at the thought of Joe waiting at home.

Alexander looks a little disappointed as I tell him I'll have to leave soon. I wish I could invite him to come along and hang out with us, maybe push Joe on the swings awhile.

Maybe one day.

"I'll see you later, yes?" he checks, and I nod.

"Of course. Delaney's at eight."

He shakes his head. "No need for Delaney's. I think we've well and truly crossed professional boundaries, don't you?"

I know this is a triumph. Waking up in his bed with him was the most amazing feeling.

"I'll come back here, then? At eight?" I'm so happy I could cry.

"Whenever you're ready."

I nod. Thank him again for the money and the breakfast. Thank him for everything.

I hug Brutus goodbye, and kiss Alexander right on the mouth in the doorway without holding back.

There's nothing left *to* hold back.

ALEXANDER

I wire the rest of Amy's money to Claude's offshore account and let him know about my impromptu evening by email.

I tell him I'll no longer be needing Delaney's while I'm at it.

His reply comes through instantly.

No venue?

No venue, I confirm. *I'll take it from here,* I confirm.

You exchanged personal information?

I don't bother replying to that one. It's none of the cunt's fucking business what I've exchanged with her.

Having the girl in my home was the final straw for me. The final scrap of my restraint has shrivelled and died. For better or fucking worse I'm all in with this insanity.

I browse upcoming music events after I've walked Brutus, but there's nothing that takes my interest.

I haven't felt alive in so long. This surge of life is addictive. It makes me believe anything is possible. *Anything.*

That's why I fire an email off to the Kings and Castles management team. That's why I ask them why their current gig listings are empty on their website.

It takes a few hours to get a response, but when it arrives it's very forthcoming.

That's what an email signature like mine gets you. That's what being a lawyer gets you full stop in fact, even if your email has nothing to do with the fucking law whatsoever.

They tell me the band are recording a new album. They tell me there will be no upcoming gigs for at least six months.

I call the mobile number listed, and a shy woman answers.

"It's Alexander Henley," I tell her. "I just emailed."

"Yes," she says. "I'm sorry about the schedule, but if you check back in six months…"

"I've no interest in checking back in six months," I say, and I have my calendar open in front of me. "I want them to perform next week."

"But that's… impossible…"

"Five hundred grand," I tell her, and her gasp of breath tells her I've gone in way too high, but I don't fucking care.

"Five hundred thousand? To play next week?!" I hear the frantic tapping of keys and imagine her looking me up from my email details.

"I'll transfer the funds on confirmation."

"I'd need to make some calls…"

"I'll be waiting," I tell her.

She calls me back in fifteen, and by then I've already confirmed a venue. An intimate little gig in Charing Cross road. The venue also cost me a pretty penny, but I don't care about that either.

I'm used to Brenda organising my entire life for me, but not this time. I'm glad I'm handling this one for myself. The thrill is exhilarating.

I'm surprised I haven't done this before, but Claire hated this band. She hated pretty much everything I loved.

"I've pulled some strings," the woman on the phone tells me.

Her words make me smile.

I give her the venue details and she writes them down. I ask her for their bank details and she reads them out twice.

I ask for an official invoice which she assures will arrive in my inbox in less than five minutes.

It takes four exactly.

I wire the funds with a smile on my face, and it takes all of my reserve not to head right on over to Amy's house to spill the crazy fucking news.

But I don't.

The surprise will be the sweetest.

MELISSA

My heart feels full to bursting as I lift Joe into the baby swing. His sweet laughter tickles me, his little bobble hat swaying in the breeze.

Dean has a quiet smile on his face as he watches us, his hands shoved into his jeans pockets against the chill.

I try not to stare at him, but I can't help it. I try not to wonder what will happen if he agrees to my crazy scheme, but I can't help myself.

I try not to imagine him taking Alexander's beautiful cock in his ass. The idea makes me lurch like a rollercoaster.

I don't know whether I can ask him. I don't know whether doing something like that would be too weird to ever come back from.

But he wants Alexander. I know he does. I know he thinks about it.

I know he'd be the perfect set-up. I know he'd enjoy it like I enjoy it. I know he'd know what to expect and not go screaming for the hills as soon as that grip landed firm around his throat.

"You're quiet," he says as we head away from the park.

"Am I?"

He smiles. "Yeah, Lissa, you really are. All Henley'd up, I guess."

"Something like that."

We buy a pot of bubbles on the walk back, and Joe claps his hands as they float all around.

He's happy. He's really happy.

And I am too.

"You out again tonight?" Dean asks as he pours us a coffee back home.

I nod. "It's Saturday. My usual night."

"What about Wednesday? Is that a usual night now as well?"

I don't know, I tell him. Because I don't.

"And Fridays?"

I don't know that, either.

"It's great money," I say. "Crazy money."

"So quit the day job."

I feel the niggle in my belly. "Maybe soon."

"Maybe right now, before he puts two and two together and this whole mess puts you on your ass."

He's got a point and I know it.

"Soon," I repeat. "Maybe."

He lets it drop.

The pressure to confess my crazy scheme is right behind my eyes. But I can't. Not with Joe chomping happily on apple slices in the room next door.

I feel guilty all over again, but this time it's not for Alexander. It's for the shit I'm going to try to drag Dean into.

It's for the crazy way I've been thinking about him.

"Do whatever you have to do," he tells me when I'm all dressed up and ready to go. "Whatever it is, just go all in and get it done. You've got to, Lissa. You've got to make this real or walk away, for all of us, not least for you."

My heart thumps.

"I know," I tell him, and I do know.

I'm close enough to taste it. Close enough to feel my dreams at my fingertips.

I just need him to help me with the last final hurdle.

"I'll see you in the morning," I say. "We'll have an us night tomorrow. Wine, takeout..."

"Sounds good to me."

"We need to talk," I tell him, and his eyes are so suspicious.

They should be. He knows me too well.

"Talk about what?"

"Alexander Henley stuff," I say as I head for the door. "And stuff about us, too. I'll tell you all tomorrow, I promise."

I kiss Joe on the way out, and dash off for Kensington before Dean can grill me for details.

ALEXANDER

My attempt at homemade paella is quite abysmal, but Amy doesn't seem to mind.

Her eyes sparkle across the dining table as I top up her wine, and I'm itching to tell her about my grandiose gesture for next weekend.

I keep a poker face regardless.

A full stomach does nothing to quell her libido. She's tearing my shirt from my chest before we've even cleared the plates.

I fuck her all the way through my house.

I push her to her knees in my hallway and ram my cock right down her pretty throat.

Her lips are still glistening with my cum as I finger fuck her asshole over my kitchen island.

She's perfectly ready for my cock as I take her tight cunt over my coffee table.

I fuck her again as we're washing up for bed. She braces herself on the wash basin as I choke her until her legs are weak. Her eyes are stark in the medicine cabinet reflection. Her skin looks so pale as I take her to edge.

I have to support her weight as she comes with my thumb against her clit.

She's still loose and limp as I carry her through to the bedroom like a perfect little doll.

And there she rests – her head snug in the crook of my shoulder as she drifts off to sleep.

I browse gay hook-up sites on my phone until sleep finds me too.

THIRTY—THREE

ALEXANDER

T he usual undertone of desolation is absent as I make the drive across to Hampshire on Sunday afternoon. Even Brutus seems to grin at me, his overbite looking especially slobbery as he pants in the passenger seat.

I think he liked having Amy in our house again last night.

Having a new cleaner in the house first thing this morning, not so much.

"You've got to stop doing that shit," I tell him, as though he stands a hope in hell of understanding. "You'll get us into trouble one day, boy."

Having to rescue a damsel in distress from behind your kitchen doorway at seven a.m. – dressed in nothing but your bathrobe – raises the heartrate somewhat.

Brutus still looks thoroughly pleased with himself.

At least our sweet Amy slept through the fracas.

My sweet Amy slept like an angel. An angel with a sore fucking asshole. I can't fight the smirk.

I'm enjoying the sensation of waking up in my own bed with her tight little body next to mine. I'm enjoying her gentle laughter. I'm enjoying the way she wants me.

I'm enjoying everything.

And I'm going to enjoy seeing my boys, too.

They're already waiting when I pull up on Claire's driveway. They rush though the front door as their mother paces out after them, but even the scowl on her miserable face can't dent my mood.

I give the boys a hug and tell them to pile on in to see Brutus, and Claire waits until they're safely in the Merc before she launches into her monologue about state school being the right option for the boys, and have I thought any more about my *silly* position on the whole thing.

I tell her *no* – in no uncertain terms – and she shakes her head.

"You're unbelievable, Alex. You need to think of the *boys*."

My response is instant. I *am* thinking of the fucking boys.

"They *are* moving schools!" she blusters.

I hold my ground. They're not moving fucking schools without my say so and she fucking knows it.

I'd strip her of her lavish lifestyle in a heartbeat, fight her through the courts with a legal prowess far more intimidating than she'll ever have access to.

She'd be a fool to fight me head-on and she knows that, too.

"You're a stubborn bastard," she says, and I nod.

"Think what you want, Claire. The boys need a decent education."

"Like *you* had? So they can turn out like *you?!*"

I don't grace her with an answer to that one. I'm already heading back to the car, fighting to keep hold of my sunny disposition long enough to smile through crappy burgers and too much football lingo.

"Ask them what *they* want!" she calls after me. "At least ask the boys what *they* want!"

So I do.

I ask them as soon as we've taken a seat with our offal-based meat products.

"Your mother tells me you want to change schools," I say. "Is that true?"

Matthew nods his head with a smile, blissfully oblivious of any potential tension.

Thomas not so much.

His eyes leave mine and stare at the table top, burger discarded.

"Well, Thomas? Is it true? Do you want to change schools?"

He shrugs.

It isn't like him to avoid a direct question, and since he *is* avoiding the question this really isn't the right place to push it, not amongst the screaming toddlers and the families out for a cheap bite to eat.

I change the topic of conversation, focusing instead on Portsmouth's goal-scoring record this season, and that works well to lighten the mood.

"I'm going to play for Portsmouth," Thomas tells me. "Terry says I'm really good."

"He does, does he?" My boy nods, and even though Terry's fucking name makes my insides grimace, I'm undeniably proud. "That's good," I say. "Well done."

It's Matthew who drops the next shitty bombshell. The poor kid has no idea.

"We're going training!" he gushes. "Terry's going to put us in kids' club!"

"Excellent," I lie. "And what does *kids' club* involve?"

Thomas tells him to shut his stupid little mouth, and I'm taken aback by the venom in his tone.

"Enough of that," I snap. "Let your brother speak."

But Matthew doesn't want to speak. Not now. His lip trembles as he holds back tears, and he looks so young sitting there. I'd forgotten how young he is.

Thomas folds his arms. "It's on a Sunday. You won't let us go anyway."

"Won't let you go?"

He shakes his head. "Mum said there's no point even asking. She said you'll *never* say yes."

My throat dries. "Never say yes to you training on a Sunday afternoon?"

They both nod, and it smacks me right in the gut. I could retch my fucking French fries all over the fucking table.

"That's what you want, is it? You want to go training?"

Thomas shrugs, but Matthew is still too young to understand etiquette. He nods so innocently, and I really do think I'm going to vomit up my fucking dinner.

"We won't go," Thomas says. "We see *you* on a Sunday afternoon."

But they want to. I can see it all over them.

I wrap up my burger and clear my throat. "If you want to go training with Terry on a Sunday afternoon, you should go."

Their eyes widen.

"But that's your day..." Thomas tells me, like I'm not perfectly fucking aware of that.

Forcing a smile is so fucking hard. "We'll make other time," I say, even though I know it's probably a fucking lie. "Maybe Saturdays, or holidays. Maybe even weeknights when the evenings get longer again."

Matthew punches the air. He hollers out a YES that gets the family to our right turning their heads, and I know it's signed and sealed already.

"What about you?" Thomas asks, and I have to pretend I'm choking on a gherkin.

"I'll be around," I say. "I'm your dad, right?"

They nod.

That's right, I'm their fucking dad. Even if they have a new one now. Even if Terry steals my Sundays, and takes them out of the school I chose for them, and gives them another cool sibling to add to their dinner table.

Even if it doesn't fucking feel like I'm their dad.

Even if it never feels like it again.

I still am.

I still am their fucking dad.

"Drink up," I say. "We'll take Brutus for a walk."

They drink up.

My fingers are shaking as I pick up my uneaten burger for the dog. My throat is scratchy as I dump the empty wrappers in the bin on the way out.

I park up at the meadow a couple of streets down from Claire's, and Brutus piles out happily, wagging his tail as Thomas clips on his leash.

We walk in silence, lapping that meadow three times before I can bring myself to speak.

"Tell me about school," I say. "What do you want to do?"

Thomas looks up at me, and I keep my expression as neutral as I can.

"You can tell me," I say.

So he does.

My boy tells me how he hates the school I picked for him. How he hates the other kids, and thinks the teachers are stuck up and boring.

He tells me how he feels sick to his stomach every time he has to go there.

How the other boys call him a common little freak because he likes football now and not rugby.

He tells me how they call him a little gay boy because he doesn't scrum like he used to.

I'm sure there's no blood left in my face as I land a hand on his shoulder and ask him why the hell he didn't tell me this before.

And now it's Thomas who has the trembling lip, wiping tears away on the back of his sleeve before they have chance to spill.

"Because... because I didn't want..."

"Didn't want what?"

It breaks my heart when his face crumples, and in some deep part of me I'm relieved to find I still have one.

"I didn't want you to be ashamed of me."

And now Matthew is crying too. My two boys stand and cry in front of me and I feel nothing but a cunt.

It's so easy to pull them into my arms, so easy to breathe into their hair so they don't see I'm right on the fucking edge myself.

"I'll never be ashamed of you," I tell them. "Not ever. No matter what. Do you understand me?"

I have to pull away long enough to check their faces.

"Boys, do you understand me?"

They nod.

I can't believe I'm saying this. I can't believe I have to say this.

Most of all I can't believe Claire is going to get her fucking way, but that doesn't matter now.

Only the boys matter.

"I'll let the school know in the morning," I say. "You can switch over next term."

I have to pull over into a layby off the A3 to vomit on the way home.

MELISSA

Dean and I have finished up half a bottle of wine before I'm brave enough to broach the subject.

He shifts in his seat as I turn to face him, knowing full well I'm about to rope him into something shady.

"No," he says, just like that. "Whatever it is, no."

"You don't even…"

He shakes his head. "It involves Henley, right? Some crazy plan? *Another* crazy plan?"

"Well, maybe… but it's not…"

"Forget it, Lissa."

We sit in silence. He tops up our wine and takes a forkful of noodles from his takeout tub.

"You want him, right?" I ask, and he stops chewing. "You said you'd do him for free. I'm saying you don't need to. I'm saying fifty-fifty, maybe just once if you want… but just think about it…"

"Are you fucking nuts?"

I shake my head. "I'm serious, Dean. He wants men. He told me."

"He fucking *told* you?"

"Yes."

He swallows. "No."

"No?"

"No, Lissa. This shit is way too fucking much."

"He wants men. And if I give it to him… if I like it too…"

"If you give it to him then what?" he snaps. "Have you even listened to yourself? Crystals and music, whatever, but this is…"

"Crazy, right?" I finish. "Maybe it's crazy, yeah. But maybe it'll be the ace in my deck, maybe it'll be the thing that makes him really fall in love with me."

He looks at me as though I've suddenly grown an extra head. "Jesus wept, Lissa. Have you heard yourself?"

My stomach is in knots as I look at him.

"I don't want it to be some random," I tell him. "I don't want to hook up with some random guy who doesn't know what he'll be… getting into…"

"Being choked half to death you mean? Sure, it might be a tough fucking sell, Lissa. No shit."

I sip my wine. "Forget it, then."

"I already have," he says, but he's lying. His eyes are wide and angry, but he shifts in his seat and crosses his legs, and I know. I just know.

"You want him. I know you do."

"Not like that, I don't."

"But you do, don't you? You can't stop thinking about him either."

"That's bullshit!" he snaps, but it's not.

I remember his face when I told him all the gory details. The way he swallowed when I told him how Alexander chokes me to the brink. How it made me feel. How Alexander makes me feel…

"The guy's fucked up," he says.

"But you want him."

"I want a lot of things…"

"Fifty-fifty," I say. "One night. You get to have him."

"And what the fuck will *you* be doing?" His jaw is so tight.

"Watching," I say. "Just watching, Dean. It's not like we… I won't be…"

He shakes his head. "Don't even talk about it. I'm gay, Lissa, I just can't even."

It's the first time he's said it out loud. His words hang in the air as I take a breath.

"You already knew." He shrugs. "It's not news."

"No," I say. "It's not news." I swirl the wine in my glass. "I mean it. I wouldn't be… involved. It's about Alexander, and you."

"There *is* no Alexander and me," he snaps. "I've never even met the guy."

"But you could…"

He gets to his feet. I know he's considering it when he begins pacing. He doesn't want to admit it, but he is.

I give him space.

I'm finding that works pretty well lately.

"How would you even swing it? What you gonna say? Hey, Mr Henley, this is Dean, my best fucking friend. He looks after my brother for me while I'm out playing hooker."

His words cut, but I don't say a thing.

"Hey, Mr Henley, this is Dean. He's a sad little virgin guy who jerks off to your picture every fucking night and thinks about taking it in the ass. Is that what you're gonna fucking say, Lissa?"

I can't keep my silence. "You're a virgin?!"

He groans. "Don't act so surprised. *You* were a fucking virgin a few weeks ago."

I feel my shot. It's a whisper on the wind. A glimmer of a chance.

"I was a virgin until him. And he was the best experience of my life. He was everything." I'm being honest. My smile is all real as I remember how he took me, how he made it feel so good. "Fine, if you don't want to do it for me, do it for yourself."

"For *me*?!"

"Yeah," I say. "For *you*. Do it because you want him. Do it because he's everything. Do it because he'll be the most amazing experience you'll ever have."

"With you there cheerleading from the sidelines?"

"You'll forget I'm even there, I promise."

"You promise?!" His laugh sounds as crazy as I feel.

I finish up my wine. "I need to go to bed. I have work tomorrow."

"I'm not doing it," he says.

His voice sounds a lot more certain than he looks, but I've said my piece. I've said it all.

"I'll find someone else," I tell him. "Don't worry about it. If you don't want him, I'll find someone who does."

"Some fucking random?!"

"I guess so."

He shakes his head. "Just quit your job. Tell him you got off on the wrong foot, he may never know, not if you give him your real name and pretend it was a false alias."

"He knows Amy is a real person. He looked her up."

I hate the way his eyes bore into me. "He looked her up?!"

"Yeah. I had no idea he would."

He rubs his temples. "She knows me. She knows *you*. What the hell if he turns up at her door? What the fuck do we do then?"

It's nothing I haven't thought about myself. Nothing that hasn't niggled me at night before I fall asleep.

"I'll tell him," I say. "I'll quit cleaning and I'll tell him my real name, just as soon as he's fucked another man. I'll tell him the very next week."

He laughs a cynical laugh.

"I will!" I insist. "I'll tell him. I just need this final piece of the puzzle! This one last thing!"

"Gay sex?!"

I nod. "So he knows I'm all in. With everything."

"Fucking hell," he hisses. "This is so fucking fucked up!"

I don't argue with him.

I squeeze his arm as I head for bed. My fingers link his and tug before I reach the door.

"Forget I said anything," I tell him. "It's cool."

He doesn't say a word as I close the door behind me.

I hear him pace around the place as I climb into bed. I hear him clear up the wine glasses a few minutes later.

And then nothing.

Silence.

I'm half asleep when the tap on my door comes.

The clock says half three a.m.

He eases the door open, and I feel the weight of him on the bottom of my bed.

I'm reaching for my nightlight when he tells me to stop.

"What is it?" I ask. "Are you okay?"

I can't see him nod. I can only hear him breathe.

"You'll just be watching? No like... touching or..."

"Of course no touching. This is just... him... with a guy..."

"Fifty-fifty?"

"You can have the whole three grand if you want it."

I'm not tired at all as I wait in the darkness.

Sleep has well and truly given up the ghost as I wait for Dean to spit out whatever he's thinking.

"I'll do it," he whispers. "Just once. So you don't need to... find someone."

I lunge for him, but he holds me back before I can hug him.

"Wait!" he snaps. "There are conditions!"

My heart pounds as I wait for them.

"If I let him fuck me, you quit cleaning afterwards. No fucking about, Lissa. If the guy fucks my ass to make your crazy fucking plan work out for you, you quit and you tell him your real name. You make this real, or you walk away."

My mouth is so dry. "Okay."

"Okay?"

I nod, even though he can't see me. "Yeah, that's a deal. He fucks you, I quit my cleaning job."

"And you tell him your real name?"

I pause for just a heartbeat. "Yeah."

He sighs. "I can't believe I'm fucking doing this."

And neither can I.

He gets to his feet, and heads for the door, and I still can't believe it. I still have to hear the words.

"You're saying you'll let him fuck you? You're saying you'll do it? For me?"

"No," he says before he closes the door. "I'm saying I'll do it for *me*."

THIRTY-FOUR

ALEXANDER

I confirm first thing Monday morning that the boys will be changing schools. Brenda draws up the letters I dictate to her, and I sign them off with a shaky hand before she faxes them through to their headmaster.

I send Claire an email telling her it's done, and also telling her the boys are free to attend Terry's shitty *kids' club* on a Sunday afternoon.

My whole world is spinning on its fucking axis.

My mouth is parched no matter how many Americanos Brenda brings me from the coffee shop next door.

I'm listless in my client meetings and I'm clumsy with the board report amendments that need my bastard input.

I hate how out of control I feel. I hate the wriggling worm of vulnerability in my gut.

I hate how painful it feels to find my heart still beating.

I'm staring into the abyss today, but whereas I normally rely on Brutus to be my sobering factor, I now have another anchor in the storm.

The insanity with Amy is the only thing keeping me actually sane.

The *Puppet Master* title the industry slapped on my head over a decade ago suits me well, but not as well as it did, and not anywhere near as well as it suits my slimy fucking father.

His grubby fingers are in everything, twisting everything.

It shouldn't come as a surprise when he blasts his way into my office before lunch. It shouldn't come as a surprise when he slaps a copy of the paperwork Brenda faxed across to the school onto my desk.

"What the fucking hell is this, boy? Have you lost your fucking mind?!"

It takes all of my restraint not to reply in the affirmative.

"The boys are changing schools," I say. "I've discussed it with Claire, I've discussed it with *them*."

"What the fuck is wrong with you?!" His eyes are angry and wired. Just as they were all those years ago in the public toilets.

Just as they've been so many times since, when I haven't played into his filthy fucking hands at every opportunity.

"It's none of your cunting business, old man," I tell him.

"Oh, but it fucking is," he hisses. "Those boys are next in line to the family business. *My* fucking business."

I laugh in his face.

And there, amongst the laughter, is the simple truth I've been avoiding my whole fucking life.

The truth of the peace I've granted my boys, even though they don't realise it yet.

I want out.

"You'll have to find another puppet to train in my stead. Thomas wants to be a footballer, and Matthew... well, Matthew doesn't have the disposition for this shit.

I see him as an artist maybe, or a celebrity chef. Maybe even a flower arranger."

"Don't test my fucking patience, boy." My father's disgust is actually etched into his features. A lifetime of scowling carved into stone under spiteful eyes. "You'll withdraw your instruction with immediate effect. I'll handle Claire and her lunatic educational preferences."

"I won't," I say, "And *you* certainly won't be doing fucking anything about Claire."

The thump of his fist on wood makes my pens rattle. "Be careful, boy. Be very fucking careful."

I don't even blink. "We're done here."

It's in my eyes and I know it. I know he sees every single flicker of hatred I have for him, and this shitty fucking business, and the way I've lived my seedy fucking life.

"We're not done," he seethes. "Not even fucking close."

"*I'm* done," I tell him, and I hate my beating heart. "I'm done with bailing out cunts and crooks."

"What the–"

"I'm done with shaking hands with addicts, and fraudsters, incompetent fuckwits with more money than sense."

"Don't–"

"I'm done with rapists and murderers, I'm done with people hiding behind expensive suits. And I'm fucking done with *you*."

"YOU'RE NOT FUCKING DONE!" he roars.

I laugh, because he looks even more unhinged than I feel.

"Oh, but I am," I say. "I'm going to off my caseload onto Hugh Lister. He's doing well. A rising star in your delightful organisation. I'm sure he'll be able to handle it."

His finger is white when he jabs it in my direction. "You don't walk away from clients like yours, boy. And you *can't* walk away from clients like *mine*."

My gut twists.

"I haven't had anything to do with clients like *yours* for fucking years."

"That doesn't fucking matter," he says. "You know things. Things that make you a fucking liability if you stop toeing the fucking line."

"Don't threaten me."

My eyes are like steel. His are like stone.

"I couldn't keep you safe, boy."

"You wouldn't try," I say.

He doesn't even attempt to deny it.

"What in the name of holy fucking Christ is going on with you?" he asks, and he's searching. Digging.

I hate the way it makes me shiver.

I force bravado. "I'm thinking I might take on some legal aid cases. Represent the good guys for a change. Who'd have thought?" My laugh comes out twisted.

His pupils are like pinpricks. "Something happened to you, boy. What the fuck is it?"

"Something happened to me a long fucking time ago and you fucking know it. You were *there*."

His smile is grotesque. "You liked it, boy. You moaned like a little fucking sissy bitch as you shot your load over that piss-stained wall."

"Get out of my office, you disgusting old cunt."

We stand-off. Eye to eye. Scowl to fucking scowl.

Hate.

So much fucking hate.

So much fucking disgust.

He shoves the paperwork in my direction before he steps away. "Retract your fucking statement to the school, boy."

"Get the fuck out of my office," I repeat.

He stops in the doorway, and his expression gives me the chills.

"I'm going to find out what in the name of Christ is going on with you, and then I'll put a fucking end to it. I promise you that."

Or put an end to me.

A chill rips up my spine.

And it's there.

It's always been right there.

The faces of my demons aren't those of porn stars, or rent boys, or drinking enough whisky to blackout into oblivion.

My demons all look like my fucking father.

And so do fucking I.

I hold my expression for a long minute after my door closes behind him, and then I rip up his fucking paperwork.

MELISSA

I'm nervous.

Of course I'm nervous.

I'm dancing a stupid crazy dance, right on the edge of a cliff, and now I'm pulling Dean along with me.

I only have a short window and I'm well aware of it. I feel the clock counting down to zero on all my stupid lies.

I heard Sonnie downstairs at Alexander's on Sunday morning. I pretended to be asleep with my heart in my throat, praying to God he didn't call me down there.

But one day he will.

One day I'll run out of luck, and no amount of gemstone trivia is going to bail me out.

Dean has his conditions and I'll keep them.

I'll hand in my resignation just as soon as my plan reaches its final destination.

And in the meantime I dance the crazy dance.

Mr Henley seems strange on Wednesday evening.

He's quiet as he takes me. Quiet as he kisses me after.

Quiet as he holds me.

"Are you alright?" I ask in the darkness.

He takes a breath before he answers. "Nothing for you to worry about."

"Okay," I say, and squeeze his fingers a little bit tighter.

I wonder if he's growing tired of me already. I wonder if he's getting sick of paying so much money to have me here.

It only makes me more determined to see this craziness through.

To be the woman his ex-wife wasn't.

To be the woman he will fall in love with.

He's all I want. *That's* all I want.

But Mr Henley is quieter still on Friday night at the soup kitchen.

He looks so brooding as he stirs the pot, and he doesn't smile on the streets, not even once.

I hate it.

I hate feeling so insecure after things were going so well.

I hate not knowing what's going on with him.

I tell him so in a roundabout way as we take a cab back to his.

"I'm sorry," I add straight after. "It's none of my business. I just... care."

He takes my fingers in his. "You're better off out of it," he tells me.

His tone gives me shivers.

"But I want to be *in* it," I whisper. "I want to be with you."

He doesn't even reply to that.

It only makes me more determined than ever.

I send a confirmation text to Mrs Stanley's daughter Helen when he's letting Brutus out for his final poop of the evening, telling her we'll be on for a few hours of babysitting tomorrow night.

I hate the niggle in my belly. I hate the thought of leaving Joe with a stranger, even though she's not one.

But it'll just be for one night, and he knows Helen. He knew her before…

She'll be fine, and he'll be asleep anyway. He's good at sleeping right through.

Mr Henley holds me tighter than ever as I drift off to sleep tonight, and I don't understand it. I don't understand any of it.

I wish I could tell him that I love him. That I'm right by his side, whatever he's facing, whatever this… is…

But not yet.

Soon. But not yet.

THIRTY-FIVE

ALEXANDER

I'm not going to let this shit with my father ruin the evening I have planned for Amy. Nor ruin it for me, either.

I shake off my mood as I get ready. I practice my smile in the mirror, making sure I can pull this off without a hint of exhausted paranoia in my eyes.

My father's not a man of false promises. The old cunt is a lot of things, but a bluffer isn't one of them.

There's every chance I'm going to pay the ultimate price for leaving this business.

But that's not for tonight.

Tonight is about Amy.

I position the knot of my tie just fucking so.

I fasten my cufflinks with a smile for Brutus.

I've just let him out for a piss when she knocks at the door.

She looks incredible in black. Her dress sparkles like the finest grade diamonds, and so do her eyes.

"Claude's message said *dress to impress*," she tells me, and does me a twirl on her way in. "Will I do?"

My throat feels scratchy as I look her over. Her shoes shimmer to match her dress. Her makeup is perfectly natural.

"You look beautiful, Amy."

She runs a finger down my tie and it makes me shiver. "So do you." She gives Brutus a scratch behind the ears. "Where are we going?"

"You'll see."

"A surprise?"

"Yes. A big one, I hope."

We've barely any time before the cab pulls up, and that suits me just fine, because any longer standing with this beautiful creature in my hallway would render me incapable of leaving this house without taking her upstairs with me first.

I set the alarm on the way out. I check the street before I join Amy in the taxi.

I feel ghosts on my shoulder, waiting for me, but I brush them off as I take her hand in the backseat.

"Are you okay?" she asks me, and I'm glad the cab is too dark to see her eyes.

"I am now."

"I'm going to have an amazing evening," she says.

"You don't even know where we're going yet."

"I don't need to." She rests her head on my shoulder and I close my eyes. Savour this moment.

Savour every moment.

Charing Cross Road is heaving when the cab drops us, but the venue I've booked is totally deserted.

She stares around in bewilderment as I stroll up to the bar.

"This is… quiet…"

"It's by design, Amy."

"It is?"

I smile as I order champagne from the solitary barman, and she raises her eyebrows as I take one for myself.

"A one-off," I say. "A celebration."

She raises her glass. "A celebration of what?"

"Life," I tell her.

Her eyes flash with pain, and I wonder why the word hurts her so badly. It's so stark to me in this one moment – how little I know about this woman. How little I know about her life.

But she *is* life.

She's everything.

And she's also a fucking mind reader.

"*You* are life," she whispers and clinks my glass.

"I'm quitting my job," I tell her, just like that. "I think it's about time I lived a little." I laugh at my own sick little joke.

Her eyes are like dinner plates. "You're quitting?"

"I'm a lawyer," I tell her, like she hasn't pieced two and two together already. "I spend my life enabling very rich people to do whatever the hell they fucking want. Destroy whoever the fuck they want. But not anymore."

She dithers as she sips her champagne. "And you can just… resign? These very rich people won't want you to leave, right?"

"How is your drink?"

She nods. "Really good."

I finish up mine, and the bubbles taste fucking divine.

"It's time for the show," I tell her, and take her hand.

MELISSA

I'm scared and I don't know why. I don't really understand what's going on, but I know it's bad.

I know it's really bad.

I also know for sure that I was wrong about Alexander Henley.

I was wrong about everything.

I thought I knew every single thing there was to know about this man, but I was a fool.

Because I know *things*. Stupid little *things*. Tiny pieces of shattered mirror I've been fitting together as I go.

But the mirror doesn't make the man.

The man is right here at my side, and he's not a collection of *things*. He's not his interests, or his divorce paperwork, or the smell on his bedsheets.

He's not the man they call the puppet master. He's not the lawyer who loves his job the way I always assumed he'd love it.

And I'm pretty sure he's a man who can't just walk away.

I'm sure you can't just walk away from those kind of people.

My heart is in my mouth as I follow him through to the back room, and the venue is still empty here. A roomful of empty tables, and only one of them has a candle on it, the one right in the middle with the very best view of the stage.

I can't make out the huddle of people setting up, not without the spotlights, but I recognise the opening notes the moment they ring out.

I've heard this album so many times. On the underground on the way to Kensington and back again. At night in bed while I'm thinking of him.

He squeezes my hand. "I had to pull some strings for this," he whispers. "Just as well they call me the Puppet Master."

I feign ignorance, but he's not even looking at me, he's looking at them. "The Puppet Master?"

"Yes."

"Why do they call you that?"

"Because my dirty hands pull everyone's strings."

I don't know what to say to that, so I squeeze that dirty hand of his and he squeezes mine right back.

I love his dirty hands.

I love *him*.

He pulls out my seat for me and takes the one at my side. His thigh presses to mine under the table, and his dirty hand is on my knee.

"This is really just for us?" I ask him, and he smiles.

"For you," he says.

"For *me*?"

"You're the only person I've ever met who loves this band as much as I do," he tells me, and I feel rotten inside. My belly is full of worms.

"I do love them," I say, and it's not actually a lie. Not anymore.

I know that for certain when they start up the set. I feel every note in my heart. I feel the sadness in the lyrics. I feel how beautiful this is.

Everything is beautiful.

But nothing is so beautiful as Alexander Henley.

I watch him as he stares at the stage, and his mouth is open just a little, his eyes wide as he takes it all in. His foot taps along to the beat and mine taps with it, and his eyes are so happy I could cry.

So I do.

I do cry.

I cry for the beautiful sadness in the music.

I cry for all the lies I've told.

I cry for my lost dreams and the parents I'd give my life for, just to see them one more time.

I cry for the way I love Alexander Henley.

I cry happy tears for the way I get to hold him at night.

I'm wiping them from my cheeks when I feel his eyes on mine. "What is it?" he whispers as Kings and Castles start up their next song.

"This," I tell him. "It's perfect."

"Yes." His thumb brushes my cheek. "Yes, it is."

I know Dean is waiting for my text with the venue location, but I can't give him this one.

I know Dean is hanging around the city for my instructions to head on in to wherever we are and give Alexander the eye.

I want to text him and tell him to go home to Joe, to tell him this was all a mistake and I'm going to tell Alexander my real name before the night is out, because I'm done with all the lies and the stupid games.

I want this to be real. More than anything in the world I want this to be real.

I'm staring at Alexander's beautiful dark eyes as the opening bars of Casual Observer ring out from the stage.

I'm smiling as he smiles, ready for his arms as he pulls me close.

And it is real.

This is real.

The way my heart beats against his is real. The love I see in his smile, that's all real too.

I sing the words as he does, and this song is all about feeling like an outsider in a crowded world, which is funny, because the world is empty tonight. It's just him and me, and I've never felt less of an outsider than I do right now.

"This was worth every penny," he whispers as the song finishes up. "I'd have paid ten times over to see you so happy."

And that's why I don't a send a cancellation text Dean after all.

That's why I keep my shit together enough to ride this crazy train right to the end of the line.

Because as much as it scares the crap out of me to take this so insanely far, it'll be worth every panicked heartbeat to give Alexander Henley exactly what he wants.

Even if Alexander Henley thinks he's doing it all for me.

THIRTY-SIX

ALEXANDER

Amy is glowing as we give our thanks to the band after the set. She tells them how much she loves them, eyes twinkling as she relays all the same stories she told me.

I love listening to them.

I love listening to *her*.

If I was a man who believed in mumbo jumbo, I'd say she and I stood as indisputable evidence that soulmates really do exist. That there really is fate at play behind the chaos of life. That chance encounters are sometimes nothing less than little miracles.

She feels like a miracle to me.

But I'm not, so this is simply an extraordinarily perfect set of coincidences.

It doesn't make it any less beautiful.

Amy can't hide her disappointment as I suggest we cab it home for the rest of the evening. It surprises me when she takes my hand and implores we stay out awhile. Suggests we *live* a little.

I'm happy to indulge her.

It's been a long time since I've been out amidst the general populous on a Saturday night. There's a thrum in the air as we step into a busy little tavern just down the road from the venue.

Amy orders a wine as I contemplate my options.

I should go for a mineral water, but she squeezes my arm before I can.

"Live a little, right?" she calls over the humdrum, and she's right.

I really should live a little.

So I do. I order the finest whisky they have, then trail happily behind my sparkling Amy as she leads us to an empty table in the corner.

The humdrum pales for me the moment she disappears to the bathroom. Tonight isn't about London, or having a few drinks in spite of my own self-imposed abstinence. It's not even about our private performance from the world's greatest band.

Tonight is all about her and this insane connection we share.

The insane connection that has me hoping I can navigate this terrible fucking mess of my life and come out the other side unscathed.

With her.

I want to come out the other side with her.

I tell her so when she returns. My voice is just a ghost in her ear. The hand I've placed against her spine registers her intake of breath when I say the words.

"Come away with me."

"Come away with you where?"

"Wherever I have to go," I answer, and her eyes flash with fear.

I really shouldn't have said anything. That's champagne and whisky for you.

"Where will you have to go?!"

I shrug. "Out of the city, certainly. Out of the country, maybe."

"What about your boys?"

My gut twists. "My boys have a new life now. A better life." I take a breath. "I'll be at the end of the phone whenever they need me. I'll arrange transport whenever they want to come."

Her stare is uncertain. "You want me to come with you? Like... *with* you? Is this..."

"You know what this is," I tell her. "Unless I'm very, very much mistaken, we both do."

She shakes her head. "You're not. I'm just... surprised..."

"You're surprised?"

"Yeah. I just... I thought I must just be a... because you pay me and I don't..."

I kiss her temple. "I've paid for a lot of sex in the past few years, but I can assure this is the first time I've ever paid half a million to take a girl to see her favourite band."

She doesn't have any words, just the hugest blue eyes. And I laugh.

It feels so fucking good to laugh.

She laughs too. She laughs the delicious kind of laugh of someone high on life.

"Just as well we have the same favourite band," she says. Her eyes sparkle as the laughter fades, and her hand snakes up my thigh under the table. "Let's finish the night with a bang," she whispers. "It's a night for favourites, right? How about we look for another?"

"Another what?"

"Another fantasy to fulfil," she tells me, and my cock twitches.

I know what she's angling for. I know exactly what filthy thoughts are flitting behind those innocent eyes.

I know full well the meaning of the fucking pang in my gut, too.

Maybe it won't feel the same with her there.

Maybe she will really make it... *different.*

"You want me to fuck another man?" My voice is just breath in her ear, but she shudders.

"Yes," she whispers. *"Please... if that's what you... if you want to as well..."*

I hate how much I want to, but that's nothing new.

"I could make some calls," I tell her. "Maybe Claude can hook me up at short notice."

Her eyes sparkle. "Or I could go and have a word with the guy who's been staring at you from the bar for the last twenty minutes straight."

I scan the crowd, suddenly well aware that I've been totally oblivious to every other person in this building. And there he is.

He's young. Way too fucking young.

Short cropped hair and piercing eyes. Casual, but not too casual. Jeans and a shirt.

He doesn't look away when I meet his eyes.

"You like him?" I ask her and she nods.

"He's cute, right?"

"Cute for me or cute for you?"

She squeezes my thigh. "You're the only man I'm interested in."

I raise an eyebrow. "Is that so?"

She nods. "That's so."

I hold the guy's stare until he looks away with a smile. Yeah, he's fucking up for it.

"He's young," I say.

"Legal though. I saw them take his ID at the bar."

She's an observant little minx. Law school really would suit her well.

"You want me to go ask him?" She's smiling, squirming in her seat, and this is a whole new side of her, one that makes my balls fucking tighten.

I shake my head. "I'll handle it."

She looks taken aback.

I raise an eyebrow. "You think I've never propositioned a guy before?"

She squeezes aside to let me pass, and I angle her face up to mine for a kiss as I go. My eyes meet his as I leave her, and seeing me with Amy does little to dent his interest.

So far so fucking good.

He clears a spot at the bar for me as I make my way over, and he's taller than I expect up close. He smells fresh. He smells like he wants my cock in his ass.

"I'm Dean," he says.

I take out a twenty from my wallet to pay for his drink.

"The name's Ted," I say.

MELISSA

I can hardly watch. My knees are shaking under the table as Alexander pays for Dean's drink at the bar.

My heart is a panicked mess as they talk.

I force a smile as Alexander looks in my direction. His mouth is by Dean's ear, and I wish to God I knew what he was saying.

I also wish Dean and I had sorted out a bail-out word, because I'd be so close to using it right now. So close to blowing this whole crazy thing off.

Downing my wine doesn't make the nerves any easier. I can hardly sit still as Alexander brings me another and brings Dean along with him.

"Amy, this is Dean," he tells me, and I'm sure my smile is fake enough to cringe as I say hello. "Dean's coming back with us," Alexander tells me, and my stomach drops through the floor.

I grip his hand under the table and he runs a thumb across my knuckles.

My silly fantasies about this evening were ridiculous, I know that now.

This is Dean. My *friend* Dean. Pretending to be some random in some London pub in order to take Alexander's dick up his ass.

But he doesn't need to, because Alexander said all he needed to say already. He's asked me to go away with him, and I'm still reeling. I need a way out of this hole I'm in, not a sure way of digging it all the deeper.

I'm digging it way too deep.

It's in Dean's eyes as he stares at Alexander. It's in the way I know he must be so nervous. The way I know he must be as terrified as I am of blowing our cover.

"We should drink up," Alexander says and my heart pounds.

Dean drinks up, downs his beer in one.

I have to take mine back in three long swigs, and my legs feel bandy as Alexander takes my hand and leads me out of this place. I can barely speak as we leave the pub with Dean in tow.

Alexander pulls me into the doorway of the very first hotel we pass. It's nothing special, nothing like Delaney's, and that makes it seem so much more real somehow. Three of us in some regular hotel room, where the man I adore is going to pound my best friend's ass.

I can't believe I set this up.

I can't believe this is really happening.

"I'll get us a room," Alexander says, and I'm left with Dean as he heads on in.

"You can go," I hiss. "This was a crazy idea, I'm sorry."

"Too fucking late for that," Dean hisses back. "It's gonna look real fucking suss if I suddenly make a fucking dash for it."

Alexander beckons us inside and I take a breath.

"You want to do this?" I ask before we go.

Dean looks at Alexander and his eyes darken. "Yeah, I wanna do this."

Fuck.

"He's rough," I say, like he doesn't know that already, but he isn't even listening, he's already swinging the door open.

I feel like a prostitute all over again as we head up to the second floor. I pretend it's taking the stairs in my heels that leaves me breathless, but that's not the half of it. I'm on the edge of panic. My ears are ringing and my head feels light as Alexander finds our room and opens the door.

Dean brushes past him on the way in, and Alexander grabs my arm before I can join him.

"Are you alright?"

I nod. Smile. "Sure."

"Don't want to call this off?"

I look into the hotel room and Dean's already perched on the bed.

He wants this.

They both do.

I shake my head. "No," I say. "I don't want to call this off."

He closes the door behind us, and the click of the lock sends shivers down my spine.

ALEXANDER

My delicious little Amy has underestimated me.

That's no real surprise, she simply has no comprehension of how astute I have to be in my line of work. My entire career has hinged on my ability to read people – the things they don't want to tell me, the subtle little inferences of their body language, the little facts between their lines.

I wasn't sure, not until we left the tavern.

I couldn't call it for certain until I watched them outside as I went to book us a room.

Dean, whatever his real name is, is no stranger to my beautiful Amy. They've met before. I'd venture as far as to say they're pretty well acquainted.

Which leaves me with a dilemma – to call them out and put an end to this dance, or push them as far as they'll go to maintain their cover.

They don't call me the puppet master without good reason.

I keep my mouth firmly shut as I lock that hotel room door behind me.

The minibar is a poor show compared to the one at Delaney's. A couple of standard bottled spirits, some mineral water and some single glass-sized bottles of wine.

I pour a glass each for the two of them, and revert to mineral water.

"Amy has a fantasy," I begin. "She wants to see me fuck another man, as I'm sure you've well gathered by now."

Dean nods, takes his wine with a thanks.

Amy flashes me a smile that's way too bright, then perches herself on the bed alongside him. Their shoulders are tense and rigid, the space between them a whole gulf of fucking awkwardness.

"The thing is," I say to the pair of them. "I've a fantasy of my own."

Oh the sweet delight as their eyes widen.

"A fantasy?" Amy asks.

I nod. "I hope we can all get what we're looking for from this evening."

I take a sip of water and neither of them says a word.

It's Dean I hone in on first, I shoot him a smile that conveys nothing but that of a friendly stranger looking to get his rocks off. "I want you to fuck my girlfriend," I tell him.

Amy squirms so hard she splashes wine onto her dress. "You didn't say…" she begins but I shrug to cut her off.

"Another surprise," I tell her. "I wanted it to be a surprise." My laugh is low and loaded. "After all, you chose him."

"But I…"

I close the distance and tip her face to mine. "I'll fuck a stranger for you, you'll fuck a stranger for me. I think that's a fair exchange."

Her pretty eyes are full of horror.

"He's cute, right?" I mimic. "You said so yourself."

"But I wasn't…"

I turn my attention to the guy whose ass I'm going to pound. "You want both of us, of course. That's why you came here."

The kid is out of his depth. He doesn't know where to fucking look. "I'm, uh… I thought this was a guy thing…"

"Oh, it will be," I tell him. "Just as soon I've watched you fuck Amy." I slap his shoulder. "I was her very first, you know. Offering her the experience of another man's cock is the very least I can do. Variety is the spice of life, don't they say?"

Amy leans towards me, reaches out a hand for mine. "I don't need another man," she says. "This is all about you."

I drop to my knees to meet her eye to eye. "Indulge me. Call it another of my guilty pleasures."

She can barely swallow. She looks petrified.

"No hard limits, remember?" I prompt, and I feel like an utter cunt, but I don't care.

The look of pain in her eyes as she realises she's still technically on the clock almost makes me change my mind. *Almost.*

I turn to Dean. "She's got a gorgeous pussy, I'm sure you'll enjoy the experience."

"I'm gay," he says, as though that matters shit to me right now.

I shrug. "I'm sure we'll be able to get you hard. Don't worry about a thing."

But he is worried. He's so fucking worried that their pathetic little front shrivels to nothing. They stare at each other in horror, and the cards are all stacked. I'm going to push this as far as it'll fucking go.

"Don't be shy," I tell them. "We're all strangers here. Just one crazy night, for the memories."

I tug my tie loose and drape it over a chair, my jacket too.

I carefully unfasten my cufflinks and roll my sleeves up as though I'm preparing for hard labour, and Dean's eyes widen, wondering what the fuck I'm planning.

"He's gay," Amy blusters. "We should find someone who isn't... for me... if that's what you want..."

I shake my head. "Right here, right now," I insist. "I'll give him a helping hand to get him nice and hard for you."

She visibly flinches, and so does he.

"Is something wrong?" I ask. "You two seem... awkward."

Amy tells me she's good, so does Dean, and their fate is sealed.

I finish up my mineral water and take a seat on the bed between them. I pull them back by their shoulders, urging them to recline alongside me while I unbutton my shirt. You could cut the tension with a fucking knife.

I kiss Amy first. I kiss her so hard she squeaks into my mouth. I palm her pretty tits and tweak her nipple until she moans, and then my hand moves across to Dean.

I slide my fingers up his thigh until I feel the bulge of his groin. I grip him through the denim, my tongue still deep in Amy's mouth as I feel him stiffen.

His breath is ragged as I break away from Amy and land my mouth on his. He's hard as I rub his dick through his jeans, and so am I.

"Have you ever been with a man before?" I ask him, and he shakes his head. I thought as much. "How about a girl? Have you ever been with a girl?"

He shakes his head again.

I suck his bottom lip until he groans, making light work of his shirt buttons. His bare chest is firm and smooth, he shivers as I pinch his nipple.

"You're going to fuck my girlfriend," I grunt as I unbuckle his belt. I pop the button and tug his cock free. He pulses in my grip. "That's it," I tell him. "Nice and fucking hard for me."

I can hear Amy's shallow breathing. I can imagine her open mouth.

I reach for her without breaking free from Dean. My tongue is soft and wet across his lips, dipping inside as he moans for me.

I jerk his fucking cock as I switch to kiss Amy. I yank down her dress to expose those ripe little tits knowing full well she's probably beside herself at the thought I'm going to make her go through with this. It doesn't make me stop.

I'm still jerking Dean's cock as I take Amy by the hair and guide her face to his. She murmurs under her breath, her mouth closed tight.

"Kiss him," I tell her.

He grunts as I squeeze his dick.

Their lips touch but stay closed and Amy's sweet face is little more than a grimace.

"Fucking kiss him," I tell her, and I feel a perverted thrill as she does.

It's a crappy fucking effort. Nothing but a flicker of tongues, like two clumsy fucking teens.

I take his hand and place it square on her tit. I hold him firm as he tries to tug away.

"You're going to fuck each other," I tell them, and my voice is so fucking sharp.

They are statue still, Dean's hand rigid on her fucking tit as I pull her skirt up.

I order her to take her knickers down. Her fingers are shaking as she obeys me.

I love how she fucking obeys me.

I slide my fingers between her thighs and rub at her clit, and she squeaks and wriggles but doesn't stop me.

I'm sandwiched between pussy and dick and I work them both. My own cock is pulsing, straining in my fucking pants as I watch Amy twist her tongue with his.

Her pussy takes two of my fingers nice and easy, she gasps as I hook them deep, and Dean is squirming in my grip, his dick nice and fucking swollen as he bucks his hips for more.

"Lie down," I say to Amy, and she does.

I wrestle her dress up and over her head, and Dean won't even look at her nakedness.

"You're going to fuck that sweet little cunt," I tell him and he winces. Amy has her eyes closed until I force her face to mine. "Ask him to fuck you," I whisper.

"But I..."

"Ask him to fucking fuck you," I repeat, and she shudders. "Unless you want to revise your hard limits," I add. "Unless you want to tell me you've changed your mind?"

She thinks about it. I know she's thinking about it. I see it all over her face.

"Have you changed your mind, Amy? Is there something you want to tell me?"

I take Dean's arm and urge him towards her. He moves slowly. So fucking slowly.

"Well?" I ask Amy again. "Is there something you want to say to me, or not?"

She tries so hard to hide the truth. It's almost pitiful.

Her voice is just a croak when she answers me, and I admire her bravado.

"No," she says. "No hard limits."

"Then ask him to fuck you."

Dean positions himself on top of her, his arms rigid as they support his weight. His cock is still nice and fucking hard. He grunts as I take it in hand and rub it against Amy's smooth little mound.

I rub him in her wetness and she wriggles.

"Ask him to fuck you," I repeat again, and there's a sickness in my gut. A perverse sense of satisfaction as she bleats out the words I've been demanding.

"Please fuck me," she says. "Please, Dean, please fuck me."

THIRTY—SEVEN

MELISSA

My heart is pounding so fast I feel sick.

I feel Dean's dick against me and I hate myself for doing this. I hate myself for taking things this far.

I know Dean's cursing himself for ever agreeing to be a part of this train wreck, but he's hard in Alexander's grip and he's in too deep to stop.

Alexander Henley isn't a man you feel like you can argue with.

I'd forgotten this side of him. I'd forgotten the side that forced me to my knees and ordered me to drink his piss in Delaney's. I'd forgotten how demanding he is.

And he is.

His eyes are dark and fierce, his jaw gritted as he rubs Dean's cock against my clit and makes me squirm.

"I know that feels fucking good," he tells me. "Don't fight it."

It does feel good. I hate how good it feels.

I hate how things will never be the same between Dean and me ever again, now, even if I really did call time out and tell Alexander I'd made a stupid mistake.

I spread my legs and turn my face to the side, focusing on nothing but Alexander. This is just sex. It doesn't have to mean anything.

But it means everything, because it's Dean. It's *Dean*.

Oh fuck. It's Dean.

I hear the wetness between my legs, and Dean's raspy breath as Alexander keeps on rubbing. Dean's cock is hard against my clit, and the rhythm is too much. I can't stop wriggling. I can't fight the urge to buck my hips and take him inside me.

I'm going to come with my best friend's cock against my clit and there's nothing I can do about it.

Not unless I want to scream time out.

But I'll never scream time out to Alexander Henley. Never.

I grit my teeth. "Fuck me," I say to Dean and he tenses. "Just fuck me."

He groans, and I feel like a crazy bitch. I tilt my hips to take him and pray he knows this is just one crazy night and it's all my fault.

His cock nudges my entrance but he doesn't push inside. He's straining. Fighting.

"Do it," I whisper. "Fuck me."

Alexander nips at Dean's ear. "Tell me you want her tight little pussy."

Dean doesn't say a word.

I hook my legs around his thighs, even though it makes me die inside. I urge him on, even though neither of us wanted this.

"Fuck her," Alexander says again, and Dean buckles.

"Alright," he grunts. "I'll fuck her. I'll fucking fuck her."

I'm braced for it. Heart in my mouth as I prepare for the thrust.

But it never comes.

Alexander pulls Dean's cock away before he can push inside me. He shunts him by the shoulder until Dean rolls onto his side, panting against my cheek.

My eyes are open wide as I search Alexander's.

"What?" I say. "I was going to... I thought you wanted me to..."

His eyes are dark and distant. They give me shivers.

"You're not going to fuck Dean," he tells me, and my mind is spinning.

"But..."

He smirks as he pulls me towards him, kisses my mouth as he climbs over me.

"You're not going to fuck Dean," he says to me again. "But I am."

I flinch as he yanks Dean's arms behind his back and slams him hard on his front. I flinch again as he tears Dean's jeans from his ass.

"You want cock," he snarls, and Dean groans for him. "You're going to get fucking cock. I'm going to fuck you until your ass fucking bleeds for me."

I can hardly breathe.

I can hardly think.

My pussy clenches as Alexander spreads Dean's ass cheeks and lands a gob of spit right on target. I hate how it flutters as he pushes his finger all the way in.

Dean cries out as Alexander pushes in another.

Alexander fucks him hard, two fingers ploughing deep, and Dean looks so vulnerable as he squirms.

I'm open-mouthed as the man I love looks in my direction.

"Play with yourself," he barks. "You fucking wanted this. Show me that horny little cunt."

Oh God, I do it. I spread my legs for him and rub my fingers around my clit, and I hate how excited I am. Hate how desperate I am to see him fuck Dean's ass.

He positions himself, his weight heavy on Dean's back as he slides his cock around Dean's hole.

"I like it fucking rough," he snarls, and shoves the head inside.

Dean cries out.

He cries out again as Alexander thrusts all the way in.

It's brutal. It's really brutal.

My fingers feel dirty as I rub at my clit.

Alexander fucks Dean hard enough that Dean's face is a grimace. The bed creaks under us, the headboard thumping against the wall as he goes.

"Your tight little ass is going to milk me fucking dry," Alexander hisses and Dean moans for him. "Take it. Just fucking take it."

Dean does take it. He groans but he doesn't protest, his asshole takes everything Alexander gives him.

I already know what's coming as Alexander snakes his arm around Dean's throat.

He holds firm, Dean's neck straining against the chokehold, his eyes wide as he realises his air's been cut.

He wriggles, gasping for breath, and Alexander punishes his asshole for his efforts. I hear his balls slapping Dean's skin. I hear Alexander's strained breath as he pounds Dean's poor virgin ass like a man possessed.

And I love it.

Oh God help me, I love it.

I hate that I love it. I hate that I love the sight of Alexander's dick in my best friend's ass, but I do.

My clit is throbbing and my breath is fast. I'm past caring about how disgusting this is, I just want it.

Alexander stares at me and I stare right back, and I fuck myself with my fingers. I fuck myself as he watches me, and I love it.

Dean gurgles and Alexander grunts.

Dean's eyes bulge wide as Alexander tightens his grip.

It must hurt. It has to. It must burn like hell, and I can't believe it when Dean starts bouncing back at him. When Dean's hips beg for more.

"I'm going to come in your dirty fucking asshole," Alexander hisses. "And Amy is going to lick you fucking clean."

I can't control my breathing.

Alexander eases them to the side just enough to reach for Dean's dick, and he's using the choke hold as leverage, fucking his ass hard enough that Dean's cock jerks in his palm.

I don't know which one of us is going to come first.

Dean's dick is twitching in Alexander's hand, and Alexander's thrusts are becoming desperate, and I'm rubbing my clit hard enough that I'm shaking.

"Come here," he calls, and I go there. I'm still playing with my clit as I wriggle across the bed to him.

I kiss him as he's fucking Dean's ass. He sucks my tongue and I know he's on the edge, I can feel it in his breath.

"You're going to take his cum in your mouth," he grunts. "Spill a fucking drop and I'm going to make you lick it from the fucking sheets."

I cry out as my clit sparks, and I move. Quickly.

I shunt down the bed and position my mouth by Alexander's jerking hand, and I'm ready. Mouth open wide to do as I'm told.

The disgusted part of me feels so far away. My clit is all there is.

"Now," Alexander snarls and I rub myself so frantically as Dean's cum spurts in my mouth. I fight the urge to retch as it hits the back of my throat, and it's too much when I hear Alexander grunt and come himself.

I ride the waves with my best friend's cum in my mouth, and it feels too good to care.

The crazy train collides with the end of the track, and it feels wild and scary to be this unhinged.

I hear Dean's frantic gulps of air as Alexander lets him go. He coughs and splutters and groans as Alexander pulls his cock from his poor battered ass, and he won't look at me.

I've still got Dean's cum in my mouth when Alexander tugs at my hair. I'm still fighting the urge to retch as he forces my face to Dean's used ass.

"No hard limits," he hisses, and my stomach lurches. "Lick it up."

Dean's asshole is glistening with Alexander's cum.

It dribbles down his ass crack like syrup.

"Lick it up," Alexander says again, and his eyes are fierce on mine.

I won't disappoint him.

I never want to disappoint him. No matter what.

I take a breath, I smile at him.

And then I lick it up.

Every last drop.

THIRTY-EIGHT

MELISSA

I lose all sense of time in that hotel room. I lose all sense of myself as Alexander goes in for round two and rubs his cum-slick dick against Dean's until they're both hard again.

I'm like a ghost of my old self as Alexander pins Dean on his back, hoists his legs up high and slides his cock right back inside Dean's poor ass.

Dean doesn't grimace this time. His grunts are full of want, not pain.

He kisses Alexander right back, like I'm not even there, and this is it, right here in front of me.

The Alexander Henley effect.

I play with myself because I want to this time, not because Alexander tells me to. It's all for me as I rub my clit until I shudder and stifle my moans on the bedsheets so Dean won't realise how disgusting I really am.

I don't think he'd notice anyway. His world is full of Alexander Henley.

He doesn't fight when the hand clamps around his throat, doesn't struggle as he chokes for the man I love.

He comes when Alexander does, spurting thick streams against Alexander's stomach under the pressure of the thrusts.

Dean's eyes are glazed for a long time as he comes down.

I feel so cold inside as he sobers up from this madness and realises what the fuck just went down.

He tugs up his jeans as Alexander watches him, and I cringe as he makes his excuses, says he's got to leave now.

"Not so fast," Alexander says and points at the smear on his stomach.

My eyes are watering with the need to retch as Dean licks him clean. I look away as Dean takes Alexander's dick into his mouth and sucks him until there's nothing left to take.

And then Alexander lets him go.

Dean barely even says goodbye, just limps from the room with his shirt still unbuttoned, shooting me a wild-eyed glance as he goes.

I flinch as the door closes behind him, collapsing onto the bed as my mind spins with all this.

Alexander pours me another wine and I take it with shaky fingers. I down it in one, even though it tastes rancid.

"I guess Dean's not one for small talk." His voice is laced with black humour, and that gives me shivers too.

"I guess not," I whisper, and my cheeks are burning.

I'm surprised when he pours himself another whisky. I'm itching to get out of here, desperate to be just about anywhere besides the place I almost took my best friend's dick.

"How do you know him?" Alexander asks, and I bolt upright.

"What?"

He smirks. "How do you know him? Don't even think about lying to me, Amy." His eyes are so dark. "I hate it when people lie to me."

My whole body is burning. The urge to crumble and confess everything is a dam waiting to burst, but I can't.

The quiet anger in his stare tells me that I can't.

I'm surprised my brain isn't too addled to think my way out of this as I swim through my options.

"It was supposed to be a surprise..." I tell him. "I'm sorry... I just..."

"You paid him?"

I shake my head, because I don't think I could pull off that lie even if I wanted to. "We were friends at school. I know he... likes men..."

"So you called him up and said *Hey, Dean, how about taking my boyfriend's cock in your ass this weekend?* Is that how it went?"

Boyfriend.

"Something like that."

"And what the hell makes you think I can't find a man for myself?"

"That isn't what I think!"

He comes closer, my stomach lurches as he climbs onto the bed alongside me. "So, enlighten me, Amy. What *do* you think?"

I shake my head as the tears prick. "I wanted to do it for you. You do so much for me... and I... I wanted to make you happy..."

"Make me happy by setting up an old school pal to take my dick in his ass?"

I shrug. "Oh God, Alexander, I don't know! I wasn't thinking straight! It was..."

"Stupid," I tell her. "Reckless to think I wouldn't fucking notice. Believe me, Amy, I notice everything."

But he doesn't.

I shiver at the thought of him ever finding out about all my lies. I shiver at the stupid idea I ever thought I could confess my real identity and still have him at the end of it.

"I'm sorry," I tell him, and I am. "Please forgive me."

"I've already forgiven you," he says. "If I hadn't, we wouldn't be having this conversation."

The relief washes over me so hard my head spins. "Thank God," I say, and my hand is to my heart as it begins to calm.

It takes me by surprise when his fingers land on my throat, steals my breath as he flattens me to my back and brushes my lips with his.

His voice is cold. Harsh.

"I don't like being played, Amy. Don't ever fucking do it again."

"I won't," I whisper, and he kisses me. His fingers stay loose, and I keep breathing, even though my insides are burning up.

"You played a dangerous game," he tells me, and I could cry. He doesn't know the half of it.

He rolls onto his back with his arm under his head, and if he's still angry he doesn't show it. The room feels bitter cold now, and I know it's probably just my own shock, but I pull the covers over myself and drape them over him too. He doesn't pull away as I lay my head on his chest.

I love listening to his heartbeat.

It's so much calmer than mine.

"That could have gone badly," he says, as if I don't already know that.

I nod anyway. "I'm sorry."

"We're done with sorry. I'm trying tell you something." It feels like heaven as his hand wraps around my waist under the covers. "I think you need to know."

My voice is so timid. "Need to know what?"

"Why I have such a... *reaction* to wanting men."

"You don't have to…" I begin, but he shakes his head.

"Just listen," he says, and I do.

ALEXANDER

My throat is dry as I opt to tell this sad fucking tale.

I can't say it's a pleasant confession. The last time I told this story it cost me my marriage – the final dying scraps of the sham it was anyway.

I'd made a note to myself in the aftermath – never fucking talk about it. But I'm drawing a line through that now.

"My parents are pieces of shit," I tell her. "I used to feel sorry for my mother, putting up with all my father's fucking crap all the time. The women, the late nights, the *work meetings* that ran on until the early hours most days. I thought she was naive. I thought she turned a blind eye to all his seedy outlets because she was scared of losing him. I thought that's why she drank herself into oblivion every fucking evening before I'd even finished my dinner."

"But it wasn't?"

I shake my head. "She knew everything, she'd just rather keep quiet and stay in the fancy house with the glitz and glamour of being Mrs Henley Snr. than do something about all the lies."

She doesn't say anything, just waits for me to continue.

"I wondered where he went at night. I was a teenager living in a house full of lies and hushed whispers. I was at a school I hated, preparing to take over a family business that made my father bitterly fucking twisted, at least that's what I thought. I thought that's why he was always so fucking angry." I take a breath.

"You have to understand. My father is a legal icon, he's one of the best lawyers this country's ever seen. Walking in his footsteps was... *hard*. But I did it. I wanted to make him proud when I was too young to know better."

"I get it," she says. "I wanted to make mine proud, too."

Wanted.

I make a note of the tense for future reference.

"I knew my father paid for sex. I'd see him at social events schmoozing with all the high class hookers on the scene. I'd see him take a feel whenever he thought nobody was watching. But I was always watching. I saw everything. I'd watch him with those beautiful women and I'd want them for myself. I wanted to be like him one day, taking whatever he wanted, doing whatever he wanted."

"With prostitutes?"

I nod. "With women I could pay to do whatever pleased me. It was the power. I saw how my father used it, and I wanted to be the same."

She takes a breath against my chest. "That's normal, right? Wanting to be like your dad?"

I laugh. "Not quite. Not when I fully realised how far his depravity fucking went."

"What happened?"

I fight the urge to grab another whisky. "I started following him. Spying." I breathe. "It's a dangerous hobby that, spying on someone. The tiny victories are... addictive. A little snippet of insight here, uncovering some seedy little secret there. I felt so fucking clever. I felt like I was so fucking in control."

She tenses in my arms, as though she knows what's coming.

"I thought I knew everything about my father. I'd been snooping on him for well over a year, rooting through the paperwork in his study, going through his phone records, his emails, trying to fit together the shadowy pieces of his life." I sigh. "I know it's hard to understand, why someone would... do that. I know it's hard to believe that someone would be so... *desperate* to please someone else that they'd take it so fucking far as to follow them across the fucking city to a public toilet in the East End, but I was all in by then. I wanted to know him. I wanted to please him. I wanted to be just fucking like him, even though he at least partly repulsed me."

Her breath is ragged but I keep on going.

"I peered in through the door to the urinals, feeling so fucking pleased with myself for my stealth." I smile. "But the cards always come tumbling down eventually. My luck ran out. It wasn't my father who caught me, it was some big fucking ape of a guy who was piling on in for the fucking show. He grabbed me by the throat and dragged me inside, and slammed me up against the wall as a couple of others laughed."

"Oh God..." she breathes, and I kiss her head.

"He said he'd got a young one. He thought it was hilarious. He told me I should have piped up if I wanted some dick in my ass, not skulked around the outside like a wimpy little queer."

"What did you..."

"Nothing. My face was pressed against the wall and the guy's weight pinned me tight."

I feel her shaking, and I realise I've got to tell her the fucking truth. The whole fucking truth.

"I could've screamed. I could've fucking yelled the place down and kicked out or elbowed him and told him to get the fuck off me."

"You were scared..." she whispers.

I shake my head. "It wasn't fear. I was scared, of course I was fucking scared, but it wasn't that that rooted me to the fucking spot. It was the fucking hard on in my pants. It was the stench of the wall, the stench of him, the way I wanted a part of whatever fucking seediness was going down there."

"You wanted it?"

"Wanted it, didn't want it… it's a fine fucking line. My dick wanted it, my brain not so fucking much."

Her voice is a choked little squeak. "What did he do to you?"

I smile. "You've seen what he did to me, I just did it to your poor little virgin friend back there. He pulled my fucking pants down and put me in a chokehold then rammed his fucking cock in my ass. Only he went in dry. I at least allowed your friend a little grace."

"He choked you?"

I nod. "Hard. He choked me hard. Fucked me hard, too."

She gasps, stiffens, and I know what she's thinking. I know she thinks I was violated, which is true. I know she thinks this shit has fucked me up, which is also probably true, but that isn't it. That isn't why I'm telling her this.

"He fucked me so hard the tears streamed down my fucking face, and I came for him. I shot my load in his hand, splattered the fucking wall with it."

"But you couldn't not…"

I laugh. "Oh believe me, Amy, I could. I fucking wanted it. I really wanted it. That fucking climax was one of the best I've ever fucking had. I shuffled out of there with my ass bleeding and my lungs on fire and my dick still wet with my fucking cum, and I loved it. I hated myself for loving it, even right there in the aftermath."

She shudders. "It's ok… to be bisexual…"

"I know it is," I tell her. "It's not that that bothers me. It's the… seediness. The brutality. The fact that I came with my face pressed to a wall that stank of piss, with a man that stank of sweat, and I loved it. I felt so fucking ashamed."

"You had nothing to be ashamed of," she tells me. "It was them."

I laugh again, and then I pull the covers back. Her eyes widen as she sees the state of my fucking dick. I'm hard enough to fucking blow.

"It's ok to be bisexual," she whispers again.

"My father knew," I tell her. "He followed me outside and clipped me round the ear and told me never to fucking follow him again."

"He knew?!"

"Of course he knew. He knew I was following him, too. The old cunt set it up. Nothing happens without my father's say so. *Nothing*. He's the fucking real puppet master. He pulls everyone's fucking strings. And I'm just like him."

"I don't think you are…" she whispers, and it's so sweet. Her faith in me is so fucking sweet. I kiss her head.

"It was the first real time he took me under his wing. He told me I should be on the other side of the fence next time, the side with all the power. He paid for hookers and brought me into his rancid network of rich clients, and taught me everything I needed to know about playing the system and enabling the rich to do whatever they fucking please as long as they're willing to pay for it."

"You were just trying to please him…"

"For a time. After that I was all in for myself." I turn to face her, and her sadness for me is so beautiful. Beautiful but misplaced. "I'm a sex addict," I tell her. "Or I was. I calmed it down when I got married, but it was always there, lurking behind the scenes. Claire wanted to know why I didn't fuck her anymore like I used to. She asked what really turned me on, what she could do. It was a mistake to tell her the truth. She insisted I should have therapy. Every time she looked at me, her eyes were full of pity and disgust." I pause. "Maybe yours will be too."

She kisses me. She kissed me hard. She tangles her fingers in my hair and presses her body to mine, and my heart pounds in my chest. "You will never disgust me," she whispers. "Never. I love you."

She loves me.

The thought makes my stomach twist, but it's beautiful. It's everything.

"I hate my father," I tell her. "I hate everything he is. I hate everything he dragged me into, but mostly I hate myself for becoming just like him. But that's going to change. I'm getting out."

She strokes my arm. "I'll come with you," she whispers. "Wherever you're going, I'll come with you."

I breathe a sigh of relief.

"Good," I tell her, "because I'll be going soon."

THIRTY—NINE

MELISSA

I would give anything to tell Alexander who I really am, but I can't.

I've played him too much. I've lied too much.

My dreams of open arms after a teary confession have shrivelled and died.

He's been so honest, and I've been such a fraud. I thought I knew everything, but I knew nothing.

He'd never forgive me and I know it.

I could die in his arms as he holds me in the aftermath of his confession. It kills me to know how close I am to having him. How close I am to making this real.

I have to make it real.

We lie in silence for a long time, just breathing. My hand rests on his hard cock but he makes no move to thrust against my touch and I make no move to bring him off.

I wish we could stay here forever, but he moves as the light begins to glow through the window.

"We should go home," he says, and I move with him. Pull my dress on and tug my knickers up and take his hand when it's offered.

He calls a cab before we leave and I lean against him as we wait.

The cards are tumbling down all around me and right now I'm numb to the whole thing. I only have one card left.

One single card left and I'm intending to play it.

I'll hand in my notice tomorrow with immediate effect. I'll say there's a family emergency, I'll say anything. I'll confess to Alexander that I lied about my name and say I was worried for my brother. Worried people would find out I was a hooker.

Maybe he'll believe that. Maybe he'll understand.

Maybe he'll never check his employee records, not since he's leaving himself.

Maybe we'll escape into the sunset. Maybe he'll come to love Joe as I love him.

It's worth a shot. It's the only one I have left.

It's morning when the cab pulls up at his. I'm ready for a few hours' sleep in his comfy bed before heading home to face the music with Dean, but as Alexander turns his key in the lock the alarm doesn't beep with the countdown.

And I know.

Of course I know.

I freeze on the spot as he steps inside, tugging away from him at the horror that Sonnie's already at work in there.

I can't.

Oh God, I can't.

He'll know. He'll know as soon as she stares at me, even if she doesn't say anything... even if she doesn't blow my cover...

"I have to go," I tell him.

He turns back. "Go?"

"Right now," I say. "I have something on this morning."

His eyes dig into mine, and there's an insecurity there I've never seen before.

"Look, Amy, if I said too much…"

I shake my head. "No! It's not that!"

I hear Brutus padding through the hallway and I hear Sonnie's voice calling him back, and I'm out of time.

"I'm sorry," I say. "It's not that, I swear, but I have to go."

"Go where?"

"I'll see you on Wednesday," I tell him. "I'll be over at eight."

He's still staring as I run from there. He takes two steps in my direction before I'm out of sight.

I don't stop running until I'm on the underground.

⚜

Dean's eyes are wild as he opens the door.

"Did you tell him?"

I shake my head and he groans.

He pulls the living room door closed as Joe watches TV with his cereals.

"What the fuck, Lissa?" he hisses. "You said you'd fucking tell him!"

"I can't!" I hiss back. "I just can't! He'd never forgive me!"

"Then what?" he snaps. "My ass is fucking bleeding, Lissa, the man's a fucking animal."

I lean against the wall, my heart pounding in my ears.

"He wants me to go away with him, he's quitting his job and moving away."

Dean's face is a picture of horror. "Away with him? How can you go away with him? He doesn't even know Joe exists!"

"You think I don't know that?!" I snap, and the tears are coming. I try to choke them back. "I'm going to resign tomorrow, I'll tell him I lied about my name and hope he forgives me, I don't need to say anything else, maybe he'll never know."

"And what if he does know?" Dean's eyes are like coals. "What if he finds out you fucking lied about everything? That even your fucking confession was a lie?"

I shrug. My laugh is deranged through the tears.

"Then it's all fucked anyway." I suck in a breath. "And so am I. I'm fucked without him, Dean. I can't go on. I can't."

He pulls me into his arms and I feel like the terrible crazy bitch I really am. I feel like hell. I feel like this is everything I deserve for lying so much and not giving a damn for the consequences. Not giving a damn about anything but getting into Alexander Henley's bed.

"I'm sorry," I whisper. "I'm so sorry I dragged you into this. I'm so sorry for what I made you do."

He breathes into my hair and he rocks me, and it makes me feel even worse to know he still cares, despite everything.

"Fuck, Lissa," he whispers. "You didn't make me do anything. I'd have done it all myself."

FORTY

ALEXANDER

I shouldn't have fucking said anything, but it's done now.

She couldn't hide the panic in her eyes, the crazy tension in her limbs as she freaked out and ran from me.

A couple of steps, that's all I took, still fucking scarred from chasing that poor fucking cleaner down my street a few weeks back.

I should've chased Amy harder. I should've dragged her inside and made her listen to me.

I should've told her I loved her.

Because I do. I do fucking love her.

It's not *Melissa* that's cleaning my house this morning, it's the girl from last week.

She's still petrified of Brutus, I hear it in her voice when she calls him, tells him to get his sorry ass back where she can see him.

It makes me smile through the fucking panic.

She looks horrified as I step into the kitchen. Her eyes are wild as she gushes out apologies.

"Oh hell, Mr Henley, sir. I didn't see you there, I swear. I'm sorry, oh drat, I'm so sorry."

I wave her apology away as I take a seat at the island.

I feel exhausted as I give Brutus a pat, and I'm starving. I'm really fucking starving.

"Can I get you a coffee?" the cleaner asks, and I'm about to say yes before I really look at her.

The poor woman looks as exhausted as I am, working her ass off to clean up after me before seven on a fucking Sunday morning.

"What's your name?" I ask, and her eyes widen.

"Sonya," she says, "but everyone calls me Sonnie."

"Well then, Sonnie," I say. "Why don't you sit yourself down for five minutes and I'll get us both one."

She looks like she's going to faint as she takes a stool. As though this is some kind of test.

It isn't. I put the beans in the machine with a smile.

And then I ask her if she wants to join me for some muesli.

Sonnie is a chatty soul. She tells me how my dog isn't really so bad when you get to know him.

She says Melissa told her so, and she was right.

I still feel a rush at the name, a debt of gratitude for the fact that she provoked the tiny spark of hope in me. Without that spark of hope I'd never have met Amy.

Without that spark of hope I wouldn't be anywhere.

"Tell me about Melissa," I say, and Sonnie grins.

"Lissa is all kinds of awesome, Mr Henley, sir. She's damn sorry she couldn't be here on a Sunday, what with her brother and all, but ain't nobody gonna be keeping her from her Monday through Friday, that's for sure."

"Her brother?" I ask, and Sonnie looks unsure. "You can tell me," I say. "She's been an excellent help to me, I should thank her."

"You haven't met her yet?"

I shake my head. "A few moments in a meeting room, that's all. She buys me bacon and orchids. I appreciate it."

Sonnie's grin is intoxicating. "Well, sir, she'd be damn happy to hear you say so. The girl thinks you're class-A amazing."

"She does?"

She nods. "Hell yeah." She leans across the island. "Between us, she met you before. She wouldn't say nothing, oh no, so I'm doing her a favour. Would make her year if you hung around one morning to give her your thanks."

I sip my coffee. "She met me before?"

"Outside some school gates. You gave her one of your fancy cigarettes."

The flash of memory is so faint. "The girl with the sparkly tobacco tin?"

She shrugs. "I don't know about that, Mr Henley, sir. Depends how many schoolgirls you been giving your smokes to."

I laugh. "I don't make a habit of it."

"Then I guess she's the girl with the sparkly tobacco tin, sir," she says.

How extraordinary.

I'd be taken aback if I wasn't thoroughly versed already in the peculiarity of coincidence.

"You said she couldn't be here because of her brother?"

Sonnie looks so sad. "I shouldn't say anything."

"Please," I say. "If I can help her…"

"Her parents died," she tells me. "Poor soul was only just eighteen, back last spring. Takes care of her younger brother now, just a wee little soul he is. So much to take on for a youngster."

I feel a genuine pang of sympathy. "She lost both her parents?"

"Hit and run," Sonnie says. "Awful, truly awful. Guy who did it got off with it, too. Some fancy lawyer to thank for that most likely." Her eyes widen in horror as she realises what she's said. "Not like you, sir. Oh no, not like you are."

I wave her horror aside. "It's fine," I say. "Fancy lawyers have a lot to answer for. I know."

"Lissa wanted to be a lawyer herself," she tells me. "Before the accident, you know. I think you inspired her back then at school. Your little talk got her all fired up."

I feel so sorry. I tell her so.

I ask her if she thinks Lissa would be suited to a place on our training program and she claps her hands in glee. "She'd love that, sir! Oh hell, yes! That would make her whole lifetime!"

I'll set it up before I leave. It's the very least I can do.

After all, I won't be needing a cleaner for this house anymore. The orchids would be well and truly wasted on this empty place, and so would *Lissa*.

I wave Sonnie off as she leaves for the day and she thanks me for my muesli.

And then I fire off an email to Claude asking him for a final settlement figure on Amy.

FORTY–ONE

ALEXANDER

'm glad I'm going to be through dealing with Claude soon, because the cunt fucking infuriates me.

Back and forth all Sunday afternoon, grilling me on why I'm requiring a settlement figure.

I give him nothing. I tell him to quote me a figure and mind his fucking business.

His one fucking million is a joke, but I wire the funds anyway, just to keep this fucking easy.

After all, Amy will end up with most of it.

I'm calm as I head into the office on Monday morning. My resolve is steely and my nerves are cold as ice.

I prepare my official resignation for the board and begin assigning my clients to capable colleagues.

I need to keep this under the radar until it's too late. Until it's too late for my father to action any fucking comeback before I'm out of here with Amy in tow.

I've no time for him when he charges into my office. There's not even a fucking board meeting on today and I tell him so.

His eyes are like pinpricks as they feast on mine, and they remind me just how much I hate him. How desperate I am to spend the rest of my life as far away from the seedy cunt as possible.

He slams a file onto my desk and jabs a finger in my direction.

"I knew there was something going on with you, boy." He laughs a terrible laugh. "I should've guessed it would be a pissing woman. Sweet tight cunt is to blame for most of men's problems. Don't I fucking know it."

"What the fuck are you talking about, old man?" I sneer.

"Claude told me all about her." He laughs and my blood runs cold. "I should've guessed it. Half a million for a piece of fine virgin snatch and it sends you all fucking doolally." He shakes his head. "Now you're after a settlement agreement for that same fucking pussy? Willing to pay a whole fucking mill for it?"

"Stay out of it," I snap. "It's none of your fucking business."

"Oh but it is," he snarls. "Because she's addled your fucking brain, boy. The woman's playing you for a silly fucking fool."

"You know nothing about it," I tell him, "and you definitely know nothing about her. Just get the fuck out of here."

"Amy Leigh Randall?" he asks, and my breath hitches. "Twenty-one years old, perfect bloodwork, lives in EC1 with her lovely parents and two delightful younger siblings, yes?"

I don't say a word as he flips open the file. He slams a photo of some random woman down in front of me.

"*This* is Amy Leigh Randall," he hisses.

I stare at the stranger on the passport copy. "What the fuck–" I begin but he slams down another.

And there's my Amy. Her hair is mousy, as it was on the passport I snooped at in her bag. Her smile is bright and so are her eyes, and she looks so young. So sweet.

"That's Amy," I hiss to my father, "as you well fucking know."

He shakes his head, and he's victorious, just as he is in the courtroom. "No," he says, and jabs a finger at my beautiful girl. *"That's* Melissa Martin. Your fucking cleaner." Oh how he laughs. He laughs as my poor spinning brain picks up the pieces.

I stare dumb and it makes him laugh harder.

"Oh good God, boy! Wise up, she fucking played you!"

I can't even think. I can't. I stare at that fucking photo and my hands are shaking. "You're wrong," I say. "This is fucking ridiculous."

"Yes it is!" he snaps. *"You're* fucking ridiculous, boy. You've been played by a fucking cleaner. By hired fucking help! I can't believe you paid half a fucking million for that, she'd have done it for minimum wage." He laughs again.

My heart is pounding in my temples as the pieces all fall into place.

And the picture is fucking hideous.

It's so hideous my stomach wants to turn inside out.

But my father keeps the blows coming. "Don't tell me you've fallen for the girl. Mother of Christ, this just gets better."

"This can't be right," I tell him. "You're a fucking liar. You've always been a fucking liar."

He shakes his head. "No, boy. I'm not. I've never fucking lied to you. You lie to your fucking *self. That's* the difference between you and I. *That's* why I'll always be the senior in this business until the day I fucking die. Because *I* have the fucking balls to own my own fucking shadow, but you, you'd rather bleat on in therapy than fulfil your own fucking potential."

"I'm going to get to the bottom of this," I hiss. "And then I'm going to leave this fucking business, and you along with it."

"I've made it easy for you," he says with a grin. "Melissa Martin is right downstairs for you. Meeting suite sixteen, where you met the wily cow in the first place, I believe."

MELISSA

I hate being here, caged in meeting suite sixteen with its big glass walls in the heart of Alexander's business domain.

I shouldn't be here.

My resignation letter is already stuffed in my apron pocket, my legs shaky as I sit beside Sonnie, wondering what the hell we're all doing in here, summoned at such short notice.

"Health and safety in the workplace," Janet begins up front. "As per the request of the management." She looks as flummoxed as we do, and it scares me.

This whole thing scares me.

"Feels off to me," Sonnie whispers, and shudders for effect. "Not like we don't have this in the handbook. Maybe some silly cow fried herself on the vacuum cleaner or some shit."

I can hope.

Oh God, how I hope.

"I hope it doesn't take long," I whisper back. "Brutus needs his walk."

"He ain't so bad, that mutt," she says, and it makes me smile through the paranoia.

"He's a good boy," I say.

"His owner ain't so bad, either." She nudges me. "I saw him yesterday. Little bird might have told him about you."

Oh fuck how my stomach lurches. "You did what?"

She can't carry on. Janet calls the room to order and starts talking through her slide deck.

I clutch the letter in my pocket, holding it like a talisman as I stare numbly at the screen. This will be my last time in this building, I swear it. I just need to get out of here unseen. Please God, let me get out of here unseen.

It seems to take forever. Janet's words blur into one, the screen fading into the background as my thoughts tumble and crash around my stomach.

I'll grab her when this is over, I'll hand over my letter and make a dash away from here.

And then I just have to wait until Wednesday. I'll tell him my real name as soon as I'm through his door.

No more lies. Not ever.

I manage to calm my breathing, counting in to seven, out to eleven as I fret in my seat. The clock keeps ticking. Fifteen minutes, twenty, twenty-five. The slide deck counts up to twenty-six, and we're almost there when the room ripples. Slide twenty-three. Only two more to go.

I don't look around at first.

Call it instinct. Call it paranoia in overdrive.

It's only when Sonnie nudges my elbow that I tear my eyes from the screen.

"There he is," she whispers. "Ain't he mighty fine? Look quick, before you miss him."

The world stops turning. My breath stops coming.

Just like that the cards collapse.

They tumble from the sky, every single one, and my final ace is burning.

My final ace is all gone.

He's staring right at me as I turn my head to the window.

His father is at his side with a terrible smile on his face, and Alexander looks as horrified as I do.

More horrified than I do.

He shakes his head so slowly, his jaw gritted as he swallows, and his eyes. Oh God, his eyes. His eyes are full of pain. Pain and hate.

Alexander Henley fucking hates me.

And I fucking hate myself.

His father gives me a wave, and he's laughing. He's actually laughing as he turns away and grabs Alexander by the elbow.

Alexander doesn't move for long seconds, just stares in disbelief as I stare right back.

I don't even hide the tears falling. I don't care how many people are staring at me, or how Sonnie is squeezing my arm.

"Sorry," I mouth, "I'm sorry."

And that breaks the spell.

He turns away with his father, then shrugs him off as the older man tries to speak.

I get to my feet as the man I love stalks off down the corridor, and Janet shrieks as I make a run for it.

"*Miss Martin!*" she screeches, but I don't even slow down.

"Alexander!" I call, but he doesn't even look at me. He slams the door at the end of the corridor, and I'm all set to charge on after him, be damned with the consequences, but I can't.

The hand on my shoulder is firm. Alexander Henley Senior's grip is brutal.

"We need a fucking word, Miss Martin," he hisses.

And I cry.

Oh God, how I cry.

ALEXANDER

I take the stairs, all sixteen fucking floors of them three at a time with my lungs on fire.

I barge past some catering staff halfway down and don't even apologise.

I can't speak. I don't want to fucking speak.

I don't even want to be alive.

The world spins as I pace through the lobby. My lungs scream for air as I barge through the main entrance doors.

My lungs scream to be out of this fucking place.

I stumble onto the street and straight into Mr Rand on his way in.

He holds out a hand and I stare mute, as though I'm a fucking lunatic. Because I am. I am a fucking lunatic.

"Are you alright, Henley?" Rand asks, and I brace myself on his shoulder, using him as leverage to walk on by. I stumble down the street with the wind whipping my tie, and the rain feels like acid against my cheeks.

A cigarette. I need a fucking cigarette.

I stumble into a tiny corner shop two streets down, and the assistant is wide-eyed as I bark out an order for anything. Sixty of fucking *anything*. And a lighter. Make that two fucking lighters.

"Do you need some help?" she asks, and I know I must look like fucking death. "A doctor, or…"

I hand over my credit card as she rings up my purchases. My voice sounds like a crazy man.

"I'm fine," I say.

She nods politely as she hands over my cigarettes.

I've torn into the first pack before I'm even out of there. I smoke it with my back to the wall and light up another straight after.

I've been played by a fucking cleaner. My own fucking cleaner.

Of course I've been fucking played.

The gemstones, the fucking band, the way Brutus was so fucking fond of her.

Of course he was fucking fond of her. He fucking knew her. He saw her every fucking day.

My hands ball into fists against the pain.

Brown hair to blonde, as though she knew I liked blondes. As though she knew about my teenage fucking crush.

As though she'd peered inside my fucking soul and not the tatty fucking memory box in the storage room.

It takes me three cigarettes before I can trust my legs to take my weight.

Three cigarettes before I feel like I can breathe without screaming my lungs raw.

I hover in the street, contemplating going back to the office and tearing the little bitch a fucking new one.

Scrap that. I should congratulate her fucking prowess and tell her she'd make a damn fucking fine lawyer.

She can have my fucking job if she wants it.

I laugh a bitter laugh as I picture her pretty face.

Oh fuck, she was fucking good.

Good enough that I actually believed she fucking loved me, which is a fucking joke in itself.

Nobody who's ever truly known me has ever come out the other side still loving me.

I hail a cab to take me home.

I've nothing to fucking say to her, and nothing to say to my fucking father, either.

MELISSA

I'm stripped of everything – my ID badge and my swipe card and Alexander Henley's house keys.

I'm even stripped of my stupid scratchy cap and apron.

Mr Henley Snr. laughs as he finds the resignation letter in my apron pocket.

"So close," he says. "And to think you nearly got away with it." He laughs again to himself. "Extraordinary. You're wasted as a cleaner, most likely as a hooker, too. You should be a lawyer."

I have to cover my mouth to stop myself being sick.

"I'm sure I don't need to tell you what would happen if you were foolish enough to contact my son," he says. "Consider your employment well and truly terminated. Please don't insult me by asking your manager for a reference."

I can't speak. I can't say anything.

His smile is a sneer. "Believe me, you don't know anything about my boy. If you've any sense at all you'll stay as far away as possible. He has a penchant for asphyxiation games, as I'm sure you well know. Something tells me you wouldn't come out the other side of the next one."

I blink away tears, and I don't care. I don't care that I wouldn't come out the other side of the next one.

I really don't.

The life insurance would be more than enough for Dean to take care of Joseph.

"Stay away from my fucking son," Mr Henley Snr. hisses. "You're fucking dead to him."

I don't say a word as he marches me to the exit with a security guard at my side.

FORTY—TWO

ALEXANDER

I call out an emergency locksmith and barricade myself in tight.

I smoke all my cigarettes and only venture out for more.

I ignore all calls. I ignore the appointments on my calendar. I ignore all the messages from my cunt of a fucking father asking me when I'm going back to the fucking office.

The pill bottles in the medicine cabinet scream my name, but I can't abandon Brutus.

His furry head on my lap is the only thing that keeps me breathing.

It's been forty-eight hours when I pull Melissa Martin's little thank you notes from my kitchen drawer. I head upstairs with a cigarette in my mouth. The gemstone cabinet clicks open with the new code.

I hold her scrawled gemstone identification card next to the note thanking me for muesli, and it's right there. Right in front of my fucking face.

She's tried to disguise it, of course. The scrawl is more slanted on the gemstone card, but the loops of her letters are the same.

It was right in front of my face the entire fucking time, I just chose not to see it.

I didn't *want* to see it.

My heart pains as I see her *lucky quartz*. What a fucking bitch. What a total fucking bitch.

I turn it over in my palm as I take the final drag of my cigarette, and then I throw it. Hard. Hard enough that it bounces off the fucking wall and disappears behind some shelving. Fuck it. Fuck all of it.

When I start I can't fucking stop.

Thousands upon fucking thousands worth of rare gemstones meet the same fucking fate. I clear the shelves with frantic sweeps of my arm, launching them at the wall together with their pretty fucking plinths. I don't give a fucking fuck. Not about any of it.

I charge downstairs and stamp on my fucking Kings and Castles CDs, because the bitch has fucking ruined them for me. She's ruined fucking everything for me.

The orchids are wilting in their fucking vase and I tear those up too.

I hate how she was inside this fucking place. I hate how she was inside *me*. Inside my fucking head.

I've never felt so fucking violated.

Not by those cunts in the public toilet, and not by my filthy fucking father, either.

And I want to tell her. I want to tell her what I fucking think of her.

I want her to see who I really fucking am. Not the fucking sap she played like a fucking fool.

The real fucking me.

The one who paid a fucking million a couple of days ago for a permanent go on her pretty fucking snatch.

I'm going to get my fucking money's worth.

My fingers are shaking as I type out a message to Claude.

Amy. Tonight. Delaney's.

I wait for the reply.

Are you fucking insane?!

I don't have time for this shit. I press to call.

"Book it," I snap. "Just fucking book it, you greedy fucking cunt."

"Jesus, Henley, calm the fuck down!" he bleats, and I laugh.

I really fucking laugh.

"My name's Ted fucking Brown," I say.

MELISSA

Dean doesn't know what to do. He wanders around the place, taking care of Joseph and trying to take care of me along with him, but I'm a lost cause.

It's too painful to eat, so I don't.

It's too painful to think, so I don't.

I lie in bed, cocooned in a smog of despair that won't lift. My heart breaks a thousand times when I think of what I had and what I lost.

I was so stupid.

And selfish, and cruel, and reckless.

I hurt him.

I'll never forgive myself for how much I hurt him.

I kiss Joseph at bedtime, and I hobble out to give him lunch, but the rest of the time I'm a zombie.

I may as well be dead.

"You need to eat, Lissa," Dean tells me on Wednesday. "Please just eat something. Some soup, or…"

I shake my head. "I can't."

"But you have to! Please, Lissa, think of Joe." His words make me cry, and he sighs. "Or don't. Please, Lissa, just get some help. I can take you to the doctors or call someone out."

"Nobody can help me," I tell him. "I don't want to see anyone."

He doesn't push it, and I go back to bed.

I shout him to leave me alone when he taps on the door in the afternoon. I tell him I've got nothing to say.

He comes in anyway, and chucks me his phone.

"I shouldn't even be fucking showing you," he hisses. "But I can't fucking bear to see you like this."

The message is blurry, I have to blink three times before it comes into focus.

Delaney's. 8 p.m.

Your client is Ted Brown.

I almost throw up.

"You can't go," Dean says. "Not on your own. He'll fucking kill you."

But I'm already up on my feet.

"I'm going," I tell him and he curses at me.

"Did you not hear me? He'll fucking kill you, Lissa. Call Helen, get her to babysit."

"I need to go alone," I say.

"No, you really fucking don't."

But I do.

I do need to go alone.

I take a shower and throw my everyday clothes on. A worn cami and a pair of budget jeans.

I don't wear any makeup and I don't spritz myself with designer perfume samples.

I just go as me.

I want him to know me. *Me.*

I want him to stare into my eyes and see *me* staring back at him.

I want to hear him say my real name.

But most of all I want to say sorry. I need to say sorry.

Even if it's the last thing I ever do.

FORTY-THREE

MELISSA

I don't bother checking into my own room at Delaney's. I walk straight through reception and call the elevator. It takes me right up to the top floor, and I head for suite twelve with frantic steps.

I'm not scared.

My heart is already broken. I already hate myself for what I've done.

My dreams are already in tatters.

My breath is ragged as I reach the door, but I make no move to compose myself before I knock.

He keeps me waiting this time, and I wonder if he's right on the other side. I wonder if he's having second thoughts.

Tears spring to my eyes the very second he opens the door. Bittersweet relief floods through me.

Black suit, white shirt, black tie.

Dark eyes. Angry eyes.

Hurt eyes.

His hair is slick and his jaw is gritted.

The fine lines around his eyes look etched in. He looks tired. Damaged.

There's a lump in my throat as I breathe him in for what might be the final time.

I soak in the shadow of stubble on his jaw. The birthmark on his cheek. The heaviness of his brow.

"*Amy*," he says, and my heart stops.

"Alexander," I say, and he steps aside to let me pass.

I flinch as the door slams behind me. "It's Ted fucking Brown," he snaps.

I nod. "Ted," I whisper.

There's no champagne this evening. He reaches into his jacket and pulls out the envelope.

"Let's get the fucking practicalities out of the way first, shall we?" he spits.

I shake my head. "I don't want your money," I tell him. "I'm not here for the money. I never have been."

"Is that so?"

"Yes."

It was the wrong thing to say. He tears into the envelope with a fierceness that makes my legs tremble. He throws the notes at me in plumes of rage. They rain down on me, landing on the floor like leaves.

"Pick it up!" he snaps. "Don't be fucking shy. You want more?"

He pulls out his wallet and empties it at my feet.

I've never felt so cheap as I do when his loose change lands on my toes.

"Why are you here?!" he seethes. "Are you that fucking greedy for more?!"

"I don't... it's not about money..." I repeat, but he doesn't care.

"I've made you a fucking millionaire, isn't that enough?! You want more?!" He takes off his watch and throws that at me too.

I can't stop the tears as his cufflinks bounce off my chest, and I don't understand it. I'm not a millionaire. I'm not here for his money.

"Pick it up!" he shouts, but I don't move. He drops to his knees and gathers notes from the floor to throw in my face all over again, and I don't even flinch. "Take it!"

"I don't want it," I whisper. "I swear I don't. I used the money for my brother, that's all, to make sure he has enough for a good life."

"Oh he'll have a good fucking life," he barks as he gets to his feet. "He'll have a whale of a fucking time with the six fucking figures I paid for you."

My eyes meet his, and I don't get it.

"Don't play fucking dumb," he snaps. "I know you get seventy fucking percent."

"I get what you give me," I tell him. "I'd have taken whatever you gave me. I'd have taken nothing."

He sneers. "What I give you and the rest of the fucking money Claude wires to your fucking account, you mean?"

But I don't. I don't mean that. I don't know what he's talking about. I tell him so and he rages all around me. He storms across the room and pours himself a whisky from the mini bar, and I just wait.

"Enough of the lies," he says and lights up a cigarette. "I've had fucking enough of it."

"I'm not lying," I tell him.

"You're telling me Claude never fucking paid you?"

"*You* paid me."

"And Claude, yes?"

I shake my head. "He said it would be cash… he said never to ask…"

He still thinks I'm lying and I know. His eyes are hostile and suspicious as they stare into mine. I don't blame him.

"If you're fucking lying to me…" he threatens.

"I'm done with lying," I tell him and my voice breaks.

He sits down on the edge of the bed with his hands in his hair, and I so much want to touch him. It pains right through me to leave him be.

"He didn't pay you?"

"No, never," I say again.

"Amy, if you're lying…"

My legs don't want to hold me anymore. I'm exhausted and empty. I drop to my knees amongst the scattered money.

The silence is heavy as neither of us speak another word. I don't care. I only care that I'm with him, even though he hates me.

He finishes up his cigarette and drops it into his empty tumbler.

"He really didn't pay you?"

I shake my head.

"I paid half a fucking million for your virginity and a five percent compulsory cash tip on top. You didn't get it? What about the million I paid for your fucking settlement fee last Sunday? What about the ten fucking grand I paid twice a fucking week?"

My jaw drops open. "You did what?!"

"You didn't get it? Not any of it?!"

"I got twenty-five grand the first time, but it was more than enough. It was more money than I've ever seen. I get the envelopes. I get whatever you give me. And I don't know anything about a settlement fee! I don't know anything about a million pounds, I swear!"

I stare numbly as he pulls out his phone. I watch him as he gets to his feet and presses it to his ear.

"Amy's fucking money," he says. "Where the fuck is it?"

I can't hear the other end of the conversation and I don't care.

"What do you mean it's fucking *pending*? What the fuck does *pending* mean?!"

His eyes meet mine for a heartbeat, and his next words are for me.

"Did you give the prick your bank details?"

I shake my head.

He turns away. "You don't even have her bank details you slimy fucking cunt. You thought her name was Amy Randall."

"I don't care," I say. "I don't want it."

He silences me with a raised hand.

"Transfer it to my fucking account," he snarls. "*I'll* make sure she fucking gets it. You have twenty-four fucking hours, Claude, or I'm pulling the fucking plug on your seedy fucking operation and I don't care who I fucking take down with me. You can pass *that* little gem onto my fucking father."

He hangs up and tosses his phone onto the dresser.

"You'll get your money," he says.

"Please keep it," I tell him. "Please, Alex- *Ted*. Please, Ted."

"You earned it."

"Being with you was the best thing that ever happened to me. You being my first was all I ever wanted."

"Shut up!" he snaps.

But I can't. "*You're* everything I ever wanted. I lied because I wanted you. I lied because I thought it was the only way."

"You lied because you scoped my fucking house out and thought you'd rip me off for some fucking cash."

I cry-laugh, because it's so far from the truth, so insanely far from the truth.

"Why are you even here?" he snarls.

And it's my chance. Maybe my only one.

"I came to say sorry," I whisper, and the tears roll down my face. "I'm so sorry,

Alexander. I never meant..."

"You're fucking sorry?!"

I nod. "You'll never know how sorry I am. You'll never know how much I wanted you."

I can hardly see him for the tears. I wipe them away and choke them back. I wish I hadn't. He looks so fucking pained.

"You've said it," he tells me. "So leave."

I shake my head. "Please don't make me go."

"Go," he snaps, but I can't. I just can't. "Get out of here, Amy. Fuck off."

"Please..." I breathe. "Please don't..."

"Please don't what?! Don't throw you out? Don't fucking touch you? What?"

"Don't throw me out," I whisper.

"Get out or give me my fucking money's worth."

My eyes widen. "You mean..."

"I mean get the fuck out of my fucking hotel room or give me what I fucking paid for. That's why I called you here, Amy. To get my fucking money's worth."

I drag myself to my feet and force back the tears. My eyes are on his as I pull my top off over my head and unclip my bra. I take off my jeans and my knickers with them, and I don't care how exposed I am. I don't care how angry he is, just as long as he lets me stay.

"You're fucking insane," he tells me.

And I am. I am insane.

"You really want to fucking go there?"

I nod.

"Walk away."

"No."

"Jesus Christ, Amy. Just fucking go."

"I won't," I tell him. "Not unless you make me. I'll never walk away unless you make me."

I half expect him to. I half expect him to turf me out into the corridor stark naked, but he doesn't.

His eyes are so cold as he gets to his feet. "On the bed," he says, and I move for him. "On your fucking front," he tells me, and I do as he asks.

I hear him unbuckle his belt. I feel the heat of him as he comes near.

"Tell me you don't want this," he hisses as his weight bears down.

"I'm done with lying," I whisper. "I do want this. I always want this. I want *you*."

"Tell me to stop," he snarls, and I shake my head.

"Never."

"Never?"

"Never," I say again.

"We'll fucking see about that," he snaps, and I take a breath as he grabs my hair. He tugs hard and I don't even flinch.

It hurts so bad as he pushes inside me. I'm not ready but I don't care. It's everything just to take him.

"You're an excellent liar," he tells me as he fucks me rough. "I believed every fucking lie you fed me. I believed you liked this."

"I love this. I loved everything."

I cry out as he slams in deep. His breath is in my ear and his fingers are rough in my hair, his body pounding mine with everything he's got.

I take it all.

I love it all.

"I fell for you," he snarls. "You took me for a fucking fool, but you're the fucking fool for coming here, Amy. You're the fucking fool now."

"I love you," I whisper through the pain. "I've always loved you."

"How about taking my cock in your tight little asshole? Do you love that as well?"

"Yes," I breathe, and I know what's coming.

I can't stop myself whimpering as he forces his way inside. It burns so bad, like my insides are on fire, but I don't care. I grit my teeth and take him. I buck back at him even though it hurts like hell.

"Tell me to stop," he breathes.

"No," I tell him. "Never."

"Tell me you don't like this. Tell me it fucking hurts."

I shake my head. "I *do* like this. I loved everything you ever showed me."

"Everything?" The word is a threat. It makes my heart pound.

"Everything," I insist, even though I know I'm playing with fire.

"You liked it when I choked you half to fucking death, did you? That got you off, did it? Don't fucking lie to me."

"I loved everything!" I cry. "I swear I loved everything! I wasn't lying, not about that! I'd never lie about that!"

I whimper as he pulls out of me. I gulp in breath as he flips me onto my back. My chest heaves as he tugs his belt from his waist.

"Tell me you don't want me to choke you," he hisses and he wants me to say it, I know he does.

But I can't.

I done with lying.

"Say it, Amy."

"I loved all of it," I tell him. "I swear."

"You'll tap out," he seethes. "Tap your fucking hand when you want to tell me the fucking truth."

My throat is already dry when he wraps the belt around my neck and links it through like a choke chain.

The leather feels so different to his hand.

I'm scared.

I'm really scared but I don't show it. I don't want him to see.

"Tap your fucking hand," he says again as he tugs on the end. I retch but my hands are balled into fists at my sides.

I'm never going to tap out. Not ever.

The moment I tap out, this will all be over.

My chest fights for air that won't come. My legs tremble with adrenaline as Alexander Henley pins me down and slides his cock back into my asshole.

The burn in my ass pales into significance to the burn in my lungs.

This isn't like usual.

I'm normally relaxed. I normally feel safe, even though I feel out of control. I normally slip beyond the fear so easily, but not today.

Today it's a battle not to tap my hand and wrench that belt from my neck.

His eyes are on mine as he fucks me. Staring into him is the only thing that keeps me still.

"Tap out," he whispers, but I don't. "Damn it, Amy, tap fucking out!"

His breath is hot on my open mouth, but I don't move. I don't tap out.

I wrap my legs around his waist to take more of him, and my hands loosen from fists to land on his shoulders. I keep them there.

"You'll tap out," he hisses. "Fucking hell, Amy, you *will* tap out."

But I won't.

My ears start ringing as my head swims. It's calmer now. Everything is so much calmer.

His cock doesn't hurt in my ass anymore. Nothing hurts.

Everything feels amazing.

I stop struggling for breath. I finally find peace.

Dots dance across my vision and it's okay here. I'm happy here.

I brush my thumb across his cheek, but he feels so far away.

Tap out, Amy. Fucking hell.

He feels so far away.

His eyes are the last thing I see before mine close.

FORTY—FOUR

ALEXANDER

My blood is on fucking fire as I pound her fucking ass.

It's a punishment fuck, pure as fucking sin. Raw and brutal and angry. So fucking angry.

I hate the way I love being inside her. I hate the way my cock still craves this.

My eyes bore into hers as I scream at her to tap the fuck out and get this over with.

But she doesn't.

She fucking doesn't.

I tug the belt tighter around her pretty throat and she doesn't even squirm. Her fingers brush my cheek and she smiles at me.

It breaks my fucking heart all over again.

Tap out.

Everything in me is screaming at everything in her.

Just tap the fuck out, you crazy fucking bitch. Stop lying to me.

Her hands fall to the bedsheets as her eyes close.

I stop thrusting the second her chest stops heaving.

"Amy?" It's a stupid question. Her head lolls limp, and she's pale, like a fucking ghost.

I yank that fucking belt free in a heartbeat. I tap her face and tell her she's proved her point. Fuck, she's proved her fucking point.

I shake her shoulders and demand she fucking answer me.

But she doesn't.

"Jesus, Amy," I hiss. "Wake up. Christ, wake up." My blood runs cold. "Amy!"

I fight the panic. Force down the terror.

"Please wake up. God fucking forgive me, Amy, please wake up."

Her eyes open wide as she gulps. They focus on mine as she splutters and gurgles.

She takes one long desperate breath and so do I. I'm shaking. Trembling as I pull her into my arms.

Oh God, how I hold her. I smooth her hair with my heart pounding against hers.

She's dazed. Confused as she orientates herself.

"Alexander?" she whispers and her breath is so fucking raw.

"I'm sorry," I breathe. "I'm so fucking sorry."

"I'm okay," she rasps. "It's okay."

But it's not. This will never be fucking okay. I tell her so, and my voice is as raspy as hers.

"I didn't tap out," she says. "I wasn't lying. I'd never tap out."

I'm the biggest cunt in the fucking world. A bigger cunt than that asshole Claude or any one of my fucking clients. A bigger cunt than my filthy fucking father.

I press my lips to her forehead and she sighs. Her body melts to mine as though she still cares, and it breaks me all over again.

I wish it was me without breath.

I wish it was *me* who'd choked in *her* arms.

"Jesus, Amy, I thought you were gone," I whisper, and my voice is lost in her hair.

Her hand buries in mine. Her fingers are so gentle.

"It's Lissa," she says. "Everyone calls me Lissa."

"Lissa," I breathe, and I feel her smile.

"You've no idea how much I've wanted to hear you say it," she says, and I must be a fucking fool all over again, because I believe her.

God fucking help me, I believe her.

MELISSA

I thought staring into Alexander Henley's eyes as I slipped away was the most blissful thing in the world.

But I was wrong.

Staring into Alexander Henley's eyes as I come back is the most blissful thing in the world.

My chest feels dry and achy. Every breath makes me cough.

Even so, it still pains when he pulls away. I'm reaching out for him as he heads for the mini bar.

I pull him close as he comes back with a glass of water.

"I'm sorry," he says again.

I shake my head. "I'm the one who came here to say sorry."

The cold water feels so nice as I swallow. I drink it down in long sips and he takes the empty glass from me.

The bed is so comfortable here, nearly as comfy as his. I curl into a ball and he lays at my side.

I want to stay here forever.

I'd give anything to make this ok.

"Can you speak?" he asks and I nod.

"It's not so bad now." I take a breath to illustrate and it's not nearly so raspy as it was before.

"Tell me everything," he says. "I'm listening."

"You don't have to," I tell him. "I fucked up so bad."

"Yeah, well. We've both done things we're not proud of. I nearly fucking killed you."

"You promised you wouldn't kill me," I whisper. "I believed you."

"Maybe you shouldn't have."

"But you didn't," I say. "You didn't kill me."

"By good fortune, Lissa, nothing more."

But I don't believe him. I saw the relief in his eyes as I opened mine, and it wasn't just panic.

I saw through the panic. His eyes still cared about me.

I don't know where to start. I'm still thinking it through when he speaks.

"Your friend Sonnie told me we met before. You were the girl with the sparkly tobacco tin."

My eyes meet his. "You remember?"

"It had hearts on it," he says. "Glittery hearts."

"I used to fantasise about you recognising me one day. But you didn't."

"You were a kid," he says. "I saw a million kids that week."

"But only one with a sparkly tobacco tin."

"You had darker hair," he said.

"I dyed it for you," I tell him. "Because I saw those pictures of Debbie Harry in your storage room."

"I gathered as much."

I take a deep breath. It feels so good to breathe. "This isn't how it was supposed to be. I was going to be a lawyer, just like you. I was going to go to uni and become the very best, and then I was going to come for a job with you. I thought if we were colleagues... I thought if I could impress you..."

"You planned that all those years ago?"

I nod. "I worked hard for straight-As all the way through the rest of high school, all the way through college, too."

He squeezes my shoulder and I know then that Sonnie told him.

I feel the tears welling up before I've even said another word.

"My parents were out for their anniversary. Dad took Mum out to the place they met, a little Italian place they loved. I was babysitting for Joe. I told them to have a good time. They were really happy, Dad bought Mum orchids, they were her favourite."

"You don't have to tell me this," he says, but I want to. I want him to know *everything*.

"It was a stupid rich kid who hit them, driving his dad's car way over the speed limit. The police said he didn't slow down, didn't even see them."

"Did they prosecute?"

I shake my head. "Rich lawyer, not enough evidence. Circumstantial, they said. He had a good college record."

"I'm sorry."

"I didn't think I'd ever get up. I didn't think I could go on living. But I have a little brother, Joseph. He wasn't even twelve months old."

"You take care of him?"

I nod. "I quit college and claimed benefits for a while, but I hated it. That isn't what I want for Joe. My parents worked hard, I want him to see me work hard too. So my friend Dean sleeps on my sofa, he said he'd take care of Joe so I could find a job. I found yours, and I hoped… I hoped maybe… if I could just be close to you…"

"You *were* close to me," he hisses. "I bought you peaches and fucking chocolate. I left you fucking notes. A bottle of wine." He sighs. "I chased you down the fucking street, Lissa. Why the fuck didn't you stop for me? Why the fuck did you choose to lie instead?"

I prop myself up on an elbow and my heart is racing. "I was your cleaner. I was a nobody. I *am* a nobody, and you're… everything."

"I chased you down the fucking street, Melissa. Jesus Christ." He's angry again. His body is so rigid. I want to touch him but I don't dare.

"I was already in with Claude. I'd already filmed that slutty video. If I'd gone back when you called, if I'd introduced myself before you'd seen it and then you did…"

"I wouldn't have fucking seen it!" he hisses. "I'd already quit that shit. I was going cold fucking turkey, going fucking insane over a cleaner I'd never fucking met."

I didn't know.

How it fucking hurts.

"I'm sorry," I say again. "I thought if I could just… be someone… if I could love what you love… maybe you'd love me like I love you."

"So you lied? Snooped on me, and dug into all my fucking things, and then lied to me? Played me like a fucking fool?"

"I'm not even nineteen. I was a cleaner taking care of her younger brother. I didn't think you'd even look at me."

"But I did!" he snaps. "I fucking did!" He rolls away from me and it pains so much to face his back. "This is so fucked up," he says. "I believed all of it, every fucking thing you said, and it was all just a fucking act."

"*Was*," I tell him. "But it isn't now. I *am* that person. I'm everything I pretended to be, I swear."

He laughs a horrible laugh. "Stop it."

"I love the things that you love. I love the gemstones and I love Kings and Castles. I loved that gig so much it made me cry, and it was all real."

"Please stop," he says.

"And I love Brutus. I love *you*."

"You don't even fucking know me," he snaps. "And I sure as hell don't know you."

"That's not true," I whisper. "It was real. Everything I felt was real." I don't want to cry again but I can't stop. "And everything you felt was real, too. I felt it. I felt *you*. I still do."

"Just fucking stop," he snaps, but I can't.

"I was going to tell you last weekend, right after Dean. But you were so angry when you found out I knew him. I was scared that if I said anything you'd never speak to me again."

"Good job you averted that fucking crisis." His sarcasm cuts.

"I fucked up," I say. "I just wanted to say sorry, that's why I came here."

"And you said it."

I want to beg for forgiveness. I want to fall at his feet and beg him to give me another chance.

But I don't.

I don't deserve another chance.

"I'm sorry about your parents," he says. "I'm sorry you had to give up on college. I'll make sure you get the money from Claude. I'll take your bank details and pay it over myself. It can be a new start. Put yourself back through college." He rolls to face me, but he feels so far away.

"And what about you?"

"I'm leaving," he says and my heart shatters. "I meant what I said, I'm done with bailing rich cunts out every day of my life. I'm done with my father and his shitty fucking business."

I wipe the tears from my eyes. "I wish I could come with you."

"Yeah, well, so do I," he says, and gets up from the bed. "Maybe in a parallel universe. Maybe somewhere there's a Melissa who turned around on the street that day."

"I hope so," I cry. "I hope that other Melissa is so much happier than I am right now."

I crawl from the bed and reach for my handbag. I dig inside for his fire opal and offer it over to him. "You should have this back," I say.

"You don't want it?"

I have to catch a sob. "I love it," I say. "But I lied to get it. It doesn't belong to me."

"Keep it," he says.

I feel so defeated when I slip it back into my bag.

He puts his belt back on and fastens himself up. He smooths down his tie in the mirror.

We're done here, and I wish I'd never started breathing again.

He drops to his knees to gather up the money from the floor. He taps it into a pile on the dresser and leaves it there.

He fastens up his watch and his cufflinks.

"I'll call you a cab," he says. "Where do you need to go?"

My stomach is nothing but pain as I give him my address. He calls me a cab and tells me it'll ten minutes, and then he lights up another cigarette.

I'm crying quiet tears as I get dressed.

I can't bring myself to say goodbye, so I don't. I stand in the middle of that hotel room looking at Alexander Henley for one last time, and he sees me.

He holds out his cigarette packet.

"For old times' sake?"

I take one and he holds a lighter to the end for me.

It's a perfectly awful end for us. It makes me smile a sad smile.

"Go to college," he says as he finishes his.

Please don't leave, my soul screams, but I don't say a word.

"Your cab should be here any minute," he says.

I nod, and then I break. I rush towards him for one last touch, and he's rigid in my arms but I don't care. I don't care that his jaw is gritted tight as I kiss his cheek.

I don't care that he doesn't hold me back.

"It was real," I whisper. "*I* was real."

"Goodbye, Melissa," he says.

And I go.

I leave his cash on the dresser, and my heart in that room behind me.

FORTY–FIVE

ALEXANDER

She left her cash on the dresser. I didn't notice until too late.

That cunt Claude will have some fucking questions to answer, and I'll get her all she's owed.

I feel beaten as I head down to the reception and hand over my key card.

I feel defeated as I call a cab of my own and wait outside.

I wanted answers and I got them, but they don't make me feel any better.

Neither does her apology.

Hope. Such a fragile thing. Such a ridiculous thing.

I'd enjoyed it while it lasted.

Hope teased me with a glimpse of another life, where I could love someone and they could love me back. A life where I wouldn't have to be alone.

I hate the thought of starting over without her.

I hate the thought of running away from my shitty life with nobody to run for.

I climb into the back of the cab and give the driver my address.

And then I change my mind.

I give him hers instead.

Melissa Martin knows everything about me, and I still know virtually fuck all about her.

She crawled inside my mind and died there, and I don't even know her middle name.

It's still there, the anger. Still bubbling under the surface.

I still feel violated.

I don't know what food's inside her fridge, or which music she has on her playlist. I don't know what colour her bedroom is, or whether she has any pets.

I don't know if she takes a bath or a shower in the morning.

I don't know what she looked like on her old school photos.

She knows fucking everything about me, and that smarts.

It's like an itch I can't get fucking shot of, this insane desire to even the score.

I almost change my mind as the cab pulls up outside her block.

It's a shithole. This whole area is a shithole.

The entrance door is covered in graffiti and the stairwell stinks of piss. I don't touch the handrail as I make my way up to her floor. My hands are in my pockets as I scope out where her flat is.

It's in a corner at the back of the top floor, number 21.

I close my eyes as I knock, and it's not really a knock at all, it's a deafening thump. A whole fucking string of them.

It's Dean who answers. His eyes widen in horror as he clocks it's me.

I'm past him in a heartbeat, my eyes wild as they feast on everything in that place.

"Where is she?" I snap, and he heads on through the living room. He taps on a door at the far end and she looks tiny and broken as she steps out. Her cheeks are blotchy and tear-streaked and her hair is a mess.

Her eyes well up afresh as she sees me, and her bottom lip trembles. "Alexander?" she says as she dashes over. "What are you doing here?"

Dean's shoulder shunts mine as he passes. He takes a coat from the hook. "Don't fucking hurt her," he tells me.

I have no intention of fucking hurting her.

"I'll be back in an hour," he tells Melissa, and she nods.

I wait until the door closes behind him.

And then I walk right on past her.

I start in her kitchen. I read all the little notes on her fucking pinboard. I flick through the cookbooks and tear through all the drawers.

"What are you doing?" she asks, but makes no attempt to stop me.

"You saw fucking everything of mine," I snap. "You snooped in fucking everything. I'm showing you how it fucking feels to have your home invaded."

I know I'm a fucking lunatic, but I don't care.

There's barely anything in her fridge. Some milk, and ham and fresh vegetables. A half-used block of cheese.

I march through to the living room when I'm done in the kitchen. I tear through the display cabinet, digging through all the letters in the top drawer.

I flick through family photos and Melissa points out her mum and dad, like it needed saying.

I look under the sofa and under the TV. I flick through her brother's DVDs and her mum's old exercise videos.

I learn nothing other than she's a girl living in her parents' wake. Picking up the pieces of a shattered life.

"Doesn't feel so great when you're not the one doing the fucking snooping, does it?" I snap, but she doesn't say a word.

She doesn't have many beauty products in the bathroom, just basic shampoo and conditioner and a kid's bubble bath.

She uses sanitary towels not tampons, and her toothbrush is pink.

"Which is your bedroom?" I ask and she points to the door at the end of the hallway. "Tell me to leave," I say, "or I'm going to tear your fucking room apart."

"Never," she says. "I'll never tell you to leave. I can't even believe you're here."

"Suit yourself," I snap, and step on in.

MELISSA

I can't believe he's really here.

I don't even dare to hope that this isn't over.

But he's here. He's *here*.

He's angry, and wound tight, and his eyes are wild and dark, but he's here.

I follow him into my bedroom and tell him to go ahead. I tell him to do whatever he wants. I'm not interested in secrets. I'd cut open my soul if I could, just to show him what's inside.

He stares at the old Debating Society certificates on my wall. He picks up the framed family photos on my dresser.

He smells my old stuffed teddy bear and opens my wardrobe and tears through my clothes. There isn't much in there, it doesn't take long.

It doesn't take him long to rummage through my makeup box, either.

The drawers under my desk are filled with old college books, he flicks through the legal ones and he swallows. "This really was your dream?"

I nod. It's all I can do.

And then he sees it, my battered old chest of drawers on the far side of my bed.

The one with all my crystals laid out on top, my Kings and Castles CD still open by the player.

"You didn't show me these," he says as he picks up a piece of bloodstone.

"I didn't have them then," I say, and I'm not lying. These additions were all for me.

He holds up the CD case. "Research?"

I shake my head. "I only bought that last week, I wanted the physical copy."

"Fucking hell, Lissa," he snaps. "You changed your whole fucking life for me."

I shake my head. "Only at the beginning. I thought I was playing…" My smile hurts. "It's funny how pretending to be someone else can help you find out who you really are."

He stares at me. "You think this is who you really are now? Amy pissing Randall?"

I shake my head. "I think she's just the start. I was nothing after they died. I was nobody. Being Amy Randall was the best thing in the world."

It really was. Being her was everything I ever dreamed it would be. Loving him was everything I ever dreamed it would be.

And more.

So much more.

"*Knowing* Amy Randall was the best thing in the world," he says.

He takes a seat on my bed and rubs his temples. "I should go."

"Please don't."

His eyes burn into mine but I don't look away. I'll never look away.

"Then you'd better put the kettle on," he says.

ALEXANDER

Her kitchen is cramped. She nudges me with her hip as she reaches for a clean mug, and I wonder how they ever fit three people in this place.

I shouldn't be here.

My threats to Claude will be working their way back to my father if they haven't reached him already.

I have no interest in taking them back, which means my window of escape is limited.

He'll be gunning for me, and so will his associates.

I shouldn't be here, I should be planning my exit, packing up the things I want to take with me.

But I still don't want to leave her. Not even after everything she's done.

"I'll be leaving London tomorrow night," I tell her. "Any longer and the chances I'll make it out reduce dramatically."

She tries to hide her fear as she stirs my coffee. It's instant crap and it tastes bitter as shit, but I don't care.

"You think they'll come after you?" she whispers.

"I know they'll come after me. I'm far too much of a liability."

"So what then? You keep running?"

I shake my head. "A few months under the radar and they'll realise I've no interest in blowing their cover. I'll slip down their target list."

"You're sure?"

No. I'm not sure.

I've become far too fond of this *hope* novelty recently.

"Would you still have come with me?" I ask her.

"Knowing what you're running from?"

I nod.

Her eyes hide nothing from me. "Yes," she says. "So long as Joseph was safe."

Joseph.

I had no idea he'd even existed. No idea she was holding so much together. A baby, a full-time job, moonlighting with me three times a week. The soup kitchen.

All of that with a side helping of crushing grief.

At eighteen years old.

She's barely even an adult, and yet she's one of the most mature women I've ever met.

Figures, of course. That's what responsibility does to you.

Melissa Martin impresses me. Learning that comes as a surprise.

Melissa Martin is made of steel. She must be to live through what she's lived through.

I remember her polishing that boardroom table all those weeks ago. I remember how impressed I'd been with her determination. With her grit. Her work ethic.

I remember how transfixed I was by her quiet apology. The humbleness in her stance.

I remember how touched I was by her kindness in my house. Her generosity with her cupcake gift for me.

The orchids.

The fact she cared.

I thought I'd fallen in love with Amy Randall, but I'd only paid for Amy Randall because I was so hung up on Melissa Martin, even though she was faceless, even though she ran from me when I called.

"You didn't need to be Amy," I tell her. "I already wanted Melissa."

I know my words pain her. She flinches as I say them. "Please don't," she whispers. "It hurts enough already. I can't bear to think I lost it all in vain."

But she hasn't.

She hasn't lost it.

As much as I want to hate her, I can't.

As much as I want to turn my back and leave her here, I can't.

I can't run without her.

I don't want to run without her.

If my father's associates don't put an end to me, I'll put an end to myself.

Today, or tomorrow, or further down the line when Brutus has long breathed his last breath.

When the boys are all grown up and don't even call anymore.

When there is only me.

She made me feel alive again, without her I'll want to die again. It's only a matter of time.

I'm about to say it when a cry sounds through the wall.

It jars my senses, just as it did all those years ago when my boys were so young.

"Shit," she says. "Joseph. He has nightmares sometimes."

"Go," I say, but she's already on her way.

I wander through her living room as the cries continue. I hear her singing and she has such a beautiful voice. Such a sad voice.

I wait ten minutes and the kid's cries are still fraught.

Fifteen minutes go by and I can't hold back. It's instinct.

Parental instinct.

The strength of it takes me aback.

I knock on the door so gently. "Melissa?"

"Come in," she says over his sobs.

412

I push the door open slowly, and there she is, rocking so gently with that sweet little thing in her arms. He looks like her. Even with his face all crumpled with tears, he looks like her.

His little nightlight glows on the nightstand, and this must have been her parents' room. Their bed is still made up neatly. A piece of floral fabric still pokes from the wardrobe doors.

It must break her heart every day to come in here.

I know, because my boys' bedrooms broke mine, even though I still saw them every Sunday.

I had to take them apart in the end. They're magnolia now. Empty.

"Matthew used to get night terrors," I tell her. "I used to point out the stars. He liked that."

She smiles. "You did?"

I nod.

"I think he still dreams of them," she tells me. "I do, too. It hurts so bad when I wake up and find they're not there."

She looks so tired. She looks fragile and willowy and lost.

I hold out my arms. "Maybe I could try?" I offer, and she bounces him on her hip before she hands him over.

"This is Alexander," she whispers. "He's very kind. He's going to show you the stars. He showed me them, too."

That little boy's eyes are so wide as they stare into mine. My heart is thumping as I take him.

"Hi, Joseph," I say. "I'm Alex."

"Alex?" Melissa whispers and I nod. "I like Alex."

So do I.

I take that little boy through to the living room and pull back the curtains. The city glows orange, but you can just about see them, the little pinpricks of white in the sky.

He forgets to cry as I point them out. His little hand grabs my finger as I gesture to the few constellations I can see.

"Stars," I say. "They're magic."

I'm aware Lissa is at my back. I feel her eyes.

"Can you count them?" I ask, and he laughs at me. His laugh is the sweetest sound.

"You're good with him," Lissa whispers.

The triumph thrills me.

"I've had a lot of practice."

"More than me," she says. "I'm still learning."

She's doing a great job and I tell her so.

"Dean does most of it," she says, and I remember he still lives here. I remember he's coming back soon. "Time for bed now," I say to Joseph, and he's happy to go back to Lissa when she takes him.

I watch from the doorway as she settles him back down and sets his twinkle mobile playing.

She eases the door closed when he's asleep.

"Thanks," she says. "Sometimes it takes hours."

I don't have hours.

I don't even have minutes.

Every breath takes me closer to disaster.

So I say it. I have to.

"Come with me," I say. "Both of you."

Her eyes fill with tears. "But I can't... you said you don't even know me, and you don't know Joe, and what about Dean? Dean's been so good to us, and he has nobody. His parents are assholes."

I know that feeling.

"Then I guess we get to know each other, Lissa. You, me, Joseph. Dean, too. We'll all go. Fresh start."

She shakes her head, and it's not a refusal it's disbelief. She crumples to the floor and I head down there with her, and it feels so nice to be back in her arms.

"It'll be scary for the first few months," I say. "We may need to keep moving."

"I don't care," she says. "We'll go wherever you go, all of us."

I hear the key in the front door, and kiss Lissa's forehead before Dean comes through.

"I need to pack," I say. "You do, too. Come over this afternoon when you're ready. Pack as light as you can. We'll leave from mine."

She nods. "We'll be there."

And I know she will be.

I'll be waiting.

FORTY—SIX

ALEXANDER

I cab it back to mine with my heart in my hands.

Make or break.

Life or death.

And I'm excited.

This rollercoaster isn't done yet.

We'll leave under darkness, when anyone watching thinks I'm all tucked up for the evening.

I'll organise a hire car and get it delivered before midnight, and we'll take off for somewhere far away. Anywhere.

Maybe the coast. Brutus will like it there. So would Joseph, I'm sure.

Brutus wags his tail as I step on in. I bolt the doors up tight and get to work.

I sort through my paperwork and take the few pieces of documentation I need.

I pack my photos and the few of my gemstones that made it through my rage unscathed.

I choose my favourite suits from the sea of black in my wardrobe, and contemplate whether I'll still be wearing them in a few months' time.

Choosing the things from my boys' old bedrooms takes the longest. It's a ladder into the loft job, rooting through boxes I'd packed in a hurry. Some finger paintings, and their first teddy bears and Matthew's reward chart that I pulled down from the kitchen door.

Two cases is all I need. My whole life packed in two cases.

The second of them is mainly filled with the contents of my safe.

My father tries to call at seven a.m. and again at eight and nine on the dot.

He leaves a voicemail at eleven, but I don't listen.

It's when I get a text from an unknown number that I know the rumour mill has started.

Ronald bastard Robertson.

I wish I could give him the scoop before I go. One last confession of my father's seedy business for his tabloid.

He attempts to call me at lunchtime. Pings an email to my work address asking for a *puppet master* exclusive.

I ignore that, too.

There are only two things I have left to do.

Order a hire car, and wait for Melissa.

I get to work ordering the hire car.

MELISSA

"We're really gonna do this?" Dean asks and I nod.

"We're really doing this."

He helps me with Joe's things, packing them into one of Mum and Dad's old suitcases as Joe tries to pull them back out again. It's a slow process but a happy one.

Dean hardly has anything for himself. One single rucksack stuffed with clothes and his phone charger.

I hardly take any care with mine, just throw in the clothes fit for purpose and my crystals along with them. It's when I get to my parents' room that things become a bit harder.

Photos and memories. Too many to pack.

But I guess I can send for them when we're settled.

Months, Alexander said.

"You're sure he's down with me coming?" Dean asks and I nod.

"Yeah, I'm sure."

"And things won't be... *weird?*"

"Not if we don't let them be. Fresh start, right? This place is so full of memories. Good and bad."

"A fresh start sounds real good." he says. "For all of us."

Yes, it does.

The cash is the last thing I pack, wedges of notes that I was waiting to deposit into Joseph's account when I got the chance.

It feels weird to pile it in amongst my clothes.

I'll give it back to Alexander. He can take care of it, for Joe.

I hope he can take care of all of us.

I hope he lets me take care of him right back.

Our things are piled up in the hallway when I call a cab. We're out of breath when we've lugged it downstairs, but I fasten Joe in with a smile.

"Wave goodbye to our old house," I say and he does. He waves b-bye.

"This is it then?" Dean asks as the car pulls away.

"This is really it," I say.

ALEXANDER

My heart thumps when their cab pulls up outside the house.

I tell Brutus to behave. Tell him to *sit fucking down* and be nice for once.

I unbolt the front door with a smile, bounding out without thinking to help them inside with their cases, and a tap on my fucking shoulder nearly gives me a fucking heart attack.

Ronald fucking Robertson outside my fucking house.

His gormless photographer snaps a shot of us with the cases and I nearly knock his front teeth out.

I send Melissa on in with Joe and wait till the boy is out of earshot.

"Don't you even fucking dare think of printing that," I say.

Ronald shrugs. "I think we can keep it out of the final draft if you'll give me a few words about what's going down? Family feud, right? Is it true you're gonna expose your father's gangland clients?"

"Like fucking hell it is," I say. "Not that it's any of your fucking business."

He holds up his hands. "Just saying what I heard, Henley, that's all. Can't believe

419

you're getting a fucking conscience at your old age." He laughs. I hate his fucking laugh. He gestures to my front door as Dean lugs the last of the cases inside. "That pretty little thing got anything to do with it?"

"That *pretty little thing* is none of your fucking business, either."

I leave him at my gate where he belongs.

"Give me a scoop!" he shouts. "Your side of the story!"

"I have no fucking side of any story," I say. "I'm fucking done!"

I close the door behind me, and close the fucking curtains so the cunt can't see inside.

MELISSA

It's so nice to be back in Alexander's house.

It's so nice to wander around the rooms and smell his bedsheets for one last time.

They won't be his bedsheets in the new place, they'll be ours. The thought makes me giddy.

I show Dean around the place I've come to know so well, and he knows we're just killing time, chasing away the nerves that are thrumming from Alexander even though he tries to hide them, but we play along anyway.

Even Brutus is a good boy as we introduce him to Joe. He doesn't even snarl at Dean either.

It's like he knows.

Dogs know their own people, just as I said to Alexander, and Brutus knows us. He knows we're all bound together, destined for pastures new. I can tell by the way he sniffs the cases, his tail thumping at the leash draped over the top, just waiting to go.

"Are you sure we can trust the guy?" Dean asks as Alexander lets Brutus out into the garden.

"I'd trust him with my life," I say, and I would. I'd trust him with anything, even Joseph's.

"Alright," he says. "This is some crazy ride."

It is, and I know it's about to get even crazier. Good crazy.

Just as soon as we've left the city behind.

"The hire car arrives at ten," Alexander tells us when he heads back in. "We should be safe to go then. We'll have to be quick."

I nod. "We will be. We'll make light work of it, the three of us."

He paces as the evening draws in. He smiles but I know he's edgy.

I settle Joseph down on the plush cream sofa, and try to settle down with him, even though my nerves are on fire.

Dean talks about everything, waffling on about inane crap to keep us all from fizzing over. His jittery fingers are the only tell that he's not as calm as he makes out.

But that's okay.

He's doing a great job.

Alexander sighs with relief when the knock comes at ten to ten.

He tells me to hold Brutus back while he takes the keys from the driver and I do. I leave Dean with Joe in the living room and take tight hold of Brutus in the kitchen. I crouch to the floor along with him and hope he doesn't drag me right out of there.

"Be a good boy," I say. "Please, Brutus, don't be a dick."

But he is a dick.

I feel it in every fibre of him when Alexander heads to the front door.

His snarl is vicious and his muscles are wound up tight, much tighter than I've ever seen him.

Alexander looks back at me as he slides the bolts open. "Keep hold of him," he says, and I nod.

And I do. Even though it's hard. Even though he's pulling like a truck and I have to dig my heels into the floor to stop him tearing his way down the hallway. Even though he's so savage he shows every single one of his teeth.

"Calm down!" I hiss but he doesn't listen. "Brutus, please," I say, but he doesn't want to know.

He lurches forward and I shunt along with him, and I have to tug him back with all my strength as Alexander pulls the door open.

I'm still tugging him back when the bang sounds.

FORTY—SEVEN
ALEXANDER

I should have known it.

I trust Brutus easily as much as I trust myself.

I should have known it wasn't mindless savagery that sent him fucking livid as I went for that door.

And I should have known my father would never just chance me disappearing into the night.

There's no hire car outside when I open the door, just a man in black with his hood pulled down low.

It's not like Hollywood when I see the gun in his hands. There's no heated showdown where he tells me how much my father wants me dead, or passes on some cryptic message.

There's just a bang. A bang and a flash.

It feels like a punch. A punch right in my gut.

Only it makes my ears ring.

And everything slows down, just like it did when that cricket ball smashed my temple at twelve years old.

The whole world slows down.

I think I stumble before I fall. It feels like that.

Melissa's scream is so far away, and I wish I had the breath to tell her to stay back, but I don't.

I notice the tiny things in those slow seconds.

The shock on the gunman's face as my shirt pools with blood. The widening of his eyes as he looks past me into the hallway, his gun still smoking as Brutus charges him down.

I'm waiting for a second shot that doesn't come.

It can't.

Because Brutus is a savage beast when he needs to be.

And in that one slow moment as I prepare to meet my end, I'm glad he is.

I feel the heat of him as he lunges between me and the man at the door.

I hear the crunch of his teeth as they sink into flesh and bone, and the bang as the gun unloads onto my doorstep.

I've already fallen by the time the gunman screams. I don't see Brutus tear his arm open and lock back on for more.

I do see Melissa, though.

Her blonde hair is like an angel's under the ceiling light. Like the inclusions in her lucky crystal as she stares down at me and pulls my head into her lap.

My hand is over my stomach.

It feels as if I've been kicked.

Only a kick isn't wet and warm.

A kick doesn't feel like your life is slipping away from you.

My life is definitely slipping away from me. I see it written in her pretty eyes.

"Call an ambulance!" she screams, and it's not at me.

It's so hard to raise my arm. So hard to brush her cheek with my thumb.

Summoning my breath is the most painful thing I've ever done, but the most beautiful release I've ever felt.

"I love you," I say, and I wish I'd said it a lot sooner.

I wish I'd have said it that day on the street when I chased her, even though I didn't know her name.

I wish I'd have told her when she turned up at my hotel room door last night, before I half killed her.

I wish I'd have told her when I still had the strength to kiss her goodbye.

But it's perfect all the same.

She's perfect.

And she was worth it.

Worth dying for.

Her fingers are gentle in mine. Her eyes streaming as she tells me I'm going to be fine, that an ambulance is on its way.

She promised me she'd never lie again, but I think I can forgive her this one.

I love the irony of this insane thing we call life. If I was a man who believed in mumbo jumbo, I'd say fate has a wicked sense of humour.

But I'm not.

It's just one of life's peculiarities that leads me to this one hilariously ironic moment.

The moment I face my end is the precise moment I least want to slip away.

But I can't stop.

Even though Melissa screams my name and begs me to stay with her. Even though her hand crushes mine and the kiss from her pretty mouth reminds me of the myriad reasons I want to stay alive with her, I can't stop my eyes from closing.

FORTY-EIGHT
MELISSA

Alexander Henley, the man who is my everything, leaves me once in his hallway, just before the paramedics arrive, and again on the operating table before they stem the bleeding.

I sit and wait in the corridor while they fight to save his life, and my hands are still bloody but I don't want to wash them.

I don't want to wash him away from me.

My tears are quiet but they don't stop, not once in all the hours I wait for fate to show its hand.

Dean only stays a little while before he takes Joseph back home to the bed we were leaving behind. He holds me tight and tells me it's *gonna be alright*.

He'll hold on, he says. *He's not the kind of guy to back down from a fight. No fucking way, Lissa.*

I hope he's right about that.

Dean tells me he'll pick up Brutus on the way home. He tells me he'll keep him safe until Alexander is back.

Brutus saved his life.

I need Alexander to wake up just so I can tell him so.

I want him to know that the dog whose life he saved from death row just saved him right back, and if that's not fate, I don't know what is.

I just pray to God it's fate that brings Alexander back to me.

I recognise Claire Henley from their wedding photos as she rushes into the ward at just before midnight. Her eyes are wide and scared and her lips are pale even though she's wearing lip gloss.

"How is he?" she asks me, and I shrug. I don't know. Not yet.

I tell her so.

She takes a seat at my side.

"The stubborn sonofabitch will pull through," she tells me, and I stare at her face as a tear falls. "I should've known his filthy fucking father would be the end of him."

I don't know what to say, so I don't.

"Are you his…" she begins, and I nod.

"We were, um… moving away."

She sighs. "About bloody time he found something he really wanted." She brushes a tear away. "I don't know how I'm going to tell the boys, if he…"

"He won't," I say. "He's a stubborn sonofabitch, remember?"

She smiles at me. "I heard that ugly mutt saved his life."

I smile back. "He's not so ugly," I say. "He's great when you get to know him."

"I never really gave the thing a chance. He smells bad."

"There's time."

"I hope so," she tells me. "And I hope there's time for you to meet my boys, too. They'd love to see their dad… happy."

So would I.

427

I'd love to see him happy, far away from all this with his feet on the sand somewhere.

We're sitting in silence as a doctor heads out to us, he tugs the mask from his face and calls for "Mrs Henley," but Claire gestures at me.

"I think this is for you," she says, and I get shakily to my feet.

I can hardly breathe as I step forward. My knees are knocking as I wait for the verdict.

But it's good. It's really good.

He shows me a diagram of the bullet they took from the bottom of his lung. He lost a lot of blood, the doctor tells me, but I already know that. My hands don't let me forget it.

My head is dizzy with relief when he tells me he's going to be just fine. That they stemmed the bleeding and fixed him back up, and he'll be weak for a while, but he'll live.

He'll live.

They're the most beautiful words I've ever heard, even more beautiful than *I love you* from Alexander's perfect mouth. Even more beautiful than the first time he used my real name.

I thank the doctor.

I thank him over and over through my tears.

And Claire is happy for me. She puts her arm around my shoulder at the happy news and squeezes tight.

"I told you," she said. "He's a stubborn sonofabitch. You'll find that out for yourself, don't you worry."

I'm not worried.

I can hardly wait.

EPILOGUE
ALEXANDER

Maybe I'm slowly becoming a man who believes in mumbo jumbo.

The dog I rescued from certain doom is the one who saved me from mine.

The girl whose eyes I stared into as I thought she'd died in my arms, is the very girl who stares into mine as I really do die in hers less than twenty-four hours later.

And what a twenty-four hours they turned out to be.

But maybe the biggest irony of all is that it's the same gormless photographer I told to fuck off a few hours earlier that captures the pictures needed to identify my shooter.

It's the story Ronald *pissing* Robertson runs in his shitty tabloid that sees the authorities locate my cunt of a hitman and take him in for questioning.

Apparently his arm needed over thirty stitches. He'll probably never regain the use of his fingers, which is just as well considering he needs them to pull the

I don't think he'll be pulling another one anytime soon.

I assumed he'd get away with it, of course. After all, my father's a better puppet master than I'll ever be.

But not this time. This time the puppet master chose the wrong puppet. This time he rushed the job and paid on the cheap. A fool's error most certainly, and one that makes me smile every time I ponder it.

I waited a long time for that filthy old bastard to ever make a mistake.

The piece of shit he got to take a shot at me on my doorstep was an amateur at best.

He was more than happy to blab the details of my father and all his cunting associates in exchange for a shorter sentence, and I was more than happy to fill in the blanks.

That's how I came to stand on the other side of the witness box for once in my life, watching my father tried for attempted murder.

That's how Melissa, Dean, Joe and I got taken into witness protection and shipped away to a nice little town on the Welsh coast a million miles from bloody anywhere.

And that's how Melissa and I ended up as Mr Ted and Mrs Amy Brown. Just regular folk going about their regular business, with a regular kid and a dog, and my friendly nephew Danny hanging around.

Melissa really did end up as a Mrs, too.

I married her in hospital the very next day after my operation, just in case my father came back for round two.

She bought me orchids for my room, and a cupcake too.

And a crystal.

The crystal.

She fished out her lucky quartz from behind the shelving at mine and handed it right back as we said our vows.

I'll never throw it away again.

I'll never throw her away again, either.

My boys are coming to visit next weekend.

It's been three months since my father was convicted, and I think the coast is as clear as it'll ever be.

I grind the beans for the coffee machine as Dean heads back from the beach with Joe. I watch them up the path as Brutus pads along behind, and I can't stop smiling, knowing that my beautiful wife is due home any minute.

From college.

My beautiful wife Amy is studying law at college.

She wants to be a lawyer one day, who'd have thought it? It seems not everything was for my benefit. Far from it.

She wants to be a legal aid lawyer at that. Good deeds for those who can't afford decent representation.

I'm proud of her.

And me?

Well, I think I'm going to take it easy awhile.

I've got a whole collection of gemstones to start over, and a wife who actually wants me at night.

I've got a family in Joseph and Dean.

I've got my boys heading over for football practice this weekend – I've even set them up a pitch in the garden.

And I've got my vicious, unlovable, untrainable dog, who's not nearly so vicious these days.

That's more than enough strings to keep me occupied.

And when it's not, I choke my wife's throat until she taps out, and she *does* tap out these days.

When the nights draw in, and Joe's tucked up quiet in bed, I fuck Dean's tight little ass until he bleeds for me.

And sometimes, occasionally, when I'm feeling particularly like my old cunt of a self, I'll pretend I want to watch them fuck each other, just to check I can still make them squirm.

They didn't call me the puppet master for nothing.

THE END

ACKNOWLEDGEMENTS

Johnny, my incredible editor, this one has been quite a ride, and I've loved every minute, as always. Thank you so much for pulling out all the stops for me.

Letitia, you always do me proud with the cover. You are amazing! Thank you so much.

Tracy, my awesome and tireless PA, I still love your face after two years, and I hope you still love mine. Thank you for all the hard work.

To Louise and Leigh for reading my early copies. Your input is so appreciated!

Michelle and Lesley, thank you so much as always.

To my amazing reader group, you ladies (and gents) are all kinds of awesome! Thank you so much for your support and enthusiasm – and your patience with this one!

So many friends to thank! Lisa, Dom, Jo, Sue, Siobhan, James, Lauren, Tom and the lovely Maria… I'm so honoured to know you all. Thank you all for putting up with my incessant book-speak!

Isabella and Demi, you changed my life, for real. I hope you know how much I love you for it.

Isa, thanks for being here for the second time in row I hit publish. I hope you realise this is going to be a 'thing' from now on. You might just have to move in…

Jon, your support means everything, as always.

My amazing family, I hope you know how important you are.

Bloggers and the amazing fellow authors who support me every day! Thank you so much! This community is incredible. I'm so honoured to be a part of it.

And of course, to my readers! Thank you for taking the time to read Buy Me, Sir. I hope you enjoyed the experience.

If you love Alexander Henley even half as much as I enjoyed writing him, I'll be a very happy author indeed. x

ABOUT JADE

Jade has increasingly little to say about herself as time goes on, other than that she is an author, but she's plenty happy with that fact. Living in imaginary realities and having a legitimate excuse is really all she's ever wanted. Jade is as dirty as you'd expect from her novels, and talking smut makes her smile. She lives in the Welsh countryside with a couple of hounds and a guy who's able to cope with her inherent weirdness.

Find Jade (or stalk her – she loves it) at:

www.facebook.com/jadewestauthor

www.twitter.com/jadewestauthor

www.jadewestauthor.com

Sign up to her newsletter here:

http://forms.mpmailserv.co.uk/?fid=53281-73417-10227

She won't spam you and you may win some goodies. :)

Made in the USA
Las Vegas, NV
13 November 2020